WATER'S CALLING

COURTNEY POLLMAN-TURNER

First published in Great Britain in 2021 by SMASHBEAR PUBLISHING.

Office 6945, London, W1A 6US, United Kingdom

www.smashbearpublishing.com

This paperback edition published 2022

Paperback ISBN: 978-1-915636-01-0

eBook ISBN: 978-1-915636-00-3

To Justin, for being unoppressive in your hereness, and for always walking beside me when the only way out is through.

WATER'S CALLING

1

―――――

'Spar with me.'

LeiRain stood with her back to her lover as she tucked in her dingy white blouse. She looked down at herself and frowned. A thick layer of flour dusted her thin shirt and roughspun brown skirt. She tried to brush them off, but it was pointless. The entire room was covered in flour. LeiRain tugged her skirt around, trying to keep her shift from sticking out the bottom. The shift shouldn't have been visible at all, but LeiRain had outgrown her skirt so that the hem stopped at her lower calf and she hadn't bothered to buy a new one. The fashion was for women's skirts to fall to the ankle but LeiRain found it easier to move around in the shorter skirt, especially since she was most accustomed to wearing trousers. She only wore a skirt when visiting Bren, anyway.

Sighing heavily, she swiped aggressively to brush off as much flour as she could without having to get undressed again and shake everything out. Feeling around her head for loose strands of hair, she located a thick wave and attempted to tuck it back into a mussed braid.

'Why do you do that?' Bren asked from behind her.

'Do what?' She felt the hair slip out again and decided it was best to redo the whole thing. She pulled free the leather strap that held her braid together and combed her hair with her fingers before tugging her locks back firmly with both hands. She turned around to face Bren as she finished the braid and began tying it off.

'That,' he said, his heavy-lidded eyes taking her in. 'Your hair. I like it better when it's mussed.'

'That's because you've done the mussing,' she said with a smirk. 'What will people think if they see my hair sticking out like I've been—' She let her sentence trail off; he had half-closed his eyes and she doubted he was really listening anymore.

Bren was sprawled lazily across the sacks of flour on which they had just tussled, wearing nothing but his tunic. He made no move to dress himself and stared absently overhead as thin fingers of sunlight broke through the edges around the door, illuminating the flour hovering in the air. Bren's head was tilted at an angle that accentuated his sharp jaw, and the little hollow just beneath his ear where he liked to be kissed. His tangled chin-length hair looked golden when streams of light hit it. He lifted a hand and tucked a few loose strands behind the pointed tip of his ear, an indication of how relaxed he was since Bren usually took great pains to hide his elf heritage.

He had still made no move to get up or dress by the time LeiRain finished tying off her hair. Instead, he took in a slow breath and closed his eyes. She watched his bare chest rise and fall, admiring his lean and muscular form. Life on a shipping vessel kept him fit and strong, but didn't afford him enough food to overcome his naturally slight build: another elf-like feature. Nibbling at her lower lip, her gaze made its way to his muscular abdomen. Her cheeks heated, the space between her thighs aching as she took him in, eyes lingering on the scar that marked his side just above the hip.

It was an old scar from when he was young and had been careless handling lines. The rope had gotten away from him, tearing through his shirt and burning his skin with friction. He was lucky. Many sailors lost a finger – or worse – to mishandled mooring lines. He'd gotten the scar long before she knew him but her fingertips could recall the sensation of brushing against it. His breathing slowed and she realized that he was drifting off to sleep.

LeiRain glared at the empty wine bottle that laid on its side, and cursed herself for having shared the bottle with him. Wine always made him drowsy, but she had more bottles than she knew what to do with. A group of local men had thrown an entire wine shipment into the harbor a few weeks ago because the wine was allegedly made from grapes harvested on a blend-owned vineyard. The men in question complained that this was taking away income from humans while paying no mind to the fact that this caused substantial financial damage to the human ship captain and his mostly-human crew and investors.

Most of the crates had been jettisoned whole and sank to the harbor floor unbroken. Bad for the captain and the vineyard owner, LeiRain had thought, but good for her. She had collected armfuls and carried them home, planning to sell them later. Much to her disappointment, the entire village was still talking about the incident and the wine itself was a scandal. Anyone she tried to sell to would know that she'd plucked the wine from the ocean floor, reminding them of the controversy while highlighting her *otherness*. So, the bottles sat in her room, collecting dust. Bren, on the other hand, had been happy to imbibe with her. She turned back to him as he began to lightly snore.

3

She reached for the blade leaning against the bulkhead only a few feet away and shifted its dented metal scabbard to her left hand. The space had a low ceiling with only six or so square feet remaining free of cargo, so she had to awkwardly angle her body to draw the blade without bumping her elbow against the wall even though the sword itself was a small, stunted thing. Gingerly, she pulled it from the scabbard, cringing as it gave a light squeal.

She looked down at Bren. His eyelids fluttered slightly but he seemed otherwise undisturbed. She glared at the blade as if she could threaten it into silence, before pulling it free. It was a second-hand piece of rubbish that she'd purchased off of a traveler. He'd been desperate to fund his departure from Harbor Village before his excessive gambling debt he'd incurred the night before had come due; she'd thought it a bargain. Her mother could have made her a much better piece, but LeiRain felt proud to have bought it herself – a mark of her growing independence.

LeiRain widened her stance and leaned over Bren, hovering the sword's tip a few inches above his nose. To her surprise, Bren reached up and gently pushed the tip of the blade away without opening his eyes. She scoffed and he smiled languidly before his eyes blinked open. He turned his head toward her and wrapped a hand around her calf. He tugged slightly on her lower leg, and she allowed herself to stumble closer to him with a laugh. She regained her posture and pointed the blade at his chest this time.

'Come on,' she pleaded, laughing one more time before forcing herself to look serious, 'spar with me. Please?'

'No second go this time?' Bren pushed his bottom lip out into a pout.

'I want to practice with the sword now that I have one.'

'We *are* practicing with a *sword*, aren't we?' Bren raised an eyebrow, his eyes darting between her and his groin.

LeiRain rolled her eyes at him and was trying to think of an appropriate comeback when they both stiffened at the sound of footsteps passing overhead. A form crossed in front of the door at the top of the short, narrow stairway that led to the cargo space they were occupying. They were cast into utter darkness as the form blocked the few threads of sunlight that illuminated the room. It was only a flicker, though, as the passerby moved on without pause.

Relieved, LeiRain took in a deep breath before realizing her mistake and sneezing out a noseful of flour. LeiRain narrowed her eyes and forced her mouth from a smile into a flat line as she shifted the blade so that it pointed at Bren's groin.

'Get up, you lazy ass. Put your pants on.'

He gave her a sardonic look, and she responded with an exaggeratedly wide smile. LeiRain shifted the sword to where his trousers lay discarded on the deck near his feet and picked them up with the tip of her blade, dropping them on his stomach.

Bren groaned in complaint as he grabbed his pants with one hand and pushed himself into a sitting position with the other. He took his time pulling on the trousers, pausing to glare at LeiRain before leaning back on his elbows and lifting his groin into the air to pull the waistband over his hips. Slowly, he tied the drawstring into a knot at his waist and stood. He shook out his thick blonde hair, causing a fresh cloud of flour to fill the small storage space like a mist.

LeiRain cleared her throat and shook her head impatiently, tossing him his own sword just as he tugged a shirt over his head. He snatched clumsily at the blade, grabbing it by the worn leather scabbard.

He didn't bother to strap the sword belt on but instead drew the blade free and let the scabbard fall to the floor. The weapon, in much better shape than her own, slid smoothly from its sheath, flashing where it caught the light. Bren, like most sailors, preferred a cutlass and his blade was roughly the same size as her own with only one sharpened edge and a very slight curve near the tip. Her own short-sword was double-edged but much dulled with heavy use and lack of attention.

Without changing his stance, Bren made a few half-hearted jabs and swipes at LeiRain. She watched the well-maintained blade flash through the air, cutting arcs through the airborne bits of flour. Bren moved so slow and lazily that she deflected his attacks with ease despite her lack of training.

'You're not trying,' she complained, shifting her weight back and forth between her front and back foot. He wasn't a master swordsman, but Bren had learned the basics of sword-fighting after years at sea. Most sailors had some amount of skill, especially those aboard merchant vessels who had to defend their cargo from time to time. He could definitely do better than this.

'Rain.' He lowered his blade and shrugged. 'This space isn't big enough for this.'

'Then let's go above decks,' she suggested then winced, knowing she'd said the wrong thing. All joviality left Bren's face.

He swallowed and his jaw flexed. There was a reason why they met secretly, and it wasn't for something as noble as protecting her honor. Bren could be himself with her, but around his shipmates and Harbor locals, he put a great deal of effort into hiding his blend status. The secrecy wasn't personal, LeiRain knew. He hid whatever this was between them because he was afraid it would invite questions. It was not because he was ashamed of her. After all, they were *both* blends. It's just that he could pass easily for human and she... Well, she had blue skin. But knowing this didn't make her feel any better nor did it stop them from arguing about it.

He ran a hand through his hair and shook his head. 'You know that's a bad idea. We've talked about this.'

They had talked about it before. So many times. LeiRain valued her time with Bren because it chased away her loneliness, if only briefly. But now loneliness came rushing back. It pressed against her eyes, threatening to bring tears. She lowered her sword before Bren could notice that her hands were shaking. LeiRain breathed slowly through her nose as she schooled her features, desperate to hide her emotional reaction, and let herself frown to stop her lower lip from quivering.

Bren was a quarter elf but looked human save for his unusually beautiful, round face, slender nose and pointed ears. She marveled that anyone could mistake him for a human given the flawlessness of his skin, which never sprouted a single freckle or patch or sunburn despite hours on the deck, and the golden shine of his blonde hair. But all he had to do was pull a cap down over the tips of his ears and everyone seemed happy to ignore these details. Both elves and humans, like many sole-bloods, were wary of allowing blends into their society. Many throughout The Continent believed blends held more power than sole-bloods as they could draw from the magic of more than one race. LeiRain didn't know if this was true for some blends, but this was clearly not always the case – Bren seemed to have inherited no magic at all and she had inherited only the ability to breathe underwater, which was probably more anatomy than magic. He had never told her much about his parents, but she knew that they had either been unable or unwilling to care for him beyond ten years of age. Despite his heritage posing no threat to either human or elf, Bren had found himself without a home and without a people, so he'd done what he had to survive.

He had discovered early that there was more sympathy for a human orphan than a blend and more job opportunities for a human boy than a blend beggar, so he'd kept his ears covered and done his best to pass. He had become so adept at maintaining the façade that even the sailors he worked, ate and slept beside forgot that he was a blend. Bren's livelihood was dependent on his ability to remain unnoticed. Being seen topside, let alone sparring, with LeiRain would draw far too much attention.

She understood. Really, she did. There was no future with Bren. No prospect of becoming his wife, and she could accept that. Their dalliances were an escape, an outlet for them both. But their relationship was the closest thing she had to real intimacy. To friendship.

She'd been so alone before they'd met nearly four years ago. Perched on top of a barrel on the next dock, she had watched as another boy teasingly pulled the cap off his head and threw it into the water. A group of local children had laughed at him while he dangled from the dock with one arm and reached for his cap with the other. Eventually, they grew bored and went about their business elsewhere but Bren was still left trying to fish this essential piece of his disguise out of the water.

When the waterlogged cap sank below the surface, Bren sat down and began to unlace his boots. This had spurred LeiRain into action. She scrambled off the barrel and jumped into the water, surfacing in front of him only seconds later. As soon as Bren had recovered from the shock, he plucked the cap from her outstretched hand, wrung it out, and shoved it back on his head, still dripping. She caught a brief glimpse of a pointed ear as it peaked out from his thick, golden hair and immediately understood.

LeiRain had known his secret from the very beginning and they'd grown a friendship based on mutual need for acceptance. The two of them could be themselves with each other and it had seemed only natural for their friendship to take on a physical element as they matured. What LeiRain hadn't expected was for this to make the secrecy more hurtful. Being secret friends had felt almost special to her, but being secret lovers felt shameful. His unwillingness to acknowledge her publicly left a deep ache in her soul and as he grew into his lie, his social circle expanded. Bren came and went from Harbor Village and he had 'friends' in other ports, too, but she only had him. When he left, there was no one.

Her face must have given away her thoughts because he snatched her around the waist and pulled her close, his sword clanking as it fell to the deck. 'You sure you don't want to go again?' he asked, leaning in to kiss her neck. Despite herself, LeiRain's body responded to his touch and she was just about to succumb to it when he whispered 'this may be our last chance' into the hollow of her neck. Slowly, she placed a hand on the center of his chest and pushed him back.

'Why?' Her brow wrinkled as she searched his face. While she had known that their relationship wouldn't last forever, LeiRain couldn't think why it needed to end so soon. She had always assumed it would continue until he was officially betrothed or she had finally cut a way out of Harbor Village for herself.

During their last liaison, Bren had casually mentioned talks of an engagement with a young woman from up north. But it had only been a possibility then, and LeiRain did not think it was likely to work out. The girl's father, a well-off merchant according to Bren, was unlikely to trust his daughter's future to a poor sailor boy. Bren's birth was questionable at best, worse if the merchant knew of his blend parentage.

LeiRain knew that Bren aspired to marriage and respected this, and they both knew that she was not the marrying type. Marriage would tie her to a home, a single place, and LeiRain longed to see the world. Most young women in Harbor Village married not for love, but because it was expected of them and there were few respectable alternatives. Having grown up without a father, and as a social pariah in her own right, LeiRain didn't think this societal expectation applied to her. Even if she had wanted to marry, there would be no proposals for her while she remained in Harbor. No one here would marry a blend.

Her stomach rolled with disgust as she contemplated the possibility that she had just lain with someone else's betrothed. Their relationship was based on a certain trust, and the understanding that they were both free to do as they wished with each other and elsewhere. But having dalliances in other ports was not the same as being affianced. LeiRain couldn't help but feel personally betrayed, having been made complicit in Bren's unfaithfulness. Heat began to spread up her neck and into her cheeks.

'We won't be coming back to Harbor Village,' he explained with a confused look at her apparent distress. 'At least, not for a long time. Captain says it's getting too dangerous. Too many conflicts between blends and Royals.'

She made no attempt to hide her derision, and no effort to subdue the temper that had been stoked by her own imagination. '*Too many conflicts with blends.*' Her voice rose.

'Well, yes, and things are getting tense—'

'*You're a* blend, you asshole!' She was yelling now and pulled back from his embrace. Deep down, LeiRain was relieved that she hadn't just become the *other woman*, but that was buried somewhere beneath her anger. And her disappointment. Regardless of the reason, the thought of Bren disappearing from her life was shattering. Her limbs shook as a dark purple flush covered her cheeks.

Only her anger showed as she glared at him, willing away the tears that pricked at the backs of her eyes. She felt a slight embarrassment over misreading the situation, but she channeled this into rage, and ignored the despairing ache in her chest.

Bren's gaze ran over her features, confusion turning to trepidation. His eyes softened to pleading as he reached for LeiRain, drawing back when he found her hands balled into fists at her sides. She took a step back.

'You know what I mean, Rain!' He ran one hand roughly through his knotted hair before holding both out in front of him in a placating gesture. 'It's just the Royals are having a lot of success recruiting here and ... whenever you get a lot of blends and Royals in the same place' – he shook his head and shrugged – 'trouble starts and trouble makes investors nervous and nervous investors don't pay captains of ships to bring loads of merchandise across miles of ocean! There are still ports where blends are well accepted, and the Royals haven't been able to get a foothold, so that's where most of the business is now.'

A chill ran through LeiRain's body, cooling the heat of her anger. The blends in Harbor Village already lived as second class citizens, and a strong Royal presence would only make things worse. The Royals, so named because of the royal blue swaths of fabric they wore to identify themselves, belonged to an organization of men sworn to uphold 'the ways of humanity'. Their membership was growing on The Continent and Harbor Village was ripe with men who wanted to join their ranks. As far back as she could remember, men in Harbor

Village had complained about blends taking their jobs and stealing their business, but it had always seemed like men just blowing off steam ... until the Royals had begun to organize them. LeiRain had thus far ignored the growing number of men and boys with strips of blue cloth tied about their biceps, but Bren's words made her recall all that she'd noticed in recent months.

One memory stood out in particular. Three weeks ago, she'd been people-watching at the pier, settled into a mess of cargo boxes waiting to be loaded, when the wine shipment had been dumped. A nearby vessel had just finished loading its last crate of supplies, and the tired crew and dockhands were making their way down the brow with jocularity when a group of men wearing the Royal mark had strode haughtily onto the pier. LeiRain had recognized one of the approaching men: Ethan. He'd grown up in Harbor Village, left to find his fortune when she was still a child, and recently returned with a blue band around his arm and an air of authority. Tension filled the air as the two groups locked eyes, so she had slid from her hiding place and into the water, surfacing beneath the pier where they were gathered. LeiRain had done her best to eavesdrop on their conversation, but the boards overhead the lapping water made it difficult to hear. She could only make out a few words and phrases, including *bloody greedy dross*, and *filthy miners*, the former being an offensive slang term for blends and the latter a common slur for dwarves.

With a sinking feeling, LeiRain realized that Bren's captain was right, Harbor Village had become too volatile for good business.

Taking her silence as encouragement, Bren closed the distance between them and brought his head down to kiss her. A part of her longed to lean into him, to tilt her head back in welcome acceptance. But instead, she stayed rigid with tension. He didn't seem to notice.

'So, let's say one last ti—' LeiRain thrust her head forward, her skull crashing into Bren's nose. He stumbled backward and fell, tripping over the flour sacks that had only recently made such a satisfactory bed. He pressed a hand to his nose as blood dripped from it.

With one hand, LeiRain rubbed her forehead where she could already feel a painful lump forming and wiped at her now-watering eyes with the other. She had never head-butted anyone before and was somewhat shocked by her own actions. A surprising amount of blood had run down Bren's chin and onto his shirt, and LeiRain felt a mild twinge of shame when she looked at him. But there was also a feeling of satisfaction at having made him hurt as much as she had been hurting.

'What the hell, Rain!' His voice was muffled as he spoke through his rapidly swelling nose. His eyes darted from his bloody hands to her face and then back.

'I suppose you'll be visiting the northern ports a bit more frequently,' she said. If rumors were true, the Royals had yet to infiltrate the northern part of The Continent, which also happened to be where Bren's intended lived. Of course, Bren had no say in what ports he visited. He was contracted to the ship's captain and obligated to serve his contract's term. But LeiRain didn't let this stop her from blaming him. Would it hurt less to lose her only friend if she had not opened herself up to him so fully? LeiRain found herself wishing that their relationship had never become physical.

'Please,' he said gently. He held out both bloodied hands in a gesture of surrender before quickly smacking one to his nose again as a fresh stream of blood burst from one nostril. 'Please,' he repeated nasally while pinching his nose to staunch the flow. He held out a bloodied hand like someone trying to soothe a distressed animal. 'You could come with us. The captain would love to have someone with your abilities.' She scoffed, irritated by his belief that it could be so simple. 'You don't have to stay here, Rain. We both know this place isn't good for you.'

'You know as well as I do what happens to females at sea,' she replied, her voice cold.

'I can...' He hesitated and then went forward with the lie he'd been about to speak. 'I can protect you.' He squared his shoulders.

LeiRain shook her head. 'No, you can't.' Her words were laced with disappointment. He'd just been bested by a girl with no formal training. There's no way he'd be able to fight off the crew if they wanted her, and no way to trust that he would even try when he already went to such trouble to hide their friendship.

'I know you've turned down other captains before,' he began. She had, it was true. 'You can breathe underwater!' He paused to spit out a glob of bloody saliva and wipe his chin. 'You'd be an invaluable crew member – hull repairs, problems with the anchor, anything lost overboard... You could handle those problems with ease. Surely you could negotiate a contract that would guarantee your protection.'

'Bren, stop.' She held up a hand in front of her and he flinched. 'These men come into port and make their way straight to the nearest brothel, not caring if they're paying for someone who's in the profession willingly or someone who has been sold into it. Not caring that most of those girls are still children. It won't matter what my contract says when I'm at sea with fifty men.'

'Not all sailors are like that,' he spat again, 'not all men—'

'Of course they're not all like that.' She rolled her eyes. 'But enough of them are. I'm a woman, and a blend. I'll fetch no respect from the crew, and I doubt that any ship's captain would have the power to guard me day and night nor the desire to do so. No captain would dare deny his men their pleasure. I have more freedom here than I would as a ship's crew. I won't trade Harbor Village for a smaller prison.'

She sighed heavily and picked up her sword belt and scabbard. Her palm was sweaty where it gripped her sword and she felt the metal vibrate when it screeched as she replaced it in the scabbard. Without taking her eyes off Bren, LeiRain strapped the sword belt around her waist. She shook her head at him one last time before turning toward the stairwell, taking the steps two at a time and yanking the door open as soon as she reached the top.

LeiRain's eyes began to water anew as she squinted at the brightness. She blinked a few times as her eyes struggled to adjust, then turned to look back at Bren. He had followed her halfway up the stairs and stood with a hand raised to shield his own eyes. A coating of flour covered the deck in his wake. With sunlight flooding the compartment, she could make out the footprints they'd left behind, which had been invisible in the near darkness. Swallowing, she steeled herself to walk away.

'Goodbye, Bren,' she said coolly, 'and good luck with your merchant's daughter.' She flashed a false smile and stepped through the door before he had a chance to reply. Before he could see the tears welling up in her eyes.

2

Anger threatened to burst out of her in salty droplets. It vibrated through her like beats of a drum and made her thoughts circle around with dizzying rapidity. She bit the inside of her cheek and squinted into the light to hold her tears at bay. Her hands shook. She wanted to scream, to stomp.

The deck of the ship was mercifully deserted. The boards beneath her feet were hot and would need to be swabbed with saltwater soon to keep them from cracking, so it wouldn't be long before sailors made their way back aboard. The lines holding the ship in place creaked softly as the vessel bobbed in the water. If she walked to the bow, she'd see dockhands taking their lunch wherever they could find shade. Harbor's streets were full of vendors pushing their wares, and long lines of sailors stood before a few of the food stalls where thin billows of smoke drifted up from their cookfires and grills.

LeiRain flinched when she caught sight of one remaining deckhand. He sat on the main deck near the brow – which he was surely meant to be guarding – with his hat pulled low over his eyes. He hadn't noticed her.

In order to accommodate Bren, LeiRain came and went using a sun-bleached rope ladder that dangled unsteadily down the side of the ship. It faced away from the pier, and her ability to breathe underwater made it an easy feat for her to come and go this way, invisible to everyone save the few on deck. She'd come aboard soaked but spent so much time in Bren's company that her thick skirt was now nearly dry. The ladder had been raised back up and left in a pile after she'd come aboard hours ago.

She put a hand on her knotted stomach, feeling angry at herself for going to such lengths to make Bren comfortable with their meetings. It hadn't seemed unreasonable before; afterall, she could breathe underwater. But now it felt as though she were coated in the same slimy green fur that grew on ships' hulls near the waterline.

Limbs shaking with barely contained emotion, she kicked the rope ladder across the deck. It scraped over the wooden planks, coming to rest only a few feet away from the crewman who was napping on his watch. He shifted and readjusted his hat but still took no notice of LeiRain. With a sigh, she bounded across the deck and took a running jump over the rail. The feeling of weightlessness was briefly exhilarating as she dropped the fifteen feet and hit the water with a loud splash. LeiRain could have landed gracefully in the water from that height, could have made nary a sound, but she wanted Bren to hear it and feel her ire.

Skirts billowed when she hit the water. They rose up and blocked her view as she let herself sink until her feet touched the bottom. With an annoyed scowl, LeiRain gathered the fabric in her fists and cinched it in knots around her thighs, not caring about the scandalized looks she would receive from village matrons once she exited the water at the edge of town. It couldn't be much worse than the scathing glances she earned when she wore pants, which is what she'd be wearing now if she hadn't been trying to look *nice* for Bren.

Fat lot of good that did, she thought to herself.

She walked along the floor of the harbor, sending up little puffs of sand with each step. She paddled her arms now and then to keep herself from floating to the surface. A stream of bubbles rippled over her face as she exhaled the last of the oxygen in her lungs and let them fill with the cool salt water. Once she'd rid her lungs of air, it was easier to walk along the bottom, and she only paddled her arms when pushed by a current.

Sunlight streamed through the relatively shallow harbor waters, illuminating the smooth rocks, bits of broken shells and lost items scattered on the sandy bottom. The moored vessels cast great shadows over LeiRain as she walked beneath them, lazily brushing her hand along the hulls with a deep enough draft. Overhead, she could see the silhouettes of birds, their tiny feet paddling frantically beneath the surface while all was still on top.

She looked through odds and ends on the ocean floor, assessing the lost or discarded treasures, occasionally nudging one with a toe before deciding if it was worth picking up. There was no coral here, and only sparse patches of seagrass as the frequent coming and going of ships stirred the bottom too often for much to settle and grow. She came across fishing hooks, coins of mostly copper and silver, and a silver hair comb adorned with delicately carved vines. The hooks she left – they wouldn't go for much and the risk of catching her own finger on one when she pulled it from her pocket was too great. She'd learned that lesson the hard way. After collecting the coins, LeiRain kept the comb in her hand, running her thumb over the carvings as she walked. It was beautiful and she would be sad to part with it, but it would sell for a good price. And when would she have occasion to wear it anyway? There wasn't any glamor in Harbor, just hard work and rough hands. The only occasion a Harbor woman had to dress up was her own wedding, and she did not have to worry about that.

LeiRain had become skilled at pricing out her finds as it was the only means she had of supporting herself independent of her mother's income. Her mother wanted her to learn a trade, whether it was working beside her at the forge or starting her own business, but LeiRain had resisted. She was a fair cook and a decent baker, but such a trade would tie her down, making it more likely that she would remain stuck in Harbor. She could scavenge anywhere, though.

When she'd first discovered that her father was tempest, a water god, and that she had inherited his ability to breathe underwater, LeiRain imagined grander things for herself. But with no one to guide her through the deep, fear had kept LeiRain from venturing too far from shore. She'd put her unique ability to use in scavenging items lost to the harbor.

Too long on land, she remembered her father saying. LeiRain had only met him once at the age of eleven and she still had nightmares about the encounter. She recalled how he'd dragged her into the surf and forced her head underwater. Until then, LeiRain hadn't known she could breathe beneath the waves. She wasn't sure if her father had known already, or if this had been his way of finding out. LeiRain could still recall the panic coursing through her as she thrashed against his grip. For a few terrifying seconds, she had been certain that she was about to die, but then her body took over and drew in that first lungful of water.

But despite everything, what she remembered most from that day was the disappointment in her father's voice when he left her, drenched and shaken, standing on the beach in her mother's arms. *Too long on land*, he had said. This was part of how she saw herself now, a part of her identity. Despite being the offspring of a water deity, LeiRain was a land-dweller, a blend whose unique ability was little more than a parlor trick.

LeiRain stopped before a discarded crate of wine. She examined it carefully, noting where the wood splintered around the broken lid. She pushed it over a few times with her foot until the broken pieces gave way further and two bottles rolled out and into the sand. A crab, which had squeezed its way into the box, scurried for cover elsewhere. The crate was full and the bottles were all intact. And much to her delight, the water-logged labels had begun to shrivel and peel cleanly off the bottles. Unlabeled spirits would have to go at a cheaper price, but given the wine scandal, LeiRain doubted they would sell at all with the labels intact. She took the two bottles that had come free, gripping their necks together in one hand, the silver comb still in the other. She'd have to come back for the rest, and maybe find a way to soak the ones she had at home until those labels came off too.

She emerged from the water at the edge of town where the cobblestone road ended abruptly and was replaced by packed dirt. Her mother's forge and her home were the only things at the end of this path, which had been formed over time by the perpetual passage of feet. Had her mother's work been less popular, the ground beneath her would have been covered with moss and ferns. LeiRain exhaled heavily, forcing the remaining water out of her lungs so that she could easily breathe the air again. She always felt a bit heavy when she first returned to land and clearing the water from her lungs light-ened that load a bit. LeiRain took in her surroundings as the water ran out her nose and over her chin. It was late afternoon and the streets were beginning to clear as people went home to make their dinners and see to the evening chores. There wasn't much chill in the air this late in spring but she still felt a bit cold as she walked home in water-logged clothes.

The buildings along the cobblestone were all fine and sturdy, housing businesses such as the bakery, the shoe cobbler, and the grocer – those held by proprietors who could afford such a prime location. Behind those buildings the establishments were less rich but the shops were still considered reputable. The structures became smaller and less well-made the further inland one went into the village. The inland portion of the village was mostly residential, but a few of the more questionable businesses resided here. All of the shops – at least those in permanent structures – were owned by humans.

LeiRain nodded her head in greeting to a heavy-set blend woman with dark skin and a black cat-like tail that swished behind her as she packed away the goods she'd been selling. Blends and non-human sole-bloods made decent coin in Harbor, but they all operated out of wagons or small booths that were easily torn down and reassembled each day. The woman waved distractedly as she finished sealing up a crate, her mule toeing the ground behind her in agitation. The animal was laden with satchels, suggesting that this woman was leaving for good, not just calling it a night. Nobody in Harbor would sell land or property to a non-human so none stayed for more than a few weeks or a month or two at most.

LeiRain left dark water spots in the dirt road as she turned left and took the path away from the village to walk home. She cradled the wine bottles and ruminated on her disappointment over the fact that Bren would not be back. Their relationship had at least been honest and direct, and being connected to him, especially physically, had allowed her to forget her loneliness for a little while. She swiped angrily at the tears pearling in her eyes.

LeiRain shoved her emotions down, tucking them safely away before stepping out of the shaded lane and onto the grassy clearing near their home. The house she shared with her mother, a single-story structure of wood and brick, was set back against tall, thick trees. Their branches hung over the roof and kept the house pleasantly cool during the summer months. The clearing was raised slightly in the middle, though not enough to be called a hill, and that's where her mother's forge sat, its fire a safe distance from the house and surrounding forest. Its metallic roof reflected the late-day sun, causing LeiRain to squint. She frowned when she noticed a horse, it's black coat glossy in the afternoon sun, tied to a post just outside the workshop. The horse twitched its ears at the sound of metal objects falling just before a man stumbled backward out the structure, clearly having been removed by force from her mother's workspace. LeiRain froze, standing slightly outside the sanctuary of the trees. She slid the comb into one of her skirt pockets and placed her hand on the hilt of the rusted blade still wore.

'Crazy bitch!' the man yelled towards Alarra's workspace.

'And best you remember that the next time you consider asking me to make a weapon for your lot,' Alarra retorted.

The man, back on his feet and standing to his full height, brushed his blonde hair away from his face. It was Ethan, she realized with a start, the man she'd recognized on the pier just before the wine crates had been tossed. What was he doing here? LeiRain continued to quietly observe.

'My money not good enough for you? *I'm* not good enough for you?'

'Money's money,' Alarra said somewhat quieter, 'but I'll not have the blood of innocents on my hands. I heard what you did.' She now stood just outside the cover of her workshop with a half-finished blade in one hand and the other resting on one of the large water barrels she kept near the forge.

The water barrels, LeiRain thought. Would her mother notice if they were half-full of soaking wine bottles? She shook off the distraction as Ethan took a step toward her mother. Alarra's grip tightened visibly on the blade she was holding and Ethan halted, his hands fisted at his sides, muscles rippling with tension.

'What? To that clan of dwarves? What do you care?'

LeiRain might have thought him handsome if not for the way his face contorted in anger. His knees bent and he leaned slightly forward, making his body look coiled, like an animal ready to pounce.

'You and your men slaughtered them. For treasure that they did not even possess.' Her mother's voice was cool and level as she drummed her fingers on the top of the barrel, but LeiRain saw the way her brow crinkled slightly, and the lines at her mouth pulled tight. Alarra was uncomfortable, she felt threatened. LeiRain hoped her mother's brave words were enough to fool Ethan, to deny him the satisfaction of knowing the effect he had on her.

They accused the clan of stealing from a caravan of merchandise, LeiRain had overheard a dockhand say a few days ago. *Said it was the dwarves who'd ambushed it. But they didn't find a single piece of the goods on them. 'Course, they didn't bother to check until they'd killed the whole lot.* There was so much gossip along the docks that LeiRain hadn't placed much stock in this, but her mother did not buy into gossip. Alarra must have confirmed this with a reliable source. LeiRein had never before heard such disgust in her mother's voice and her own stomach turned to think that it may all be true. The men had allegedly taken what little wealth the clan had and killed every last dwarve – male, female and even their young.

LeiRain's hand tightened on the scabbard of her sword as she recalled another rumor claiming that the shipment was never ambushed and the humans responsible for transporting the goods had stolen from their employer, claiming highway robbery to cover their tracks.

A droplet ran down her brow, sweat or seawater she wasn't sure, but she remained intensely still and squinted at the man her mother had thrown from her workshop. Could he be a cheat and a thief? A murderer? She'd seen him roughing up those dockhands and dumping wine crates into the water. The two bottles she clasped now felt excessively heavy and she wished she'd left them in the harbor.

'What do you care for some thieving, sub-human beasts? They weren't even at work mining, which is all they're any good for.' The muscles in his jaw jumped and he held out a hand. 'If you're not going to fill the order, give back the drawing.'

Alarra lifted her chin. 'I know what this is, what it will do' she said, holding up a piece of paper that LeiRain hadn't noticed until now because it had been crumpled inside her fist. 'A weapon like this shouldn't exist,' her mother said, crumpling the paper still more.

'*Larra*,' Ethan's voice was quiet and laced with warning. He held out one hand, palm up. 'Give it to me.'

Her mother turned and threw the balled paper into the forge. A streak of orange flame sprouted up as the paper was incinerated. LeiRain looked at Ethan. His hand was still held out but the open palm had curled into a first and his face had gone red. A blue vein jumped out at his temple as he breathed heavily through his nose.

LeiRain couldn't stand watching any longer. She cleared her throat and stepped further into the sunlight, away from the trees.

Her legs shook slightly but she held her chin high and partially withdrew her sword from the scabbard, stopping just before it screeched in protest against the blade.

Ethan turned to look at her, eyes moving slowly from her head to her feet and then back up to her face. His gaze was cold and made a shiver run up her spine, but she refused to let him see her fear. She took him in as well, noticing his fine clothes, new boots and the royal blue strip of cloth tied to his right upper arm. A knife was strapped to his lower leg and there was a shortsword on the belt at his waist. Judging from the elaborately carved hilt, his sword was expensively made, though not as fine as anything her mother could forge.

LeiRain strode forward with her heart thumping so forcefully that she could feel it pulse in her ears. She tried to keep her eyes on Ethan but allowed herself a brief glance at her mother. Alarra met her gaze and LeiRain caught a brief flicker of fear behind the hardness in her face. Her mother shook her head, the movement so subtle that LeiRain would have thought she'd imagined it if it weren't for the warning in Alarra's eyes.

LeiRain's footsteps faltered and she halted a good ten paces away from where Ethan stood. Wildflowers and thick clumps of grass covered the clearing, and to LeiRain's mind, marked the end of the village's influence. It was a welcome place where she was safe from ridicule. She looked at the patch of purple flowers that Ethan had trampled while stumbling out of the workshop, and couldn't help but think of him as a blight. A poison that had somehow spread from the village and threatened to eat away their peace.

'Gods.' He looked back at her mother, disgust warring with amusement on his face. 'You kept the drossling.'

LeiRain was glad he'd looked away from her because she'd been unable to hide her flinch at the slur. *Drossling.* It was a derogatory name for blends, so foul that people only said it under their breath. She'd rarely ever heard it spoken so freely.

'I thought you would have tossed it back in the sea years ago.'

Drossling. It. LeiRain narrowed her eyes at him, cheeks flushing with heat.

'Maybe if I were a filthy dwarve or a drossling blend my money and my cock would suit you fine.'

Alarra took a step toward the man, hands on her hips. LeiRain could have sworn that Ethan flinched.

'Go fuck yourself, Ethan,' Alarra said with a snarl. 'Nothing's changed in the years you've been gone to make me want you.' LeiRain's eyes widened in surprise. Her mother wasn't one to be delicate with her language, but LeiRain had never heard her talk like *that* before. It made her stomach twist and her breath catch

'Hoy, what's that about dirty dwarves?' LeiRain jumped as a familiar voice boomed from the road behind her. She cast a glance over her shoulder at Ron, one of her mother's regular customers, who stepped out of the shadows and into the sunlit clearing. The dwarve's chainmail was a pristine dark gray but the long-sleeved shirt beneath was a sun-faded green. His barbuta helmet was so highly polished that the sun reflected off of it, making it difficult to look him in the eyes. The helmet, which Ron never seemed to take off, covered most of his face, revealing only his dark eyes and a thin strip of his lower face from nose to hairy chin. Wide and solid-looking, he made an intimidating figure, standing with his hand nonchalantly resting on the hilt of a sword – not the ax she was used to seeing him carry. Sprigs of bright red hair sprouted out of the chainmail on Ron's chest as his lengthy beard struggled to escape its confines.

The dwarve took another step forward and LeiRain felt a

wash of relief at his presence. When she glanced back at her mother, something about the set of Alarra's shoulders told her that she felt the same way.

Ethan lifted his chin slightly and tugged at the bottom of his tunic, straightening it for the first time since he'd stumbled. He shot a glare at Ron, and then LeiRain. The look in his eyes made her head spin as she struggled to hide her fear. She was accustomed to some mistreatment or lack of consideration from the villagers, but Ethan's glare held more than just the common disregard for blends. It felt personal: he hated *her.* Without another word, he untied the reins of his horse, hopped on the mare's back and took off riding for town, the horse's hooves kicking up a giant cloud of dust as he went.

3

_____

LeiRain breathed a quiet sigh of relief and pushed her sword all the way back into its sheath, shifting one of the bottles of wine to the hand that had been gripping the pommel. She adjusted her hold on the bottles to compensate for the slipperiness of her sweaty palms. She and Ron fell into step with each other as they approached her mother's workspace.

The fire in the forge had gone low, but she could still feel the heat radiating off of the dark red bricks that made a circular frame around the blaze and marked the boundary of the workspace. Tables piled with tools and partially formed weapons pressed against the walls on either side of Alarra. On the back wall, the light of the fire glinted off of several finished weapons. The clearing surrounding the workshop was alive with thick grass and wildflowers, but where Alarra stood, the ground had been repeatedly trampled and singed by escaping sparks, leaving it barren with packed dirt.

Alarra's back was to them and LeiRain took a tentative step forward, uncertain of her mother's state of mind. Alarra stared into the flames, hands on her hips, shoulders rising and falling with each heavy breath. Her mother reached for an iron poker and stoked the fire. The heart of it quickly flared from orange to blue, then purple before fading back to orange. Even several paces away, LeiRain still felt a wave of heat roll over her.

Ron broke the silence. 'Real piece of work that one, 'Lara. Not been back here for nearly ten years and thinks he can walk in and take what was never really his before he left.'

Her mother replied with a grunt, still turned away from them.

'Demi,' he said, turning toward Rain with a nod. He put his hand in his pocket and withdrew it, his fingers closed around something. LeiRain smiled and, setting the bottles of wine down in the grass, extended her hand to him. Ron opened his fist and deposited a small rock onto her waiting palm. It was tan, flecked with spots of white, gray and a very light pink. 'From the southern part of The Continent.'

She examined the stone while recalling all she'd read about the southern reaches. It was warmer there and the ocean waters were a different shade of blue. Her most prized book had colored illustrations, one of which depicted the water as a bright turquoise rather than the darker gray-blue of the waters off the coast of Harbor Village.

'Thank you.' She squeezed her hand shut around the stone and smiled at Ron. LeiRain hadn't realized she was still tense until her shoulders began to relax. It had been quite a while since she'd seen the dwarve and with Ethan's unwanted presence, it seemed that he couldn't have come at a better time. LeiRain looked again at the rock he'd given her before placing it lovingly in a pocket. Then, recalling the wine she'd been carrying, LeiRain bent down and picked up the two bottles. 'Wine?' She held them out to Ron in offering.

'Ah,' his eyes brightened when he saw what she offered.

'Thank you, Demi! This will cut down on the bar tab.' He winked at her.

At last, Alarra turned to face them, her sharp eyes narrowing on Ron. In the bright sunlight, it was easier to see that her mother was aging. There were fine lines on her brow and the corners of her eyes and creases had begun to form on her once smooth neck. But aside from this, and a few strands of white hair amongst the auburn, Alarra seemed untouched by the years. Her bright green eyes, the ones that she'd passed down to her daughter, still burned with the same intensity they had for all of LeiRain's childhood. 'What will it be this time, Ron?' There was a note of exasperation in her voice, but also a bit of playfulness. Ron had been one of her mother's customers for as far back as LeiRain could remember, and there had always been a bit of banter between the two of them. It seemed to LeiRain that this was the closest thing her mother had to a friendship.

'Well, errr...' Ron hesitated a bit, his voice losing some of its usual bravado. 'I was hoping you could fix this.'

The dwarve turned out a canvas sack he'd been carrying and two jaggedly broken parts of an ax blade landed in the dust. The metal was a darker gray than LeiRain's blade, the pieces glinting with a bluish hue where the sun hit them: sorcerer's steel.

LeiRain held back her gasp at the rare and expensive metal. Sorcerer's steel was known for its ability to hold enchantments and for being notoriously difficult to forge. Only the dwarves knew where to mine it – perhaps that was how Ron had come by so much of it. But how had he managed to break such strong material?

Ron gave the bag another shake and the splinters of a thick handle, made from the same material, landed in the dirt beside the shattered blade.

'How?' Her mother's eyes widened, and she shook her head as she took in the state of the weapon. 'That ax did not break with ease. What magic did this?' She looked up and examined Ron with her lips pursed, hands moving from her hips to cross over her chest.

'Oh, you know,' the dwarve said gruffly, fidgeting with his fingers like a young child caught in the act of mischief-making, 'just dragon hyde... It was a mighty beast, alright.'

'You saw a dragon?' LeiRain breathed out the words without meaning to, and she examined the remnants of the ax with much greater interest than she had moments ago. Dragons were believed to be extinct, killed off in the great war, just like the fae. It was known as the War of Sorrows for this very reason – it had brought about the end of two great magical species. But if Ron had seen a live dragon...

She looked up at him, uncaring that her mouth had fallen open.

'Uh,' he said, raising his hand up to ward off questions, 'to be honest, I didn't actually see a dragon. I faced a foe who wore dragon scale armor.' LeiRain frowned. 'Sorry,' Ron said, seeing her disappointment. He looked away from her as he reached inside his helmet and scratched his chin. 'For the record, though, he was still a mighty beast. And quite difficult to overtake given that he was covered in dragon scales.'

Alarra's eyes widened still further as she looked back and forth between the jagged bits of steel. 'The scales... The magic was still intact?'

It would take a powerful magic to shatter sorcerer's steel. A dragon's magic lingered in its remains for some time after it died, or at least that's what LeiRain had read. Since most dragons were believed to be long dead, it was rare to encounter any such magic. Ron gestured to his dismembered weapon, indicating that this was answer enough.

'I don't know if I can fix this one, Ron.' She knelt over the pieces to get a closer look.

'Aye, you always say that. But you know how important this piece is to me and my family. And you always find a way.'

LeiRain knew that weapons were often passed down from one generation of dwarves to the next. She wondered how old this ax was. How many hands had it passed through before Ron's?

'I'll pay double. You're the only one along the coast who can...' He looked around the clearing before lowering his voice. 'Renew the enchantment.' And it was true: it was believed that magic ran through the blood of all creatures, but that it ran too thin in human blood to be of any use. LeiRain didn't know if there were others like her mother, but Alarra... She could use magic.

It wasn't much. LeiRain had never seen her do more than imbue her metal work with magical enhancements, and she only did that for a few select clients – those she trusted with her secret. But it was enough that the villagers would both envy and fear her if they ever found out.

Alarra stood, her face serious. She was only a few inches taller than Ron when she straightened her shoulders and met his gaze, but he was afterall tall for a dwarve, standing just over five feet high.

'No, no. I mean it this time. It's not about the money, though you *will* be paying at least double for my efforts. This must have taken a great deal of crafting. I'm not sure I can ever restore its integrity.'

LeiRain nudged a piece of the ax blade with her toe, trying to imagine the strength of a blow that would shatter sorcerer's steel. She'd seen bits of the material in her mother's workshop before, but had never touched it until now. Given how strong the steel was, she expected it to be heavy, but it moved easily when she nudged it.

'Ah, well, you'll find a way. You always do,' he said, setting a bag of coins on a nearby table. 'Here's a down payment, in platinum. I'll bring the difference when I return in…?'

'A month, no earlier,' Alarra said and Ron smiled with gratitude and satisfaction at having convinced her to do the repair. 'You'll have to stick with a sword for a bit.'

'Ack, it's no bother. It forces me to stay proficient in both,' he glanced at LeiRain and winked. He patted the sword hanging from his belt. 'Right then, I've got to head out for my next job, anyway' he said. He turned, nodding towards Rain. 'And before you ask, Demi, I'm not at liberty to disclose the details. You'll have to wait until the job's done to hear about my adventures.' He smiled, holding up the bottle of wine in thanks before shuffling back into the trees from where he had emerged.

With Ron gone, LeiRain made to head for the house and change out of her damp clothing. Their small home was tucked into the trees on the far side of the clearing, a good fifteen feet from the forge just in case the fire ever got out of control.

'Rain.' She stopped at the sound of her mother's voice. It was soft and questioning. 'Tomorrow's your birthday.' LeiRain stood still, holding her breath in anticipation of her mother's next words. She would be nineteen tomorrow, reaching her majority according to The Continent law. Would Alarra press her to learn the iron work trade? Or to turn her talent for cooking into an occupation?

Her mother had mentioned both before and seemed to think that one of these paths would lead LeiRain to find her place in Harbor Village. But she didn't want a place in Harbor Village. She longed for the life that Ron had, moving from one job to the next as a sell-sword. He could turn down or accept jobs as he pleased, and most importantly, he didn't have to stay in one place. In fact, his occupation hardly allowed him to settle anywhere.

But Alarra dismissed the idea, warning LeiRain that there were things in the world she should fear more than the villagers' bigotry and a life of monotony.

Alarra had thus far ignored all of LeiRain's pleas for a sword, which is why the daughter of a skilled blacksmith carried around such a sorry excuse for a blade.

She waited for her mother to turn around, to at least ensure that LeiRain was still standing there, listening. But Alarra remained facing the other way, inspecting the broken ax. 'I was thinking I could take the morning off and go with you into the village. We could buy some pastries and tea and watch the ships come and go, maybe talk about plans for your future.'

LeiRain's insides twisted, her throat suddenly dry. They never spent their time together talking. Even when they actually ate together, they sat in silence save for the sound of their silverware scraping the plates.

'Alright,' she said, her tone of voice indicating otherwise. She'd never forgotten her mother's words after the terrifying encounter with her father. Alarra had told him that she'd been *afraid to love my own daughter.* When Caspian left, her mother refused to speak about his visit and so LeiRain had no idea what she had meant by this statement. Her mother had sacrificed a great deal for her, working at her forge, hot and soot-covered, sometimes for as long as ten hours a day to keep them in comfort. Most of the time, LeiRain believed her mother's words to be only an indication of how much she feared Caspian. Alarra had been protecting her from the moment she'd known a babe grew in her womb. But at other times,

LeiRain thought about her mother's words and wondered if she'd ever been able to overcome this fear, if she'd ever been able to love her daughter.

When her world felt suffocating, LeiRain tried to remind herself of her mother's sacrifices and her father's terror. After her encounter with Caspian, LeiRain had hoped life would change. That her mother would change. As LeiRain stood on the beach, shivering in her mother's arms all those years ago, she'd learned that her father had been responsible for the death of her grandparents. And that he had ordered her mother never to leave Harbor. *He* was the reason why she'd been trapped here, in this miserable village. But then her father had declared that he would never return, and LeiRain had thought this might free them to leave. She'd believed that Alarra would take them from Harbor Village and her world would open up. This hope, this belief that things would change, had eased the hurt of her father's rejection. And things had changed. But not enough.

Alarra had become more attentive, but only minimally. It was as if her mother had been unwilling to acknowledge LeiRain as a fixture in her life until she was certain her father would not take her away. They'd begun to take their evening meals together, and her mother had started to talk about LeiRain's future in a way she never had before.

But in the ways that really mattered, Alarra remained unreachable. LeiRain desperately wanted a close relationship with her mother, one where they talked about things beyond the practicalities of daily living. What had her mother's child-hood been like? Who were her grandparents? She knew the forge had belonged to her grandfather before his death. Had he, too, been able to wield magic and work sorcerer's steel? If not, how had Alarra learned to use this gift?

Her mother could be warm and conversational when

they discussed trivialities, but the moment LeiRain asked about her family or her mother's past, Alarra became a wall of ice. How might her world have been different if her grandparents were still alive? She imagined sharing a kitchen with a doting grandmother who would teach her the secrets of baking so that LeiRain did not have to learn them through trial and error. She pictured a grandfather who would ruffle her hair affectionately. LeiRain tried to imagine Alarra in such a world, to picture her mother smiling at her affectionately, planting light kisses on her forehead before bed each night but that's where her imagination found its limit.

Worse than Alarra's coldness was that her mother kept them in Harbor Village. Even after Caspian's promise that he would not return, Alarra had insisted on remaining in place. Surely this must have released Alarra from his original command to stay? If he wasn't returning, what was there for Alarra to fear in leaving? But her mother was full of excuses when LeiRain begged to leave. *My business is established and it would be too difficult to build it elsewhere,* and *there is no guarantee that another village will be any kinder to us.*

So, they stayed and the last few years her mother had spoken to LeiRain about learning a trade, insisting that she should have started apprenticing already. She knew better than to suggest LeiRain seek employment in the village. No one in the village would hire a blend, so she pressed LeiRain to shape a skill that allowed her independence.

When LeiRain had finally told her mother of her aspirations to become a sell-sword, Alarra had dismissed the idea immediately. *It's far too dangerous for a woman to go about on her own like that, not that anyone would hire a woman sell-sword anyway. And who will train you? Surely, anyone skilled with a sword began their training well before the age of their majority.*

And, *no, I will not make you a weapon to aid you on this path. Choose a more sensible occupation.*

Her mother was probably right, though LeiRain refused to admit this aloud. Despite this, the more her mother pressed, the fewer hours LeiRain spent at home. Instead, she spent most of her days scavenging the detritus on the harbor floor where her mother's nagging words could not reach her.

LeiRain picked up the water pitcher that sat outside her mother's workshop and drank deeply from it until there was nothing left. 'Um, pitcher's empty,' she croaked, her throat somehow still dry. She turned without another word and walked toward the barrels of rainwater. She carried the pitcher with her, its cool handle turning warm in her tight grip. Her cheeks flushed in irritation as she thought of her mother's desire to celebrate her birthday by forcing her into a conversation about a future she did not want.

Instead of refilling the pitcher and returning to the forge, LeiRain kept walking toward the house at a clipped pace. She yanked open the large wooden door to their home and stepped inside, sighing in relief as she stepped into the quiet privacy. It was dark and cool compared to outside, and it took a moment for her eyes to adjust to the low light. Walking through the kitchen and sitting area, she halted at her open bedroom door. Her jaw tightened – the door had definitely been left closed when she left. LeiRain scanned the room.

Her bedsheets were still askew from this morning, and the books on her bedside table remained in the same order she'd left them. Alarra likely opened the door to better air out the house, and indeed there was a nice breeze slipping in through the front windows and out the window in her bedroom. In her already irritable state, however, she cursed at that perceived invasion of her privacy. LeiRain pulled the comb out of her left pocket and set it down on top of her dresser, where she kept a small mirror. Maybe she'd put it in her hair later, just to see how it looked on her before she sold it off. LeiRain's regular trips into the ocean left her wavy hair perpetually stiff with salt water residue. It was difficult to comb and she kept it in a braid most of the time, but LeiRain couldn't help thinking the silver of the comb would look lovely against her blue-green waves. She sighed and turned away from the mirror.

From her other pocket, she withdrew the stone that Ron had given her and turned it over in the light from the window. She marveled at its otherness, the suggestion of adventure that it held, before kneeling down in front of her bed and withdrawing a heavy metal box. Her mother had made it to hold valuable items, and there was a lock that came with it, but the items the box held were valuable only in LeiRain's eyes. She flipped open its lid and took in the contents. Dozens of rocks, the largest as big as her palm, all different in color and texture. All representing another place, another exciting experience that she hoped to one day have. Ron had been bringing her these tokens from his travels for as long as she could remember, and she'd kept them all. Carefully, she placed this new one inside the box and closed the heavy lid, making sure it latched. She sighed as she pushed the box of daydreams back beneath her bed.

4

LeiRain remained kneeling on the floor for several minutes, absorbing the weight of today's disappointments. After swiping at her eyes a few times, she stood. She unclipped her sword belt and set the belt, scabbard and weapon to lean against the wall. She uncinched the ties that held her skirt in place and let it fall to the floor, pulled her shirt over her head, and then tugged off the thin shift she'd been wearing underneath. With a grand sigh of relief, she loosed the laces on her half-stay and let the supportive garment fall from her torso to her hips. The skin beneath her breasts bore red creases where the garment had been cinched tightly to carry the weight of them. She loosened the laces further and pulled it down over her hips and stepped out of it. Finally, she tugged off her dingy-white, knee-length stockings. Naked, she tossed the discarded clothes into a corner to await laundering. Pulling open one of her dresser drawers, she withdrew a long, wide strip of cloth and began to wind it around her chest.

Her breasts weren't overly large, but as she'd transitioned to womanhood over the last few years, the weight of them had begun to feel uncomfortable. She wore them unbound when she slept or wore her half-stay, which was only when she visited Bren. The half-stay cut a much more flattering figure than the band of cloth, but binding with cloth was much more comfortable and less restricting of her movement.

Once the band was tied off, she pulled out a sleeveless white blouse. It was actually meant to be worn as an under-garment but the band around her breasts kept it from being overly immodest. LeiRain then donned a pair of slim, brown pants lacing the waist over the bottom of her sleeveless blouse. She pulled on a fresh pair of stockings and slid her boots back on.

Next, she walked to the mirror and undid her braid. LeiRain ran a brush roughly through it, dropping fingerfuls of green strands on the floor as they came loose with the brush-ing. Loose like this, LeiRain's hair hung in thick waves that fell halfway down her back. Dividing her locks into two halves, she braided each tightly and then pinned the braids in a circlet around her head, tucking in the ends of each.

LeiRain took a book from the tall stack at her bedside table and carried it into the kitchen. It was a bit too early to start dinner so she sat down and placed the book on the table where it would rest in one of the patches of light from the window. She ran her hands over the thick tome. It was bound in brown leather with gold filigree on the cover. The title, *Before the War*, glistened in gold print, which was still legible but had begun to wear away with frequent touching.

All of her books were second hand and she'd largely taught herself to read. Alarra had instructed her in what she knew of math and angles, which was more than most as it was an important part of smithing. She'd also taught LeiRain her letters, but only the basics of reading. The rest, LeiRain had taught herself, with the help of Bren once their friendship had formed. There was a school in town, but it was only for boys and while she wished she'd had a better education, she was also somewhat relieved to have avoided formal schooling in Harbor. The village children could be mean to one another, especially to those who were different or judged inferior. If she'd been forced into a school with them all, surely she would have been the focus of their ire.

The book creaked as she opened it and she was careful not to force a bend in the spine. She liked how plainly books gave her information. Unlike her mother, they revealed histories with no evasion. *Before the War* was one of her favorite books because, in addition to detailed descriptions of past events, it also had illustrations, artists' interpretations of the world that had existed before The War of Sorrows.

Thinking of her encounter with Ron, she flipped through the pages until she found one of the illustrations that featured a dragon. The colors were faded, but her imagination was vivid enough to visualize the light reflecting off the scales of the great serpentine beast. The bright green dragon soared over a battlefield, leathery wings spread wide, an open maw with rows of sharp teeth on display. On its back rode one of the fae, his image nothing more than a shadow.

The War of Sorrows had taken place hundreds of years before LeiRain was born, and while dragon scales remained in circulation, providing artists and historians some clue as to what they looked like, there was no trace of the fae. Sometimes, they were depicted as dark, vague figures while other times they were painted as blurs of yellow light. No one knew what they looked like, and no artist seemed willing to attempt a more definitive rendering.

LeiRain examined the figure on the dragon's back, enjoying the mystery of it. She wondered if the fae would be remembered with such awe and respect if they weren't wrapped in enigma. The only certainty about the fae was that they had brought the war to a close – and they had done so at the cost of their own extinction.

She flipped until she found notes on the very end of the war and the beginnings of the current post-war world. There was a bit about 'the King's peace' and how a human king had come to rule most of the continent. She wondered how true that had been when this book was written, because the King's Men, the guards meant to keep his laws, never made it as far as the coast where she lived. The King's Men were meant to replace the vigilante justice that had risen up before the war. Toward the end of the chapter, there was an illustration of Ronland the Red, his fiery red beard and the large scar across his cheek were drawn in almost the same shade, making the slash look more like a fresh wound than a scar. Most books depicted Ronland as a hero, but this author viewed the dwarve more as a cautionary tale against vigilantism. LeiRain looked at the picture and ran a hand over her own cheek feeling the smooth skin where Ronland would have felt the raced edges of the blemish.

LeiRain flipped to an earlier section about the peace that preceded the fighting. A world where dwarve, shifter, human, and all other manner of creatures lived in close harmony. Resources were shared and intermarriage was common, which is how blends had come to be in the first place. Despite the commonplace nature of interspecies families, during what was known as *The Long Peace*, the author asserted that the term *blend* wasn't coined until sometime after the war. When resources became more scarce, these divisions began to arise.

She looked up from the book and stared blankly at a scratch on the table's surface, trying to imagine a Harbor Village where humans shared homes and had children with magical beings.

Perhaps that was a world in which she would be content to take on an apprenticeship. Maybe she would have studied with the pastry chef whose shop sold the little *sun cakes* she liked so much but couldn't quite replicate on her own. Not caring about her blue skin or freakish ability to breathe water, he would teach her the secret to making the perfect honey glaze to pour on top of the cakes and let her practice her hand at sprinkling the sugar crystals over the pastries as the glaze dried.

This made her stomach growl, loudly, bringing her back to the real world. The stream of sunlight through the window had turned from the bright white of late afternoon to the gentle orange glow of early evening. She closed the book and pushed her chair back from the table. It was time to get to work on dinner.

She rose and lit the oven, uncovering a roll of dough she'd left to rise this morning as it warmed. LeiRain scored the dough with a fine blade her mother had made just for this purpose. Alarra had refused to make her daughter anything she might use in combat, but had contentedly honored LeiRain's request for kitchen tools. By the time Alarra came in for dinner, the sun had faded to the point that LeiRain had lit a few oil lamps and the kitchen was filled with their warm radiance and the inviting smell of fresh, hot bread. Her mother's sleeves were still rolled up but her forearms were clean and glistening. She'd also washed off her face, slicking loose hairs back in the process. Her clothes were still sooty and scented of smoke as she sat down at the table. LeiRain poured wine into two metal cups and Alarra reached for one, taking a long pull from it before speaking.

'The bread smells good,' she said.

LeiRain put the steaming loaf on the table in front of Alarra, her only acknowledgment that her mother had said anything. Compliments were rare between them and it seemed to LeiRain that they came when her mother thought it was to her advantage to give them. She ladled them each a heavy bowl of stew before sitting down at the table herself. Alarra began cutting the bread and a thick curtain of steam rolled off the cutting board in between them. Regardless of her mother's agenda, the bread really did smell good. Both the stew and the bread were too hot to bite into without burning her mouth, and her mother stared at her seriously while they waited for the food to cool.

'I have money set aside for you,' Alarra said, breaking the uncomfortable silence. Her mother brought a spoonful of hot stew to her mouth and swallowed it without so much as blowing on it first. LeiRain poked at hers with her own spoon, still waiting for it to cool. 'I know you hate the forge, and I don't blame you.' Alarra went on. 'You don't have to come work with me.' The tightness in LeiRain's chest eased a bit and she dared to feel hopeful. With enough money, she could travel, hire someone to teach her how to fight. Steam coiled in front of Alarra's face as she tore her piece of bread in half. 'It's enough to get you started with your own food cart in town.' The tension in LeiRain's chest began to twist tight again, as she fidgeted with utensils. 'It could get you started, and once you figure out what sells best, we can work on finding your business a permanent structure.'

Even if she wanted to sell her baked goods, only the travelers would buy from her. She saw how poorly the vendors – who were almost exclusively blends – were treated by villagers, and it was easy to understand why none stayed for more than a few weeks. Did Alarra not know this because she spent so much of her time in the forge, or was she ignorant of it because her own humanness protected her from seeing such things? No one would rent LeiRain building space, and

44

she'd earn the ire of the entire village if she tried to compete with the local bakery. Alarra must have noted her skepticism as her mother raised a hand up in the air to halt LeiRain's speech.

'I know it won't be easy. Do you think it was easy to establish myself as a blacksmith?' Alarra took another bite of stew and stuffed a chunk of bread in her mouth. Her eyes were fixed on LeiRain as she chewed and swallowed. LeiRain was doing her best not to cross her arms in a pout. 'No one wanted to trust their weaponry to a female. I had to work hard, prove myself, and look for the right clients.'

LeiRain couldn't help herself at this. 'Yes, but you have magic! You are literally the only blacksmith on the coast who can work sorcerer's steel and place enchantments on your goods. Are you going to enchant my bread rolls for me?'

LeiRain tore off a piece of the bread slice that was cooling next to her, dunked it into her stew and then ate it, not allowing herself to flinch when its heat scorched the roof of her mouth. Alarra's days in the forge seemed to have made her immune to the heat, but LeiRain had no such advantage. She let the food rest on her tongue as she glared across the table at her mother who, by the set of her mouth, appeared infuriatingly unaffected by LeiRain's outburst.

Alarra reached for her own bread and picked up the slice thoughtfully, blowing on it before taking a small bite. When she'd finished chewing, she took another swallow of wine and then looked back at LeiRain.

'You won't continue to live under my roof without an occupation, so I suggest you discover a reasonable path forward in the near future. You're too old to be playing lost and found with the trash on the harbor floor. If you can't find a way to support yourself, then you'll have to leave.'

LeiRain had finally chewed and swallowed the too-hot bite

she'd taken, and she could feel a loose flap of burned skin on the roof of her mouth as she spoke. 'Great,' she replied. 'I'll take that money you've saved up to get me started and be on my way.'

'I'm not going to invest in my daughter's *death*,' Alarra said. Her tone hinted at disinterest, but there was a bit of fire in her eyes now.

'Staying here is just a slower death,' LeiRain replied. She'd meant to say this under her breath but it came out louder than intended. It was the truth in her mind, and judging by the way Alarra now pursed her lips, she wondered if it wasn't how her mother felt sometimes too. Alarra took another spoonful of stew, staring at the bowl now instead of LeiRain. When she looked back up, the heat in her gaze had vanished.

'Think about your options. We can talk about it in more depth tomorrow morning, over *sun cakes*.' Her mother tried to sound bright when she said *sun cakes*, as if buying her daughter's favorite pastry would make up for the life of drudgery she wished her to assume. LeiRain made no retort and they finished the meal in silence. Alarra wished her a good night as she headed to her room to undress and wash. LeiRain carried the dishes to the sink basin, set them down, then lifted one hand to brush her fingers lightly against her forehead. Right where she imagined that, in another life, her mother might kiss her goodnight.

LeiRain washed all the dishes save her cup, into which she emptied the rest of the bottle of wine. She drank it down quickly, pacing the kitchen as she did. Her mother was an early riser, and LeiRain would have to start her morning before dawn if she wished to avoid contact. She chided herself for letting hope seep in when Alarra had said there was money set aside, that she'd be allowed to do as she wished with the savings. The hope had only been a flicker, but it had been enough to make the reality hurt all the more. The money was not to be LeiRain's, rather, it was to be her mother's way of luring her into the life she had so far rejected. *Well,* she thought, cheeks warmed by anger and alcohol, *it isn't going to work.* She washed her empty cup and went to bed, hoping that the wine would lull her to sleep.

5

─────────

Despite the wine, sleep eluded her; her thoughts and feelings wouldn't settle enough to let her find rest. Anger, loneliness and disappointment swirled around inside LeiRain as she tossed and turned. After trying for hours to fall asleep, she finally kicked off the sheets and sat up. She'd left her hair braided, knowing that the morning would be a rush to get out the door before her mother woke. A few curly tendrils of hair had broken free in her restlessness and now clung with sweat to her face and neck. The thin shift she wore to bed stuck to her skin and she had to peel it off herself before pulling it over her head.

With a resigned sigh, she swung her feet over the side of the bed and onto the cool floorboards. She stood, walking over to her dresser. Bright moonlight shone through her window, illuminating the room without an oil lamp. The clothes she'd donned earlier were in a heap next to her small mirror and she threw her damp shift on top of the pile before methodically wrapping her chest. She caught a glimpse of herself as she reached for the sleeveless blouse and frowned at the dark purple circles under her eyes, contrasting sharply against the light blue of her skin. She drew the string tight on the waist of her pants and carefully tucked her pant legs into her boots before lacing them tightly. Pants were, in general, more convenient for underwater wear than skirts, but none of her clothes were really designed for such an environment, so she did her best to keep the loose ends securely tucked when possible. She picked up her sword and sword belt to don once she was outside. She was still getting used to wearing it and didn't want to risk waking her mother if she bumped into things with the scabbard as she navigated out of the house in the dark.

Slowly, she opened her bedroom door and stepped into the sitting room and kitchen area. The door to her mother's bedroom was closed and she was likely fast asleep, having been up with the sunrise the previous day. Nevertheless, LeiRain stepped lightly, trying her hardest to avoid the floorboards known to creak. She clutched her sword belt tightly in her arms, pressing it against her chest. As she made her way to the door, a flash of light caught her eye and she turned toward it. To her surprise, a polished broadsword, scabbard and shield rested on the kitchen table, along with a note scrawled in her mother's slanted, unschooled handwriting. She picked up the note and held it in a thread of light.

To my daughter, on her Majority. Happy birthday, Rain.

She set the note down, blinking back tears as she examined the weaponry. It was some of Alarra's best work, LeiRain thought. It was also one of the most affectionate demonstrations her mother had ever made, second only perhaps to Alarra's desperate embrace the day her father had taken her to the ocean. She brushed away the memory, focusing on her mother's gift. LeiRain had thought the blue hue of the shimmer she'd seen was a trick of the light, but now realized that all three pieces were made entirely of sorcerer's steel.

Her heartbeat quickened as she wondered what enchantments her mother might have placed on them. Stepping closer, she examined the details of the metal work. The sword looked small on its own, but when LeiRain picked it up, the length and weight felt perfect for her. The blade had a subtle curve to it, making the single sharpened edge slightly longer than the dull-edged backside of the weapon. The hilt felt as though it were formed to the arc of her grip and she was delighted to see that it was detailed with a pattern of tiny, shimmering scales. Where it looped around and met with the hilt again, it ended in the shape of a wide fluke, like the tail of a large fish.

There were intricate embellishments along the blade of the sword too. Sea creatures were etched into the metal, looking almost alive, but when she ran her finger across the flat of the blade, it felt entirely smooth, no trace of carvings. The creatures appeared to shift as light hit the sword at different angles, just like her father's robes. LeiRain found herself suddenly lost in memory.

It was a hot summer day and she was napping in the sunny clearing outside the forge. There was a loud clang, a break in the usual rhythm of her mother's hammer against steel. LeiRain opened her eyes and thought, for just a moment, that she might still be asleep. The tall, broad figure standing over her, skin as blue as her own, must be a dream. His richly embroidered robes, decorated with underwater scenes, glimmered in the sunlight. But then he spoke and LeiRain knew he was real. 'So we have a daughter,' the man standing over her said. Not just any man, but tempest. A water deity. Her father.

Coming back to herself, LeiRain slid her palm carefully over the lively carvings, tracing her hand along the blade once more before examining the scabbard. Lines that resembled rolling ocean waves ran down the length of the sheath, and just like the blade, the steel was smooth to the touch when she traced the lines with her fingers.

Nearby sat the shield, which was shaped like half an oyster shell. Its surface was etched to give the illusion of the front edges curving outward. It was so precisely designed that LeiRain had to touch the edges to be certain that they curved slightly back and not out as the carvings would have her believe. She shook her head in awe, having not realized before the true depth of her mother's artistry. Most of Alarra's commissions were requested with urgency and something like this must take a great deal of time, or at least a great deal of planning and magic.

In the center of the oyster shell, where a pearl might be found, rested a large, iridescent opal. When she touched it, the stone was flush with the metal, though it was smoother and much cooler to the touch than the steel. Its aquamarine swirls felt familiar but it took her a moment to understand why.

Jeweled pendants hung from her father's neck as he loomed over her in the clearing. The most striking was a large opal, its shifting shades of blue and green like a bit of ocean captured and contained.

LeiRain shook her head and let out a slow breath. She stared into the dark hallway, blinking, until her heartbeat slowed and her body remembered that she was here, in the kitchen. She was no longer that frightened eleven-year-old. LeiRain swallowed, looking back down at the weapons. She studied the opal again, then the carvings. Her mother had taken those terrifying memories and crafted them into something beautiful.

'Thank you,' she said to the empty room. In that moment, she felt like she might actually be able to let her mother in, to trust her with her affection. *I love you,* she thought, and maybe if Alarra had been there, she would have said it out loud. But, her mother had not been brave enough to give her this gift in person. LeiRain began to wonder at her mother's motivation in crafting her these pieces. She certainly hadn't given up dissuading her from pursuing the life of a sell sword. Could this be her mother's way of compromising, offering an olive branch? Perhaps Alarra simply thought that the weapon her daughter had been carrying reflected poorly on her as a metal worker. But as much as she appreciated the gesture, LeiRain would not, *could not*, compromise on her future.

Gently, LeiRain sat her sword belt down on the table. She unlocked the leather straps that held her scabbard to the belt, and removed her old sword and its sheath. With care to maintain stealth, she laced the straps through the loops on the scabbard her mother had made before picking up the sword. It was lighter than the one she'd been using, but she would still have to build up her strength to wield it properly.

LeiRain slid the blade gingerly into its sheath, trusting her mother's work not to groan and squeal like her old sword and scabbard. LeiRain could make out something else on the table that must have been laying beneath the shield. It did not reflect the light as the metal work had and she was unsure what she might find when she reached out with her right hand. Leather. It was a leather strap. She picked it up and held it in the moonlight streaming through the window. It was a guige, a heavy strap that would allow her to carry the shield more easily by sliding it on to her back. She kept it in her right hand with her sword and held the shield in her left hand as she crept outside.

Once clear of the house, she walked to her mother's workspace and set the shield face down on one of the tables; it was so highly polished that LeiRain didn't want to set it on the ground. She draped the guige over her left shoulder and adjusted the buckle to fit just over her right hip, then took it off and ran the strap through the loops on the back of the shield before buckling it again. With some awkwardness, she held onto the shield with her left hand while pulling her head and right arm through the guige.

LeiRain used both hands to guide the shield over her left shoulder where it hung against her back. She held her arms overhead, then out in front of her, and then raised her shoulders up and down a few times to accustom herself to the weight and the pull of the leather strap across her chest. Once it was on her back, the burden was much easier to bear, but LeiRain would need to become more practiced at handling this piece of equipment. It would take time for her to get used to it.

Now that she had donned her new weaponry, LeiRain felt a pang of guilt at leaving. She hadn't left a note for her mother, and normally wouldn't have thought much of it but... She looked at the sword on her hip. No, this is what her mother wanted. She wanted LeiRain to feel a sense of obligation at such an elaborate gift. It might have been crafted with love, care and the best of intentions, but it was still a manipulation and LeiRain would not be forced into compromise. If her mother was right about anything, it was that LeiRain did need to find her independence, to identify a path and choose it. She was nineteen now, an adult. It was time to find her way.

She took in a deep breath, filling her lungs with crisp night air, then let it out in a determined sigh as she began to walk toward the village. Her pace quickened and her breaths came faster, creating little puffs of steam that she could just make out in the starlit. It was darker on the heavily wooded path between their home and the village, and the fact that any light broke through the trees at all was a testament to the fullness of the moon. Having not slept, LeiRain expected to feel a heaviness in her steps but instead she was energized. Perhaps it would catch up to her later, but right now she couldn't remember when she'd ever felt so alive.

She could have entered the water at the beach closest to her home, but LeiRain disliked the idea of walking beneath the ships at night, their long shadows replacing what little moon and starlight could make it past the water's surface. Instead, she decided to cut through the village and make her way to the southern beach. LeiRain walked briskly through the empty streets. Harbor was eerily still at this hour. It was too late for the revelers and drunks to still be about, and too early for the shopkeepers, vendors and dock workers to be setting up for the day. There were bits of trash scattered about the cobblestone street, remnants of the day before. A few rats gnawed at someone's dropped pastry, scattering to the shadows as she passed nearby, then slinking back out to finish their meal when they deemed her no longer a threat.

Her steps halted and LeiRain took in the stillness. For a brief moment, in this quiet emptiness, Harbor Village felt like something else. It was full of possibility and newness, a strange land ready to be explored. She imagined this was how travelers saw the village as they passed through. LeiRain continued walking, the spell cast by stillness and quiet dissipating when she stepped over the remnants of a shattered wine crate, a reminder of the cruelties found in daylight.

The cobblestone paving came to an end just past the last pier where it met with the beach. She stepped off of the road and onto the coarse sand. In the low light, the sand looked white rather than the tan she knew it to be and her feet sank a few inches with each step until she reached the wet packed sand at the water's edge. The tide was starting to go out, leaving shallow pools as it pulled away from shore. She could make out a few anemones in the pool closest to her, and the slick shells of crabs skittering beneath a large boulder that was entirely submerged an hour ago.

None of the normally bright colors were observable. The nighttime muted them to shades of brown and gray. LeiRain paused for a moment, the cold water lapping at her ankles, and took in the expansiveness of the ocean before her. Some part of her knew that she was being reckless, but it felt like she couldn't stop, propelled forward by her drive to break free of Alarra's expectations.

She didn't know if she was trying to convince herself, or her mother, but LeiRain had to prove that there was more out there for her and she could not do that over sun cakes and tea. She had never left the shores of Harbor, had never even gone more than a mile offshore on her most adventurous day. LeiRain swallowed and took another step forward. She wouldn't return until she'd at least visited another village, seeing for herself what opportunities she might find elsewhere. The bright orb of the moon reflected off the water like a beacon, calling her to the depths. LeiRain sucked in a lungful of cool night air, steeling herself for what lay before her, then walked confidently out into the surf until her head disappeared beneath the waves.

6

———

LeiRain headed south, scanning her surroundings as she went. The human detritus littering the ocean floor near the village became less common as she walked along an uninhabited part of the coast. She heard the little clicks and whirs of tiny aquatic creatures as they moved to feed and breed in the more fecund waters nearer shore. The sounds both comforted and disconcerted; there was a certain normalcy about the comings and goings of creatures along the tideline, but the way sound carried in the water always made her second guess how near she was to the source. Occasionally, a click or a pop came to her ears so loudly it would make her jump, expecting to find the source within arms reach, but there was never anything there when she whirled around to look.

With the added weight of a shield, she no longer had to flutter her arms to keep her feet on the ocean floor, but it did add a bit of surface resistance as she pushed forward through the water. The muscles in her legs began to burn within the first hour and she had to switch between walking and swimming to give her thighs an occasional break. The water was relatively clear and shallow but with occasional pockets of darker water, filled with tiny organisms too small to see but numerous enough to make the ocean cloudy.

She was working her way through one of these pockets when she remembered the rocky cliffs lining this part of the shore. On a clear day, you could see them from Harbor, and she knew from talk amongst the sailors that there was no beach here. If she tried to exit the water along this part of the coast, she would meet with a high-reaching wall of stone. It would be impossible to climb without the right gear, and the land would be inaccessible to her. LeiRain pushed off the sandy bottom and kicked her legs to swim upward until she was treading water just below the surface. She scanned the shoreline for a shallow inlet or anything resembling a beach, but all she saw were miles of steep, smooth rock face. If she wanted to exit the water, she thought with a rapidly beating heart, she would have to walk further south or turn around and return to Harbor. LeiRain let herself sink back to the ocean floor and pushed the thought from her mind; she'd never been so far away from the safety of land before. Her steps quickened in search of clearer water. She didn't want to give fear the chance to dissuade her from her purpose.

The water became much deeper and eventually the waves were crashing nearly fifty feet overhead. It was the deepest she'd ever been and it was terrifyingly dark with thin streams of early morning sun just barely cutting through the surface. She moved forward more slowly now, giving her eyes time to adjust to the strange way shadows moved at such a depth.

LeiRain felt a wave of relief as she realized the sun was growing brighter. Golden streaks of light reached down from the sky and began to spread across the ocean floor. It hit the sand in little patches, creating mesmerizing patterns of light and shadow beneath the waves. Colors she couldn't see before were now vivid, the small rocks and shells on the ocean floor more clearly visible. The effect was eerie, and though she welcomed the increased visibility, the play of light made this new world seem all the more alien.

Sound moved differently here as well, the frantic noise of the teeming coastal life having long faded away. In its place were groans and clicks that sounded less hurried, almost sluggish, as if it took more effort to move through the much colder waters of the deep.

LeiRain's breath quickened, the cold water rushing into her lungs and back out slightly warmer. She strained her eyes toward the south where she thought she could see the ocean floor moving up in a gentle slope, returning to the shallower depths that were more familiar to her. Pausing, she cast a glance toward the open ocean. A deep blue world stretched out before her, full of mystery and danger. LeiRain's stomach tightened against the invisible tug that tried to draw her forward. She hadn't had much of a plan, just the idea of finding her way to another village, spending the day somewhere new and returning to Harbor the next day. Now, she found herself drawn more to the sea than land. Why hadn't she explored beyond coastal waters before? Fear? Yes, there was fear. But also, LeiRain realized, she had let herself fall into habit.

She'd told herself that she would not be lulled into the routine of village life, and without realizing it, she'd turned her rebellion into a routine of its own. Never venturing further out to sea, treading the same path each day. Never daring. Never growing. Today, she'd reached her majority. She was officially an adult. If LeiRain didn't push herself now, step outside of what was comfortable *now*, how could she ever hope for things to change? Did her own fear keep her just as rooted in Harbor Village just as much as her mother's?

The sun found a clear path through the waves in a way that made her certain there were shallower waters ahead. She thought she could hear the soft scraping noise of sand crabs skittering between submerged rocks, and the splash of a bird diving for fish. If she kept moving south, she would find herself somewhere different, but still familiar. Safe.

LeiRain's heart fluttered and her hands balled into tight fists as she made her decision. The water before her was such a deep, dark blue that she couldn't tell if she was seeing far off into the distance or only a few feet ahead. There were reassuring patches of brightness across the sand, but they were separated by larger swaths of shadow. She fought the urge to glance once more south, knowing that it would cause her to second guess herself. Anyone could make their way to the next village, but she knew no one else with the ability to explore the secrets of the deep ocean. She rested a hand on her sword, gripping the hilt for reassurance, as she followed her curiosity into the darkness.

She pushed forward into the deep, body humming with equal parts fear and wonder. Her arms and legs burned, her body carrying more weight than she was accustomed to. She'd been moving west for what seemed like hours now. The ocean floor had appeared largely barren with only small clumps of stunted sea grass and the occasional shape of some hidden creature shifting beneath the sand.

After traveling a mile or so out, LeiRain began to relax. She stopped expecting something to dart out at her from every shadow and actually fooled herself into believing that her visibility stretched for miles. She was staring at the ocean floor as she walked, growing bored with the lack of scenery when she felt a flutter of movement. Flashes of silver appeared only a few feet in front of her and streaked past her face. Her heart stuttered as they brushed against her cheeks, then surrounded her entirely, rippling the water around her arms and legs.

Seconds later, she laughed with relief. It was only a school of fish, swirling around her in a mad, semi-organized tornado of fins and scales. They were small, no bigger than her hand and yet their presence was still intimidating as they slashed through the water around her. It was over in less than a minute and the fish disappeared into the darkness behind her just as suddenly as they'd arrived. After that, she moved more cautiously, her heart speeding up each time she felt movement within the depths.

She wasn't certain how, but she could sense where the water ended and dry land began. It was like closing your eyes and still having a good idea of where your hands were, even though you couldn't see them. It had always been this way in Harbor Village, but she'd thought that was just because the waters were so familiar to her. Yet, even here in this strange new place, she knew intuitively where the water ended.

LeiRain estimated that she had moved three or four miles away from the shore by this point. When she turned her senses to the west, to the open ocean, she could still find the water's end, but the distance was so vast that it came to her with a sort of fuzziness. Thinking about the expanse before her felt overwhelming, almost incomprehensible, so she withdrew her focus from the water's western limit. As LeiRain was recoiling from the immensity of the waters ahead, she noticed something else. It was a widening expanse of water, but in a different direction. Her already cautious pace slowed further and she came to a halt just as her toes met with the floor's end.

She looked down to where the ocean's bottom dropped away. Of course, she knew it wasn't really bottomless, she could sense the edges of it, but in only slightly better focus than the ocean's westward limit. The water was somehow both clearer and darker here, an inky black seeming to radiate from the drop-off. She felt every part of her body recoil. Her arms and legs hummed with energy and her mind screamed that she should flee. She deliberately slowed her breath to ward off the threatening panic. LeiRain imagined taking another step, falling and sinking into the blackness. Even surrounded by cold water, she could tell that she was sweating. She could feel the heat radiating from her cheeks into the chilly vastness.

LeiRain wondered if she would still have her sense of place if she slipped into the darkness, or if she would be lost, with no awareness of what was up and what was down? That was silly, of course she would still have her sense of the water's limit, but something deep and instinctual warned her away from the blackness. She shoved down the primal urge to flee and forced herself to walk further south along the jagged edge. Her heartbeat pulsed in her temples and her breaths came faster as she urged herself on. There was a thin line, she realized, between thrill and terror, and she liked the rush that it gave her to be so near to something that felt so dangerous. It reminded her very much of how she'd felt in her father's presence, and this more than anything spurred her on.

LeiRain walked and swam south for what seemed like hours and saw no sign of the drop-off ending. She had just begun to entertain the idea of turning back east, toward the shore, when a spot of brightness caught her eye.

Across the chilling void of the drop-off, light danced on white sand. Sea grass and thick, bright kelp grew strong and tall. The ocean floor on the other side seemed to rise and fall like rolling hills. Though the water in this oasis was just as deep as where she now stood, bright rays of sunlight penetrated through. Flickers of colorful movement caught her eye and she knew that the terrain before her was flourishing with life. Aquatic plants with orange and purple blooms swayed with the currents and small, iridescent fish darted about. It was lively and inviting like nothing she had seen before. She imagined being close enough to run her fingers gently over the blossoms, or to see the detailed patterns on the fish. But the inky blackness of the drop-off still loomed, a barrier between her and the wonder beyond.

LeiRain clenched and unclenched her fists, took a steadying breath and pushed off the edge before she could second guess herself. There *was* something different about the way the water moved in and around the edges of the drop-off. Instead of smelling of life and organic things, it stunk of death. She dared to look down and saw nothing in the dark waters yet still imagined rotting things and gnashing teeth. The water she inhaled here was almost debilitatingly cold, and LeiRain wasn't sure if that was because of the actual temperature or the necrotic scent that came with each lungful. Fear and exhilaration propelled her over the yawning chasm, allowing LeiRain to stave off the effects of the unnatural chill.

She swam more quickly than she would have thought possible considering her fatigue, but adrenaline sang through her veins and gave LeiRain uncommon speed. She became acutely aware of her sword and shield and how much they weighed her down. Still, she pressed on. The distance across the drop-off was greater than it had looked, greater even than she had felt with this special sense of hers.

She arrived at the other shore panting, the tightness in her chest making it difficult to take in full breaths. LeiRain sank to the floor, hands and knees buried in the sand, gasping and fighting to maintain consciousness. The bright colors of coral and undulating sea plants she'd admired now spun around her as she fought off dizziness. She finally composed herself, but not until the last bit of foul water from the drop-off had been forced from her lungs. She exhaled its cold sourness and drew in a deep breath of the warmer, cleaner water of the kelp forest. By the time her head stopped spinning, her eyes had mostly adjusted to the brightness and she could better appreciate the beauty of her surroundings. LeiRain heard the whoosh, click and scraping of aquatic life; could feel it humming around her.

Her visibility stretched for miles. Rolling ocean valley laid out before her, dotted with clumps of bright and thriving coral, plants and clusters of kelp that occasionally grew so tall they must have broken the surface. She glanced back over her shoulder. Beyond the oily black of the drop-off was deep blue water and white sand from which she'd come. LeiRain looked down at her hands as she pushed off the floor to stand and blinked as it sparkled with tiny flecks of gold. Green sea grass and purple seaweed covered large patches of the floor near where she stood, tiny fish slipping in and out of their gracefully swaying tendrils.

More fish, most brightly colored and sporting spots, stripes or other daring patterns not found in the waters of Harbor Village, darted around coral structures in shades of pink and blue. She marveled at her surroundings, the colors more vivid than any art in her books. Even the anemones tucked within the coral branches were brighter than those back home. LeiRain jumped slightly at something large sliding atop the sand next to her, but it turned out to be only a shifting shadow, cast by some of the high-reaching kelp as it swayed in a ripple of current. She walked forward, so enthralled with the tall plants that she caught herself only seconds before nearly bumping into a large cluster of purple-black sea urchins.

When another flicker of movement caught in her peripheral vision, she both cursed and laughed at herself as her head spun around reflexively. She expected to see nothing more than shadow, but it was obvious that the sun touched everything in front of her. LeiRain's eyes narrowed, moving from the brightly lit ocean floor to the dark folds within the kelp. There was something there and perhaps she was just being paranoid, but it felt like something intelligent. It felt like something was *watching* her. LeiRain crept closer to one of the kelp plants, studying the shadows between the tall strands. Her pointed ears strained for any out of place rustling sounds, but it was difficult to hear over the noise of her thrumming heart. A school of fish swam contentedly nearby, the mass of bodies swishing through the water audibly, but she was listening for something larger. The school of fish passed and disappeared into the plant life.

LeiRain noticed more movement in the water as her senses came alive in a way they never had before. Her limbs tingled with readiness and a primal reaction overpowered her exhaustion. She could close her eyes and instinctively know where things were around her. She could feel the kelp, even sense some of the individual strands and know how high they reached. It was the same way she knew where the ocean ended and could feel it lap against the far shore. But if that sensation felt remote, the sensation she felt now close, almost intimate.

LeiRain jerked her head around as something moved from within one of the kelp plants to her right. She squinted at the dark space between the swaying strands— The kelp let out a playful giggle.

LeiRain jumped. It was difficult to discern the source of a sound underwater, but she was almost certain it had come from somewhere between the kelp's skyward-reaching leaves. LeiRain didn't move, didn't breathe, as she searched the space in front of her. More movement, within the shadows of the tall growing seaweed, out of sync with the swaying of the kelp.

She brought her hand up slowly and clasped the pommel of her sword, pulling it free of the scabbard. It was weighted differently in the water, the sword becoming both lighter and also more difficult to wield as the force of the current pushed against the flat of the blade. With a turn of her wrist, she shifted the blade so that the current ran smoothly over its thin edge. She took a step forward and pointed its tip at the small humanoid figure hiding within the plant life.

LeiRain's stomach was a mess of knots as she spoke. 'Step into the light,' she commanded, forcing her voice to project smooth confidence.

The figure obeyed, and LeiRain's eyes widened as she took in the being before her. Her grip on the sword loosened and she began to lower the blade. The creature looked at her with wide, black eyes above a slender nose. Curls of dark blue hair floated around the creature's head and sharply pointed ears framed either side of her cherubically round face. Only four feet high, the girl was clad in a weave of green and brown seaweed that just covered her chest and groin. The rest of her skin was bare and its light blue color helped her fade into the shadows.

On closer inspection, LeiRain realized that the creature's skin was not a solid blue like hers, but dappled with spots of green, tan and a light pink. It was a perfect camouflage among the coral and seagrass. The child did not cower under LeiRain's inspection but returned her gaze, the large, dark eyes unblinking. Her tiny mouth turned up slightly on one side in a smirk. The confidence with which the creature stood her ground told LeiRain that there was a fierceness the dainty appearance belied.

LeiRain examined the fingers that curled around the kelp and noticed that they were several inches longer than what would be considered proportional in most humanoids. The delicate fingertips were capped with thin, sharp-looking fingernails akin to claws and there was webbing between the girl's fingers and toes. LeiRain wondered what those claws might be meant for and failed to hide her shudder. The girl's smirk turned into an even smile, then, and she laughed, the sound like tiny bells ringing underwater. Something in the depths of those black, staring eyes and the coolness of the girl's grin sent a chill up LeiRain's spine. This creature might be small and young, but she was not helpless, and she was much more comfortable in this environment than LeiRain.

'Who are you?' LeiRain asked, biting off the urge to say *what* instead of *who.*

The creature opened her mouth to speak. LeiRain wasn't expecting the strange, piercing sound that the girl emitted and she flinched at the initial notes, which were reminiscent of whale song. A cold, hard knot formed in LeiRain's stomach and her throat felt tight as she swallowed. She'd heard numerous languages spoken before, but the otherness of this creature's speech made LeiRain want to slink away.

Without consciously deciding to, she drew back her sword arm and readied a strike. Then, just as abruptly as it had come, the sound cut off. The girl's round eyes seemed to grow even wider just before she darted away into the thick foliage. LeiRain stared after her, feeling slightly guilty. Perhaps she'd misread the creature and frightened her away when she'd braced for attack. Or perhaps LeiRain's fear had been so apparent that it had been offensive?

She chewed on her lower lip as she worked out how to proceed. Fascination and curiosity tugged LeiRain forward. But fear and caution held her back. What was this creature? Had she been trying to communicate? The girl was far better adapted for this aquatic world, and there was no way to know her intentions, or if there were more just like her nearby. But if

LeiRain let this opportunity slip away, she might never encounter such a creature again. She *had* to learn more. LeiRain, having made up her mind, bent her legs to push off the ocean floor and follow the girl into the aquatic forest. At the last second, something made her hesitate. Something felt ... wrong. A chill ran up her spine, again, and this time goose-flesh sprouted along her arms. Her newly discovered senses shrieked with warning. Another presence disturbed the water behind her. Something *big*.

7

LeiRain swallowed back the bile in her throat as the smell of decay rippled through the water. She hadn't yet turned around, but could sense the creature's presence as it slithered up from the abyss of the drop-off.

Her heart thundered as she pivoted on her heels and her breaths came fast. She took in the menacing gray figure in front of her. Its large maw was stuffed with yellowed teeth, row after uneven row of them. They filled the beast's mouth so thoroughly that LeiRain doubted it could close all of the way. Behind the head, at least six feet of its slimy, narrow body had become visible and still its full length hadn't yet slid into view. It moved with an obscene grace.

LeiRain's stomach lurched as the creature finally finished its ascent – the eel-like beast was close to ten feet long. Its lissome undulations were made more grotesque by the sickly pallor of its gray flesh and the smell of rot that accompanied it. Some atavistic part of LeiRain's mind screamed at her to flee, but her speed could not possibly match the beast before her. And what of the girl?

She forced down her rising panic and remembered her sword. Hands shaking, she fumbled to adjust the grip on the pommel. Water rolled off the beast's great body, the movement powerful enough to create a current of its own. She stood, half-frozen with her blade held in front of her as the milky pale, bulging eyes and gaping, putrid mouth moved closer. She shifted her weight between feet, stirring up the ocean floor as she waited for the attack but instead of meeting with her blade, the beast swept past her. She felt a rush of relief and then confusion as she watched it slither into the kelp forest. It had ignored her entirely, but why?

Strange cries rose from the darkness. *The child.* LeiRain's fear boiled over into anger, and adrenaline urged her to move. There was only a brief moment to consider her course of action before she crouched low and shoved off the ocean floor, propelling herself toward the monster's gray underbelly. Focusing all of her anxious energy into her sword arm, LeiRain swung, thrusting against the water's resistance.

It was unskillful. Sloppy. But it accomplished the task. She nicked the narrow end of the creature's tail. The beast made a sound that was half roar, half squeal, and a thin stream of oily, purple blood began to leak from where her sword had made contact.

LeiRain braced as the beast wheeled on her, maneuvering through the water with an ease that made her wonder if she'd just made a terrible mistake.

If nothing else, she consoled herself, at least the child might have a chance to get away.

The beast gnashed its teeth at her but did not immediately attack. She took the opportunity to widen her stance and tug her shield over her left shoulder. As the monster slithered around her in increasingly narrower circles, LeiRain saw that, in addition to translucent gray fins, the beast possessed four scrawny arms. They were short, maybe only a foot long, and dangled limply at its sides. The arms hardly looked functional; perhaps they were just a vestigial feature passed down from the beast's ancestors. But then LeiRain saw its spindly fingers flexing and knotting into fists, over and over again, sharp claws clacking together as it did so. With each pass, the monster came closer and those claws looked more threatening.

Time seemed to slow as she watched the monster's dorsal fin cut through the water. LeiRain's breathing steadied and her awareness shrank until there was nothing but her and the beast. Though adrenaline still surged through her body, she felt no desire to flee. The moment for escape had passed and her fear shifted into something new; a peculiar sense of calm. Her mind became clearer, her vision sharper, and her muscles coiled, ready to respond. She turned in circles where she stood, following the monster's movement, not daring to take her eyes off of it.

Again and again the beast circled her, and still it did not attack. LeiRain could feel the weight of her sword and shield, the slight quiver in her thighs, and still she remained poised for action. Her discomfort was just a white noise in the background of the stand off, but LeiRain became aware that she was gripping her blade too tightly. If her fingers went numb, it would be hard to maintain her grasp. Keeping her eyes on the beast, LeiRain adjusted her hold on the pommel. The tip of the blade bobbed slightly as she did so, two of her fingers peeling away from the metal. Fearing she might drop her sword, LeiRain's eyes darted briefly to her right hand—

No sooner had her eyes wandered than the beast struck out. LeiRain looked up in time to see its mouth yawning open only inches away. Its jaws slammed together, just barely missing her shoulder and sending a wave of putrid water rolling over her face.

LeiRain stumbled back, eyes wide and shield held in front of her. Just as quickly as it had struck, the monster darted back to the perimeter of the circle it had been making. LeiRain blinked away her shock and tried to regain the focused calm she held only moments before. *Too close, Rain*, she thought. *You can't take your eyes off of it again.* There was something different about the way the beast circled now that made LeiRain swallow the thick lump in her throat. It slashed through the water with an air of haughtiness and satisfaction. *It's toying with me.*

Adrenaline still sung through her limbs, feeding LeiRain energy, but it would not last indefinitely. She could already feel her strength waning. The creature seemed to sense this too. It took its time, wearing her down. LeiRain followed the beast's movements, her throat thick with dread and her ears filled with the thunder of her own heart.

While she focused on the creature, her feet caught on a clump of seagrass and she stumbled. As LeiRain tilted forward, the creature struck again. Her shield, in place by chance rather than skill, deflected the large teeth but her body shuddered with the impact. LeiRain's shoulder groaned from the contact but she willed her left arm to keep the shield aloft.

The beast lunged again and LeiRain batted it away with the bulwark, panting with exhaustion as she did so. Before she could even reset her stance, it struck once more. She had to use the strength of her entire body to heft the shield into place this time, but nevertheless managed to deflect the attack.

It knows I'm growing tired. There was a deep ache in her left shoulder where it had absorbed the previous strike. She blinked away the tears that welled up with the intensity of the pain and refocused her eyes. LeiRain's lungs burned and her breaths came fast and shallow. The beast's pace quickened as it continued to circle. She struggled to match its speed. If she didn't strike soon, it would wear her down so much she wouldn't be able to.

LeiRain noted the urgent flicks of the beast's tail and knew – a fourth attack was coming. It lunged. The beast darted through the water toward her as she pushed off the sand, thrusting her shield up with a grunt. It collided with the beast's open mouth, the sharp teeth making a whining, scratching noise as they hit and then slid over the sorcerer's steel. She gritted her own teeth, ignoring the pain, and swung her sword wildly where she'd expected the beast to be. The blade cut through the water without making contact.

LeiRain blinked in surprise as she looked over her shield and saw a great distance between her and the creature. She had felt a rush of water when her shield made contact, but hadn't realized that it took the monster with it. Its long, slender body rolled end over end as it was pushed away by the force she'd generated. The beast fought against this unnatural current to right itself and she sank back down into a fighting stance before the rush of water could dissipate. The monster was nearly fifteen feet away from her by the time it was able to reverse momentum. It sliced hastily through the water, now, agitated by this set-back. The *clack clack clack* of its nails rever-berated through her skull as she watched it swim toward her with purpose.

LeiRain tried to recreate whatever she'd done before to send the beast rolling away. She bent her legs and inhaled sharply as it tore through the water toward her. LeiRain had no idea how she'd generated such force, and even less of an idea on how to recreate it. She wasn't entirely sure she could even withstand another attack, but she had to try. A brief pang of worry surfaced as she remembered the little girl – and

LeiRain hoped the child would escape the creature, even if she did not.

Her limbs were shaking with exhaustion now and her head spun. It was a struggle to remain upright, but she was determined to at least do damage to the beast before it took her down. LeiRain squeezed her eyes shut and braced for another impact. With her eyes closed, her other senses sharpened further and she let the water tell her a story. It painted a picture of the space around her, every ripple a brush stroke that added detail to the whole. Even the monster, she realized with a start. She could sense its location and movement with her eyes closed. The ocean didn't like the beast anymore than she did, and LeiRain could feel the water itself recoiling from the gray-skinned monstrosity. Steeling herself, she adjusted her grip shield and sword. LeiRain gave out a harsh cry and hurled herself into battle.

The monster's teeth scraped down the front of her shield again, but this time she caught the beast with the tip of her blade before it spun away. She wasn't sure how she did it, but LeiRain generated another powerful current and sent her opponent rolling end over end once more. It let out a shrill cry as it spun. A thin ribbon of deep purple blood trailed behind it, blooming into dark clouds as it spread out through the water.

A giddy, almost manic laugh escaped LeiRain. Her lungs burned as she watched the monster slowly begin to break free of the current. It was so far away now that its form almost disappeared against the darkness of the drop-off. She slid the tip of her blade into the sand, her weight resting on it as she caught her breath. LeiRain watched the creature struggle free from the current she'd created. It shook its head and for a moment, she thought the beast might retreat. But then it turned back to her, jaw snapping in agitation. She'd hoped to scare the monster away, but she'd only succeeded in pissing it off. It gnashed its teeth one more time before starting toward her again, moving with impossible speed. LeiRain closed her eyes and pulled her sword from the sand. Before she could do anything else, a clammy hand wrapped around the wrist of her sword arm and the world around her went black.

8

The heaviness of sword and shield disappeared as LeiRain fell through darkness. Her head spun and her body felt weightless. The sensation was oddly familiar but it took her a few seconds to place. Where had she felt this before? Then it came to her: it was the same sensation she'd experienced as a child when she'd stood in the clearing outside her mother's workshop, looking up at the sky, spinning in ever-faster circles until all sense of balance was lost and she tumbled to the ground, giggling. For a brief moment, the elation nearly made LeiRain laugh out loud, but the cool fingers gripping her forearm were a sober reminder of the present danger.

The blackness dissipated and her body sagged under the sudden weight of her weapons. She staggered slightly but avoided falling as the world slammed back into existence. LeiRain found herself looking into two sets of dark, lidless eyes. The hand that encircled her arm withdrew.

One of the figures before her, the girl that had darted into the kelp, smiled widely. Her earlier grin had been toothless, but now her lips peeled back to reveal rows of thin, sharp teeth. LeiRain's brows rose as she took a step back and the girl's smile faltered. A man stood beside the girl, one webbed hand resting protectively on the child's shoulder. It had been his hand around LeiRain's wrist. He watched her now, brow creased and face solemn.

LeiRain looked back and forth between the two of them. She would have been less concerned about protecting the child from that beast if she had seen the girl's teeth earlier. Those were the teeth of a predator.

But where was the beast now? LeiRain's head whipped from side to side, searching for the eel-like creature that had been charging toward her. The beast was nowhere to be seen, and neither was the drop-off. She turned back to the girl and her companion.

Warning bells rang in her head as she studied them. Her chest was still heaving from the encounter with the eel-monster and she did her best to remain upright as her legs shook beneath her. Whatever the man had done to her, whatever that blackness had been, it had left LeiRain dizzy and nauseated. Still, she did her best to stay alert and take in her surroundings. Coral and aquatic plants decorated the ocean floor around them, but they were no longer in the kelp forest where she'd first discovered the child. Both of her arms ached, and she wanted desperately to sheath her sword and slide the shield onto her back, but LeiRain kept them at the ready, uncertain if danger had passed.

The man stood before her, unashamedly naked save for a small knife made of broken oyster shell strapped to his thigh with braided seaweed. His skin was the same mottled blue as the child's and they both had green hair the color of sea grass, though his was cropped much shorter than the girls.

LeiRain felt her cheeks warm slightly at his nudity but was too exhausted to thoroughly blush. Long arms hung loosely at the man's sides and he said nothing as she looked him over. LeiRain had come to rest with her feet on the ocean floor, but the creatures before her floated a few inches above the sand. Their webbed feet kicked lightly every few seconds to maintain their position. The round eyes at first appeared lidless and unblinking, but with further examination, LeiRain observed a translucent film sliding over the glassy orbs for a few seconds at a time before snapping away again.

The man's head cocked to the side and he returned her exploring gaze. His round face was framed by a set of dramatically pointed ears and gill slits on his neck flared as he examined her. The gills intermittently presented dark red lines of flesh as they expanded and contracted rhythmically.

LeiRain was beginning to suspect that this man had rescued her from the monster, so, she reasoned, his intent was unlikely to be nefarious. She offered him a tentative smile. Seeing this, his brow softened and he opened his mouth to speak. Just like the girl before him, what came out was not words – at least none that LeiRain could understand – but an odd series of sounds that vibrated through the water and made her want to cover her ears.

How can I communicate with them? She shrugged her shoulders and shook her head.

'I don't understand,' she said with little hope of being understood herself. But the man straightened at the sound of her voice.

'I speak the common tongue as well,' he replied in a deep and melodic voice. 'Though I lack practice.' He didn't have an accent so much as an unusual way of varying his pitch. She wondered what those variations might mean in his own language, and how much nuance she missed in being unable to recognize their significance.

'My name,' he went on, 'is Orca. This'– he nodded toward

the girl, who now peered out from behind his leg – 'is my daughter, Delphine.' Then, in a less friendly voice, he said, 'My daughter, who should *not* have been near the deep, especially not on her own.'

The girl looked shame-faced, cheeks flushing a deep lavender before she darted out of view behind Orca's leg.

'We owe you a great debt, daughter of tempest.'

LeiRain shifted her weight back and forth between her feet as she waded through the torrent of questions that rushed through her mind. Before she could ask any of them, a wave of nausea crashed over her. LeiRain bent forward, sliding her shield over her left shoulder as she did so and clutching her stomach with the now free hand. She took another step back, feeling as though she might be sick.

The nausea passed and LeiRain pulled herself upright again and sheathed her sword. Orca looked at her with open concern on his face. 'I'm okay,' she said, waving him off with a sweep of her hand.

She smiled weakly, and tried to decide what to ask him first. Alarra had always been so guarded, so unwilling to answer LeiRain's questions about her father. And there had been no one else to ask. The man before her now was familiar enough with tempest to recognize LeiRain's heritage. What other knowledge might he possess? She opened her mouth to speak, but closed it again, not knowing where to start. Were there others like her? What about the tempest themselves – how many of them were there? Would Orca know how to find them? Could her father be nearby?

Orca spoke before she could gather her thoughts. 'I would not have been there in time to prevent Delphine from coming to harm. The sheel have voracious appetites and an unfortunate preference for water elves.'

Water elves, she thought excitedly! LeiRain had seen forest elves come through Harbor before, and some of their features – the round face, the sharply pointed ears – were similar to those of the creatures before her. Water elves were mentioned in some of her history books, but most authors seemed to think that elves were only terrestrial. It was widely believed that, if anything resembling a water elf did exist, it was likely the result of tempest and elf mating. She did not think the creatures before her had been born of tempest; LeiRain did not have gills or webbed digits, nor had she seen any such features on her father.

'Thank you,' he finished. LeiRain nodded.

'Um, you're welcome, and thank *you*.' She swallowed, her throat feeling tight. 'I … don't think I would have lasted much longer if you hadn't…' She looked around again. There were miles of rolling ocean floor ahead of her and behind her. Occasional clusters of kelp reached for the sky, but these were thin and widely dispersed, unlike the forest in which the girl had sought refuge. The area around them was thick with tall clusters of coral and a wide variety of flowering plants. 'Actually,' she looked back at Orca, her brow crinkling. 'Where are we and what happened? How did you bring me here?'

'We swifted,' he answered matter-of-factly.

LeiRain shook her head and narrowed her eyes. The corners of his mouth lifted in a close-lipped smile.

'It is a gift that most water elves possess,' he explained, seeming to recognize her confusion. 'We can travel very long distances instantly. And we can hear each other's cries from anywhere in the same body of water. That is how I knew that Delphine was in danger, and how I found you both quickly.'

A useful gift, LeiRain thought, *even if it does have a downside.* Her dizziness was receding but she still felt a bit nauseated.

Looking down at the girl who peeked around her father's

thigh, LeiRain did her best to ignore his all-too-visible groin. The girl, Delphine, had seemed so mischievous before, unafraid when she'd met with LeiRain. The... what had he called it? The *sheel* attack must have frightened her terribly for the girl to show such timidity now. Or perhaps it was her father's scolding. LeiRain recalled the awe and fear she'd experienced in her own father's presence and wondered if Delphine might feel the same way. Or did fathers lose prowess in their daughters' eyes when they lived daily in each other's presence?

'You will excuse her silence,' Orca said, running the sharp tips of his fingers affectionately through his daughter's hair. 'Delphine understands the common tongue but does not yet speak it.'

Of course she must understand, LeiRain thought. The girl had followed her order to step out of the shadows. She had also blushed at her father's rebuke, which he'd spoken in the common tongue.

'She is just nine years of age, still learning.'

Nine years old, only two years younger than I was when I met my father. LeiRain recalled her eleven-year-old self. Had she looked as small and breakable as Delphine? She imagined her father's thick fingers wrapped around the bicep of the child in front of her. Imagined what that would have looked like to all those they passed in the village as he dragged her, confused and afraid, toward the beach. She examined the way Delphine's cheek rested against her father's leg, how her small fingers reached up to grasp his hand as it combed through her hair.

No, this little girl would not feel for her father the way LeiRain had felt – *still* felt – toward her own. She saw now that the girl must feel something far more powerful than the awe LeiRain's father had inspired. Delphine trusted her father.

Delphine felt loved.

LeiRain pulled her eyes back up to Orca's face. 'Where are we?' she asked, realizing that he had not yet answered her question.

'We are just outside of Corallis,' he said, adding 'our home,' in explanation. He tilted his head to the side again and examined her. 'You have not been around water elves before?'

'No.' She wondered if she should admit that she hadn't known water elves existed until moments ago.

'Most of your kind are familiar with us, our ways, our dwellings. You have spent most of your time on land, I see.' He said this with a smile, revealing his disturbingly sharp teeth.

LeiRain resisted the urge to reach for her sword. Though she was beginning to believe that the two of them were no threat, her instincts continued to scream warnings every time she saw their needle-thin teeth.

'Even your weapons,' he said, as if reading her mind, 'are made for land combat. Nevertheless, you seem to have wielded them to your advantage with the sheel.'

'Yes, I have spent most of my life on land. My name is LeiRain, by the way,' she said, realizing that she had not yet returned this courtesy. 'Thank you for getting me away from that ... from the sheel. I hate to impose, but do you happen to know where I can rest safely and find something to eat?'

'Of course,' Orca replied, his voice moving up in pitch in a manner that suggested excitement. 'You will be our guest tonight. There is food, drink, and we will make sure you rest safely.' His brow creased, and he gave her the same concerned look she'd seen on his face earlier. 'We should treat your wound before anything else, though.'

Now that he mentioned it, LeiRain became aware of the pain in her left arm. Like her other muscles, it ached from the effort of bearing her shield, but there was also a more localized throbbing in her shoulder. She looked down at the arm and the stinging cut visible on her shoulder. She didn't think it was from one of the monster's enormous teeth; the sheel must have snagged her with one of its claws.

LeiRain turned her arm so that she could better see the wound. The cut ran from her shoulder through her bicep, nearly down to the elbow. The gash was not deep, but it oozed blood, a tiny cloud of red swirling out from it and disappearing into the sea.

'It's not that bad,' she said as much to reassure herself as to convince the water elf. 'I just need to bandage it for now to stop the bleeding.' She smiled but Orca did not look convinced.

'I will take you to a healer,' he said with finality. 'And she can decide how best to treat the wound. Sheel are foul creatures. Your wound should be cleaned as soon as possible.'

LeiRain looked at the gash again and recalled the stench of rot that had emanated from the beast.

'I've never heard of a sheel before today,' she said. 'Are they common here?' It was hard to imagine that such a thing existed in the waters and had never once been pulled up by a net. It had come from the deep, dark drop-off so perhaps the sheel remained out of the reach of most fishermen. Still, it seemed remarkable that she hadn't heard any stories about the beasts.

'They are not natural things,' Orca said, his voice dropping several octaves. 'The tempest created them, using magic to merge the most vicious of sea creatures into one beast. They are so repellent that even the ocean itself recoils from them.'

LeiRain recalled the strange disturbance she'd sensed in the water around the sheel, even before she'd seen it.

'All other life in the sea lives in connection, partnership. Even prey and predator exist in a kind of harmony. It is not so with the sheel. The one that you wounded will likely die of infection. No other ocean life will come to clean its wound as they might for another creature. It is the great weakness in the tempest's creation.' He paused and looked back at his daughter. Her tiny hand was still entwined with his larger one. 'Most of the sheel are well-controlled. They are unquestioningly obedient to the tempest who claims them, but sometimes they roam wild when their master goes ashore for a long period. Or when their master dies.'

'Dies?' She scrunched her face in surprise and confusion. Tempest were gods. Her father was a god. Could gods really *die*? LeiRain swayed with renewed dizziness and Orca reached out to steady her. Suddenly, her questions seemed less urgent and all she wanted from the world was a solid meal and a long nap. She'd pushed the limits of her own endurance. LeiRian had not eaten anything since the night before and had foolishly left without food. It wouldn't have mattered so much if she'd stuck to her original plan and gone to another coastal village for the night, but instead she'd headed for the vast unknown of deeper waters.

'Are you alright?' Orca reached out to steady her.

She swallowed, trying to find her voice, and glanced at her wound. Blood still seeped steadily from the gash. It was really quite difficult to tell how much blood you were losing underwater, she realized. Did the edges of the cut look swollen now? Infection couldn't set in so quickly, could it? When she didn't respond to him right away, Orca mistook her silence for reluctance.

'I understand that we are strange beings to you, but we will not harm you, especially not after you've protected our youngling. If you come with us to the city, you can find rest and be around others of your kind.'

LeiRain focused on him, ignoring the ache growing in her

temples and her churning stomach. 'There are others like me there? Other ... children of tempest?'

'Of course,' he nodded. 'There are sons and daughters of tempest who dwell in the city. You will not be alone, and I promise that you will be safe.'

Her throat felt thick and her vision blurred slightly as she swallowed back tears. She'd been so alone for so long, and she knew so little about her father, about tempest. At that moment, there was nothing that could keep her from following Orca to his city. She would go, even if he hadn't promised safety.

She slowed her breathing, hoping to steady herself. With the world still spinning around her, LeiRain gave him a nod to indicate that he should lead the way to Corallis.

9

L eiRain took in a sharp breath as she caught sight of the tall coral spirals. It was like nothing she had ever seen before. Though the city was planted in deep waters, it was also kept warded, Orca explained, to ensure that the dangers of the outside world could not intrude on their peace. Even from this distance, Corallis seemed to radiate light, its edges glowing in the same pastel shades as its pointed towers.

Or perhaps that was just her vision blurring as the headache worsened.

'The buildings were carved long ago from the rock of mountains that rose out of the ocean floor. You'll see when we are closer, but those colors are from the coral and plants that grow thickly over every surface in Corallis. The reefs give us beauty and sustenance, and in turn we live in a way that sustains them.'

LeiRain tried to imagine the amount of work it had taken to create such an elaborate living space from hard rock. Thousands of water elves would have had to chip away one little piece at a time to create these impressive structures.

LeiRain thought of the little box of stones she kept under

her bed. Tiny pieces of far-off lands carried in Ron's pocket for hundreds of miles before being deposited into her eager palm. She had studied each one for hours, becoming familiar with every edge, color patterns, and the weight. With little to go on, she had held each one and done her best to imagine its place of origin. LeiRain doubted that any stone could effectively represent the majesty of Corallis.

'It is beautiful, is it not?'

'It truly is,' LeiRain said, smiling and nodding her head in agreement.

She pulled her eyes away from the city in the distance to look at Orca. He was smiling – thankfully with his mouth closed. He seemed to stretch taller now, shoulders pulled back and chin high as he looked at his home. LeiRain tried to imagine what it might be like to feel proud of where she lived but it was too much of a stretch for her imagination.

Orca began swimming again. LeiRain trailed behind him while Delphine swam in energetic loops over and beneath the two adults. LeiRain, who continued to struggle against fatigue and pain, envied her energy.

She could see in detail now the thick branches of coral that lent the towers their color. Every structure was teeming with life both large and small. LeiRain, who had grown used to seeing the same sea life nearly every day in Harbor, was fascinated by the diversity of life surrounding her. The same brightly-colored aquatic plants she'd spotted earlier decorated not only the ocean floor, but nearly every inch of structure that wasn't already covered in coral. Fish of varying sizes and colors flitted about, more comfortable with her presence than she expected them to be. The fish in Harbor always darted away the moment she'd drawn near, but here she could swim straight through a school of them, their fins brushing lazily against her skin, and they would make no move to avoid her.

She held out her uninjured arm, opening her hand and extending the fingers. A small, orange fish stopped briefly to nibble on her palm while several others swept in and out of the loose strands of hair that had escaped from her braid. She felt warm and safe, the flutter of fish reminding her very much of the annual butterfly migration in Harbor, when droves of butterflies overtook the outdoors. Each spring, the orange and black-speckled wings covered nearly every available surface as the butterflies returned from their winter breeding grounds in the more temperate south. LeiRain loved to lay in the clearing during migration season; if she could lay still for long enough, butterflies would alight on her, their tiny feet whispering against her blue skin.

The fish's nibbling tickled her palm and, reflexively, she began to pull her hand away, one corner of her mouth turning up into a smile. Lost in memory and wonder, LeiRain's eyes began to close but she caught herself and forced them open – she really did need to heal. And she could really use something to eat and drink. And some sleep.

Water elves came and went from all levels of the structures, swimming in and out of openings in the smoothly carved rock, careful not to disturb the thickly growing coral covering the exterior. Many were dressed like Delphine, their bodies partially covered with weaves of seaweed, but many more wore nothing save a small weapon or a bit of jewelry fashioned from sea glass and shells. The elves added their own splash of color to the scene with skin in shades of blue and green, mottled with purples, tans, and pinks. They were clearly visible as they moved about, but LeiRain had no doubt that they could fade into their surroundings if they so desired. She shuddered as she realized how easily these creatures could have hidden, observing her from the shadows with their sharp teeth and clawed hands resting on daggers.

She shook her head, dismissing the thought. They had shown only kindness so far, and Orca claimed that they lived side by side with others like her.

Still, her eyes shifted to the elves with many blades strapped to their legs and arms. Those with the most weapons had noticeably shorter hair, even the women. Practical, she thought, if one is expecting to fight in the water. Her own hair was intermittently clouding her vision as rogue strands floated in front of her face. The majority of the elves wore their hair quite long and free, great curtains of blue and green that trailed behind them as they swam. LeiRain was certain she would get lost in the tangles of her own hair if she did not restrain her locks, but the elves seemed accustomed to the loose strands. They cut smoothly through the water with the help of their webbed feet, their hair swaying gracefully as they went.

LeiRain startled when Delphine let out a sudden, high-pitched squeal and then darted ahead of them to meet a pair of youngling elves swimming out from one of the buildings. Delphine moved through the water with impressive speed, darting around much like the bright little fish. LeiRain knew then that the pace she'd been struggling to maintain must have felt painfully slow to the elve. The younglings barely had to kick their feet or paddle with their arms to send themselves soaring through the water. LeiRain had kicked furiously to keep up with the two of them, her own feet encased in leather boots and lacking the webbing that made the elves so adept at moving through this environment.

The younglings darted around each other, changing directions quickly and with only the slightest flick of their wrists, the webbed fingers putting great force behind each movement. Eventually, they flitted out of sight leaving LeiRain feeling clumsy in their wake. She'd come to think of herself as a good swimmer, moving comfortably through the water. Now, LeiRain felt self-conscious of the way she paddled her hands to keep herself steady, the lack of fluidity in the way she walked across the ocean floor and the graceless manner in which she kicked her feet to move forward. When she compared her own movements to the underwater grace of the elves, swimming suddenly felt impossibly difficult. She sighed. Maybe it was just hunger and fatigue.

Haunting music became audible as they moved further into Corallis, passing between a pair of large boulders that seemed to mark the city's limits. She could suddenly hear the back and forth whale-like speech between elves both near and far. At almost the same time, a savory scent reached LeiRain's nostrils. She couldn't quite place the smell but it was somehow both familiar and foriegn ... salty, and ... meaty? *Of course it would be meaty,* she thought, remembering the elves' sharp teeth. Orca had mentioned that wards prevented him from swifting directly into the city – there must also have been wards that contained the sounds and smells of life in Corallis.

When her stomach rumbled, Orca glanced at her. She smiled at him dismissively, but her mouth ached as she salivated. LeiRain was so dizzy with hunger that it would have been impossible to remain upright on land, under the full force of gravity. She was grateful for the press of water supporting her.

LeiRain tried her hardest to observe all her new surroundings as she followed Orca through the maze of tall assemblies, but her mind was fogged by fatigue and the urgent need for sustenance. She was plagued with sharp hunger pangs that shot through her stomach at regular intervals. The smell she'd detected reminded her of the venison stew she made every winter when the forests were overrun with mating deer. At this point, it could be salted starfish and she'd hardly care –

she just needed to eat something. And to rest. Her aching muscles, especially her legs, felt in danger of giving out. She tried to get by with less frequent kicks, dropping back even further behind Orca. Without a word, he slowed his own pace to match hers.

The elves they passed nodded politely to LeiRain but did not seem particularly surprised by or interested in her presence. This was somewhat reassuring as it made her feel more confident that Orca had been telling the truth about others of her kind residing in the city. The passersby greeted Orca in their whale song language, and he responded in the common tongue, for her benefit. But LeiRain was so tired now that she hardly cared what they said to each other.

'Where are the other blends – I mean, children of tempest?' She asked as they passed a couple of elves who were so besotted with each other that they didn't acknowledge LeiRain or Orca. Part of her had expected to run into another blend almost immediately, and as her wonder at being amongst the elves began to wear off, her desire to see someone like her grew stronger.

'There are only a few who live with us now. Many of them leave upon their adulthood.'

'Why would they leave?' She asked. 'How do they end up here?' LeiRain's tongue felt heavy, her words slurring as weariness began to win out over her curiosity. It was getting harder and harder to follow Orca, the muscles in her legs threatened to give out entirely.

Orca chuckled softly, and LeiRain's cheeks grew warm, thinking he was laughing at her.

'I'm sorry, LeiRain,' he said, sounding sincere. 'It is just that I am amazed at your ability to maintain such intense curiosity even while you are faint from hunger and suffering a potentially mortal wound.' She wrapped her arms around her stomach as it growled again. Then his words sank in.

'Mortal wound?' She felt more alert than she had since combating the sheel. 'It's just a scratch!'

'As I said, sheel wounds are prone to infection. That is why I am taking you directly to Lana. She is a healer.'

'Oh.' LeiRain looked at her arm. She gasped as she observed the cut, which was now purple and oozing. She pushed herself to continue moving forward as the pain in her arm and the heaviness of her limbs warred with burning hunger for her attention.

'The sons and daughters of tempest who live within the borders of our city are here because this is where their mothers chose to abandon them. Many leave because they are not able to find themselves at home here. We almost never see them again once they leave, and I do not know where they go, though I suspect that many seek out the parents that discarded them.' He frowned as he said this. LeiRain found herself appreciating her mother a bit more after hearing this; at least she'd had one parent. Guilt stabbed at her – she should have at least left her mother a note – but pain and exhaustion quickly distracted her from this thought.

Orca was polite but brief with the other elves as he hurried LeRain through the city. The open waterways between the carved stone structures were narrow compared to the streets in Harbor, but she quickly realized that they were employed very differently than roadways on land. The deep water allowed the elves to swim not only beside one another but above or below them if needed.

For now, she and Orca stayed near the ocean floor where LeiRain could push off the hard surface with her feet rather than trying to maintain the frantic kicking of her legs. She was grateful for this as she trudged along, wincing at the pressure of the water against her open skin. Her vision was beginning to turn black around the edges and Orca had taken to looking over his shoulder at her every few seconds to make sure she was still upright.

Finally, they stopped before one of the stone structures. Orca floated upward, gesturing for LeiRain to follow. With a grunt, she pushed off the ocean floor, kicking her legs as furiously as she could to propel herself up to meet him. He swam next to her, his feet kicking lightly every few seconds as her own legs churned. They came to stop on a small lip of stone, high up on one of the rock structures and LeiRain guessed that the opening in front of them was a door. She had tried to keep track of each turn they had taken, to notice unique features that might serve as landmarks, but the city was so large and strange to her tired eyes that she only had a rough idea of where they were. Her mind held on to a vague idea of bright colors, sharp coral, shimmering plants, and smoothly hollowed out stone.

Orca reached out and tugged gently on a rope of kelp that weaved its way through the branches of coral. A light tinkling sound issued with each tug, coming from somewhere inside the building. Orca placed a bracing hand on LeiRain's back as they waited. She opened her mouth to tell him she was fine, but instead swayed on her feet as her vision narrowed and expanded, her consciousness flickering. LeiRain felt her breaths coming faster now and there was a tightness in her chest that made each inhale feel shallow and strained.

A female elf appeared, her face peeking out from behind a curtain of seaweed that filled the doorway. Loose green curls billowed around her cherubic face and her large black eyes stared at LeiRain. Her lips were a dark red that seemed incongruent with the rest of her pastel coloring and LeiRain drew back slightly as her tired mind imagined them stained with blood. The seaweed hid the woman's body from view and LeiRain got the eerie impression that a disembodied head was floating in front of her.

'My mate's sister, Lana,' Orca said, gesturing to the head. 'She's a healer. She will mend you.' He pressed a gentle hand on LeiRain's back, nudging her toward the woman with blood-red lips. 'Lana,' he began, 'this is LeiRain. She has been wounded by—'

'A sheel. Yes, I can see that, given that she's oozing infection in my doorway. I'm busy.' The female ducked back behind the seaweed, disappearing from view. Her voice was somewhat muffled when she spoke from the other side of the doorway, 'I don't have time for a silly god-child who thought she could take on one of those filthy beasts.'

'Lana.' Orca's voice held a sharpness she had not heard before. 'She saved Delphine from a sheel. If she hadn't been there, I would be mourning my daughter – your niece – right now.'

Lana's head popped into view again, the rest of her body materializing this time as she moved through the seaweed and approached LeiRain. 'Fine,' Lana said as she studied her. The woman exuded a dangerous kind of beauty as her dark eyes focused on LeiRain's wound and her graceful, webbed fingers probed the tender arm. Lana wore more clothing than any of the water elves LeiRain had seen thus far, though the garb provided no additional modesty. The garment was sheer and sleeveless, white with a purple hue to it when she moved. It reminded LeiRain of dragonfly wings, and she briefly wondered what it had been made of as she resisted the urge to reach for the fabric and rub it between her fingers.

Lana examined her carefully, starting with a soft touch at her shoulder and working her way down. LeiRain flinched at the first touch, surprising even herself with the intensity of her reaction. It was incredibly painful. She followed Lana's eyes as they scanned the gash on her arm. The bleeding had slowed, but the flesh surrounding the cut looked angry and swollen.

'Come,' Lana said, placing a hand on LeiRain's back to urge her through the doorway. Lana's fingers felt cool against her skin. 'You're already feverish,' the woman said, confirming LeiRain's suspicion. 'Sheel are nasty things. Your body is trying to fight the infection.' Orca made no move to follow them inside and LeiRain looked over her throbbing shoulder, eyes wide and pleading.

'She will care for you well,' he said as Lana pulled her through the doorway. 'I will check on you, soon.'

LeiRain opened her mouth to reply but clamped it shut when a loud gurgling sound issued from her stomach. She wrapped her arms around her torso, letting out a gasp when the motion tugged on the tight skin around her injury.

'I'm ... sorry,' she stammered. LeiRain wasn't sure if she was apologizing for her growling stomach or for taking up Lana's time.

'Eat,' Lana replied flatly as she pulled from a bowl of odd-looking fruit and handed one to LeiRain. She took it from the elf and turned it over in her hand, inspecting it carefully. It was the size of her palm, tan in color with small black spots. The weight and texture of the skin reminded LeiRain of a pear, but aside from the coloring, it was like nothing she'd seen before. Its skin was in layers that resembled the petals of an unopened flower. Was she supposed to peel it? Eat the whole thing? Her stomach grumbled again.

The elf was rummaging through a shelf of tincture bottles, each one plugged shut with a mass of seaweed. LeiRain was watching her, debating whether or not to ask these questions, when Land spoke. 'You just bite into it, daughter of tempest.' LeiRain jumped slightly at the sound of her voice, having not realized that Lana was paying attention to her. But she was grateful for the direction and bit into the fruit without further hesitation.

The moment her teeth cut into the fruit, LeiRain's mouth began to ache with a burst of salivation. She forced herself to chew despite the urge to eat as quickly as possible. The fruit had a familiar flavor, something she could feel as much as taste. It was like the sun cakes she so loved from the baker's shop in Harbor Village, the bite in her mouth buttery and rich with a hint of honey. She'd tried so hard to recreate sun cakes at home and could never get the recipe quite right, yet somehow this fruit replicated the taste perfectly. *Except,* LeiRain thought, *somehow much better*. She studied the fruit in her hand – the inside was soft and white. She poked at it with a finger and found the texture to be a bit gummy. But when she took another bite, LeiRain could feel the flakiness of the pastry crust, the stickiness of the honey drizzle and the coarseness of the sugar crystals as she chewed.

She continued to examine the fruit as she ate. There was no evidence of anything that would mimic the textures of a sugared-pastry. She took another bite, her fascination with the experience overcome by her intense hunger. It only took a few more bites to finish it off and, without asking, she reached to take another from the bowl. LeiRain paused, fingers hovering over the fruit, as she realized that her hunger was sated. How could such a small piece of fruit be so filling? Still, she was tempted to eat another just to enjoy the taste of it, but the fullness of her stomach warned her not to.

'What does it taste like to you?' Lana asked as she turned around, fists full of tinctures.

'Sun cake,' she replied. 'It's a pastry. A dessert,' she clarified, wondering if the elf had ever eaten a pastry. It seemed unlikely given how poorly a pastry would fare underwater.

'It is called *longing fruit*,' Lana said as she looked carefully at one of the bottles she held. 'It only grows in our cities. It tastes to each person like the most delicious thing they have ever eaten, so it tastes differently to everyone.'

'What does it taste like to you?' LeiRain asked. Lana looked at her and smiled. LeiRain had to force herself not to back away from those unnerving teeth.

'You don't want to know, little godchild.' LeiRain shivered. 'You show restraint,' Lana said. 'Many who taste longing fruit gorge themselves for the enjoyment of it, despite the fullness they feel. It is a poison if you consume too many. And if you eat them one after another, each piece of fruit tastes better than the last. Many people will eat and eat until they've poisoned themselves.'

LeiRain looked from Lana to the bowl of longing fruit, fascinated and terrified. She felt a flash of anger as she realized that Lana had not warned her of this before she'd begun to eat. What would the elf have done if she had taken a second, and then a third? How many could she eat before they became poisonous to her?

'Of course,' Lana went on, 'It only has that effect on mortals, and you're only half mortal, so it's *hard* to say how it would affect you.' The elf looked up at her. 'Perhaps that is why you were able to restrain yourself with such ease.' Lana passed a small vial to Leirain.

'Drink,' she commanded.

LeiRain took the vial and began to pick at the seaweed that held the bottle closed. Without a word, the elf snatched the vial back from her.

'No, not like that. If you do that, the contents will be lost to the ocean,' she said, annoyed. 'You suck the seaweed into your mouth, along with the contents of the bottle. You can swallow it all; the seaweed is edible.' Her tone was more patient as she finished. Lana handed the bottle back to LeiRain.

The thought of sucking down the seaweed wasn't particularly appetizing, but Leirain did as instructed. She wrapped her lips around the mouth of the vial, eyes flitting to Lana as she did so. The elf's expression was unreadable as she watched. LeiRain squeezed her eyes shut and drank. To her surprise, the seaweed had a pleasant, salty taste to it. It required chewing, but only a bit. The liquid had no flavor at all as it filled her mouth. She swallowed it in one big gulp, and it burned as it went down her throat. She stuck out her hand to give the empty bottle back to Lana, and felt her grip on the vial loosen as the feverish heat of her body turned to a warm sleepiness. Her head bobbed in the water. The little vial floated away from her open palm and LeiRain watched it drift away. Its surface caught the light and its sparkle was almost hypnotizing. LeiRain fought to keep her eyes open, to keep watching the tiny star of the bottle as it floated into Lana's hand. But her eyelids were too heavy.

'I must remove some of the surrounding flesh,' Lana's voice sounded far away. 'It has already begun to corrupt. It would be much too painful if you remained awake.'

LeiRain's eyes were closed, though she still imagined she could see the floating vial. Some part of her thought that she should respond to Lana. She should acknowledge her words. But when she tried to open her mouth, her tongue felt as thick and heavy as her eyelids. The immensity of this long day weighed on her fully, now, and she gave into the fatigue. Her muscles relaxed in a way they never had before as all worry faded from LeiRain's mind.

'Sleep well, godchild,' Lana whispered from somewhere far away.

10

Leirain couldn't see anything; her eyes were sealed shut. She could tell that there was no ground beneath her and she was breathing water, not air. LeiRain fought against the fogginess of sleep to remember where she was, where she had been. She'd never fallen asleep in the water before and the sense of weightlessness was disconcerting. LeiRain tried to force her eyes open, reaching for them with her hands, but she met with resistance when she attempted to move her arm. Something held her wrists. Her heart beat wildly against her ribs as LeiRain strained to regain her sight. Finally, she managed to peel one eye partially open. Her vision was too blurry to be of any use. She squeezed her eyes shut again and tried to blink, which eventually pried the other one open as well. Her eyelids were tender and swollen and felt scratchy each time she blinked.

The water around her hummed with music. She smelled something medicinal, like alcohol combined with soap. LeiRain looked from left to right and saw that her arms were held in place by multiple strands of seaweed, wrapped around her from elbow to wrist. Any traces of drowsiness were lost now as panic surged through her body.

She yanked hard with both of her arms, trying not to make any sound as she did so. Nothing gave. LeiRain tried to sit up. If she could find purchase with her feet, it would add force to her attempts to pull free. Her throat tightened when she realized that her legs, too, were restrained. *Where am I?* And then she remembered. The drop-off, the sheel, the water elves. All of her worst fears about elves, the ones she ignored when she chose to follow Orca, came back to her. *Teeth like that are made for tearing flesh*, she thought. And still she had followed him. How could she be so stupid? So trusting?

LeiRain tried to press back the panic, to think through the situation. But something primal in her couldn't be contained. She began to thrash against her bindings. With all her strength, LeiRain pulled herself into a ball, tugging on all four restraints as she did so. They shuddered under the pressure but still did not give way. Her breath quickened. LeiRain began to rock her body from side to side, hoping she might be able to build enough momentum to break the bindings. It wasn't easy, and her muscles were still sore from her travels and combat, but she had to free herself before any of them could come back.

'Hey, woah, hey,' a male voice said from nearby. 'Calm down.'

LeiRain stopped her frenzied movement as a chill ran up her spine. She wasn't alone after all. Then, anger flared. Who would tell someone to *calm down* when they were physically restrained? Her head snapped from side to side, trying to locate the source of the voice. At first, she saw no one, but then there was a flicker of movement in her peripheral vision. LeiRain turned her head toward the movement, her sight still slightly clouded. Slowly, a pair of bright green eyes drifted into view, then a nose, a chin and finally a man floated in front of her.

There was a smirk on his blue face, which was quite handsome, and his eyes glinted with amusement. Green eyes, like hers, not the black, seemingly lidless eyes of the water elves. His hair was also green like LeiRains and cropped short. There were no gill slits on his neck and his skin lacked the mottling of the water elves. Instead, it was a smooth, solid blue, slightly darker than her own. It reminded LeiRain of the sky after a summer storm. As she studied him, the young man reached for her hand. She tried to pull away from his touch, but the bindings held her in place.

Relief flooded LeiRain as the man's fingers worked to free her from the knotted seaweed. Her body still rang with alarm but she was beginning to feel the pull of curiosity. He was like her, the offspring of tempest, and he was helping her. He freed her right hand and moved onto her left. His face was lean, which would have made him look very young if he didn't have such a strong jawline. Floating above her now, his whole body was visible. He wore no shirt, but with a pair of roughspun pants, he was more modestly dressed than most of the water elves. The legs of his trousers ended mid-calf and were cinched at the hem and waist with tightly braided seaweed. His bare chest was thick and muscled, as were his shoulders. His strong build reminded LeiRain of the young dockhands in Harbor, muscles swollen from days spent lifting and pulling.

She studied him as his fingers worked to free her arm, the panic she felt at being restrained was replaced entirely by excitement now that she was with another of her kind. He did not seem to experience the same awe at her presence, and she wondered how commonplace it was for him to interact with other offspring of tempest. She did not know what to say to him, and his handsome features did not make this any easier.

LeiRain could see thick strands of her own hair floating loose around her face and was suddenly aware of how awful she must look. Even without a mirror, she was certain that her eyes were puffy and bloodshot and her braid mussed. The fever that had been coming on before she'd fallen asleep seemed to have broken, but LeiRain would be willing to bet she looked wan.

'Does that really work?' She blurted out as she remembered his first words to her. He looked at her with his brow creased, so she clarified, 'Telling someone to calm down. Has that ever actually worked for you?' She felt angry, again, remembering it. The anger made her nervousness fade, so she clung to her indignation.

'Well—'

'Because,' she said, cutting him off, 'I find that it has quite the opposite effect, in fact. It's a very condescending and unhelpful thing to say.' She swallowed, curling her body into a more upright position now that he had loosed the ties on both of her arms. She let her mouth remain curved in a frown as he looked up from where his fingers worked on the knot at her left ankle.

'I...'

She raised her eyebrows at him, expectantly.

'I'm sorry,' he said, his face turning a light shade of purple as he flushed. He looked away from her and back to the knot at his fingertips. 'The seaweed was just to keep you safe while you slept. The elves don't really sleep the way we do so they don't think about it. They just, well, I don't know exactly but it's like they shut off only half of their mind at a time so they can still swim. They can even talk while they are sleeping. I mean, the conversation gets a bit dull when their minds are half asleep, but,' he swallowed. It was LeiRain's turn to smirk. 'But the seaweed keeps you from drifting away.'

He glanced up at her briefly as he moved to free her right leg. 'Before I learned this trick, I would just float all over the place when I slept. Once, I woke up outside of the city with the current pushing me toward the deep ocean. It was very … disorienting. So, I learned to strap myself in, I guess you could say. And I didn't mean to be condescending, I just… I guess I didn't think how strange and scary it might be for you to wake up like this. I suppose this was just as disorienting as waking up five miles from where you first fell asleep. Though much safer,' he added with a lift of his chin.

He smiled sheepishly and LeiRain felt her face heat up. She quickly glanced away..

'I'm Riv, by the way.'

'Rain,' she replied. Her stomach fluttered as she pulled herself into a standing position in front of him.

'A water-themed name,' he replied, rolling his eyes. 'What a surprise for the offspring of tempest.' Riv winked at her and LeiRain's stomach did a little flip.

'My father is tempest,' she said, 'which of your parents…' Her sentence broke off as she remembered what Orca had said to her, that the tempest offspring in Corallis were here because this is where their mothers had chosen to abandon them. LeiRain worried that her misstep would upset him, but Riv was still smiling.

'My mother is tempest,' he said, leaning back. He put his arms behind his head and kicked his feet up to float horizontally beside her. 'My father was a human. I believe, in this way, we are the same? Your mother was human?' He looked at her out of the corner of his eye.

'I… Yes,' LeiRain blinked rapidly, fighting off the dizziness that overtook her. She was now entirely vertical and wasn't sure if this was what caused the room to spin, or if it had been Riv's words. Perhaps it was a bit of both.

We are the same.

Her heart fluttered as she replayed the words in her head. LeiRain braced herself with a hand against the stony wall. Riv said nothing but continued to watch her, head turned toward LeiRain. There was a teasing half-smile on his face that invited her to say more.

'Where are your parents? Do you know them both? How long have you been here? Are there many more like us in Corallis?' LeiRain's face immediately grew hot and she knew there was no hiding her blush. Were her cheeks the same purple that Riv's had been just moments ago? The words had tumbled from her mouth so quickly, she'd barely had time to consider how rude it was to ask so many questions at once, and such personal ones at that. He laughed in answer and her cheeks cooled slightly, her embarrassment mitigated by his apparent lack of offense.

'We can talk while we get you something to eat,' he said brightly. At his words, LeiRain's stomach roiled and her middle spasmed with hunger pangs. She'd felt so full after eating the longing fruit but now her stomach was painfully empty. How long had she been asleep? As if reading her mind, Riv spoke again. 'You've been unconscious for about twelve hours, though Lana said the tincture she gave you should have only lasted for four. You must have been very tired.'

'Twelve hours,' she said it out loud without meaning to. She'd planned to be heading back to Harbor Village at this point. LeiRain had only meant to be away for a day and a night. She wondered how her mother would react when she did not reappear the day after her birthday. *I should have left a note*, she thought.

'Orca stayed with you for several hours,' Riv said, still floating on his back, 'but when you still did not wake, he had to tend to his family. That's when he asked that I come sit with you.' Riv gave her another wink. LeiRain couldn't help but note how comfortable he seemed to feel in his surroundings. This was the longest she'd ever stayed beneath the water, but for Riv, this was home. 'He said that it was your first time meeting water elves and it might be comforting to have one of your kind nearby when you woke. Do you have any pain?'

She glanced at her forgotten wound. It had been wrapped on the outside with long, wide strands of kelp. She could see thick, orange leaves from some underwater plant peeking out from the edges of the seaweed. There was no hint of the aching, burning sensations she'd felt before. Moving gingerly, LeiRain tested her arm. She extended it, then lifted it over her shoulder. Cautiously, she bent her arm at the elbow and then straightened it again.

'No!' She said, eyes widening. 'It doesn't hurt anymore! What is in these leaves?' She twisted her arm so that she could examine the wrappings further.

'The leaves are medicinal, but I have no idea what is in them. They are nicknamed "life saver," though that's probably not what the healers call them. I'm not a healer, though, so,' he held out his palms and shrugged. 'But it's your tempest blood that makes the healing so rapid.'

LeiRain thought about this. She'd always seemed to heal quickly, but she'd never really had a serious wound before. As a bit of an outcast, she wasn't around other villagers enough to know whether or not their healing differed from hers. Her stomach groaned again, interrupting her thoughts. She looked up at Riv, feeling embarrassed at how loudly her body had proclaimed its hunger, but he seemed nonplussed. Riv extended the crook of his arm to her.

'Come on, let's find you something to eat.'

She returned his grin but did not accept his arm. A man had never offered her his arm before. Thoughts of Bren pushed their way into the forefront of her mind. LeiRain had, on occasion, wondered what it might be like to walk arm and arm with him through the bustling of Harbor Village. She'd never let herself dwell on this for long, knowing that it wasn't an option, but she had felt some envy at seeing the courting couples of Harbor do this. The memories stung and she shoved them away, bringing herself back to the present moment. The thought of being so close to Riv, of touching him, made a warmth bloom in her chest. But she didn't know how to be the girl on someone's arm and she was already taking in so much that was new. Riv was staring at her now, one eyebrow raised, so she held out one arm to indicate that he should go ahead. His smile faltered slightly at this, but he quickly regained his composure and turned to lead the way with LeiRain following closely on his heels.

They exited Lana's workspace, where LeiRain had been left to recover. Free of pain and well-rested, she paid more attention to the beauty of her surroundings than she'd been able to before. Coral in shades of orange and pink grew thickly on the outside of the buildings. Occasionally, she saw clusters of purple coral branching out into long, thin fingers. The waters outside of Harbor did not contain anything so colorful. She swam behind Riv as they weaved between buildings, so distracted that she nearly ran into him twice. LeiRain made a deliberate effort to keep her mouth from hanging open as she took in the vivid colors, the friendly nods and smiles of water elves, the background noise of whale song conversations between the residents of Corallis. In her refreshed state, she noticed details she'd missed before. The water was a more comfortable temperature than what she had previously experienced at these depths and brighter than the deep waters she had traversed on her way here.

Despite the robust population of sea life, the water did not smell overly fishy as it often did in Harbor. Instead, it had a clean, salty scent with the occasional hint of something floral. She could smell again the savory stew-like food she'd noticed upon entering Corallis and she felt her mouth begin to water. Riv moved forward with purpose, swimming quickly, but not too fast for her to keep pace. He looked back over his shoulder every few minutes to ensure that she was still following. LeiRain heard the music grow louder as if they were moving toward it. At first, LeiRain thought it was instrumental music, but as she continued to listen, she recognized the threads of whalesong language used by the water elves.

Riv led her through a narrow gap between two buildings and then stopped so suddenly that LeiRain almost swam into him again. She paddled her arms wildly to slow her movement as she stared at the back of his head. When Riv moved to the side and turned back to smile at her, she gasped. The tall structures within Corallis blocked much of the sunlight from reaching the ocean floor. but now LeiRain squinted at the bright space before her. She felt her mouth fall open as she took in a sight like nothing she'd seen before.

11

————

Strands of light swept the ocean floor, reflecting off of golden sand. The entire clearing sparkled, making light dance across the faces of the elves within. LeiRain did not want to blink, afraid she might miss some aspect of the beauty. Elves were clustered throughout the clearing, their own ornate jewelry winking in the brilliant sunlight. There were no plants here, no coral, but the dazzling sand and play of light were decoration enough. Elves moved around the area at varying depths, but the center of the space was left open for what looked like dancing. Elves slid through the water in time with the music, the grace and quickness of their movements unthinkable to anyone except for those who called the ocean home.

Groups of elves milled about on the periphery of the clearing, and LeiRain saw that they were picking food from long, flat stones that framed the space. The stones were being used like tables, displaying baskets that overflowed with food. Despite being unable to recognize the majority of the dishes on display, LeiRain's mouth watered. It had been twelve hours since she'd had the longing fruit, and probably twenty-four hours since her last proper meal. She swam forward, studying the way the elves pulled from the baskets, trying to understand the protocol. She was a guest here and didn't want to be rude ... but she was *starving*.

LeiRain was so taken by her hunger that it was a few minutes before she thought to question the physics of the space. How did the contents of the basket remain in place when they ought to have bobbed about in the water and been carried off by currents? The elves seemed not to notice that this was odd and, just as strangely, LeiRain now saw that they drank from goblets, the contents sloshing about within the cups just as they would have on dry land.

LeiRain turned around to look at Riv, to ask him how all of this was possible. Her lips parted to ask the question but he interrupted her before the words could make their way out.

'It's elf magic,' he said with a shrug. The corner of his mouth turned up in a familiar smirk as he observed her confusion. 'Don't ask me for an explanation. I don't know how it works. I've just gotten used to it.'

'How long...' LeiRain's question trailed off as an elf swam by with an aromatic piece of food in his hand. Her eyes followed him as he moved away, and then flitted back to the table in search of what he'd held. She felt the gentle press of a hand on her back and looked up to see Riv beside her.

'Pretty much my entire life,' he said, as he nudged her forward toward the food. 'Like all the others, I was left here as a baby.'

'Are there many others?' She asked without taking her eyes off of the table. He hesitated before answering the question and LeiRain glanced up at him to see his lips pursed thoughtfully.

'There are some others here,' he said, looking more serious than she'd seen him so far. 'There are three of us now, grown and living in Corallis. Infants are usually left here a few times a year, so there are younglings as well, but most do not stay long into adulthood.'

'Why do they leave and...' she paused, wondering if her question would feel too personal. She took a deep inhale and went on, 'and why do the tempest leave them? Why even have a child if..." She couldn't bring herself to finish the sentence. *If they will just abandon them.* He nodded, understanding her meaning.

'Tempest women are believed to become more powerful through the bearing of children. I don't know if it's true; I've never spent any time around tempest and we rarely even see the mother when a child is left.'

They approached one of the tables overflowing with food and LeiRain fought the urge to begin helping herself as her stomach cramped and the muscles in her jaw ached from salivation. That stew-like smell came to her, again, making her stomach growl loudly, protesting her self-control. She gave Riv a look that she knew must have been something between a wince and a smile. It felt rude to begin eating while he was speaking of such personal things, but she'd never felt this hungry before.

'It's okay,' he said, smiling warmly this time rather than offering his favored smirk. 'Go ahead and eat. It's the sheel venom,' Riv replied. 'It demands a lot from your body. Even with tempest blood, you still need the energy to heal.' He gestured toward the table. 'You'll feel much better once you've eaten, and even more so after you've had another night of rest.'

Tentatively, she picked up a piece of longing fruit. She knew it wasn't the source of the savory smell that had made her mouth water so enthusiastically, but it was the only thing on the table that was in any way familiar to her. She began to nibble on it as Riv continued speaking.

'Many children of tempest grow up in Corallis, but very few stay. There is little here for us. Our immortal blood makes us longer-lived than the elves and as far as I've seen, water elves and tempest half-breeds are unable to have children together.'

'Why?' This was so surprising to LeiRain that she'd spoken with a mouthful of food. She quickly clamped a hand over the bottom half of her face while she awaited his answer. Blends had children with other races all the time on land. Why would this be any different? He looked away from her, eyes glazing over as they stared into the distance.

'No one knows for sure, but the elves believe it is a magic done by the tempest to prevent the birth of any creature that might rival them in power. As you can see,' he looked back at her, and gestured toward the table of food and goblets of wine, 'the elves have a great deal of control over the water and all things in it. Including,' he added, gesturing toward a cluster of blue and silver fish that swam in a shimmering spiral at the center of the clearing, 'the life within the water. But water elves cannot survive on land, and they cannot control the sheel because tempest magic was used to create them. Water elves also cannot control the wind and the clouds as tempest do, at least as far as we know since they cannot stay long above the water.'

LeiRain swallowed the last of a longing fruit. Even the unnaturally satiating fruit wasn't enough to conquer her hunger, but it did help her to feel slightly less ravenous.

'If water elves and tempest were able to mate productively,' Riv continued, pausing to pluck a piece of food, bright-orange and star-shaped, from the table in front of him.

'The resulting offspring might be more powerful than the tempest,' LeiRain finished for him as he chewed.

'Exactly,' he said, popping another piece of food into his mouth.

LeiRain began to reach for a second longing fruit, her hand pausing mid-reach when she recalled Lana's warning. *If you eat them one after another, each piece of fruit tastes better than the last. So people eat and eat until they've poisoned themselves.* Her tempest blood seemed to have saved her quite a bit these last few days, but she didn't want to press her luck. She pulled her hand back from the fruit.

They stayed on the periphery of the clearing, outside of the buzz of activity. She took pieces of food from several different baskets, sampling each dish until she eventually found the source of the savory, venison-stew-like smell that had greeted her upon entering the city. Greedily, she devoured several tiny, seaweed wrapped balls of fish and crab meat. LeiRain had to force herself to chew slowly and swallow each bite before taking the next. She ate messily and was grateful that Riv's focus was on scanning the crowd rather than watching her. Occasionally, she would glance up between bites and admire the swirl of activity in the clearing. Elves mingled and danced and it was a delight to watch, but LeiRain wasn't prepared to enter into it. LeiRain was so focused on admiring the revelry and consuming her meal that she nearly choked on a piece of crab meat when Orca suddenly appeared beside her.

'LeiRain, you are looking well. Do you have any pain?' he asked. Orca's voice was soft. She thought she read warmth on his face, in his posture. It was difficult to be sure, though. His wide, unblinking eyes were so unlike the facial features she was accustomed to. He was dressed the same as he had been when she'd met him, wearing only his knife and the barest amount of braided seaweed. Most of the elves in the clearing wore nothing but decorative pieces of jewelry, so his near nakedness no longer surprised her, though she still couldn't say it was something with which she was comfortable. She realized, then, that she hadn't felt fear at seeing such a large group of the elves together. There was still something disconcertingly *other* about them, but having Riv by her side was more of a comfort than she'd realized.

She shook her head enthusiastically while struggling to finish chewing a mouthful of food. She swallowed so that she could reply. 'No, no pain,' she said, moving her arm around as if to prove it. 'I'm really, *really* hungry, though.' She wiped her face with a hand and felt her cheeks go warm as she noticed the bits of seaweed still clinging to her fingers. Orca smiled in return, and though the teeth still alarmed her, LeiRain found that she was becoming less fearful of the elves.

'I told her it was the sheel venom,' Riv broke in, voice slightly muffled as he said this over a mouth full of food.

'And what is your excuse,' Orca laughed as Riv downed another bit of stuffed seaweed.

Riv shrugged and once he'd chewed and swallowed, replied, 'I didn't want her to feel embarrassed.'

LeiRain laughed at this, his gluttony indeed easing her feelings of discomfort. She took another handful of stuffed seaweed and followed the two males around the clearing, shoving bits of food into her mouth as discreetly as possible and nodding while they introduced her to others.

Each new face was just as round, beautiful and wild as the last with large, almond-shaped black eyes and dramatically pointed ears. The gills on their necks were dark slashes of blue, purple and red depending on the elf. Many of them wore a weapon of some kind, all of them shaped from bits of shell, stone, fishbones, or teeth; things that were readily available along the ocean floor. More rarely, she saw weapons made of iron, steel and even a spear that looked like it had been made from the plank of a ship. She knew from personal experience that such things were often lost to the deep, but the salt water would degrade them over time. This likely explained why the elves preferred items that originated in the sea. The elf-made weapons were much smaller than what she was used to seeing on land, none of them any longer than the length of her hand from wrist to fingertips. Their sheaths were simple, usually a thick strip of braided seaweed tied around some part of an arm or leg. Just as she'd noted on her way into Corallis, the more weapons an elf wore, the shorter they kept their hair. Practical, she supposed, and thought of her own hair. It had been braided in a tight crown around her head when she entered the water but was now coming loose, thick strands floating in her peripheral vision.

The more peaceful looking elves, like Lana, wore their hair long and free or let it float about their heads in intricate braids, with shells, pearls and sea glass woven within it. Many of them wore nothing but the strips of seaweed that held their weapons, but some elves wore weaves of seaweed like Delphine, covering their groins and, for the women, their chests. A few wore translucent gowns like Lana's, including one of the elves who was dancing. The delicate, white fabric shimmered like dragonfly wings in the light of the clearing.

She followed Orca and Riv until they brought her to a stop in front of a small circle of female elves. The nearest one turned to face them, opening up the circle. The elf had dark red lips just like Lana's. She wore weaves of seaweed over her chest and groin with small beads of green and blue sea glass dangling across the bottom of the bodice that swayed when she moved. Similar glass beads were threaded into her hair, which floated free except for a thin braid that wrapped around her head like a diadem. Her breasts were a bit larger and her hips a bit wider than most of the other women, but she was still long and lean. Despite the strangeness of her eyes, and the sharp teeth that slid into view with her smile, LeiRain thought the elf was possibly the most beautiful woman she had ever seen. Orca took a step forward and came to the female's side, his arm brushing against hers.

'This is Marina, my partner,' he said, gesturing to the elf at his side. Orca's face was full of affection as he looked as he said, 'this is Delphine's mother.' His eyes remained on the elf as he took up one of her hands and brought it to his mouth. He planted a light kiss on the back of her wrist and, still holding her hand, looked at LeiRain. 'Marina,' he gestured to LeiRain with his free hand, 'this is LeiRain, the one who saved our daughter's life.'

Marina's black eyes grew wider, which LeiRain had not thought possible given the absence of eyelids. The elf slid her hand out of Orca's and reached for LeiRain's, clasping both of them in hers as she bowed her head. Her nails, LeiRain noted, were somewhat longer than Orca's and she felt them scrape lightly against her palms and the backs of her hands.

'Thank you,' she said. Her brow creased as she shook her head subtly from side to side. 'I am in your debt, Lei-Rain.' She broke LeiRain's name into parts as she said it.

'It was nothing,' LeiRain replied. She averted her gaze as her neck and cheeks turned warm, unused to such display of emotion, such gratitude. Her efforts to save the child had nearly resulted in her own death and, frankly, she was embarrassed by the rashness of her behavior. If it hadn't been for Orca, LeiRain was confident that she would not have survived the sheel. She swallowed, willing the flush away from her skin as she waited for Marina's focus to shift, but the elf continued to hold her hands tightly.

'You're welcome...' LeiRain swallowed the lump in her throat. She hoped these words would signal Marina to release her. But when she looked up, the elf's head was bowed in gratitude. The heat that had begun to dissipate from her cheeks rushed back. They remained this way for several long seconds and LeiRain was relieved when Marina finally lifted her head. 'And you can just call me Rain,' she said, trying to erode some of the formality that existed between them. The drawn out way that Marine said *Lei-Rain* made it feel especially formal.

'Rain,' the elf said, looking into her eyes, 'I do not think you understand. Our daughter would have been dead if you had not distracted the sheel.' Her eyes shone with emotion as she went on. 'Younglings among our kind are ... rare. We have more than a thousand adult elves in the city, but only eleven younglings. Not only are the younglings dear to us because they are our children; they are our most precious resource, ensuring the continuation of our race. We,' she looked at Orca, 'tried for over a century before we had Delphine. She is our life's purpose and our future.'

LeiRain couldn't hide her surprise at this, eyes darting back and forth between Marina's face and Orca's. A small group of elves had begun to cluster around them, nodding solemnly and studying LeiRain. If what they told her was true, her actions did not just impact Delphine's family, but they could influence the future of the water elves as a whole. Her breath caught for a few seconds as she realized the heaviness of what she'd done. It felt disrespectful now to be standing there with her fist full of crab and seaweed. Her stomach twisted with nerves and discomfort at the gratitude they heaped upon her. She was grateful when Riv broke in, suddenly, grabbing one of her hands away from Marina. LeiRain stole a glance at him. His smile looked somewhat forced, and she realized that Riv had picked up on her discomfort and was jumping in to save her.

'Let me get Rain some wine to wash down her dinner,' he said, directing his comment toward Marina.

'Of course,' she replied with a toothy smile. LeiRain shivered at this and Riv's fingers interlaced with hers more tightly. He tugged her away and Marina turned to Orca. LeiRain let the remaining bits of food float from her hand as they weaved through the carousing elves, her appetite dulled by the seriousness of the exchange with Marina. Her stomach felt leaden and her distress must have shown on her face because when Riv looked over his shoulder to glance at her, his smile faded into concern. He squeezed her hand and winked at her before he turned back to face the direction they were headed. Riv's attention made her feel giddy and her heart fluttered as she allowed him to drag her through the mass of bodies. A few times, he slowed and pulled her close to him as they maneuvered through tight bundles of elves. His body against hers made LeiRain's core ache with longing and when Riv finally released her hand, she resisted slightly, letting her fingers separate from his slowly. She clasped her hands together in an effort to warm her fingers, which now felt cool in the absence of his touch. Hands no longer linked, the two of them drifted apart slightly. LeiRain turned away to hide the disappointment on her face.

12

Once she'd schooled her face, LeiRain lifted her head to look back at Riv and let out a surprised gasp. In the space between them, a small shark, maybe two to three feet in length, now swam. The predator carried a tray of silver and gold chalices on its back, just forward of the dorsal fin. It cut through the water with ease, its tail slashing lazily from side to side. Magic must have kept the tray in place. There were no visible ties connecting it to the shark and each flick of its tail should have disrupted the tray and upended the glasses, yet they did not so much as tip.

LeiRain eyed the shark as it came near, taking in its rows of sharp and abundant teeth. Riv had said that the elves could control all the beasts of the ocean, save the sheel, of course, but it was one thing to have this knowledge and another entirely to see this power exercised. She had never been this close to a shark before, and took the opportunity to look into its eye as it came by. There was something both beautiful and chilling about the cold indifference with which it looked back at her. LeiRain realized her mouth hung open and snapped it shut. Riv, on the other hand, seemed entirely unmoved by the sight. He reached up and casually snatched two chalices as the beast swam by.

Riv took a long drink from one of the chalices as he held the other out to LeiRain. She accepted it, wincing slightly as she brought it to her nose and caught the sharp scent of fermentation. Hesitantly, she sipped. Despite her relatively new wine collection, she didn't have much experience with alcoholic drinks. She had tried mead, as well as wine, but had never tasted a drink as sweet as the one she now held. There was something smooth in this drink that reminded her of honey and lavender, though she knew that neither of these existed under the sea. Enticed by the flavor, she took a longer pull from the glass. There was only the slightest bite of alcohol as she swallowed and a warm sensation as the draught traveled down her throat, spreading into her chest and eventually her belly.

The feeling reminded her of days spent napping in golden sunlight, and as she drank more, the sensation spread, reaching her arms, her legs, even her fingers. She hadn't realized how sore her muscles were until she felt the discomfort fading, replaced by a feeling of relaxed warmth. Even her thoughts felt softer. She looked out at the water elves and couldn't quite remember why she'd found their sharp smiles so unnerving. And Riv, standing beside her... She suddenly felt entirely comfortable in his presence. How could she have felt anything but comfortable next to such a handsome, friendly...

'Woah,' he said, looking back at her just as she drained the chalice. He pulled the cup from her now loose fingers and examined its emptiness. 'I guess it's a bit too late to suggest that you slow down on the wine.'

She already missed the feel of its glow on her tongue. LeiRain reached for the chalice in Riv's hand. He pulled it back and looked at her with that charming half-smile and one eyebrow raised. LeiRain, flushed with drink, smiled back at him. Whatever embarrassment she'd felt at her mussed state was gone and her cheeks didn't heat the second Riv grinned at her. This affect was accompanied by a subtle, lightheaded feeling, but even that wasn't altogether unpleasant. Pursing her lips, LeiRain took a step forward, reaching again for his glass. He didn't have to move to evade her this time as she lost her balance and tipped forward in the water. She caught herself and managed to get her feet back on the sand. LeiRain swayed where she stood and let herself believe it was just the push of a current. Even this did not embarrass her as it usually would. *I love wine*, she thought, as a giggle slipped out of her.

LeiRain's laugh was cut off by a hiccup and she brought a hand up to cover her mouth. Some still rational part of her brain realized that she might not be proud of her behavior once the wine wore off, but it wasn't enough to make her regret anything yet. She pulled her shoulders back and steadied herself against the current in an effort to look more composed than she actually was. The clearing was beginning to fill with elves, the crowd becoming so thick that the movement of bodies through the water further disrupted her balance. Some of them, noting her inebriation, laughed softly as they passed and smiled indulgently. LeiRain felt gratitude toward the salt water that buoyed her. She had no doubt that her knees would have buckled under the press of gravity if she were on land.

Riv pulled her to the edge of the crowd, just outside of the circle of tables. The music and the squeak and chirp of elf-speak was duller here. She noticed that even the smell of the food had become faint, though it was only a few feet away. *Elf magic is strange*, she thought.

'You've just thrown back an entire glass of elf wine in a

matter of seconds. It's some of the most potent drink there is.' His brow furrowed and his smile drooped, slightly. 'I should have warned you. I just didn't realize you would drink it so quickly. Now you're a bit of a mess.' He looked her over with a frown.

A hint of embarrassment echoed in the distant reaches of her mind, but LeiRain let the feeling slip away as she settled snugly into the coziness of her wine-induced stupor. For the first time, she saw the appeal of heavy drinking and understood why such enthusiastic sounds of revelry emanated from the inns and pubs each evening in Harbor. The only answer she gave Riv was to nibble on her lower lip and bat her eyes at him. He raised an eyebrow and laughed, the sound renewing the pleasure of her drunkenness.

'We'll have to find Lana before you retire for the evening or you'll feel much less jolly in the morning.'

Riv sipped from his chalice and she looked into her own empty cup, which she'd managed to ply from Riv's fingers while he was laughing. He was staring at her when she brought her eyes back up and, with feigned exasperation, he sighed and passed her his own glass.

'Just a sip!' His voice sounded stern but his eyes sparkled with amusement and his lips were pursed in a manner that suggested he was fighting the urge to smile. She obeyed, taking what she thought was a very dainty sip from his wine before passing it back. Another drink-laden shark swam by just inside the clearing. Riv reached over and plucked a full chalice from its back. 'This one is all mine,' he said, winking at her. 'I've got to catch up to *you*.'

'Drink up.' She was surprised at the laughter she heard in her own voice. They floated together in silence for several minutes as Riv drank. LeiRain watched the elves in the center of the clearing dance as Riv took big gulps from his wine. 'I can't believe I'm here.' She broke the silence without meaning to.

'Well,' Riv said, now taking long pulls from his second glass of wine, 'the elves don't let just anyone into their cities. I mean, they can't exactly say no when a tempest dumps an infant on their doorstep, but they don't usually let wanderers in, so I almost can't believe you're here either.' This made both of them laugh. 'It uh… It really is quite a big deal to be owed a favor here,' Riv went on, 'especially a life debt. If you're ever in need, call them. They *will* come to your aid.' He finished the contents of his second goblet and LeiRain looked sadly into her empty one once more.

'You mean, I just yell?' She scrunched up her face in confusion. 'How do I *call them*?' She wiggled her fingers, except for those still clutching her empty chalice, on these last two words.

'Well, I mean,' his words were beginning to sound a bit slurred, 'if you're in the same body of water, yeah. You can just yell. They will hear you. Before you ask, no I don't totally get it. It's not that their hearing is that excellent, it's another bit of their magic. That's how Orca knew Delphine was in trouble so quickly.' He tossed his empty cups back into the clearing. They both made slow arcs as they met with the water's resistance, but Riv made a pushing motion with one of his hands and a current swept them into the clearing. LeiRain blinked in surprise as a long, purple tentacle reached up and snatched both. The octopus scurried away with the empty chalices before LeiRain could even express her surprise.

'How many of us are here? I haven't seen any others.'

'Ah, well,' Riv looked at her with glassy eyes as he scratched his chin. 'There are four of us now, I think. Many come and go, but a few of us have been here for most of our lives. Cordelia and I grew up together here, along with a few others. But they've all left, except Eaton.' LeiRain couldn't imagine why anyone would leave such a place. 'He spends all his time courting an elf by the name of Pearl so we don't see him much these days.'

'Where is Cordelia?' LeiRain craned her neck to look around the clearing. She couldn't help but feel a bit jealous of the girl who'd grown up with Riv.

'Cordelia isn't a big fan of revels,' Riv replied, rolling his eyes. 'She's probably off by herself somewhere, admiring her own reflection.' *So she's pretty then,* LeiRain thought. 'I'm sure you'll meet her tomorrow.'

His voice was still light and playful, but there was something slightly off about his smile when he said this last bit. She was reminded of her last conversation with Bren. There was bitterness in Riv's words that he couldn't entirely hide. LeiRain felt another pang of jealousy. She wasn't sure if it was the memory of Bren or the thought of Cordelia that brought the feeling on, but LeiRain disliked the way it detracted from the soothing hum of her wine-soaked innards.

'What are they celebrating, anyway?' It was quite a party they were throwing.

'Uh,' he gave her a smile that looked a bit like a grimace, 'you.'

'Huh?'

'You saved the life of an elf youngling. It's kind of a big deal, Rain, remember?'

She was startled by the way he said her name. They'd only known each other for the better part of an hour and her name on his lips felt uncomfortably but excitingly familiar. This, along with the realization that the great celebration was in her honor, caused LeiRain's already wine-flushed cheeks to burn uncomfortably hot. Her face and neck felt prickled with heat and any smile she'd had faded.

'Not to downplay the significance of what you did,' he shifted in the water so that his shoulder bumped against hers, 'but they *do* like to celebrate. The elves throw a party for pretty much anything and everything. That's why Cordelia and I don't usually go... We'd be attending a party every other night.' *Cordelia and I. Blheck*, LeiRain winced internally.

'Oh,' LeiRain felt an odd mix of relief and disappointment. No one had ever before thrown a party in her honor and it was a let down to learn that this was so commonplace in Corallis. At the same time, it was uncomfortable to think that she and her unskilled fight with the sheel were the focus of everyone's attention. 'Oh!' she said, again, as memories of the sheel encounter flooded back, 'I... When the sheel was coming at me...' She looked up at Riv who was taller than she was but also floating with his feet several inches away from the ocean floor. LeiRain could feel her eyes go large in excitement. 'I did something with the water. I've never done it before and I don't know... I moved it somehow? Is that – can you do that? Is that something we can *all* do?' She waved her hands back and forth between them to indicate that she was speaking about offspring of tempest in general.

'Of course,' he looked at her, his own eyes wide now but with surprise, not excitement. 'Was that the first time you'd ever used your magic?' His eyes narrowed as he looked over her and said, more to himself than her, 'I suppose that you wouldn't have had anyone to show you, especially on land.'

LeiRain felt her shoulders tense at these words. *Too long on land*. The welcoming embrace of the wine seemed to be pulling away from her and she peeked around Riv to see if any drink-carrying sharks were passing by the edges of the clearing. She saw only elves, crowding around freshly replenished baskets of food. She turned her attention back to Riv.

'You said there were four of you in the city. You've only told me about three, and you're all the same age. Who taught all of you?'

'Ah, the fourth would be Cove. He is the eldest demi here, much older than I am.' Riv's eyes darted away from hers and his voice grew softer, less enthusiastic.

'Demi?' She immediately thought of Ron, how he had always called her *demi*, when no one else did.

'You know,' he waved his hand around to indicate the two of them much like she had a few moments before, 'demi-gods, half tempest, half whatever else...'

Demi.

Ron had known. He must have. All of those years, long before she'd met her father, he had known of her heritage. The realization was uncomfortable. He'd always seemed like more than just a client of Alarra's. He was a family friend, almost like an uncle. LeiRain felt a cold hurt at realizing that he had withheld things from her, had likely conspired in this with her mother. She imagined herself having some words with Ron the next time she saw him. What else did the dwarve know about her father, about what her mother had been like before LeiRain came along? 'I need more wine,' LeiRain declared.

13

'Hang on,' Riv said, and disappeared into the swirl of elf activity before she could respond. He wasn't gone long before reappearing, paddling his legs while both of his hands carried full glasses of wine. LeiRain set her empty glass down on the nearby table and took one of the cups from his hand. 'Don't say I didn't warn you,' he said, eyeing the glass in her hand, 'when you wake up feeling like your head has been bashed against a rock.'

'I take full responsibility for my actions,' she said, smiling as she took a drink and felt the liquid burn down her throat and into her belly once more. The thoughts of her past, of Bren and Ron and her father, began to blur around the edges once more and she closed her eyes briefly as she savored her next sip.

'So,' she pressed on, 'you were saying... Cove?'

His smile faltered briefly and his joyful expression was replaced with something else. *Sadness*, LeiRain thought. There was something about Cove that made Riv sad.

'He did teach me how to use my power and for the first several years of my life, he was almost like a father to me.

Really, he seemed to take it on himself to look after all of us younger demis, but he had taken an elf partner and when he died...'

LeiRain, emboldened by the wine and the empathy she felt for someone so like herself, reached out and took Riv's hand in hers. He didn't seem to notice at first, but she squeezed his hand gently and his eyes came to rest on their clasped fingers. He squeezed back, then cleared his throat and let her hand drop. LeiRain might have felt hurt, if the wine hadn't banished such things for the time being.

'He likes to keep to himself, now. I guess, at least he stayed in Corallis. When it first happened, I was afraid he would leave.' He shrugged, and smiled at her, 'So after that I just had to teach myself.'

Riv grew quiet, his eyes losing their focus, the smile slipping slightly. LeiRain was about to ask him if he was alright when she began to feel her feet slide out from under her. She put her hands forward to catch herself but she was being pulled away from the ocean floor, lifted up and away from Riv. Churning water held LeiRain aloft. She touched the boundaries of the swirling water with one hand and gasped as the churn beneath her moved forward. *A horse*! The water beneath her swirled in the shape of the animal, held within boundaries carved out by Riv's mind. The edges of the horse glowed a faint blue, as if a wall of light contained the roiling water. LeiRain put her fingers through the mane and laughed as the rivulets of water tickled her palm. The horse carried her in circles around Riv, who stood with a satisfied smirk on his face, arms crossed over his muscular chest. She tried not to look down as she circled. The water moved so quickly within the silhouette of the horse that it made the body opaque, but she could still see through it enough to catch disorienting glimpses of the ocean floor. She pulled her fingers from the mane and tried to stroke the horse's neck, finding a wall of water that pushed back.

'Amazing,' she said.

'I'm sure you can do that, too.'

'No,' she said, drinking from her wine as the horse trotted about with her on its back. She'd never ridden horseback on land before, but suspected it wasn't quite as smooth a ride. 'I can't do *anything* like this.' She shook her head.

'Of course, you can,' he said confidently, 'you just haven't had any training. We can remedy that easily enough.'

'I've... I've tried,' she said, feeling embarrassed. 'But nothing ever happened, not until yesterday when I was fending off the sheel.'

'Were you using that shield of yours?'

'Yes, but ... oh!' She hadn't even thought about her sword and shield when she'd woken up. She'd been too distracted by her restraints and then by Riv himself and her hunger. 'Where—'

'They are still at Lana's,' he said, holding up a hand. 'They will be safe there, but we can go get them whenever you'd like, right now if you want.'

'No,' LeiRain said. She was relieved, but also felt a bit guilty that she had so easily forgotten such an extravagant gift. 'That's okay.'

'Well, the stone,' he went on with what he'd been saying before, 'the white stone in the middle of it, it's enchanted. It focuses your magic. Had you ever tried any water magic with the shield before yesterday?'

'Actually, no. My mother just gave it to me.' She stopped herself before she added, *for my birthday*.

An image of her mother came to mind but LeiRain was too drunk and enthralled to think much on what Alarra might be doing now, what she might think about LeiRain disappearing on the eve of her majority. She would smooth everything over with her mother when she got back.

'That had to be it, then. You have the magic, just haven't trained. The shield, its stone, it will help you wield your powers. I can show you some things,' he said, and then caught her as she almost floated off of the water horse and into the current, 'But maybe tomorrow. I think we've both had a bit too much wine to do anything tonight.'

'Oh, that's ... that would be fantastic,' she said, stumbling as the water horse dissolved. She was left floating awkwardly a few feet away from Riv. 'Can I meet some of the others?'

'Cordelia? Yes. Eaton? Maybe, if we can convince him to take a break from courting. Cove,' he shook his head and frowned. 'Unlikely.'

Another question came to LeiRain, her drunk mind moving slowly as it sifted through the bits and pieces of information she'd gleaned about elves and *demis* in the last day. 'Riv?'

'Yes?' There was a bit of laughter in his voice as he examined her creased brows and sternly shaped mouth.

'You said that sons and daughters of tempest – demis,' she corrected herself, 'don't often take elf partners because we live for so much longer.'

'Well, yes but when you have a bunch of demis growing up surrounded by elves, it still happens sometimes.' He had misunderstood where she was going with this inquiry.

'Right, of course,' she replied, her words coming out with a sharpness that gave away her impatience. 'But Orca said they'd been trying for... I don't remember, exactly, but I think he said a century to have a child. So, if elves live for more than a century and demis live longer than elves... How old are *you*?' It was indelicate, but she couldn't stop herself.

'A hundred and four years.'

She felt her mouth fall open. He let out a loud, unrestrained laugh.

'I've been told I age well,' he said with a wink.

'How? Will... Will I...'

'We are only part mortal, Rain. The elves, and Cove, tell me that I will live as long as wisdom permits.' Needing something to wash away the thick knot in her throat, LeiRain finished her wine.

'Meaning,' he went on to clarify, 'that as long as we are not wounded so severely that our immortal heritage cannot heal us before we bleed out, as long as we are not beheaded, burned to ash, or otherwise brutally maimed, we will live on.'

LeiRain had never before considered this possibility and she drank deeply from her wine as her mind whirred. Did her mother know this about her? Did Ron? Surely, her mother could not expect her to spend such a long lifetime chained to a trade in a village like Harbor. No, Alarra must not know. She couldn't even imagine what her mother would say when she shared this information.

'My mother is not going to believe all of this,' she said, as much to herself as to Riv. 'I hadn't meant to be gone this long, actually,' she admitted, 'but I'm sure she will understand when I tell her all that has happened.'

Riv continued to smirk, but his eyes were half-lidded now and he bit his lip before he spoke.

'Going back and forth is tough, Rain.'

'Between water and land? No, I do it all of the time,' she assured him.

'No,' he shook his head and his smile disappeared entirely, now. 'Time is different here. If you return, I... No one who has anything, or anyone, outside of Corallis ever comes back.'

'What do you mean? Of course, I'll come back!' If the

thought of living in Harbor had been painful before, it was intolerable after experiencing the wonders of this civilization.

'It's hard to explain, but time moves differently here. It is part of the magic that wards this city.' He shrugged, 'You'll see once you go home.'

She flinched at the word *home*. She dared not say it, but Corallis, this city, Riv, it all felt more like home to her than Harbor Village ever had. She'd found so much here for her in such a short time. How much worse would it be to dwell in Harbor Village now that she knew cities such as Corallis existed?

'But you don't have to go, *yet,* right?' The smile was back on Riv's face. 'It will only take a few days for you to learn some of the more basic stuff, jumpstart your training. Your mother can wait a few more days, right?'

LeiRain thought she could. Certainly, Alarra would be happy once she learned that LeiRain had found others like her, that her daughter had found the companionship and acceptance that was absent in the village. At least, LeiRain hoped that her mother would be happy for her, content to let LeiRain embrace this new life. Always before, Alarra had objected to LeiRain's proposals because they were unsafe or uncertain, but Corallis was neither of those things. What if her mother didn't approve? *She can't stop me*, LeiRain assured herself.

'Yes, of course she can,' LeiRain replied. She felt herself smile broadly, drunk on elf wine and possibilities.

14

R iv tipped backward in the water, arms wheeling as his feet lost contact with the sandy bottom. LeiRain's hold on the water dissipated and Riv floated back into a standing position as the force that had been pushing him disappeared.

'It's a good start,' he said. His voice was serious, but his face beamed at her.

LeiRain smiled in return and glanced over at the three young elves, including Delphine, who were watching from the edge of the clearing. They were the same younglings who'd come to greet Delphine on her return to Corallis, and this was the same clearing that, only two nights ago, had been filled with revelry. LeiRain looked beyond the younglings to where Cordelia drifted through the water on her back, tying off a tight braid she'd made with a thin strand of hair. She wasn't quite sure why the girl had come; she'd said barely a word to LeiRain beyond their meeting and had appeared utterly bored the entire time she'd been practicing with Riv.

She brought her attention back to the middle of the clearing, which seemed infinitely large now that it was empty of dancing water elves and their underwater servants. There was so much open space that the younglings who'd come to watch were now playing a game that seemed similar to one the Harbor children played. *Tag*, she thought she'd heard it called. The younglings darted forward, backward, up and down as they evaded each other, still leaving plenty of space for LeiRain and Riv to train without crashing into them.

LeiRain looked back at Riv and saw that he must have followed her gaze to Cordelia. His smile had faded but otherwise his face gave away nothing of his thoughts. LeiRain had been trying to figure out the relationship between the two demi-gods ever since Riv had first mentioned Cordelia, but all she'd been able to decipher was that their attachment to one another involved feelings of annoyance and an undetermined brand of affection. Cordelia was *very* pretty and much more feminine than LeiRain had ever been. She was trying *very* hard not to let this bother her, but when she continually caught Riv staring at the girl with an unreadable expression on his face, it was difficult not to feel a bit overlooked. LeiRain reminded herself that she was new to the company of other demis, while they were common-place to Riv and Cordelia, so perhaps that was why she was so riveted by the young man in front of her. Part of her also wanted to pretend that her admiration for Riv could completely replace any feelings of affection she had for Bren.

After all, her adventures here over the last few days should have made the end of that relationship seem inconsequential, a distant memory. But the truth was that every time she caught Riv looking at Cordelia, she imagined the merchant's daughter. She saw Bren, looking admiringly on a similarly beautiful face. It made her burn with jealousy. When LeiRain thought of the tantrum she'd thrown when he'd told her, she felt an embarrassment now that she hadn't been able to feel for the first few days after the encounter.

It seemed that her feelings were determined to follow her, even to a place as breathtaking as Corallis. LeiRain looked back at Cordelia, watching the girl braid a new section of hair. Cordelia seemed oblivious to the disruption her presence had caused to Riv's concentration. She let out a long, slow breath, water rippling past her chin as she did so, determined now to concentrate on the task at hand and to regain Riv's focus as well. *He's not Bren,* she told herself.

LeiRain drew her eyes back to the center of the empty clearing, to the space between her and Riv. She'd begun to feel a bit fatigued from the magic use, which Riv had said was normal, especially since she was new to it. But the flare of jealousy and memory seemed to produce a new pool of physical and mental energy. She clung to her shield, gathering focus from the opal it held, and reached for the water with her mind. She'd always felt some sense of how the water moved, where it began and ended, but in the last few days with Riv, she'd learned to connect even more deeply with this feeling. Now that she knew the power of the shield, and had Riv's help, she was beginning to realize the breadth of her connection with the water, and the immense control she had over it.

Blood ran hot in her cheeks and neck as she closed her eyes, pulling energy from her swirl of feelings. She reached for the water with her mind and found it, but the water seemed to recoil. LeiRain took in a deep breath and let it out very slowly. Some of her resentment dissipated with the exhalation. The jealousy was still there, but it was more hurt now than anger. LeiRain tried again to take control of the water, and this time, it didn't pull away. She opened her eyes. The column of water she had reached for with her mind was spinning rapidly in the middle of the clearing. It obeyed her instantly, spinning off in Riv's direction. Her mouth quirked up in a half-smile that mimicked his. He seemed to sense something in the water behind him but just as he began to turn and look, the funnel swept over him. Riv was caught off guard. He'd been distracted by Cordelia, but also LeiRain had sent this rush of water with more force than any that she'd commanded so far. He was pulled off his feet and sent tumbling backward. Sand swirled up from the ocean floor as Riv spun end over end. It was several seconds before he was able to slow his movement using his own magic. He floated in a horizontal position for several seconds before sitting upright where he hovered over the sand. LeiRain studied Riv's face. It bore a look of confusion as he blinked rapidly, eyes staring straight ahead. Had she gone too far? Was he going to be cross with her? She watched as he squeezed his eyes shut for a few seconds and shook his head from side to side. When he opened his eyes, he was looking directly at her. She swallowed, her throat feeling thick as she waited for his response. To her relief, his face cracked into a broad smile.

'Well done, Rain!' He brought his hands together in a clapping motion. It made only the dullest of sounds underwater, but his excitement was clear. The flush of irritation she'd felt before had dissipated, the energy refocused into her magic. The way Riv looked at her now made her think that perhaps she'd misread his feelings for Cordelia. LeiRain smiled back at him, pleased to have shown so much mastery over this new skill and almost as pleased to have broken Cordelia's hold on Riv's attention.

'You should try it without the shield now!' There was a note of anticipation in his voice. LeiRain's smile faltered.

'I don't think I'm ready.' Her grip on the shield tightened involuntarily. She'd been in Corallis for three days now and she never felt the same connection with the water when she wasn't holding the shield. Riv had assured her that she was just as capable without it, but how could she have only discovered this power now if that were true?

'I agree,' Cordelia said, sounding bored.

Surprised at her contribution to the conversation, LeiRain turned to look at the demi where she now floated. Cordelia hovered in the water on her stomach, her chin resting atop her hands as she studied LeiRain. The look on her face was distinctly unimpressed. LeiRain continued to watch her, waiting for some explanation of her opinion. The demi looked up from the hair she was braiding and met LeiRan's gaze.

'I mean, you've only just started. *We've* all been doing this stuff since we were younglings.' Cordelia shrugged her shoulders and flipped over to float on her back. Eaton was locked in an immodest embrace with his elf partner, Pearl, and seemed entirely unaware of the exchange.

LeiRain's shoulders tensed. She tried not to look at the stone in her shield, the stone that was responsible for her ability to access magic. It was the opal that had allowed her to fend off the sheel when she would otherwise have been killed. LeiRain wondered if she would have ever discovered her magical abilities without it and where or how her mother had found such a stone. Did her mother have any idea of its purpose? Had Alarra enchanted it herself? Was it possible that this was the same stone she'd seen hanging from her father's neck so many years ago, resting against his broad chest? Regardless of its mysterious origins, it was her link to water magic. LeiRain lacked confidence in her ability to command the water without it. She would have to ask about it when she returned home.

Her stomach knotted at thoughts of her mother and *home*. Riv had convinced her to stay these few days in Corallis, using the lure of training to convince her. When Cordelia wasn't around, Riv seemed genuinely intrigued by LeiRain and his charms were nearly irresistible. She'd begun to think that he knew full well the effects of his half-smile. *This* was more home now than Harbor had ever been, but her mother did not deserve to be left wondering, maybe even worrying, about her well-being. She'd snuck away in the night with her mother's gifts in hand, with this magical stone that had opened up an entirely new world to her, and had not left so much as a *thank you.* Of course she would have left a note about where she'd gone if she'd had any inkling that she would be away for so long, but her mother wouldn't know that until she returned to Harbor and explained everything.

'No harm in trying.' Riv's words pulled LeiRain back from her reverie.

She shook off thoughts of her mother. She'd be going back to her soon, anyway, she told herself. She would explain everything and right the wrong she'd done Alarra, and then return to Corallis with her mother's blessing. She could humor Riv for now, especially since he was looking at her with one corner of his mouth curled up and a sparkle in her eyes that made her temporarily forget how distracted he'd just been by Cordelia. With a huff, LeiRain put down the shield. She shoved it into the sand so that it stood partially buried but upright and then took a few steps away from it. Closing her eyes, she felt for the thin line in her mind that tethered her to the water. Without the shield, the stone, her mind felt darker, the tether harder to find. LeiRain felt as if she were fumbling around, blindly feeling for her magic. Finally, she sensed it! Slowly, carefully, she began to wrap her mind around the tether.

It was there, in her grasp, all she needed to do was tug on it and she would have that connection with the water, again ... without the shield. Just as she began to pull on the connection, her mother's worried face came to mind. She saw Alarra at her forge, putting down her work to look over her shoulder at the dusty road that led away from their home. The image was fleeting, just the barest of moments, but it was enough for the tether to slip through her grasp. She felt it sliding through her fingers back into the blackness.

Eyes still closed, she gritted her teeth and swallowed her frustration and disappointment. Angry, that gentle hand, those mental fingers were no longer probing lightly in the dark; they were clawing. Her mind gripped at hints of the tether as shame, hopelessness, and loneliness broke loose in her mind... All the feelings she hid from herself, from the rest of the world, temporarily freed from their prison. The harder it became to find the tether, the more aggressively her mind reached for it, clawing and clawing until... Until she realized ... the water was retreating, pulling away from her. It was as if her magic, the water, sensed those ugly feelings and recoiled.

'I can't,' she said, her voice tight with frustration. She opened her eyes and saw concern on Riv's face. LeiRain forced her hands to loosen from the tight fists they had been in, and willed her features to relax, smoothing out the creases she could feel in her forehead and around her eyes and unclenching her jaw.

'You've come really far in just a few days, Rain,' he said, reassuring her. 'You just need practice. You'll be able to do that, and a lot more, without the stone. Soon.' She raised an eyebrow in disbelief. 'I'm sure of it,' he said, and winked at her.

She looked away from him so that he couldn't see the doubt in her eyes or her flush at his wink.

'Your escort will be ready, now.' She looked back at him and saw that he was frowning. 'So, we should finish up anyway.'

LeiRain called a farewell to the other demis. Cordelia

didn't even bother to look her way but responded with a half-hearted wave. Eaton, to her surprise, broke from Pearl and smiled at her so earnestly that his eyes crinkled around the corners. Eaton was handsome, beautiful even, but not in the same way as Cordelia or Riv. His body, though muscular, was very thin and he was at least a foot taller than Riv, who already seemed to tower over LeiRain. There were thin patches of red fur on his chest and stomach and the tips of his ears. Riv had explained that his father had likely been a shifter, though it was impossible to know for sure since he had been abandoned at Corallis as an infant, just like the rest of them.

'We have enjoyed your visit.' He moved his hand up and down Pearl's side affectionately as he looked at LeiRain.

His partner, Pearl, said nothing but nodded her agreement. She was more diminutive than any of the other adult elves LeiRain had met, and looked even more so next to Eaton. Pearl did not have the same ethereal beauty as Orca's partner Marina and her sister Lana, but she was beautiful in her own right. Her small stature reminded LeiRain of a pixie she'd seen in Harbor a few years ago. Pearl floated several feet above the ocean floor in order to keep her head at the same height as Eaton's. Her hair was cropped to what would have been shoulder length if it had been subject to gravity, which also seemed unique. The warriors kept theirs only a few inches long, and most other elves looked as if they'd never had a haircut in their lifetime. LeiRain thought about inquiring after this choice, but worried it might be rude to ask such a direct question.

Cove, the eldest and most reclusive of the demis, had remained inaccessible. Just as Riv had predicted, the older man kept to himself. He had left Corallis at one point, after his elven mate died and when Cove returned many years later, he had been an entirely different person. Riv's eyes were downcast, and his voice soft when he relayed this to LeiRain. Riv assured her that she'd meet Cove eventually, though, when she returned to Corallis.

Riv had managed easily to convince her to stay these additional two days in the city. By the time LeiRain returned home, she would have been gone for three full days, which was as long as she could stay away without guilt eating her up entirely.

The elves had agreed to return her to where she'd crossed the drop-off and to provide protection while she crossed, but they would go no further. Water elves, she had learned from Orca, were even more reclusive than forest elves. All of their cities were warded just as Corallis was, and even Orca had refused entirely to discuss the location of other such places. To return to the underwater city, LeiRain would have to swim back over the drop-off and call out. *They'll hear you*, Riv assured her. *Orca will know. He'll come get you.* The elves seemed to rarely venture outside of the wards' protection and were content to spend their very long lives within the confines of the city. When she mentioned things that were unique to land or the populated areas near shore, they seemed to be entirely unaware of them.

She freed her shield from the sand and slid it onto her back. Her sword belt and scabbard had been discarded nearby as well; it was no use to their exercises and she was still adjusting to the feel of it in the water. She picked it up and buckled it around her waist, nodding solemnly at Riv once she was ready. He swam silently next to her as she approached the edge of the city and stayed by her side when she passed the wards. LeiRain could sense the wards humming. It was faint, and easy to miss, but with her newly honed magic, the presence of wards was clear. The two of them stopped just shy of where a group of tough-looking elves stood waiting. All three of them had short hair and blades of some kind strapped to each limb.

'I'll be back,' LeiRain said, 'soon.' They stood facing each other, no more than a foot apart. Her fingers itched to take his hands in hers but she resisted the urge, tugging on the front of her tunic, instead. '*Really*,' she went on, 'I've never been so happy as I have these last few days. This is… I want this to be my home.' She hadn't meant to lower her voice, but this last part came out in a whisper.

Riv inched closer to her. He took one of her hands in his and lifted it to his face. LeiRain's heart beat an unsteady rhythm against her rib cage. Riv brought her hand to his lips, kissing the back of it. He cocked his head to the side, gave her his crippling half-smile and said, 'You'd better come back, and soon.' He had kept her hand only a few inches from his lips so she felt the flutter of water as his breath moved it across her skin. He winked, then lowered her hand and released it.

LeiRain turned away from him to face the elves then stopped and looked over her shoulder. She ran her gaze over Riv, who was flashing a smile that didn't reach his eyes. LeiRain smiled back before looking past him to take in Corallis one more time. The city was aesthetically magnificent. She'd at first been taken in by its colorfulness and beauty, but in her tired and wounded state, LeiRain hadn't been able to fully appreciate its greatness. The wards, now that she could sense them, seemed to pulse in a tall arc over the city. Tall spires of rock and coral teemed with harmonious life. Sea grass and anemones swayed in the current. Faint lines of music managed to drift through the wards, audible only because she strained to hear them.

This city had given her something that Harbor never had; peace. A sense of home. No one had jeered at her in Corallis. Homes had been open to her. She'd been treated like someone of value. She had met others like herself. Even Cordelia, who had only managed to show LeiRain indifference and disapproval, was more respectful than most residents in Harbor ... because they were the same. She looked fondly at the large boulders that marked the entrance into the city and the beginning of the wards and thought about how confused and even frightened she had been as she'd first entered Corallis. The water elves might have frightfully sharp teeth, but they had shown her more kindness than she would have ever expected from the humans in Harbor.

When she finally turned back to her elf escorts, she was crying. Not at the thought of leaving Corallis, but at the realization that for the first time in her life, she felt truly seen. LeiRain nearly laughed at the absurdity of it – she'd never cried from happiness before. The futility of blinking away tears while underwater seemed suddenly hilarious as well. She was surprised that she could even tell she was crying, but the blurred vision and stinging eyes were familiar.

'It is hard to move between our two worlds, Rain,' Riv called after her, 'but there will always be a place here for you should you choose it.'

She glanced over her shoulder briefly and saw one of the warriors, a lean-muscled female, swimming toward them. She turned back to Riv to insist that nothing could possibly dissuade her, could make her stay in a place like Harbor Village when she was now welcome in the city of Corallis. Her eyes met with Riv's as the elve's hand closed on her shoulder and before she could speak, the world went black.

15

Leirain blinked away her confusion and grabbed at the elf nearest her, to steady herself. She had forgotten how disorienting the swifting was, though it had been much worse last time, perhaps due to her injury. She looked at the elf whose arm she gripped and saw a sharp-featured face staring back at her. The elf was naked except for her array of weapons and LeiRain thought briefly of how impractical it would be for a woman warrior to roam bare-chested on land. The smallness of the elf's breasts and the lift lended to them by the water seemed to make this an entirely acceptable practice in the ocean depths. LeiRain laughed to herself as she realized how far she'd come in accepting the lack of modesty amongst the elves in only a few days' time.

'We will watch you cross to ensure you make it safely to the other side,' the woman said. She seemed to be interpreting LeiRain's hesitation as fear. The other two escorts, both men, nodded in confirmation. The dizziness had dissipated and she released the elf's arm, turning to face the expanse of the drop-off. The unnatural blackness had seemed ominous on her first crossing, but felt even more so now as she remembered the sheel that had come up from its depths.

'Thank you,' she said, the sound coming out of her more timidly than she'd intended. She nodded at each of them before stepping closer to the drop-off. She had expected the elves to swift her to the other side, but this side of the drop-off must be as close to land as they were willing to go. She walked past the edge of the kelp forest, to where the white sand ended and blackness began, fighting the urge to look back at the elves one more time for reassurance. There were a brief few seconds of hesitation and then LeiRain pushed off the edge, forcing herself to cross the void before fear could get the better of her.

LeiRain crossed the gulf as quickly as she could, legs paddling madly, arms taking large scoops of water to propel her along. Her muscles were on fire, her lungs burned. She envied the elves for their webbed digits that helped them move with such ease through the water. Once across, she sighed with relief. She used her arms to push herself toward the ocean floor and then planted her feet in the sand. LeiRain turned to look back at the sandbar that had initially drawn her attention three days ago. She could just make out the three tall figures who had swifted her here standing on the other side of the yawning darkness.

One of them, the female, she thought, waved her hand and then all three of them winked out of existence. Utterly alone now, the blackness was more daunting. LeiRain wrapped her arms around her middle, feeling dwarfed by the dark expanse of the drop-off. She slid her right hand over her abdomen and down to her waist, feeling for the reassurance of her blade. She left the sword in its sheath but brushed her fingers lightly over the pommel. It was enough to know that it was there. Her hand moved from the hilt of her sword to her guige, the leather strap that held her shield. Gripping the guige, she pulled the shield over her shoulder and held it in front of her. She told herself that she was imagining things, but still couldn't help thinking that the inky blackness was spreading, crawling up from the edges of the drop-off. Her body grew cold, and heavy. She missed Riv and Orca. Maybe even Cordelia.

Despite her fear of the hidden depths of the drop-off, she hesitated, her feelings making it difficult to leave. Without Riv, without the elves beside her, it was easy to believe that she'd imagined the entire thing – Delphine, the sheel, Riv, Corallis. But standing here, she could see the kelp forest and the bright patches of sunlight on the other side of the drop-off. Proof that what she'd seen and experienced had really happened. She'd been there. Fought there. Bled there. *It was real*. But she couldn't remain here indefinitely. The drop-off was too dangerous. And anyway, the sooner she told her mother about everything, the sooner she could return to Corallis for good. LeiRain forced her feet to shuffle backward as she moved away from the drop-off. She walked backward like this, shield in hand, feet dragging through the sand, until she could no longer see the brightly lit kelp or the drop-off.

She moved inland before she began to head south, no longer interested in exploring the depths alone now that she knew the extent of their dangers. There was something comforting in the busy whirl of sounds that carried through the shallows. There was life there. Small and, if not friendly, at least not dangerous. It made LeiRain feel just a bit less isolated. As always, lost and discarded treasures and trash lay scattered on the seafloor near the shoreline. Out of habit, LeiRain scanned them as she walked, but her mind couldn't seem to focus on assessing their worth.

Her interest in such things had dulled. LeiRain passed

by an unopened chest, intricately decorated with gold filigree, and looked at it with unfocused eyes and a distant
mind before continuing on. It didn't seem like these things
would be of much value in Corallis. From what she'd
observed, the entire community worked together to ensure
that everyone was fed and sheltered. Even the younglings
contributed in gathering plants and small mollusks, and all
of the elves seemed to know how to fashion their own
weapons. The only elves set apart in any way by their skills
were the healers, and even they took part in the gathering
and preparing of food when they were not busy caring for
others.

After the better part of a day, LeiRain drew close to Harbor
Village. She found herself having to step or swim over crates
and clusters of wine bottles. The labels all seemed to have
been eaten away and many of the bottles were in a sorrier
state than she remembered them. Maybe everything in
Harbor would look just a little bit drearier now that she'd seen
Corallis. LeiRain's mouth watered as she recalled the sweet-
ness of the elfwine. This made her think of the collection of
bottles she had stacked in the corner of her room. Would her
mother keep the bottles when she was gone? Sell them?
Would she be cross if LeiRain left them for her to deal with?
Her mother...

Now that LeiRain drew closer to home, her guilt at disappearing for the last few days had turned into an abject fear.
She tried to reassure herself that Alarra would be happy to
hear of Corallis. She would be pleased to hear of the life her
daughter could make in such a place. But all she could muster
was a vague hope that her mother would at least be happy to
see her alive. Would Alarra be disappointed at her decision to
leave? She hoped she'd understand, but now that she was fast
approaching her childhood home, it was hard not to think of

all the ways in which her mother's expectations and wants had differed from her own.

I can visit, though, LeiRain thought.

Riv had said that it would be difficult to move between places but she could overcome her anxious feelings about the drop-off, especially if she continued to master her control over the water. Many sons and daughters moved much further away from their childhood homes, having to travel days in order to visit with their parents. Some even had to come by boat because the distance took too long to cross overland, so she could come back to her mother. Not to Harbor, but to her mother. And she would bring tales of great underwater adventures and the life she had built among those who treated her as one of their own. She could make up for all the time spent on land, for all the years she'd missed in the water. How could her mother possibly be anything but happy for her?

16

LeiRain's head broke through the waves as she swam toward the shoreline. Rivulets of water ran down her face and damp strands of hair clung to her forehead. Her skin felt bare as the air hit it for the first time in days. LeiRain squinted at the intense afternoon sun, much brighter now that there weren't several feet of water dimming the shine. Once the water was only waist deep, she stopped swimming and began wading her way to shore. Everything felt heavier than she remembered as the buoying effects of the water gave way to the increased effects of gravity on land. She picked her knees up high as she sloshed her way to the sandy beach. LeiRain had expelled most of the water from her lungs by the time she reached the shore. She breathed out forcefully to rid herself of the rest of it. A thin stream of ocean water ran out of her nose and another trickled from the corner of her mouth. Her wet clothes and hair felt burdensome as she walked beside the docks. She hadn't anticipated this, hadn't thought of how strange it would feel to be on land again after so long in the water.

LeiRain jumped as a groan echoed through the empty street, but she quickly realized that it was just the sound of wind sweeping through the village. There was a bite to the wind that cut through her wet clothes and made her bare skin sting. She folded her arms over her chest, tucking her hands beneath her biceps, and wondered if there was a way to draw the water out of her clothing and hair. It wasn't something that Riv or Cordelia would have cause to worry about, since they spent almost all of their time in Corallis. She continued walking, shoulders hunched in an ineffective attempt to ward off the cold, and began to reach for the water with her mind, just as Riv had taught her.

LeiRain could feel the water, could touch it with her mind, but this small amount of water was more difficult to isolate. She felt the ocean nearby, where it met the shore. She could feel the height of each crashing wave. This blurred the edges of the water that clung to her, like trying to pick out a single voice from a room full of people singing the same song. It was a more precise business than any magic she'd done so far and she would definitely need the aid of her shield and its enchantments to accomplish such a delicate task. But the thought of pulling her hands out from beneath her arms, where they were slowly beginning to warm, was unappealing. LeiRain imagined her fingers wrapped around the cold metal and shivered violently. Even with the shield, she didn't know if she'd be able to draw the water out her hair and clothes. It was better to just hurry home, change into something dry and warm herself by the fire. Perhaps this was why the streets were so empty today; no one wanted to endure this weather.

By the time she'd reached the edge of the village, the cold had begun to make the pointed tips of her ears hurt, and she was looking forward to the sanctuary of the trees along the path home. They would shield her from the worst of this unseasonably cold wind and it was only a quick half mile or so of walking until she could dry herself. She imagined standing in front of her mother's forge and letting the waves of heat roll over her body, the dampness in her hair turning to steam. Her mother always said the forge was for working, not warming, but LeiRain imagined Alarra might make an exception after her three-day absence. Thoughts of warming herself distracted LeiRain. She walked the path to her mother's workshop for several minutes before she felt the wrongness of her surroundings.

Brittle leaves crunched beneath her feet, and the colors that she'd only half-noticed in her peripheral vision were the reds and yellows of fallen leaves, not budding flowers. She had left Harbor Village on the eve of her birthday, when the air had just begun to warm and the first blooms of spring were visible among the weeds that edged the path. There were no blossoms now. The trees, which should have been thick and full with green leaves, were instead covered with thinning patches of russet and gold. As many leaves littered the ground as hung from the branches. A shiver passed through LeiRain that had nothing to do with the cold. It wasn't unheard of for storms to bring in unseasonable weather, even in the warmest of months, but the fallen leaves were the mark of a long-standing chill. The air even *smelled* like autumn, she realized with a start, noticing the light scent of ripe apples and wood smoke for the first time.

She stood there, unmoving, for several minutes as she thought about her passage through the village, the stillness of it all. It was just past midday, a time when the shops and vendors were normally buzzing with activity, but the Harbor had been as empty as one might expect in the predawn hours.

The way the wind had swept between through the streets, groaning as it passed between the awnings of closed businesses... There should have been bodies there, blocking its path, making such acoustics impossible. What had she noticed on her walk? The same gray and brown cobblestones beneath her feet, the same storefronts and awnings, in the periphery as she had walked. Even if it were deemed too cold for street vendors, shouldn't she have seen some foot traffic along the piers? There were always ships coming and going and the vendors who did well enough to have a storefront on the main road *always* had *some* customers. She could recall no evidence of these things in her memory... No tempting smells drifting out from the bakery, no stench of freshly caught fish or live lobsters.

She walked with a new wariness, taking in the details of her surroundings more carefully now. For the first time since stepping onto this path, she observed sets of overlapping footprints, visible between the patches of fallen leaves. It was unusual to see more than a few sets of prints on this road at any given time. Her mother made most of her living by selling special pieces, sorcerer's steel that few could work and even fewer could enhance with enchantments. Customers paid handsomely for these works so few could afford her. Alarra did pieces for the villagers occasionally, but not enough to necessitate such extensive foot traffic. LeiRain kicked aside some of the leaves and studied the imprints. There were so many that it looked as if this road had been trampled by half the inhabitants of Harbor. Many of the prints were old and faint, left in damp soil that was now dry and cracking, but some of the prints looked freshly made.

Now that she was aware of the strangeness around her, LeiRain felt compelled towards caution. She could not say what she was being cautious of, precisely, but remembering the way her senses had alerted her of the sheel's approach, LeiRain decided to trust this feeling. She swept leaves over overtop her footprints in the dirt, and stepped off the road and behind the tree-line as she continued toward her home. The wind could barely touch her now as she moved between the thick tree trunks, but the cold still made her teeth chatter. LeiRain wanted to turn around, to go back to the village. She wanted to examine Harbor without her mind on other things, but she recoiled from the thought of stepping back out into the unmitigated wind. And the fresh footfalls on the road made her press on with haste.

Thick brush caught on her clothes and snagged her hair, pulling more damp strands loose from her braid. It slowed her progress each time she stopped to disentangle herself. She stepped as lightly as she could, cringing every time a leaf crunched under foot, unable to ignore the intense sense of foreboding that followed her. LeiRain could barely feel her fingers now, even as she kept them tucked between her arms and torso. She desperately hoped that her worry was misplaced, that all would be well at her mother's workshop, their home, and that she could go about the business of thawing herself unbothered. But as she neared the clearing, she could make out the sound of a male voice. No, *voices*.

She peered through the brush and into the clearing where she saw several armed men milling about. She counted at least fifteen, but it was difficult to get a precise number as they moved, ducking in and out of her mother's workshop, in and out of their home. Many of their faces were familiar, villagers. There were men of all ages and backgrounds, the style, cut and cleanliness of their clothing telling of their varied social status. LeiRain recognized one man from the altercation on the docks, the incident that had resulted in hundreds of crates of wine being thrown into the harbor. She'd watched this man draw his blade on a dockhand, a blend who was only trying to do his job and protect the merchandise. LeiRain saw that same blade on his hip now, the man's hand resting lazily on the pommel. She surveyed the clearing and saw that all of the men carried one type of blade or another. LeiRain took a deep, slow breath. The clearing smelled like sweat and steel, leather and mead – like men readying for a fight.

The baker whose sun cakes she favored emerged from the house carrying a curved blade in one hand and, curled under the other arm, a stack of books. Belatedly, LeiRain recognized them as the ones she'd had on her nightstand. His arm wrapped around the texts and rested them against his generous middle. The man's paunch seemed to have grown larger since LeiRain had last seen him. She'd never seen him outside of the bakery and noted that he looked much younger without flour coating his dark beard. He wore no apron, and his clothes were similarly free of flour dust, his shirt a crisp white linen that spoke of his wealth and made the smoothly cut strip of Royal blue fabric on his right arm all the more noticeable. The scowl he wore seemed more menacing in the light of the clearing than it ever had inside his bakery where the scent of fresh pastries softened his expression. Always before, his fearsome demeanor had seemed confined to the walls of his business. Watching him loot her home, LeiRain could see that he was more dangerous than she'd ever given him credit for. That scowl could follow her home, take what was hers, destroy what she loved.

Then there was Bren. Her eyes grew wide and LeiRain slapped a hand over her mouth to keep herself from crying out. He stood on the periphery of the activity, his shirt dingy in comparison to the baker's. There was a blue cloth tied to his arm, as well, though it looked like it had been torn from some-thing rather than cut. Its edges were uneven with threads hanging loose, and even its color was less than uniform, but it was still an unmistakable Royal blue. LeiRain's mind was briefly clouded by a memory of those arms wrapped around her. She shook her head, willing the memory away, and took in the rest of him.

His blonde hair hung down to his chin, and he wore the woolen cap that hid the pointed tip of his ears. His face looked pinched, as if he were smelling something unpleasant, and he shifted from foot to foot as he watched the other men swarm the clearing and ransack the house she shared with her mother. On Bren's hip, LeiRain saw the same shortsword he'd carried for years. He picked up the pewter water pitcher that sat outside her mother's workshop and drank from it, water spilling down the front of his shirt as he did so. Despite the cold, she could see sweat breaking out on his forehead. Bren's eyes darted around the edges of the clearing as he put the pitcher down. If she stayed still, she told herself, he might not notice her, but she had already made the mistake of trying to shrink back further into the trees. The motion caught his attention.

LeiRain stood frozen for several seconds as she stared into his eyes. Bren's eyes had gone wide in recognition. His tan face had gone white and the pitcher now shook in his hands. When he did not move or speak, did not point her out to the others, she continued to move back into the shadows, more slowly this time. For a few seconds, Bren stared at the space where she'd been standing then forced his gaze to move on. What was he doing here?

When she'd left him last, he'd said that his ship would not return to Harbor for some time, and that they'd been sched-uled to get underway the following morning. Had the ship's departure been delayed? How had he, a blend, come to join the Royals? LeiRain was shivering uncontrollably now, though she no longer felt cold. Her mother had to be there, somewhere, either in her workshop or in the house. LeiRain had to get to her, to see that her mother was alright, but the way Bren had looked when their eyes had locked... He hadn't given LeiRain away, at least not yet, but she couldn't assume that he wouldn't if he was now with the Royals. Maybe Alarra was gone, out on errands. Maybe she was off looking for her wayward daughter. But LeiRain knew that was unlikely, even before she heard her mother's scream.

She jolted at the sound, nearly losing her balance and tumbling from the brush. She caught herself at the last second, digging her nails into the dry bark of a nearby tree. LeiRain fought against the lightheadedness that threatened to overtake her. She'd never heard her mother scream before, not like that, and yet she knew that it was Alarra. Fingernails pulled away from skin and sharp pieces of bark scratched her palms as she fought to support her weight. She took a quiet, steadying breath once she had righted herself, not bothering to glance at the fingertips that were now bruising, blood pooling in the nail beds.

Her stomach turned when her mother called out, again, but she was braced for it this time. LeiRain felt one of her fingernails begin to pull away from the skin as she clutched the tree. Four men staggered out of Alarra's workspace. They were bent over, hauling something between them. It was difficult to be sure since their faces weren't visible, but they didn't resemble anyone LeiRain had ever seen in the village. The man who led them out walked backwards, bent over slightly, his thick body blocking her view of what the men were carrying. His skin was dark and the sunlight glinted off of his bald, sweating head. Even bent over, he was quite tall, dwarfing most of the men in the clearing. His clothes were neither as rich as the baker's nor as rough as Bren's, but the expensive-looking hilt of a shortsword hung from the scabbard at his waist.

The men who followed him out of the workshop were less impressive in stature, their arms corded with muscles that flexed as they strained against... Against her mother. That was her mother they were carrying, kicking furiously at the two men in front who held her legs. Her skirt was hiked up immodestly to her thighs, either a sign of the men's careless-ness or their lascivious intent. When her mother screamed again, LeiRain knew that it was not a scream of fear but one of fury, her battle cry as she fought against their hold. A life at the forge had made her mother strong and though she feared what they would do with her, LeiRain couldn't help but feel some satisfaction that it took four men to restrain Alarra – and even that was barely enough.

One of the men stumbled backward as her mother managed to smash her knee into his chin. The man, whose dark hair stood on end as if he had a habit of running his hands through it, released Alarra's leg. He clasped his hands over his mouth. Blood now ran down his neck. He pulled his hands away briefly and, spraying a deep crimson on the grass, spat something out. The dark-haired man tried to say some-thing but his words sounded garbled and he cried out in pain. LeiRain looked at the bloody lump he'd spat on the ground. It was small and plump. LeiRain stifled a gag when she realized what it was. Her mother had caused the man to bite off the tip of his tongue. As if she could sense LeiRain's thoughts, Alarra bucked and kicked out, again, more forcefully this time now that she had a leg free. Someone yelled at the bleeding man from inside the work space. Reluctantly, he released his hands from his mouth and grabbed at Alarra's free leg. The look of agony on his face was unmistakable, even as he wrapped both arms firmly around her mother's thigh. The motion pushed Alarra's skirts up even further. Some of the dark-haired man's blood dribbled onto her mother's thigh.

It was difficult to get a good look at her mother as she struggled against her captors, but LeiRain could see that Alarra's auburn hair had come almost entirely loose from its braid. It was streaked with more silver than LeiRain remembered, though perhaps it was just the light. Her mother's blouse was torn so that her left breast was on clear display to everyone in the clearing. Her head fell back and she sagged slightly in the violent grip of these men, her chest moving up and down rapidly. LeiRain did not think the fight had gone out of her mother yet, but Alarra did seem to be tiring, slowing as she fought to catch her breath. She could see the faces of the men holding her mother's arms now. They watched her with wariness. A bite mark was visible on the side of one man's chin and another man's lip was swollen and bleeding. The men finally managed to drag her mother out of her workshop and into the center of the clearing. With the bright light, LeiRain could see her mother's face more clearly. It was a puffy mess of cuts and bruises. One eye was swollen shut and there was blood on her mouth. Whether it was Alarra's blood or that of the man wearing her teeth marks, LeiRain could not tell. Her mother's nose looked a bit crooked as well, possibly broken. It was a wonder that Alarra could continue to breathe at all, let alone fight, in this condition.

A fifth man walked out behind them, apart from the fray, his shoulders tall and stride arrogant. Ethan. The man who had been here days before, provoking her mother to curse. The last time LeiRain had seen him, his face had been red with anger. Now, he was flushed with power. His blonde hair had been cropped short and he was handsomely dressed in a pair of well-shined black boots, black pants, and an olive green tunic. A matching traveling cloak hung over his right shoulder. His clean-shaven jaw clenched and unclenched, making the muscles in his cheek twitch. There was a long sword at his waist, its intricately carved hilt reflecting back the sunlight as he stepped forward to stand over her mother.

17

H old her still,' he commanded, as if the four men were intentionally failing to maintain control of her mother. 'Just,' he waved a hand at them, 'put her feet down and hold her still.'

They did as they were told. Alarra attempted to take advantage of the situation, struggling to push herself free of their grasps as soon as her feet made contact with the ground. The men were expecting it, though, and the two holding her arms had braced themselves. The men who had been holding her legs moved to grab her shoulders before her feet had even made contact with the brittle grass. Alarra now stood upright, her hands pulled tightly behind her back. There was an auburn halo around her mother's head where the sun bounced off her tousled hair. She should have been terrified, but LeiRain thought the look on her mother's face spoke more of anger than fear. Alarra's green eyes flicked from one face to another as she took in the scene before her.

'Come, young man,' Ethan said to Bren, gesturing for him to approach. Bren had managed to inch his way closer to the woods since he and LeiRain had locked eyes, and he responded to the command reluctantly. Ethan noted his hesitation, misreading it as nervousness. 'Come, just to observe. I want you to learn how a man makes his way in this world.' He looked around at the others. 'Make room for him,' he said. The men dispersed slightly so that there was a clear path from Bren to Ethan ... and her mother.

Bren swallowed and cleared his throat. He shifted his weight back and forth between his feet for a few seconds before finally stepping forward. He cast a glance over his shoulder. LeiRain stopped breathing momentarily, as she realized that he was looking for her. *Look away*, she thought, *you'll have them all notice me!* Finally, Bren did look away from the trees. He put his head down, clenched his hands into fists at his sides and walked forward to stand next to Ethan.

'That's my boy,' Ethan said, clapping him on the shoulder. 'Royals make it a point to nurture our younger members.' He directed this last comment toward the crowd of men, receiving a few grunts of approval as heads nodded in agreement.

Ethan released Bren's shoulder and took a few steps closer to Alarra's side. He reached a hand toward her face, running his fingers gently over the bruises and lacerations on her cheek. Alarra stared straight ahead, unflinching.

'Alarra,' Ethan's voice was so soft that LeiRain could barely hear it. He leaned into her mother, brushing a section of hair back over her shoulder where her blouse had been torn and bare skin was visible. 'Alarra,' he said once more as he bent forward and pressed his mouth against her throat. Her mother did not acknowledge this either, but the veins in her neck began to stand out and LeiRain knew from experience that this was a mark of her rage. As Alarra stared straight ahead, LeiRain saw fire in her eyes. Ethan brought his face away from her exposed skin and caressed her once more with his fingers, letting his hand slide over her neck to cup the back of her head. He looked for a moment like he might kiss her on the mouth.

Instead, he wound his fingers through her hair and *yanked* her head backwards with great force. This time, her mother couldn't help but cry out, probably as much from shock as from pain. Ethan maintained his grip on her hair and, with his other hand, unsheathed a knife. He cocked his head to one side and looked her mother over before taking the knife and running it up what remained of her blouse. There was a ripping noise as the knife sliced through the fabric. Ethan grabbed at the linen with the hand that held his blade, pulling it free until both of her breasts were bare. A line of red appeared where the top of the blade had grazed her, running vertically in between her mother's breasts.

'Pretty Alarra,' Ethan said, drinking in her bare skin. LeiRain dared not look away from her mother but even with her eyes locked on Alarra, she could sense that Bren stood nearby. She could see him out of the corner of her eye, shaking. Ethan brought the knife back up, running its flat side over the dark pink of her mother's nipple until it hardened at the touch. He then slid it up slowly, turning the blade until its point rested against her neck, just below her jaw. Alarra became entirely still. The slightest of movements could be the death of her.

LeiRain clenched her jaw to stop her teeth from chattering. Adrenaline sung through her veins as she stood there, frozen to the spot. She saw a tiny drop of blood swell at the knife's tip and watched it move slowly down her mother's neck. The blood made an uneven line down her mother's throat and over her half-bare chest, its course diverted by the tiny creases in her mother's skin. LeiRain could suddenly see these creases from where she stood, could see the pores in her mother's bruised and soot-stained face, and the tiny blonde hairs on her mother's arms, even though such details should be imperceptible to her at this distance. Her body hummed with an energy that seemed to enhance all of her senses, but still she stood in the shadows. She could not think what to do, could not force her feet to move. There were so many of them and she had only barely survived her encounter with the sheel, a single opponent. Could she wield her water magic to her advantage here on land? Her mouth was dry, and her thoughts rushed by so quickly she couldn't grab hold of a single one.

'Where is it?' LeiRain nearly jumped out of her skin when Ethan spoke. She moved one hand to the hilt of her sword. She could feel her hands, her whole body, shaking. Alarra said nothing but swallowed, a motion that caused the knife tip to briefly press into her flesh again. Another rivulet of blood began its slow and indirect journey down her body. Her mother's face was beginning to look strained, the fire in her eyes now replaced with a look of exhaustion.

Ethan repeated the question. 'Where is that daughter of yours?'

'I don't know where *she* is.' Her mother replied, with a note of finality. Ethan's eyes grew narrow.

'I don't believe you.' A wheezing sound emanated from Alarra. *She can't breathe like that,* LeiRain thought. *He's pulled her head back too far.* It took her a moment to realize that Alarra wasn't gasping for air, she was laughing. The sound was made husky and strange by the strain on her windpipe.

'She left. She's gone. She's been gone for a long time,' she laughed again. It was a cold sound, hiding nothing of her derision for the man who now held her hostage. The sound made the small hairs on LeiRain's arms rise. Her mother was goading him... Didn't she realize what that would do to a man with such fragile pride? LeiRain recalled how Ethan had looked the day he'd come tumbling out of her mother's work-shop, face twisted in anger at his own embarrassment.

No, no, no. LeiRain's stomach threatened to empty itself. The world in front of her seemed to wobble slightly, just as it had when she'd drunk too much elf wine. But there was no pleasant buzz to accompany this dizziness, no water to slow her stumbling. She dug her nails even further into the bark of the tree and squeezed her eyes shut. She could feel the skin on her fingertips tearing as she held onto the bark like a lifeline. Her mind whirred as she tried to reason her way through this situation. LeiRain opened her eyes, scanned the clearing and still saw nothing she could do to help her mother. Not without bringing herself into immense danger. Even if she were to reveal herself, her mother was still in Ethan's power. There were so many men… Would Bren help her if she tried to free her mother? No, she couldn't count on that. Even now she saw him shrinking back from Ethan and knew that he was too afraid to be of any use.

Her mother's hoarse laughter stopped abruptly as Ethan tugged on her hair, pulling her neck back further. He shook his head.

'And the work, Larra? I might be able to justify letting you live, if you were willing to apply yourself to our cause. Will you reconsider the work?'

LeiRain thought of the crumpled paper she'd watched her mother throw into the fire, the weapon she refused to create. Alarra's neck was so strained now that her response was only a whisper. Thin wheezing breaths came between each word. Even so, her reply was unmistakable.

'*Go … fuck … yourse—*'

Ethan yanked violently on Alarra's hair, cutting off her words. Her mother's throat was too strained to emit much of a cry but there was a soft gagging sound as her head fell back even further. A violent chill ran up LeiRain's spine as she studied Ethan's face. There had been a subtle smirk on his face before, a haughtiness to his gait. But that had been when he believed himself to be entirely in control of the situation. Her mother had mocked him in front of this gaggle of other men, and even though she told the truth, her tone and lack of deference made it impossible for Ethan to believe her. The lines on his face smoothed out until his expression was almost blank. He scanned the clearing and LeiRain, frozen in place, willed the shadows to swallow her up. But his eyes were on his men, taking in their reaction. He looked back at Alarra, and, for a brief moment, went entirely still except for the exaggerated rise and fall of his chest.

It was only a few seconds, but the pause, Ethan's hesitation, felt like an eternity to LeiRain. Like a space during which she should have found some solution. But her mind still reeled and, though her body hummed with the unspent energy of terror, it seemed unwilling to move. If anything, LeiRain felt her body trying to pull back further, to evade detection, even though it was her mother who was in danger now. She wasn't the only one who seemed to notice Ethan's unnatural stillness; the men shuffled their feet and murmured to one another. The noise they made faded into the background as LeiRain's ears filled with the sound of her own breathing, her frantically beating heart, the rush of blood. A copper-colored leaf fell from the tree overhead and seemed to hang in the air as the moment dragged on. LeiRain shook as she fought a very primal urge to retreat. She watched, helplessly, as a muscle twitched in Ethan's jaw and his knuckles paled. He tightened his grip on the blade.

LeiRain knew what was coming and yet she did nothing. She thought she might collapse, that her heart might explode as it rapped against her ribs uncontrolled. LeiRain was shaking now, shivering almost violently as some primitive survival instinct kept her rooted in place. She distantedly wondered how the men did not hear the sound of her teeth chattering.

'Wait...' Bren pleaded over the noise of the other men, but it was too late.

With one fluid, sweeping motion, Ethan ran the knife across Alarra's throat.

18

L eiRain cried out. She clutched her chest, trying to hold together the piece of her that had just broken. Until this moment, LeiRain hadn't even been sure that she loved her mother. Now, there was no doubt. It had taken a five inch boot knife for her to realize how deeply she cared for Alarra. Her breaths came in short gasps as LeiRain tried to convince herself that her mother would survive this. She wanted to go to her, to comfort her, but still she could not move and instead, LeiRain stood frozen in the brush.

None of the men heard LeiRain's cry as so many in their ranks gasped in surprise at the same time. A few of the men swore loudly, seemingly taken aback by the finality of this act. LeiRain Stared at the coal-smudged skin of her mother's throat. At first, nothing seemed to happen. Maybe LeiRain had been wrong, her eyes had deceived her, and her mother was unharmed. But just as she began to hope, a wet gurgling sound broke through LeiRain's thoughts and Alarra fell to her knees. The two men who had been holding her shoulders released their grip.

Her mother's eyes were wide with an atavistic panic. Alarra's calloused hands came up to her throat where a line of scarlet blood bloomed and then poured. Her mother tried to cover the wound with her hands but to no avail. Within seconds, those hands were covered in blood. Alarra could do nothing to prevent the crimson life force from rushing out of her body. Blood covered her arms as it ran over her wrists and down her elbows, then dripped onto the grass. Her dingy white shirt turned crimson as it became saturated. LeiRain's legs gave out beneath her and she dragged her fingernails through the bark of the tree as she fell to one knee. It hurt. Watching her mother die was somehow a physical pain. And there was nothing she could do. *I'm sorry*, she thought.

LeiRain knew this was her fault. If only she'd shown herself before Ethan had acted – it had been her they wanted, after all. LeiRain tried to quiet her breathing as the clearing became eerily still and quiet. One man scanned the bush where LeiRain hid. He'd looked over at the noise she made when her knee hit the ground. Brittle, fallen leaves had crackled beneath her weight. But LeiRain had no room left to feel the panic that his notice should have provoked. After a few seconds, the man returned his gaze to Alarra, watching her mother die just like the other men were.

Alarra's face became pale, whiter now than her blouse had been, and her shoulders slumped as she fell forward in the grass. The men closest to her took a few steps back. The spatter of blood, left behind when the man had spit out his tongue, was no longer discernible as her mother's own blood spread out to stain the ground. Alarra's fingers loosened their grip and fell away from her throat. Her eyes remained wide, though now they were still and unseeing. The flow of blood slowed. It had come so quickly at first that it had pooled, too much for the ground to absorb all at once. She watched the edges of that pool expand to meet the toe of Bren's boots. He wretched and the acrid smell of stomach bile mixed with the coppery scent of her mother's blood. LeiRain felt her own stomach lurch and swallowed it back when Bren looked in her direction. She had sunk back into the trees far enough that he couldn't possibly see her now, but there was a rawness in his look that made her feel more seen than she had before.

LeiRain was vaguely aware of the tears that blurred her vision as she scrambled to stand up. The dizziness she'd felt before was replaced with a feeling of unrealness, as if she were no longer connected to the world around her but instead an outside observer. The sensation made her feel almost invulnerable; if she were not a part of this world then none in it could harm her. All reason had gone from her at the sight of her mother's slit throat, replaced with an unyielding anger that, combined with the feelings of dissociation, drove her to act. She wanted to cut them all down, starting with Ethan but not stopping until they were all lying in a pool of blood just like the one that surrounded her mother. She felt her lip curl in a snarl. Her body still shook, but with rage now instead of fear. Her fingers, sweaty and trembling, slipped on the hilt of her blade. She again tried to unsheathe her weapon. A growl of frustration escaped her lips. The sound was lost amid the ruckus of the Royals. They filled the clearing with swearing and laughter. *Laughter!*

Her eyes watched the pool of deep red spread out from where Alarra lay. She watched the blood inch forward and then slow its progress. She watched the puddle diminish as it was absorbed into the ground. She still struggled with her sword belt. Her hands were numb, that was the problem. All rationality had fled from her and LeiRain took a deep breath as she prepared to step into the clearing and avenge her mother's death. Just as she managed to grip the scabbard firmly, just as she found the correct angle to pull free her sword, a thick, meaty arm wrapped around her body. A calloused hand covered her mouth before she could even gasp in surprise. LeiRain's arms were pinned to her sides, her sword only half drawn. Stunned, she did not react for several seconds. Once she registered the severity of her situation, LeiRain prepared to fight back. She leaned forward against the attacker's grip, hoping to throw him off balance. LeiRain was yanked off her feet before this could succeed.

B ranches scraped her cheeks as she was pulled backward into the trees. LeiRain kicked and thrashed. There was still a sense of invulnerability, but it was fading. Vaguely, she was aware of how similarly her own struggle mirrored that of her mothers when the men had dragged her from the forge. The physical contact with another being brought LeiRain back into her body. She was no longer the distant observer. The numbness in her hands spread. *Her mother's blood, soaking into the ground*. She kicked backward at her captor. *Alarra's face, pale and still*. LeiRain fought against the arms that held her, throwing her body weight from side to side. *Alarra's eyes, still open. Someone needed to shut her eyes.* She had to get to her mother.

M aybe there was a flicker of life left in Alarra. She didn't want her mother to die so alone. She'd been so awful the last time they spoke and now... *I didn't even leave her a note.* She had to get to Alarra. *Why didn't I stop him? Why didn't I do anything?* This couldn't be it! She had not just watched her mother die. There had to be more – there had to be something she could do. She had to at least hold her mother's hand. She needed to close her eyes. She had to do this before the Royals could drag her away.

L eiRain worked her mouth open just enough to bite at the hand that covered it, but the fingers were thick and rough and clasped her jaw too firmly for her to find much purchase. She jerked her head backward, knocking off her assailant's helmet. Encouraged by this, she kicked backward, hoping to hit a kneecap or shin. At first, she met only air. She kicked again. And again. Finally, her heel made contact with something hard. There was a crushing noise followed by a sudden intake of breath. With her back held tight to the attacker's chest, LeiRain felt the rumble of a growl as the man swallowed his scream.

'Gods damn that hurt. Stop your flailing, Demi!'

It was a voice she recognized, gruff and guttural, with the accent of one who'd been raised in the mountains. It was a voice she'd always thought of as friendly. Now, as she struggled to reach her mother's side, it was tinged with betrayal.

She could feel Ron's breath on her cheek, hot and smelling of beer and meat. She kicked backward again but met only air, Ron having adjusted his stance to avoid further damage to his knee caps. She planted her feet on the ground and tried to lean forward, jerking from side to side in an effort to loosen his grip. He was strong. Very strong. She moved little within the circle of his arms. The confinement brought on a new wave of panic and LeiRain struggled to breathe. The edges of her vision began to turn black as her breaths became shallow.

'You're going to get yourself killed, Demi.' Ron loosened his hold slightly and LeiRain sucked in mouthfuls of air. The dark edges that ringed her vision began to recede and she shuddered with relief.

'Demi...' There was warning in his voice as he loosened his arms further and turned her to face him. He kept his left hand on her bicep but brought his right hand, finger pointed, to his lips to indicate that she should be quiet. 'They will hear you,' he rasped and nodded toward the clearing. His fingers let go of her other arm and he slowly drew back from her, eyebrows raised, his right finger still held to his mouth.

'They have her.' LeiRain's body shook as she leaned forward, her face crumbling and she choked on a sob. 'They have her.'

'Rain, *quiet*!'

She stilled, ignoring the tears that tracked down her face. He'd never spoken to her in that tone of voice before, and had never, not even once, called her by her real name until now. The strangeness of it was enough to bring her back to some semblance of rational thought. She stared up at Ron, hand still on the pommel of her sword. His presence reminded her that there was something she'd meant to ask him about, something she'd realized in Corallis. It seemed so insignificant now, but she couldn't stop the memory from coming to mind. He had always called her Demi until now. She had always assumed that Ron was no more privy to details about her father than she was. When she'd learned that the other sons and daughters of tempest called themselves 'demis,' short for demi-gods, she'd wondered if Ron hadn't known of her heritage all along. Her mother had always been so guarded, so unwilling to talk about LeiRain's father, and so she'd hoped that Ron might tell her the things her mother would not. With a start, it occurred to her that her mother had kept many secrets and there would be no more opportunities to wrest them from her. They were gone, lost, fading into nothingness like the blood that seeped into the soil.

Ron stood before her bare-headed, his face revealed to her

fully for the first time, his helmet having been knocked off in her thrashing. A massive red beard sprang from his chin and his lightly freckled face was pale from being so often hidden away. A scar ran from just below the outside corner of his left eye all the way down to his chin. Its slick purple surface left a strip of face bare where there should have been facial hair. The corner of his eye pulled down with the scar so slightly that it hadn't been noticeable with his helmet on.

She gasped. She knew that scar. *Everyone* who'd ever seen a picture book knew that scar. Ron, this friendly, jovial dwarve that she had known all of her life was ... famous. Ron was the great warrior, Ronland the Red. She had always thought he was just another sell-sword but ... Ronland the Red was known for his great feats, for his determination to defend those who could not defend themselves. He was also rather well known for being dead.

'You're Ronland the Red.' It was a declaration and one he didn't refute, though the only response he offered was to once again signal that she should keep her voice down.

How was it that everyone believed him dead and what had brought him here? And how could Ronland the Red have let this happen to her mother? Surely he could have prevented this.

'They have her, Ron,' she said more quietly. 'You have to get her back.'

He looked at her, brows creased, and shook his head.

'I'm sorry.' His whisper was raspy and thick with grief. Eyes shining, he quietly cleared his throat. 'I'm so sorry. I—' he shuddered as he took in a breath. 'I came too late. It's too late for your mother.'

She stared at him, shaking her head from side to side. She knew it was true but ... *no*. Things couldn't just end like this.

'But,' Ron took a step toward her. Instinctively, she

recoiled. Hurt flashed briefly over his face, but it was gone so quickly that LeiRain wondered if she'd imagined it. 'It's not too late for you, Demi.' He held a hand out toward her.

'No.' She started to turn around, preparing to rush to the clearing. She just needed to close her mother's eyes. She could at least do that much. Ron's arms were around her again in an instant. He lifted her feet off the ground and carried her further away from the clearing. Further away from her mother. She tried to twist and kick her way out of his grip, but it was unrelenting. He was careful this time not to hold her as tightly, but she made no progress in her efforts to break free. She heard someone saying *no no no no no* over and over again, not realizing at first that it was her.

'Don't let Larra have died for nothing, Demi.' Ron said, not unkindly. He held her against his chest and whispered his words directly into her ear. 'They came for you. If you go out there, they will get what they came for and her resistance will have been pointless.'

'I just...' She was panting as she caught her breath, 'I just need to close her eyes. *Please.*' She swallowed and hiccuped through her tears. 'You're Ronland the Red.'

'There's too many of them, even for me. And I won't risk you by going back. Your mother wouldn't have wanted that.'

The fight left her then as the hard reality of loss hit her at full force. Ron seemed to sense the change and relaxed his hold on her, but instead of pulling away, she turned to stare at him. Tears were falling so rapidly now that she could barely see what was in front of her, just the bright red blur of Ron's beard. And then she was seeing that red stripe bloom on her mother's neck all over again. Watching her mother clutch helplessly at her throat. Ron was right. She knew he was right. But how could she walk away and live with the knowledge that she had done nothing? Not even so much as closed her mother's eyes or moved her from the crumpled position in which she'd fallen. How was she supposed to just accept the absence of her mother? Despite their troubled relationship, Alarra had been her one constant, her security. Food had been on the table because of her mother, and a roof over their head. No matter how much she'd rebelled against her mother's expectations for her, Alarra had never turned her out, had never left her basic needs unmet. And now her mother would never know of Corallis, of the life that LeiRain hoped to make there.

The smell of wood smoke drew her attention back to the moment, back to her surroundings. She wiped at her eyes until she could see clearly, Ron coming into focus in front of her. She looked at him, beseechingly. They were going to burn her mother's body, set fire to the home LeiRain had shared with her. He set her down gently on a layer of crisp, fallen leaves. She took one of his large hands in hers and squeezed it. *Please,* she thought as she looked into his eyes, *bring her back. Save our home.* He shook his head slowly, as if reading her thoughts. He placed his free hand on her shoulder, whether as a comfort or to prevent her from doing something rash, she did not know.

LeiRain stood there, her body feeling heavy and yet somehow hollow at the same time. Her chest felt as if someone had scooped everything out and sent her away with nothing but skin over a pair of ribs. Her stomach felt so sour that she doubted she would ever be able to eat again. Suddenly, all she wanted to do was to lay down and sleep; the mere thought of continued existence was enough to bring on a wave of exhaustion. The smell of smoke became heavy around them and the crackle of flames more audible. Men laughed and yelled and she hated it, but had become too tired to hate it properly. It became a muddle of sounds that was too much to process. It was all too much and she wanted to curl in on herself and retreat from it all.

'Come,' Ron said, giving her shoulder a light squeeze. 'Best move away while they are noisy and satisfied with themselves.'

She let her hands drop from his and when he turned and began walking, she followed. The leaves crunched loudly beneath her feet as she shuffled clumsily through the woods behind Ron. She remembered some version of herself that would have cared, that might have tried to tread lightly. This LeiRain didn't have the capacity to worry about stealth. She might not have the capacity to care about anything, ever again.

19

LeiRain watched the back of Ron's head as she walked. He held the helmet beneath his right arm and his unruly red hair spilled over his shoulders, catching on branches and collecting bits of brush. After a while, it began to look like the nest of a small animal. Some time within the last year, she had grown slightly taller than Ron. LeiRain walked so closely behind him now that she could see her blurred reflection in his helmet when she looked down. LeiRain was shivering again, her teeth chattering as she trudged on behind him. Some time after the voices of rowdy men had faded into the distance, her mind began to work again. Slowly. Wading through her thoughts was a bit like trudging through thick mud. The kind that sucked on your boots every time you pulled a foot free. She grabbed at the first coherent thought that found its way to the surface.

'Why are you back here so soon?' Ron had been there the day before she'd left and he wasn't supposed to return for a month. What had brought him back early? It occurred to her for the first time that he might have been aiding those men. Unlikely as it might be, given the distaste that he and Ethan had shown for one another, and the fact that the Royals didn't care for dwarves much more than they cared for blends, it wasn't impossible. How else did he come to be there just as her mother was murdered, and why hadn't he stopped them? She might be following him to something worse than her mother's fate, but there was a part of her that felt she deserved no better. After all, she'd stood by and watched her mother die, had done nothing as Alarra was murdered.

Ron's voice was gentle when he replied, as if he thought that the wrong words could break her. But it was too late, she was already broken. His tender voice stung all the places where she was wounded. It was like peeling an orange and having the citrus burn all of the small, invisible cuts on her fingers. She had been slipping in and out of despair into numbness and the sting was almost welcome.

'Don't know what you're talking about.' He gave her a quizzical look over his shoulder. 'I've not been to see your mother for months, not since I came back for this.' He gestured to the ax that hung from his hip. The ax, LeiRain realized, whose shattered pieces her mother had been inspecting only days ago. It was now whole.

'No,' she replied, surprised at how cold her voice sounded. 'No, I just saw you four days ago. Your ax was in pieces.'

Ron's steps faltered at that. He turned to face her, his eyes searching for something as they took in her face. His brow wrinkled in concern.

'Where have you been, Rain?'

'I...' It seemed too much now, to tell him all about Corallis, what had happened, who she had met, so she just said, 'I've been in the water.' Her jaw clenched. 'Why didn't you stop them? You could have stopped them.'

'She was gone before I got there, Rain.' She still wasn't used to him using her real name. It was another way in which he seemed to be trying to hold the pieces of her together. 'I got there just as you did,' he motioned to the sword that still hung at her hip, 'you were going to put yourself in their hands.' There was a catch in his voice at that. He shook his head.

She stood staring at him, the numbness settling over her again. 'Your ax was in pieces a few days ago,' she said, her voice flat.

His eyes narrowed at her again. 'Where've you been Rain? You've been somewhere magical, haven't you? Somewhere that's warded against time.'

Warded, yes, but against time?

'Rain,' Ron went on, 'I last saw you *six months* ago, when I brought this to your mother in pieces.' He gestured to the ax on his hip. 'When I came to pick this back up,' he looked away from her briefly, then met her eyes again, 'you'd been gone for over a month. Alarra... Your mother had no idea where you were, where you'd been.'

'No,' LeiRain shouted with such sudden force that Ron startled. He made a shushing motion with his finger. They were still too near the Royals who'd murdered her mother to start shouting. 'No,' she said again, more softly but with a hard emphasis on the word. 'I've been gone for just three days.'

She'd no sooner spoken these words than she realized that this couldn't be true. The chill in the air, the fallen leaves that she'd been tromping through. She took in the thick woods around her and noted the russet tones throughout the brush that should have been a luscious green around the time of her birthday. The gray sky overhead was clearly visible when there should have been a thick canopy of leaves. They were largely shielded from the wind, but she could still hear it whistling through the branches overhead. It was not the wind of spring or summer, but the cold gusts that always came through Harbor at the end of fall, carrying winter with it.

Riv had said that time worked differently in Corallis, but LeiRain had never imagined... *Six months*? Two months had to have passed in Harbor Village for every day she'd spent in Corallis. Even with their cold relationship, Alarra wasn't impervious to worry and disappearing for six months certainly would have driven her mother to concern. And now she was gone. LeiRain would never be able to apologize, would never be able to thank her for the carefully made birthday gifts. The gifts, she realized with a start, were now the only possessions she had in the world aside from the clothes on her back. They were the only things she had to remind her of her mother, now their home had turned to ash.

She looked back to Ron. When she spoke, her voice was pleading, as if somehow he could fix this.

'It was only three days for *me*.'

Tears began to fall from her eyes as something like regret enveloped her. Her stomach churned and she had the urge to expel the sourness. She leaned over and emptied its contents onto the forest floor. She stood and wiped her mouth with the back of her shaking hand. The tears ran in thick tracks down her cheeks, some spilling onto her neck and some finding their way onto her lips. She bent over and heaved once more but there was nothing left to expel save for a bit of bile and saliva.

Ron took a tentative step toward her, placing a hand on her back. He might have been considering whether or not to embrace her, but he just kept his hand there, his fingers squeezing slightly on her shoulder. Her nose dripped and she wiped it with her sleeve, which was still damp with ocean water. This realization made her cry harder until her chest was racked with such thick sobs that she could barely catch a breath through them. She didn't know how much time passed as they stood there, but Ron remained steadfast at her side until her sobs became more subdued and turned to gentle hiccups. Tears still ran down her face, but they came much more slowly now.

Ron offered her a water skin. She took it from him, squeezing the water into her mouth. She swished it around for a few seconds and spat it out. It did little to rid her mouth of the bitter taste of her own vomit, but it was better than nothing. She rinsed her mouth one more time, then took another few mouthfuls to drink. The tears on her cheeks had evaporated and her eyes were dry. Vaguely, she was aware of all the emotions that she'd just cycled through: the flash of anger she'd directed toward Ron, the regret at leaving her mother without even a thank you for the sword and shield, the guilt she felt for causing Alarra worry, and then a deep sadness as she tried to comprehend the magnitude of her loss. A hollow sensation settled over her, a complete emptiness that made her feel as if she could be blown away by a strong breeze. The hollowness in her chest and stomach were painful, but there was a numbness around the edges that made it all just bearable.

She passed the water back to Ron and he took it from her with one hand while offering her food with the other. She refused, her stomach turning at the thought. He insisted she drink from his water skin once more before they resumed walking. Any suspicion she'd had of Ron had vanished, replaced by the shock of learning that she'd missed six months of life in Harbor. Even the realization that he was Ronland the Red lost its significance. She didn't much care where he was leading her; any place was as good as the next. She had nowhere to go.

Except Corallis.

The thought made her wince. Riv had said that time moved differently there, but had he known the extent of it and withheld that from her? He had been the one to convince her to stay a few days longer. And when she thought of her time in Corallis now, she couldn't avoid the realization that her mother had been left to worry about her welfare for six months, to fend for herself for six months as well. LeiRain had taken over the responsibility of cooking for the two of them as soon as she'd been old enough to light the stove on her own. With LeiRain preparing the meals, Allara could work the forge until she ran out of daylight. And her mother was a terrible cook, anyway, and an even worse baker. It was her mother's terrible loaves of bread, usually slightly burnt and always dry and over-salted, that had motivated LeiRain to assume responsibility for their meals in the first place. Allara must have been eating sandwiches on over-salted bread for the last six months. This sent an ache through the hollow spaces in her stomach and chest. How could she ever return to Corallis when her memories there were now tainted with the knowledge of her mother's suffering?

They walked on, neither of them speaking, their feet falling heavily on the dry leaves. The air around them felt unnaturally still, especially with the sound of wind ripping through the branches overhead. There was the occasional rustle of small animals rooting for sustenance, but mostly LeiRain's ears were filled with the sound of her own breathing and the thumping of her heart. Her heartbeats reverberated inside her in a way they never had before, almost as though her rib cage rattled with each pump of blood. *Because I'm so empty now.* An invisible twig cracked loudly under Ron's foot and her heart picked up pace for a few seconds before returning to its usual rhythm.

They were far enough away from the clearing now and the woods were thick enough that even Ron seemed no longer concerned with maintaining silence. So their uncareful footfalls said everything that they could not; that they were tired, and sad, and so many other things that it was impossible to name them all. LeiRain's steps faltered often as she stared into the distance, seeing only her mistakes over the last few days and not the clumps of dirt, tree roots or divets in the ground that tripped her up. Her pants tore on thick brambles as they forced their way through the brush. There were no footpaths this far into the woods and their progress slowed as they pried their way through. Instinctively, she knew Ron had chosen this path because there was no other foot traffic.

Though they couldn't help breaking branches and tearing bushes as they navigated their way through the woods, she saw that Ron was careful not to cut his way through. When LeiRain looked over her shoulder, back to the direction from which they had come, there was little to indicate the two of them had been there. The smell of the now-distant wood smoke made its way to their noses and LeiRain pictured her home burning. Her mother's body on fire. She felt as if she might be sick again. Bile rose in her throat, stinging as it came up. But she was too tired, her abdomen already sore from her earlier violent heaves. So she did her best to swallow it back down. LeiRain thought of asking Ron for the water skin, but she couldn't seem to produce the words. She just kept moving forward, wrapping her arms around herself as she walked to hold the torn pieces of herself together.

She thought of the box of stones, hidden away beneath her bed. That box and its contents had been her most prized possessions, at least until her mother had gifted her the sword and shield. The collection had grown slowly but steadily over the years as Ron steadfastly retrieved them from every place he visited. Sometimes he returned with several, sometimes only one depending on how long it had been since he last commissioned work from her mother. LeiRain thought of the gold veins that ran through the stone he'd given her just a few days ago. No. Not a few days ago. The stone he'd given her months ago. Six months ago. It sat untouched and unappreciated for six months and now it was surrounded by flames. Would the metal box melt? That treasure had been more than just a rock collection. It had been a box full of possibilities and hope. Every time she opened the box and admired the stones, she was touching a piece of another world, some place she had never seen but might hope to one day. Even if the box withstood the fire and the collection survived, it would be just a pile of unrealized dreams among the ash.

The woods began to grow dim, the brightness of the gray sky overhead fading quickly. It had been morning when she'd left the water, and there was a distant realization that they'd been walking for nearly a full day now. LeiRain had been tripping frequently, not careful of her footfalls at all, but Ron only now started to stumble with regularity.

'We should stop for the night. It's too dark to move carefully through these woods, and you need the rest.' Ron began to kick forest debris out of the way with his foot, making a space for them to bed down. 'The going will be rough,' he said, glancing at her periodically as he continued his work. 'I'm afraid I've passed a few too many ransacked campsites along the roadways the past few weeks. The Royals have little trouble finding an excuse to execute blends and even sole-bloods these days.' Ron's voice caught and he paused to clear his throat. 'We'll stick to the woods. Too much foot traffic along the roads.'

LeiRain's only acknowledgment was to sit down on the piece of ground he'd cleared. Her clothes were dry now, but still offered insufficient protection from the cold, especially as day gave way to night. She knew they wouldn't have a fire, not if they were going out of their way to avoid notice. LeiRain tried not to think about how miserable she would be as she suffered through an unsheltered evening of an oncoming winter. Ron held out a satchel, offering her dinner in the form of salted meats and dried fruit. She shook her head, lips pressed tightly together, refusing. It wasn't long before her fingers grew entirely numb, then her toes. The cold she felt seemed to come from inside of her as much as from the chill fall air. She doubted a fire would have provided her any comfort tonight, even if they had been able to light one.

Part of her wished that she could go back and see what they had done to her mother's home. Had they destroyed the workshop, too? She longed to see it, to feel the heat of the furnace, to run her fingers over the beautifully carved pieces her mother had made. LeiRain traced her fingertips lightly over the curves in the pommel of her sword. Even as she clung to any traces of her mother, another part of her wanted to erase it from memory entirely. Perhaps she could put it away in her mind, in her own little lockbox, just like the one Alarra had made for her rock collection. She would keep it sealed, untouched forever so that her mother was not gone entirely but safely stowed away where thoughts of her could not cause so much pain.

At some point, LeiRain had gone from sitting to lying down. She now rested on a bed of leaves and forest debris, mostly soft but some with brittle edges that scratched at her face. Ron lay down with his back touching hers, the heat that emanated from where their backs touched the only thing that kept her from freezing entirely.

'Demi,' Ron spoke into the dark, 'would you like my cloak?'

He must have felt her shivering. It was a kind gesture, and the guilt and regret she'd been wrestling with all day told her that she did not deserve it. She pretended to be asleep to avoid answering him. She liked that he had called her Demi, again. It was a tiny piece of normalcy in an otherwise entirely abnormal day. He waited several seconds for her response and when he did not get one, Ron sat up and draped the cloak over her anyway. It was warm with his body heat and, despite herself, she liked how it made her feel to be looked after.

Ron laid back down and nestled into the leaves behind her, pulling the edge of the cloak over him as well so that they continued to share a good amount of body heat. She was grateful for the cloak, for the refuge it offered. Her shivering didn't stop, though it became less constant, appearing in fits and starts. It wasn't long before Ron was snoring, the sound accompanied only by the wind in the high up branches and the occasional hoot of an owl hunting for its breakfast.

She could feel the stiffness in her body now, the hardness of the ground. After several nights of sleeping in the water, even her soft mattress might have felt hard in comparison, if it hadn't been set ablaze. She stared into the darkness, her eyes so dry and swollen that there was a small twinge of pain whenever she blinked. As much as she wanted to sleep, longed for the escape of it, she couldn't imagine that she'd be able to find such a reprieve tonight. She was too achy, both in body and heart, and too cold. LeiRain thought that she might never be warm again.

20

Threads of sunlight peeked through the trees and pierced the dark fabric of the cloak that LeiRain had pulled over her head. She blinked, feeling raw, swollen, and stiff. Sleeping on land was less comfortable than she had remembered. After a few seconds, she pieced together that the hard, brittle surface she laid on was not her mattress. The leaves beneath her crinkled as she sat up. Without the shield of fabric over her head, the sunlight seemed excessively bright. Her right hip ached from where she'd been lying atop a thick tree root in her sleep. She wiped at her eyes, trying to remember why they were so tender. Her stomach growled and she felt the jolt of a hunger pang.

Slowly, the fog of sleep rolled back from her as she looked down at her clothes and the cloak that now covered her legs. LeiRain rubbed at the sore spot on her hip and tipped her head from side to side to stretch out the stiffness in her neck. She froze, head tilted to one side, as memories came flooding back. The reality of the last day crashed into her all over again, blotting out the sunlight and stealing the breath from her lungs. She had been thinking of her bed just moments ago, and now she imagined the roof on her childhood home buckling as the walls burned away, her mattress nothing but kindling. Where there had been the pangs of hunger there was now a sharp pain around the edges of her emptiness. The knot in her hip and the stiffness of her neck could not compare to the deep ache in her chest. She shut her eyes, squeezing them tight against the memories.

'Morning,' Ron said, and her eyes shot back open. He was holding out a piece of salted meat. LeiRain stared at the offering, feeling queasy at the thought of eating. She looked up at him and shook her head to indicate she did not want it, but he only waved it in front of her again, not taking no for an answer. She took it but did not bring it to her mouth. He watched as she worried the strip of meat between her fingers, the fat leaving a greasy sheen on her fingertips. 'You need to eat,' he said with his own mouth full. Chewing, he walked away to relieve himself behind a thick copse of trees.

LeiRain looked at the jerky. A part of her wanted to lie back down, close her eyes and never open them again. But there was also a distant part of her that agreed with Ron, that told her that she needed to eat something. She stared blankly ahead as she tried to decide which voice she should heed. She heard the rustle of leaves as Ron returned and could feel him looking at her, probably at the uneaten bit of meat in her hands. She turned slightly to face him, watching him drink from the waterskin. He eyed her with a cautious expression, thinking carefully before he spoke.

'I know ... how hard it is to keep on living right now, but you need to eat.'

She turned away from him again, and stared into the thick trees. How could he possibly know how hard it was? What... Who had he lost? The telltale scar on his cheek, the one he usually kept hidden under his helmet, was vivid in the morning sun, making it impossible for LeiRain to ignore his true identity. He would certainly understand loss. Nobody, at least in the stories that she had heard, had seen Ronland the Red since his family, his entire clan, had been slain some thirty years ago. The telling of the story varied, but all of them seemed to agree that his clan had been sought out by the vengeful lover of a slave trader that Ronland had killed. Few creatures had power enough to take out an entire clan of dwarves, but the stories all said that the attacker had been verdaant, a forest deity equal in strength to tempest. Equal in power to her father. If Ronland had not died along with his clan, then he had indeed suffered their loss?

'What happened to you, then?' she asked. Her voice sounded distant and cold, as if it belonged to someone else. Wind suddenly cut through the thick woods, sending a shower of red and gold leaves falling around them. LeiRain felt the cold air sweep through the neck of her blouse. Her skin dimpled with the chill but she did not bother to wrap the cloak around her more tightly. As the fallen leaves settled, LeiRain wondered if she had been too vague. But she could tell by the way Ron's eyes softened that he had gathered her meaning. Only a few days ago, she would have thought it too impolite to ask and she would have avoided such upsetting questions out of common decency. Now, the void inside her called to like, and she couldn't help but think his grief would make her feel a bit less alone.

He held her gaze and she saw his eyes narrow as he swallowed. His hesitance made her wonder if she'd gone too far. *Don't leave me alone in this*, it said. *I will be lost here forever.*

'Eat,' he nodded at the strip of meat still in her hands. 'And I will tell you. And then we have to keep moving.'

It seemed a fair enough trade, especially since she knew deep down that her body required sustenance. Without looking at the strip in her fingers, she brought it to her mouth and bit down. LeiRain caught him looking over his shoulder into the woods. *It isn't safe here.* She could read it in his posture, the way his eyes never stopped scanning. When she began to chew, Ron nodded in approval and sat down on the bed of leaves where he'd slept. He would give her this, and then he would expect her to press on.

'Thirty-two years ago, I killed a very powerful blend.' Ron's voice was steady and she felt the deep rumble of it in her own chest. 'He was a slave-dealer and the worst kind; young males and females, most hadn't even reached their majority yet.' LeiRain's face tingled as the blood drained from it. Her mother had always told her to be careful around the harbor, especially when she'd been younger. There had been a dark undertone to her mother's warning, something in her mother's voice when she said this that made LeiRain believe she really did need to be careful, even when she challenged nearly everything else Alarra told her to do. Eventually, she'd seen them for herself. Little boys and girls, younglings, being passed between adults on the docks. A handshake with a palm full of gold and then the child shuffling off with one a cloaked figure. Sometimes they cried, but usually they just stared blankly into the crowd or at their own shoes. Ron pursed his lips and looked away from her as he continued.

'His name was Galad and he possessed a unique ability. He could shape the wills of others, direct their minds. It made his work as a slave-dealer, a sex-trafficker, that much easier for him. Once he had a grip on their minds, the young ones were his.' Ron paused, scratching his nose. He sniffed and his mouth twitched. For a moment, LeiRain thought that he would refuse to tell the rest of the story. Then he cleared his throat and went on. 'There were families looking for their children. I had hoped to break them free, reunite them with their parents, all without bloodshed. I hadn't planned to kill him, but I hadn't realized the hold he had on those he'd taken – I would have had to drag each child away kicking and screaming. As much as a man like that doesn't deserve to live mercy, I was reluctant to take a life.' Ron ran a hand over his face and inhaled deeply.

'Why couldn't you hand him over to the King's Men?' LeiRain was not squeamish about the idea of such a man dying, but she *was* genuinely curious. The Continent was loosely ruled by a human king. He lived very far inland, and his rule did not always reach the coast, but she'd heard of law breakers being taken to him, to his guard. The King's Men were supposed to be the enforcers of law, at least as far as they could reach, which hadn't included Harbor. And they were responsible for keeping law breakers as prisoners until they could be judged by the king.

Ron swallowed. 'Well,' he tugged on his beard and ran his hand over his face. 'Demi, there isn't actually a law forbidding this type of trade.'

She blinked. Her brow crinkled. She was no expert on law but she knew men could be taken in for the crime of thieving. That seemed a much lesser wrong than swiping stray children to sell for pleasure. LeiRain suddenly felt very ignorant in her understanding of Continent law. The king's laws were only loosely enforced along the coast, so she supposed it wasn't her fault if she was ignorant on the topic, but it was difficult to imagine that such a thing was allowable.

'Those slaves, those *children*, there were so many of them when I got there. Rooms and rooms full of abused, misused and neglected younglings.' His voice cracked and he paused to clear his throat. 'Blends, humans, elves, dwarves ... Galad's *business* was more extensive than anyone had known or imagined.' He swallowed hard, and took a sip of water before offering her the waterskin. LeiRain took it from him as the story continued.

'I couldn't only take the few whose parents were known to me and leave the rest. I couldn't leave any of them there. No one deserves to live that way, but especially not children.' His eyes were distant now and his eyebrows knitted together. 'But I could not remove that many younglings without their coop-eration and as long as Galad held their minds, they would not cooperate. So...' His voice grew quieter, 'I took out his guards easily. He was so confident in his own power that he had almost no security.' Ron paused and spat onto the ground. 'I killed that sorry sack of dragon shit in his sleep.'

Ron looked at her now, his head tilted to one side, waiting to see how she would respond. LeiRain realized that she should probably be reacting to his story, looking horrified, impressed ... something ... but all she felt was a hollowness.

'It sounds like,' she said, trying to piece together a response, 'like you gave him the only justice available.' He nodded and she realized then that he'd been worried she might disapprove. 'Was it hard? He sounds ... powerful.'

'It was actually surprisingly easy.' A rasping laugh, edged with bitterness, escaped from him. 'The bastard was asleep and reeking of alcohol, easy to kill where he lay. It almost felt dishonorable, though I'd have taken dishonor over leaving those younglings under his power. As soon as he was dead, they were free of his control. Most of them came easily, though a few were so fearful of everything that I had to throw them over my shoulder and carry them out. I hated doing it – I could see the fear in their eyes as I gathered them up, but at least I could take them to safety.' He frowned and looked down. 'Those kind of *conditions*... They leave a scar on the mind.' He shook his head and his shoulders sagged.

'So, I returned as many of them as I could to their parents

and found suitable homes for the rest. I worked as quickly as I could, but it took months to place them all properly. And it wasn't easy, either, dragging a bunch of scared and disoriented children all over The Continent.' He looked up at her. Ron's hair had a coppery tint to it in the morning light and it shimmered when his head moved. There were dark circles under his eyes; it seemed that neither of them had slept well. 'You've read the stories? About me?' She nodded. 'Then you have some idea of what happened while I was out searching for the parents of these lost children. I had no idea—' His voice cracked and he took a second to collect himself. 'I had no idea that Galad had been involved with such a powerful lover, a verdaant. I didn't know,' he shook his head, his eyes glazed over with memory, 'she'd begun hunting down my own family in retribution.' He was silent for a long moment. LeiRain shifted where she sat and the rustle of leaves seemed to bring him back to her.

'Jade. That was her name. My people,' again his voice cracked but he didn't pause this time. 'They are fierce and strong, but they could hardly be expected to withstand such power. Most of them died before I even knew that they were threatened. The rest ... uprooted everything, found prosperity in a new home, as best they could with so many of their loved ones, my loved ones, dead.'

LeiRain saw the way his eyes clouded over and recognized it as not just sadness, but guilt. Though she knew it was wrong, part of her reveled in seeing it there, in knowing that he suffered as she did. 'I became less conspicuous,' he went on, 'took to wearing this thing all of the time.' He held up his helmet. It was a simple helmet, with none of the flourish she was used to seeing in her mother's metalwork. Smooth, save for a raised ridge that ran from the nose piece to the very back. He looked at it, watching his own reflection in the well-polished metal. 'Took jobs anonymously. Rarely visited them, though I missed my family dearly. It worked. For many years, it was enough to keep them safe. It helped, too, that there were rumors circulating that I was dead, that the entire clan was dead.' He let out an amused grunt. 'But Jade knew they were false. She knew that some had gotten away. And she found them again. Twelve years ago, she found them while I was away protecting others, fighting for others.' A few thin tears fell from Ron's eyes, tracking down his cheeks until they disappeared into the whiskers of his beard. 'She killed my entire clan. Everyone that she could find. I failed them, again.'

LeiRain wrapped her arms tightly around her torso, hugging herself. She wondered how he could laugh and eat and drink the way she had always known him to.

'My sister's husband sacrificed himself to save his family, to save her and his unborn child. He could have gotten away, but he wanted to be sure, to know for certain that they would disappear unnoticed. She is all I have left, along with my nephew, who escaped in her womb.' He locked eyes with her and the swirl of emotions she'd been trying to sort through slipped out of her awareness and back into the dark.

'We're going to them now.'

The feeling of solidarity vanished and LeiRain was alone in her suffering, again. There was a wall between them, one built of loneliness and remorse. Her mother was all she'd known in the world, the only family she'd ever had, aside from a brief and terrifying encounter with her father when she was eleven. Unlike her, Ron still had someone left.

'Where?' she asked, her voice cold and sharp. LeiRain looked at the cloak that still covered her legs, the rest of it balled in her lap. Ron's cloak. Even though she was still very cold, she pulled it from her lap.

'We'll stay with my sister in the mountains for now,' he

said. His voice was softer, more careful. He sensed the change in her and when she looked at his face, his brow was wrinkled in confusion. He held out a hand to help LeiRain stand up. 'We'd best get on. Don't want to spend another night in these woods if we don't have to, so go take care of your business and we'll be on our way.'

She drew back from the hand he offered, shifting her weight to lift herself from the ground without aid. The cloak was now balled up in her right hand and she threw it at him as she walked by to relieve herself in the woods. Where was the sadness that had been in his voice a few moments ago? Did Jade, that vengeful verdaant, still look for him? She weaved her way through the brush, noticing the shadows cast by trees as the sun continued to rise. There were rustling sounds, chirps and scratches that she hadn't noticed before and she couldn't help but wonder if she was being watched. She had only seen drawings of verdaant, but she tried to imagine what the tall, slim, green-skinned creature might look like in person. She recalled the imposing figure of her father, imagined someone like that finding them in the forest, and shuddered.

They set out with tired legs and hunched shoulders. Ron continued encouraging her to eat, handing her pieces of dried meat or fruit at regular intervals as they walked. She held a strip of dried fruit in her left hand now and thought of the longing fruit she had enjoyed in Corallis. She imagined her mother's worry when she didn't return in a day, then a week ... then months. Thoughts of Alarra, distracted at her forge, were now interspersed with what had once been only pleasant memories of the water elves' sanctuary. She saw Riv laughing with her as he held an empty wine goblet, then her mind flashed to her mother pulling burned, barely-risen bread from the oven before sitting to eat her dinner alone. She recalled the way Riv had encouraged her as she learned to use her magic, and then saw the pool of blood spreading out from her mother's crumpled body. The way her mind snapped back and forth between these two realities was disorienting and the feelings she associated with each began to bleed together so that she could no longer experience her guilt without a sense of yearning for Corallis, nor recall her contentment in Corallis without the sting of shame she felt at abandoning her mother.

For the first time since Ron had dragged her away from her burning home, it occurred to LeiRain that she could have simply gone back to Corallis. Her mother had been the only thing tying her to the village, the only reason she had come back. She had only returned to assuage Alarra's worry, to say thank you for the beautifully made sword and shield, and to say goodbye.

Where is it? Ethan's words echoed in her mind. If LeiRain had been home, would they have taken her instead and spared Alarra? How much harassment had Alarra endured from the Royals before they finally came to take her life?

As they walked, Ron filled the silence with news. He told LeiRain what had occurred in her absence: how the Royals had become bolder and more prominent throughout the Continent. They had recruited more members from Harbor Village, more humans, happy to blame their problems on anyone who was different from them. Sea traffic through the village had decreased with rumors of the violence on the coast spreading. Throwing crates of wine seemed tame compared to the way they now harassed any blend who tried to set up a cart of wares in Harbor. In other villages, too, Ron told her. The Royals no longer seemed to have any qualms with physical intimidation, sometimes beating a blend to an inch of their life as a warning to others. They then blamed the loss of business – caused by their own violence – on blends and other sole bloods, anyone so long as they were not human.

Why did my mother stay? She knew the answer, knew that it was because Alarra had waited for her to return.

LeiRain's throat became tied and pressure built in her chest as she tried not to wail in renewed grief. She managed to stifle a whimper but couldn't entirely fight back the tears. She swiped them away with the back of her hand. Ron sensed the change in her pace and the heaviness of her mood. He looked back over his shoulder but she avoided meeting his gaze. His steps slowed to be in pace with hers. Seeing this quiet thoughtfulness brought an upsurge of warmth, something that filled just a small piece of the emptiness in her chest. Even though she was not prepared to have someone witness her grief, Ron seemed determined not to deprive her of it. LeiRain quit fighting her tears and let them flow freely as she followed her friend deeper into the woods.

21

————

I t was late afternoon when they finally reached the base of the mountain. Ron announced that there were still hours of trekking ahead of them and passed her the waterskin. The terrain, he said, would become much more challenging as they finished the climb. LeiRain's head throbbed and the rest of her body ached as she experienced the effects of taking too little food and water over the last few days. On top of that, she had very little. The hard ground was not a welcoming bed and her thoughts always got the better of her at night.

LeiRain struggled to keep pace with Ron as he led her on a diagonal path up a seemingly endless slope. There was no clear trail and she tried to step into his footprints to avoid any loose rocks or crumbling patches of dirt, but his stride was wider than she could manage so LeiRain often stumbled anyway. The technicality of the climb was a welcome distraction, as was the sting of raw skin on her knees and palms from her many trips and falls.

As they trudged on, the air became thin, cool and dry. The skin on LeiRain's lips pulled tight and threatened to split if she opened her mouth too wide. She longed for her mother's burn salve – a necessity for a smith – and imagined the relief it would provide if she could apply it to her cracking lips. Ron paused frequently, making sure she caught up with him and drank enough water. She'd been timid in drinking from the waterskin before, but now she took long, deep gulps whenever she had the chance.

Ron stayed near LeiRain all day, looking over his shoulder often to monitor her progress, but just as the sun was beginning to set the dwarve went on ahead of her and disappeared over the top of a rock scramble. LeiRain had become progressively clumsier as the day went on, and the oncoming dusk combined with her fatigue to make the rest of the climb particularly challenging. The heels of her hands were scraped and bleeding as were her knees. She heard Ron call her name from somewhere above and pushed herself to keep climbing.

'I'm coming,' she answered, just before she slipped and slammed her knee into the ground again. But LeiRain didn't let the scrapes and bruises slow her. On the contrary, the pain was the thing that kept her upright and reminded her that she was still alive, even if her mother was not. Finally, she pulled herself over the top of the precipice and rested her hands on her raw knees while she caught breath.

She stared at her feet for a few minutes, panting, until Ron passed her the water skin. When she stood to drink from it, a gasp escaped her lips. Before them, the terrain had opened up and flattened out. They stood on the edge of a lush green plateau with thick grass beneath their feet. A patch of tilled soil was visible to her left, and LeiRain could just make out the rows of green sprouts dotting the dark earth. Two goats meandered in front of a small house, the warm, yellow glow from one of its windows illuminating the grass on which they grazed. Darkness obscured any other details of the structure as the sunlight continued to fade. Another stream of golden light came from the house, spreading over the ground in front of them as a door opened. A small figure stood in the doorway, silhouetted, a bucket hanging from one hand.

'Oy,' Ron called, suddenly, making LeiRain jump.

'Uncle Ron!' The door swung halfway closed him as the young dwarve dropped his bucket and sprinted toward Ron and LeiRain. The youngling stopped a few feet from them, his face still mostly obscured by the dark as light shone from the doorway behind him. LeiRain could make out a wide smile on the boy's face and the youngling's bright red hair was apparent even in the dim lighting.

LeiRain saw the boy's smile falter slightly when he noticed her standing just behind his uncle, but he didn't back away. He examined her, the tilt of his head and the tension in his body suggesting a combination of interest and wariness. LeiRain stared back at him, trying to make out the details of his face in the dark.

'This,' Ron said, gesturing towards LeiRain, 'is our friend, Rain.' The boy's shoulders relaxed. He stared at her for a few more seconds before dipping his head slightly.

'Nice to meet you, Rain. My name,' he seemed to stand a bit taller as he said this, 'is Rayand.'

Before LeiRain could say anything else, Rayand looked to his uncle and asked, excitedly, 'Did you bring it?'

'Had to leave in a bit of a hurry this time, I'm afraid.'

Even in the dark, the boy's disappointment was evident. His shoulders slumped and his head turned to the side and looked at the ground.

'We'll get you a proper ax, Ray.' Ron said in an apologetic tone. 'Things got a bit complicated this time, but I'll find someone who can make ye' a proper weapon.' He reached up and tousled the boy's hair. LeiRain looked at Ron, her eyes a bit wide with surprise at his statement. An ax? She looked back at the boy. LeiRain guessed that he wasn't more than ten or twelve.

Ray made a sound in the back of his throat that came out like 'ahck,' as he swatted Ron's hand away. The boy combed his fingers through his hair to straighten it.

As she watched this interaction, a violent shiver ran through LeiRain's body. She wrapped her arms around herself but they did little to warm her. The air had gone from cool and crisp to downright cold. LeiRain's clothes, damp with sweat, did nothing to protect her from the weather.

'We'd best go warm ourselves up,' Ron said, casting a sideways glance at LeiRain. 'Your mother's inside?' The boy nodded.

They walked toward the door, which Rayand had left standing open. At first, LeiRain could only make out the rising face of the mountain behind the inviting glow. As they drew closer, she could see a bit more of the building's detail. The structure was made of both wood and stone and irregularly shaped, which made it blend into the landscape almost perfectly. Another figure appeared in the open doorway as they approached.

'Who's that?' the woman called. 'Your wild uncle come home with more tales of misadventure?'

There was a playfulness in her voice, and a warmth, too. The woman stepped back to welcome them in and LeiRain studied her. Ron's sister-in-law was stout, with a round and pretty face. She had thick, light brown hair that was scooped back into a messy bun that sat low on her head. A few strands of white hair were visible, catching the light a bit differently than the brown. The sleeves of her blouse were rolled up above the elbow. Where her arms were visible, they were tan and rippling with muscle, just as Alarra's had been. She looked directly at LeiRain when she smiled, the skin around her dark brown eyes crinkling. LeiRain liked her instantly.

'Welcome,' she said simply. 'I'm Brya. I'm Ron's older and wiser—'

'And better looking,' Ron added.

'Sister,' Brya finished with a wry smile. 'By marriage of course, but sister none-the-less.'

'I'm...' She swallowed. LeiRain's throat was dry and felt suddenly nervous. Still holding the water skin, she brought it to her mouth, buying herself a bit of time as she drank.

'This is Rain,' Ron said for her as she swallowed the last of what was in the skin. 'She will be staying with us indefinitely.'

Brya nodded, seeming to catch the significance of this last word without any further details. LeiRain stood feeling stiff, clutching the empty skin in one hand. She was too tired to be self-conscious about her tattered state and how long it had been since she last bathed. Of course, Ron had not bathed in the last few days either but he'd not been covered in the leavings of salt water as LeiRain had been. She thought perhaps she should offer to shake Brya's hand, but LeiRain's hands were filthy, her palms scraped and bloody and her fingernails black with dirt.

'Come on then, you two.' Brya made a motion with their hands to usher them the rest of the way inside. Even in the doorway, LeiRain had begun to warm. Once inside, she stopped shivering and her posture relaxed. 'There's a basin over there where you can wash up,' Brya said, pointing. 'Ray, add a bit of the water I've just heated to that ewer. Once you're washed,' she said, looking back and forth between Ron and LeiRain, 'I've some fresh bread for you both and I'll warm some milk.'

Ron gestured for LeiRain to have the first go at the basin. She moved carefully through the room, taking in the details as she went. There was a long rectangular table with six matching chairs, the wood stained so dark they looked almost black. A single discarded napkin sat crumpled in front of the only chair that hadn't been pushed in to meet with the table's edge. There was a small stove and a few pots hanging from hooks overhead. She noticed that everything here was a bit lower to the ground than she was used to. LeiRain was slightly above average height for a young human woman, around the same height as Ron – at five and a half feet he was rather tall for a dwarve. She didn't have to duck, but there wasn't much clearance between her head and the pots and pans. She thought she could fit comfortably into the chairs, but anyone taller than her would likely feel a bit cramped. The basin that she'd been directed to had a small stack of drying dishes sitting to one side of it and a small bar of soap. She was careful not to brush against the clean dishes as she washed, not wanting her filthy clothes or dirt-caked hands to sully them.

'S'cuse me!'

LeiRain jumped as Ray brushed up against her and poured hot water into the basin. Steam rolled off the top of the bowl and LeiRain nearly groaned with pleasure as she plunged her hands into it. Warmth seeped into her fingertips and then the rest of her. LeiRain didn't realize just how cold she was until she began to thaw. She rubbed the soap back and forth between her hands, wincing as it ran over the cuts on her palms. It took furious scrubbing to debride her wounds and she gritted her teeth through the discomfort. The water in the basin turned quickly to gray-brown as dried blood and dirt came away from her skin.

'Here,' Ray was back at her side again. He pulled a chain that had been connected to the bottom of the basin and the water began to drain rapidly. 'It drains into our garden,' he said, brightly. 'They call it a sink.' He smiled up at her and added, 'it can pump water in from outside, too. But only cold water, so we have to heat it up for washing.' LeiRain nodded. She'd heard of such things, but no one in Harbor had been wealthy enough to set up indoor water pumps. It was impressive, and very useful, she thought, as he replaced the plug he'd withdrawn in the now empty basin. Ray refilled the sink with hot water.

'Thank you,' LeRain said, but the boy had already darted away. She could hear him chatting excitedly, receiving an occasional grunt of acknowledgment from Ron.

LeiRain finished washing her hands up to the wrist and drained the basin herself this time. She used the remaining water to usher residual bits of dirt down the drain. Ray had placed a thick rag beside the ewer while she'd been washing and LeiRain used this now to dry her hands. Her nose had been filled with the smell of the lavender soap while she'd washed, but now that her hands were no longer lathered in it, she was overwhelmed by the scent of freshly baked bread. A few feet away from her, Brya withdrew two loaves from the oven and placed them on a metal rack to cool.

Ron replaced her at the basin without prompting, another pitcher of hot water in one hand and a fresh rag in the other. Though his hands certainly weren't clean, they were not nearly as soiled as LeiRain's had been. *He* hadn't fallen repeatedly on the climb, nor had he relied as heavily on his arms to navigate through some of the steeper passages. Brya placed a delightfully warm cup in LeiRain's hands as she turned away from the sink, then took her elbow and led her to a set of chairs near the fire.

The home was much roomier and more comfortable than she had expected when she first viewed it from the outside. The carefully crafted furniture was clearly designed with a dwarve build in mind, but as she'd suspected, LeiRain was able to fold herself easily into one of the chairs. It was built for a much broader body, which gave her the room to pull her legs up and rest her chin on her knees as she sipped the warm milk. She winced with her first mouthful, finding it more sour than expected, and recalled the goats she'd seen outside. Used to cow's milk, LeiRain took another sip, this time with adjusted expectations. She would get used to it, eventually.

Rayand came to sit near her, folding his legs together on the floor by her chair. He held two plates in his hands and passed one to her. She set her cup down on the floor and took the offered plate, her mouth beginning to salivate as she looked at the soft, warm bread. There were two thick pieces on the dish and both had been slathered in fast-melting butter and drizzled generously with honey. She took a delicate bite and chewed carefully, minding her manners. But hunger became more demanding once she'd tasted the bread and she soon found herself taking large bites and chewing less before swallowing. The bread was gone in moments but LeiRain was still hungry. She was licking honey from her fingers and looking sadly at the empty plate when Ray popped back up from where he'd been sitting.

'More?' He asked this with a knowing smile and LeiRain felt her own lips curl up slightly at this. She nodded and he snatched both the plate and her now empty cup before heading toward the kitchen. LeiRain brought her fingers to her lips in surprise. Had she just smiled?

Rayand returned a few seconds later with another serving of honey-covered bread and a full cup of warm milk. She hadn't eaten much over the last few days, and though she knew that her body wanted more, LeiRain's stomach quickly began to fill. She ate the fourth piece of bread slowly, chewing carefully, and was barely able to down the last of her milk without feeling like she might explode.

Rayand had vacated his spot on the floor to shadow the adults in the kitchen area. She heard the murmured conversation of Brya and Ron, with periodic interjections from Ray. The words were muffled by the crackling of the fire next to her, but she heard Ron say her name a few times, then her mother's. There was a long pause after he said her mother's name.

LeiRain shifted in her chair, trying to ignore the distant conversation. She felt her eyelids grow heavy as she leaned back into the plush upholstery. Her limbs slowly grew limp, and eventually she succumbed to the coziness and drifted off to sleep.

22

Alarra's screams filled her ears.

LeiRain could barely see through the smoky haze, her mother's figure just visible through the glassless window. Alarra's cries for help rang through her, calling LeiRain to action. She thought of the barrels of rain water they kept near the iron workshop. She could feel the water, touch it with her mind. LeiRain reached for her magic. But when she commanded the water to rise, when she directed it to extinguish the flames, it would not obey. It would only slosh around inside the containers, splashing out over the sides, mocking her. She tried again, and again, until the magic began to withdraw from her. Her mother's screams continued. LeiRain clawed at her ears as she desperately tried, again and again, to compel the water to put out the fire. But every time, the water refused to cooperate.

In desperation, LeiRain gave up on her magic and ran to the barrels. She searched through the smoke for the pitcher they always kept nearby but it was nowhere to be found. She cupped her hands, instead, and ran with palms full of water toward the burning structure. But when she reached the house, her hands were empty. She tried again and again, but always by the time she reached the fire, *the water was gone save for a few droplets that clung to her palms and fingertips. The heat turned those to steam as she neared the blaze. After several failed attempts, she stopped trying and stood dazed, her eyes moving between the water, the fire and the steam rising from her hands. LeiRain watched, helplessly, as the tendrils of steam turned to smoke and she, too, began to burn. There was no one to hear her, no one to help, but still she screamed as flame consumed her.*

LeiRain jolted awake, sweat beading on her forehead. Her breaths came hard and fast and she scanned the unfamiliar space in which she found herself. A low fire popped and sizzled in the nearby hearth. A blanket had been draped over her where she'd fallen asleep in the chair but it was now damp with sweat, as were her clothes. She remembered Brya's warm eyes and Rayand's innocent curiosity, Ron's protectiveness. She was alone, the others must have gone to bed.

I am safe, she told herself and her heartbeat slowed slightly.

LeiRain stood. She was wide awake now, her body charged with energy. As she turned her head, she felt the light tug of damp hair sticking to her neck. She looked around the room, still trying to get her bearings. The blanket that had been thoughtfully laid over her as she slept now pooled at her feet. She stepped over it and moved toward one of the tiny windows in the kitchen. The night sky was visible, though it looked unlike any sky she'd seen before. The stars were brighter here and the sky a more thorough black. Its beauty had an otherworldliness to it that reminded LeiRain of Corallis.

Loss and guilt floated to the surface of her mind, warring for dominance with the intense anxiety that had jarred her awake. She preferred the anxiety. She looked back at the plush chair and the blanket on the floor. Even if she could relax enough to go back to sleep, LeiRain didn't want to risk having another nightmare. She scanned the room, looking for a way to spend her time, looking for a distraction. Her eyes fell on her sword and shield where they lay propped against the wall by the front door.

D espite being underdressed and unused to such weather, she stood facing the night, undeterred. LeiRain kept the shield on her back and held the sword in front of her face. Her eyes were beginning to adjust and she examined the sword's intricate designs in the moonlight. She thought of the hours her mother must have spent making this piece for her, the care she had taken in every detail. A manic determination, bred of fear and anxiety, hummed through her limbs. She was constantly turning away from the wind, but it seemed to change directions and follow her. Gusts hit her full on in the face and, eyes watering in response, she'd have to blink frantically to clear her vision.

She adjusted her grip on the sword, the skin on the back of her hands feeling tight with cold as she did so, and shifted to a fighting stance. She collected all of her misplaced energy, the hyper-alert feeling with which she'd woken from her dream, and channeled it into her muscles. She was risking injury by not warming up, but LeiRain didn't care. She began to move fiercely through a series of sword drills, things she'd picked up over the years from Ron, other sellswords, even books. She knew her form was sloppy, wrong, reckless. But what did it matter? She only wanted the release.

LeiRain began to sweat again, the cold air more welcome as her body's temperature rose. Her arms ached as she lunged and blocked, over and over. LeiRain went faster, harder, as she recalled the way she'd stood frozen. How the blood pooled in the beds of her fingernails as she clung unhelpfully to a tree, while her mother bled out on the grass. With every jab and swipe, she imagined herself barreling out of the woods and taking down one Royal after another until they all lay dead.

Ron emerged from another house built into the mountain, just as the sun crept over the horizon. In the light of dawn, LeiRain saw that there were several such structures built into the face of the mountain. She paused briefly to look up at the dwarve. LeiRain took in his bed-mussed hair and sleep-swollen eyes, eyes that narrowed in concern as they looked back at her. She saw his jaw working as if he were chewing on a question. Not wanting to answer any, LeiRain turned abruptly away and resumed her exercises. She saw Ron approaching out of the corner of her eye and did her best to ignore his presence. He cleared his throat.

'May I show you something?' He asked as he reached for his own blade.

It's not what she'd been expecting. LeiRain had thought he would express his worry or scold her for being out in this cold. Relieved, she nodded and turned to face him straight on.

'When you shift your blade to block like this,' he explained, moving his weapon to hold it diagonally in front of his body, 'don't shift all of your weight to the back foot. Try to spread the weight evenly between both feet.' He demonstrated, standing as she had been with a slight backward lean and then showing her how it should look, 'else you'll be easy to knock off balance.' He modeled this again, exaggerating his movements for her benefit.

'Like this?'

LeiRain swore under her breath as she tried to mirror him. She hadn't realized how much she'd been leaning into her back leg until she tried to shift forward. She tottered slightly to the right with the weight of her sword, throwing her left hand out as a counterbalance just in time to save herself from falling.

'Yes, yes,' Ron's tired eyes lit up with excitement. He nodded his head, 'Everyone's a bit wobbly at first. It just takes practice, but you've got the idea, Demi. Now it's just a matter of repetition.' Ron's smile was broad.

He was referring to her with that pet name, again. It felt normal, a little piece of sameness in her upside-down world.

'And, uh, something else?'

LeiRain nodded, giving him permission to go on.

'This is a single-edged blade. The drills you're doing – those are for double-edged blades. With a weapon like that, you'll want to start with this drill.'

Ron demonstrated with his ax. He slashed up and diagonally in front him before turning his wrist so that the back of the blade met his shoulder, then repeated the move in the opposite direction.

'When you're not striking,' he said as he watched his own blade move through the air, 'you'll want the weapon as close to your body as possible. Makes it harder for someone to disarm you.' He met LeiRain's eyes and winked. She couldn't bring herself to smile, but nodded in acknowledgment.

Ron repeated the movement beside her several more times, slower, then faster again. LeiRain watched and did her best to mimic him. Once she had gotten it right a few times in a row, she demanded that he show her something new. He mumbled under his breath about breakfast, but acquiesced and they spent another hour moving through drills. The sun was fully risen when he tucked the ax back into his belt. LeiRain reluctantly sheathed her own blade and looked around the clearing, seeing it for the first time in full daylight. She turned to follow Ron inside, her limbs shaking slightly as she walked, and cast one last glance at the mountain sky before stepping into Brya's kitchen.

Rayand sat at the table with mussed hair, rubbing the sleep from his eyes and shivering at the wind that whipped through the door as they entered. Brya was cheerily slopping porridge from a pot over the fire into a set of earthen bowls, the smell of cinnamon filling the air as she scooped. Ron took the bowls from her as she filled them, carrying two at a time to the table. He motioned for LeiRain to sit and she obeyed, observing Rayand as he drizzled honey into his porridge. The boy passed her the jar of honey and LeiRain followed suit. The sweet, warm gruel went down easily and her bowl was soon empty.

Just as LeiRain scraped up the last spoonful of porridge, Brya set a large mug of hot, dark liquid in front of her. Its bitter smell, like black tea but more pungent, was a sharp contrast to the honeyed warmth she'd just consumed. She eyed the mug suspiciously. LeiRain took a few tentative sips, mostly to avoid appearing ungrateful, and winced at the acrid taste the drink left on her tongue. LeiRain let steam from the mug float up over her face and felt her eyelids begin to droop as she did so. She took another sip. Despite the bitterness, or perhaps because of it, the drink was bracing. The hot liquid warmed her from the inside out, and each sip seemed to lend her an energy she hadn't had before. Rayand looked at her mug covetously as he sipped from his own milk.

'Can I have some coffee, Mum?' he asked.

'The last thing *you* need is coffee, Rayand. You've already more energy than the rest of us put together.'

The boy quickly shrugged off his disappointment and refilled his bowl with more porridge.

LeiRain helped clear and wipe down the table after breakfast, feeling the coffee hum through her. The bitter taste was a small price to pay for the energy it gave her. She listened to Ron and Brya chatter as she pulled the plug on the sink and watched the dirty water drain. Once the basin was empty, she wiped it out with a rag and then draped the rag over the edge to dry. Behind her, the three dwarves bickered playfully over who would do which chores for the day. LeiRain closed her eyes. Something loosened in her chest just a bit as their laughter filled the kitchen.

'Spar with me,' LeiRain demanded of Ron.

Brya had been gone for a few days now, having traveled to the nearest village for a supply run before heavy snow came. LeiRain's shoulders were tight and her jaw ached from clenching as she worried over the dwarve's safety. The normal business of the day hadn't been enough to keep her distracted and she'd spent the last two nights fretting over Brya's absence rather than sleeping. She needed something to distract her, even if it was only temporary.

'I think I will,' he replied.

LeiRain blinked at him in surprise.

'Uh...' she stammered. Ron had never before agreed to spar with her. She had become so used to his rote response – *you're not ready yet, Demi* – that it took her a moment to find her voice once he'd agreed. 'Um okay,' she answered, finally. LeiRain swallowed, adjusted her footing and looked up at Ron as a grin stretched across her face. She flexed her fingers, anticipating the ring of blade on blade.

The air was biting cold and LeiRain's fingers felt numb on the pommel of her sword, but they quickly warmed with the activity. The only thing that kept the clearing from being perpetually covered in snow was the intensity of the sun at this altitude, which began to feel hot on her skin as she struggled to keep up with Ron. Sparring was not quite what she had expected. The form she'd spent these weeks perfecting was lost in her frantic attempts to parry and any time she saw an opening to strike, the opportunity was gone before she could take it. LeiRain had lusted for this moment, for the feel of metal on metal, but she was quickly realizing that her expectations of the experience diverged significantly from reality. Despite his girth, Ron was fast and light on his feet. Within minutes, she was panting and clutching at her side to rub away a cramp. Ron sheathed his weapon and handed LeiRain a waterskin. He was breathing hard, but not nearly as winded as she was.

'Ready for another go?' Ron asked after a few minutes. The cramping in LeiRain's abdomen had subsided and her breathing had mostly returned to normal. She nodded and reached to draw her weapon, but Rayand's excited shriek cut through the clearing before her hand had touched the pommel of her sword.

LeiRain followed the child's gaze and saw a wobbling lump of cloth, just visible at the edge of the clearing. As she watched, Brya crested the steep incline and came into full view. She was so laden with the goods she carried that only the sun glinting off her brown hair made her recognizable. Swordplay forgotten, the three of them walked toward her to offer their help. Brya swiped a hand dismissively through the air as they approached.

'Ooof,' Brya said, waving them off. 'I've made it this far haven't I? I can carry the lot of it to the front door,' she said, continuing past them.

Brya dropped her pack in front of the house. The size of its load made it too large to fit through the door so the three of them began unpacking. LeiRain paused briefly when the smell of coffee beans rose up from one of the packages she dislodged. She brought it to her face and inhaled deeply, savoring the rich aroma. They had restocked the honey a few weeks ago but began to run out of coffee shortly thereafter. They were also low on flour and the oats they relied on for breakfast. They'd started rationing all of it, with a very intense disagreement breaking out over how to stretch out their use of the coffee. Ron had suggested that they have it more often, but use fewer beans, but Brya had scoffed at him, saying that she'd 'rather have no coffee at all than have a weak brew.' LeiRain agreed with Brya. If you were going to drink weak coffee, it might as well just be tea.

'How were things in the village?' Ron asked.

He sniffed at a fragrant bag of dried fruit as he scanned her face. Brya was bringing them the first news they would have of the world beyond this clearing in almost six weeks. She didn't answer immediately but instead looked at Rayand.

'Ray, go boil some water for tea, would you?'

The boy complied, though he cast an annoyed glance over his shoulder before he closed the door behind him. Brya swiped at the strands of hair that were plastered to her face with sweat. Dust from the journey had settled on her cheeks and the movement left a brown streak across one of them.

'Not good, brother.' She looked at LeiRain warily before continuing. 'The Royals have all but taken the village. Their poison continues to spread.'

23

———

'D ammit,' LeiRain spat out a mouthful of blood and dirt, pushing herself off the cold, hard ground. She had anticipated an attack from straight on but Ron weaved and came at her indirectly. She'd blocked him clumsily and subsequently lost her balance, landing face-first in the morning dew.

'You told me to shift my weight onto the front foot when I block,' she yelled as she sat up on her knees, one hand clutching her sword and the other her shield.

'Ah, yes, that was if the blow was coming from the front. And you were pivoting on the heel of your foot. You've got to pivot—'

'On the ball of my foot! *I know.*'

Ron watched LeiRain brush herself off. His dingy-white tunic clung to him with sweat and he had his sleeves rolled up above his elbows, revealing thick and muscular arms. The dwarve ran a hand over his beard, ringing sweat from it as he did so. The rest of his long hair was pulled back into a tight braid. A few rogue strands of hair sprang free and shimmered in the sunlight. He shifted impatiently from foot to foot as she collected herself. The corners of his mouth upturned slightly in response to her frustration.

She knew he was right, that the mistake was entirely hers, but Ron's smile infuriated her.

'I didn't know you'd shift and come from a different direction.' LeiRain rolled over onto her bottom and crossed her arms. She narrowed her eyes at Ron and tilted her chin up in a defiant gesture, even as dampness soaked into her slacks. He didn't seem to mind, though. If anything, her obvious irritation made his smile grow wider. Ron took a step forward and stood over her, offering his hand out to LeiRain. One side of her lip curled up in a scowl, and she flicked her sword at his hand. The flat side of her blade smacked his palm lightly as she dismissed his offer. Ron shook out his hand and arched an amused eyebrow at her as she continued the ungraceful scramble to a standing position.

LeiRain thought that she would be better able to fend him off by now. Afterall, her body had changed. She'd trained hard all through the winter. Even when snow fell and left thick blankets of white over the clearing, she rose early and trained. Over the months, her body reshaped itself to the weight of sword and shield. Like her mother who had spent so many hours hammering steel, her arms were now knotted with lean muscle. Her legs had grown thicker, more powerful, the fabric of her pants straining at times against her thighs. Her tunics now fit more snugly on her broadened shoulders and hung looser at the waist than they had so many months ago. But while physical strength was essential for sparring, it wasn't sufficient by itself. LeiRain was learning the importance of technique, and how much of it she lacked. Her most recent attempt at an offensive move had resulted in Ron smacking the back of her calves, painfully, with his weapon.

'Aye, well,' he said with a wink, 'your enemy doesn't always give you the courtesy of sharing such information.'

LeiRain closed her eyes, gritted her teeth, and wiped blood from her nose with the sleeve of her sword arm, then swore to herself as she realized she'd just stained the only decent tunic she had left. She was going to have to accept Brya's offer to stitch new clothing for her. LeiRain took in a long, deep breath, releasing the air slowly through pursed lips.

'Again,' she said.

Ron nodded, signaling his readiness. LeiRain lunged. He deflected her strike and she lunged again. He blocked the blow. LeiRain's arms were growing heavy. Her thighs were burning. She felt her elbow dropping, her arms shaking. LeiRain's frustration grew as she fought to keep her form while Ron moved easily around her. She was preparing to lunge again, when Ron acted so swiftly that she could barely track the movement with her eyes, let alone her blade. His weapon hit hers at an angle that made LeiRain's wrist bend back painfully. She dropped her sword. Before she could reflect on how easily he'd disarmed her, Ron swept his leg beneath hers and LeiRain found herself once more laying in the wet grass.

She allowed herself a few moments before lifting her head to look at him. LeiRain still clung to her shield, but only because the guige kept it strapped to her body. Her sword hand was empty save for the grass she was clutching in her fist. LeiRain looked to her right and saw her sword lying several feet away. Seconds. It had taken only seconds to disarm her and bring her to the ground. Rayand giggled from where he sat watching in the doorway. She swallowed another curse, mindful of her audience. Brya must have given up on forcing his studies, the sparring far too entertaining to compete with mathematics.

LeiRain turned to give Rayand a dirty look and saw a flash of movement in the doorway as Brya pulled him behind her, against his protests. Brya's face had gone pale and she stared past LeiRain. She shushed Rayand in a tone that LeiRain had not yet heard her use with her son. Nearby, Ron adjusted his grip on his sword while removing the ax, his preferred weapon, from his belt. LeiRain was halfway to standing when she saw his face, too, had turned ashen. His lips trembled as he looked toward the edge of the clearing.

Registering his fear, LeiRain jerked her head around to follow his gaze—

Her blood ran cold.

A tall, slender figure stood at the very edge of the clearing. The sun was at his back and its light reflected almost blindingly off of his silken, silver hair. She squinted, trying to make out the facial features that were hidden in shadow. His stature, his long and lean muscles, and the pale green skin made him unmistakably *verdaant.*

'A daughter of tempest learning to fight with sword and shield? How interesting,' said a voice that was rich and smooth.

'Who are you?' Ron's voice quivered as he spoke.

LeiRain's heart beat fast and a tight knot formed in her chest. She pulled herself to her feet, keeping her eyes on the verdaant as she did so. She'd never seen Ron afraid before. Was this man a friend of Jade, the verdaant who had single-handedly slain Ron's clan?

'I am Silversgleaming,' replied the forest deity. He did not move any closer, nor did he reach for a weapon. His voice sounded formal, but there was a gentleness to it that reminded LeiRain of wind whispering through leaves. Still, she adjusted the grip on her sword.

Ron pulled his shoulders back and lifted his chin. 'And what do you want with us?'

'I'm looking for you, Ronland the Red.'

A growl emanated from Ron's throat, and he took several steps toward the man, putting himself between Silvers-gleaming and LeiRain. Instinctively, LeiRain took a few steps backward, moving away from the verdaant.

'How did you find me?' Ron demanded.

'A locator spell, not typical magic for my kind, but I made it work. You've hidden well and it took great effort to find you.' The verdaant took a step forward. Ron's fingers twitched on the hilt of his ax. As he moved closer, Silversgleaming's face became visible. His eyes sparkled silver, much like his hair. He had high cheekbones, a long, narrow nose and his face was smooth with no sign of stubble. There were no lines of age on his face, either. The verdaant looked to be only a few years older than LeiRain, though this was no way to judge the age of an immortal.

He's beautiful, she thought. His face had an otherness that reminded her of the water elves, though their faces had been round and his was lean with sharp angles. His beauty was so severe that she thought it predatory, and LeiRain scolded herself for feeling drawn to it. For feeling drawn to *him*. He was dangerous, not lovely.

'I do not mean you or your family any harm, Ronland the Red. I come to seek your aid. I come to beg for your help.'

24

The two dwarves, axes in hand, formed a wall of muscle and metal between Silversgleaming and what remained of their family. Ron paced back and forth in front of the intruder. In colorful language, he demanded that the man leave. In gentle, almost musical tones, the verdaant implored him to listen. Not once did Silversgleaming raise a hand to draw a weapon or call on any magic. When Ron drew closer to him, his ax intimidatingly held at the ready, Silversgleaming's gaze remained steady. He did not flinch away, nor did he make any move to protect himself. There was something about this steadfastness that made LeiRain want to hear the man out. In between Ron's invectives, the verdaant asserted his need for assistance.

It took hours for Silversgleaming to convince Ron to invite him in, to hear him out. The sun's rays had grown intense and there was no hint of dew left on the grass. Ron had finally given in, convinced that the man would not leave until he was heard out. The breakfast hour had come and gone but hunger was an afterthought. LeiRain had shrunk back near the door and Rayand had been shoved inside by his mother, though

LeiRain could see him out of the corner of her eye, craning his neck to view them all from the window. The boy had still been in his mother's womb when his father and the rest of their clan were murdered by Jade. LeiRain wondered if he understood the seriousness of the situation.

'It has to be you, Ronland the Red,' he said, his voice even. 'The fate of many lives may rest on your aid.'

'How did you even find me?' Ron muttered this sentence more like a curse than a question, but LeiRain saw one of Silversgleaming's eyebrows lift.

'Hear me out, and I will tell you.'

Ron halted his pacing. The muscles in his cheek jumped, making his beard twitch as he worked his jaw. Without warning, he took a few running steps toward Silver, his ax coming up as if to strike. LeiRain held her breath. In the moment, she forgot that Silversgleaming was more than capable of defending himself. She did not want any harm to come to Ron, and she did not want to watch this beautiful creature be struck down. But Ron did not strike. He halted suddenly only a few feet away from the verdaant and froze with his ax aloft, a statue of a warrior. A few tense seconds passed before, slowly, Ron lowered the ax. The air left LeiRain's lungs in a rush of relief as the dwarve studied the man before him. Silver's arms still hung loosely at his sides. He had not so much as raised a hand.

'Are there more coming?' Ron asked. 'Does anyone else know how to find me? How to find my family?'

Spit flew from his mouth as he spoke, catching the sunlight as it fell to the ground. The muscles in his shoulders were visibly knotted. Brya inched her way forward to flank him.

'I will answer all of these questions, if you will just listen. Please.' At this, Silversgleaming's chest rose and fell with a deep breath. The corners of the verdaant's mouth pursed slightly. 'Please, just hear me out.'

His words were smooth and warm. *What harm could come from listening to him?* LeiRain shook her head, reminding herself that this was a god of the forest, not a helpless traveler.

'If I hear you, you will tell me these things. And,' there was a pause as Ron cast a brief glance at his sister-in-law before looking back at the verdaant, 'you will leave.' It wasn't a question.

'If,' the verdaant took a step forward glancing briefly at the ax in the dwarve's hand, 'you do not wish to help, if you wish me to leave once you hear the news I bring, then I will go.'

Ron didn't say anything, just lowered his ax and turned abruptly toward the house. Silversgleaming followed him and Brya brought up the rear. Her eyes narrowed at the stranger as he took long, graceful steps toward her home... Toward her son.

LeiRain was eager to hear the news this man brought, but a brief shudder ran through her as she reminded herself of his power. *He must be as powerful as my father,* she thought, recalling the way the skies had darkened as Caspian strode away from her and into the sea. It had stormed for days in Harbor after he departed. Though the verdaant had demonstrated none of it, LeiRain knew that Silversgleaming teemed with power. She stepped back as the two men approached, folding her arms protectively over herself. Ron threw the door open with so much force that it banged against the outside wall where LeiRain had been standing just moments before. It was a wonder he hadn't torn it from the hinges.

'Rayand, out.' Ron's voice did not invite protest and the boy scurried past and toward the garden just as Silversgleaming reached LeiRain. The verdaant's attention had been focused entirely on Ron since their tense dialogue began. But now, the man stopped at the threshold and turned to face her. For the first time since his arrival, LeiRain's body realized the true magnitude of the threat and her limbs buzzed with energy.

Her world narrowed to the few feet in front of her as she took in his height, his strong build, his smooth sage skin. Though his body and muscles weren't thick like her father's, there was no question of his strength. His eyes, now that they met hers, looked like the bright silver of the mountain stream in the sunlight. His gaze was intense enough to make her want to look away, but she forced herself to hold it. LeiRain's breath hitched as she felt him see through her, into her. Silversgleaming tilted his head to the side as they studied one another, and the tightness around his mouth softened.

No one had ever looked at her this way before. Men had leered at her, whenever she walked through Harbor after sunset and the dock hands were deep in their drink. This was different. It was a complete nakedness, one that made LeiRain feel as though no one knew her better, saw her more clearly, than this lethal creature in front of her.

Even more astonishing was the way that she saw into him as well. When she looked into his eyes, it was as if the core of Silversgleaming was laid bare. There was something about the way his eyelids fell slightly closed, the way he held his mouth, that spoke of sorrow and tenderness, hope and bravery ... and lust. She watched his silver lashes flutter slightly as he looked briefly at her mouth and then back into her eyes. The magic that had been so dormant the last few months rose up inside her. It was as if the power in this man was so immense that her own magic was forced to react to it. LeiRain felt it as a tug deep in her belly, pulling her toward him.

She saw a faint glow emanating from him as Silversgleaming pulsed with power. LeiRain could feel it, warm and crackling, sliding over her skin. Without meaning to, she shuddered. The verdaant's eyes widened slightly and the spell between them broke.Silversgleaming looked away and the pull vanished just as quickly as it had appeared. Now she knew, or at least some part of her knew, exactly how powerful this being was. No longer able to see into his soul, the man before her was once again a stranger whose intentions couldn't be trusted. LeiRain took a half step back and Silversgleaming's brows creased slightly as he watched her feet. The verdaant wore a look of confusion for a fraction of a second before he dipped his head in acknowledgment and followed Ron.

Brya walked past LeiRain then, face stern, and she followed the dwarve inside. LeiRain's knees shook as she walked, weak from what had passed between her and the verdaant.

Inside, LeiRain and the dwarves watched the verdaant struggle to fold into a dwarve-sized chair. Even as he did this, Silversgleaming somehow managed to look graceful. Eventually, he settled with his hands resting in his lap, the chair a bit too wide for him to comfortably use the arm rests. He had pulled the chair away from the table to allow room for his knees, which were looking uncomfortably high compared to her own. LeiRain nearly collapsed into her own chair, though she tried to hide the way her legs quivered. She did not want Silversgleaming to see how affected she'd been by their brief … connection? Of course it was a connection. He had to have felt it, too. The tug between their magics was too strong to have only been felt on her end.

If LeiRain fell into her chair, Ron threw himself into his. His face was still pale, and his body coiled as if he might spring to action any minute. He was perched on the edge of his seat and though he had sheathed his sword, his ax was still in hand. For the first time since the verdaant had shown up,

Ron seemed to remember that LeiRain was there. His eyes narrowed and his mouth became pinched as he noticed her, lips twitching slightly like he was about to say something. She squared her shoulders and lifted her chin, daring him to suggest that she leave. Ron looked at her for another moment but said nothing and turned his attention back to Silversgleaming.

'First,' Ron said, 'I need to know exactly how you found me.'

'As I said, I will share these things with you if you hear me out.' Silver's eyelashes flashed in the kitchen light as he blinked at Ron.

Ron's face turned a shade of purple nearly as vibrant in color as his beard. Brya scoffed from where she stood, leaning against the wall near Silversgleaming. Her arms were crossed and one of her hands still gripped an ax. LeiRain had never seen her wield it before today.

'You're in our home, forest god,' Brya said, shifting her weight between feet. 'We've shown our willingness to listen. Have enough respect for our honor to answer my brother's questions.' She looked eyes with the verdaant for several seconds. 'He will hear you out. *We* will hear you out.'

'As I said, I used a locator spell.' He flourished his hands gracefully, as if presenting something of significance, but this only raised more questions.

'That is witch magic.' Ron's free hand balled into a fist on the armrest of his chair. 'Did you employ someone to do this for you? Can others find me here?'

Silversgleaming tilted his head slightly to one side as if Ron had said something curious. LeiRain had heard little of what "witch magic" could do beyond the enchantments her mother had been capable of weaving. Witches, magic humans, were nearly impossible to find given how much other humans resented their power. How would he have found such a powerful one? Just as LeiRain's lips parted and she prepared to pepper him with her own questions, Silversgleaming spoke.

'Of course not,' his voice sounded harsher than it had so far. LeiRain studied his face, noted the way that he sat up slightly taller in his ill-fitting chair. He was offended. 'A witch would need a good quantity of your blood to cast such a spell. Unless you've been trading vials of your blood, which I highly doubt, finding you would not be possible for anyone less powerful than a verdaant.'

'I've never heard of the gods using this magic.'

'I'd guess that's because you've had a rather limited exposure to my kind. We don't generally advertise the extent of our abilities.' Silversgleaming shifted slightly in his chair. LeiRain thought he was going to give them a demonstration of his abilities, but he only brought his hand to rest in front of him on the table. 'I have given you this information as a token of my trustworthiness.'

'I would like to know more about this spell,' LeiRain said. She avoided looking at Ron, whose frustration and anger were becoming palpable.

'It is not pertinent to this conversation,' he said, his voice flat and his face stern. She refused to break eye contact with him and his gaze grew more intense by the second. It was different from the intensity she'd felt when they'd locked eyes outside. This was colder, more business-like, and she suspected it was meant to be intimidating. It was working. She felt her heart speed up again and she desperately wanted to look away. But there was a stubbornness in her, something she'd inherited from her mother, so she held firm. LeiRain worked her jaw as she stared back at him, unwilling to yield. Several tense seconds passed before the verdaant raised an eyebrow and sighed heavily. It was the most mortal expression she had seen on his face thus far she blinked in surprise. He broke their eye contact and looked back at Ron when he answered and he spoke so quickly that his words nearly ran together.

'It is highly unlikely that others will find you here. It took me many months to find what I needed for this spell and the magic requires a great deal of knowledge, practice and power.' LeiRain looked at the man's face and saw no emotion there. She was certain she'd feel annoyed by Ron's reluctance if she were in Silversgleaming's position, but there was no outward sign of distress. There was not a single line of irritation on his face and his hand rested on the table, unmoving.

'The spell,' Silversgleaming went on, 'also requires something of the person in question: a tooth, a fingernail clipping, something like that. And since you have clearly had this place warded, it also required a great deal of power. So, as I said, it is unlikely that a witch could perform such a spell. I also spent much time and quite a bit of money finding and acquiring an old tunic of yours. Relics of a dead legend are quite expensive.' Ron shifted in his seat. He knew that the world believed him dead, and he preferred it this way. 'They are also almost always fake so it took many months for me to find something that had in fact belonged to you. You might say that the spell also took a great deal of patience. In my experience, this is something that most people lack.'

Silversgleaming's eyes flicked back to LeiRain and their gaze locked again for a brief moment. She marveled at the flash of his quicksilver irises and felt the rumbling of the verdaant's magic even as he turned away from her and back to Ron.

'After many failed attempts and wasteful purchases, I was able to recover a few hairs from a tunic you had discarded. This eventually led me here, though my initial attempt led me to an abandoned barn some miles west. Apparently, your tunic had at some point come into contact with a particularly vicious feral cat, its hair a strikingly similar color to your own.'

LeiRain watched the corner of the verdaant's mouth twitch upward, hinting at a smile.

'The second hair,' he continued, 'led me to a rather upscale house of ill repute near the northern coast.'

LeiRain was surprised to hear this and her head snapped to Ron. His eyes flicked to her and then abruptly away, making her regret the obviousness of her gesture. It was known that he enjoyed a bit of drink, but she had never taken him to be the kind of man who would frequent prostitutes. Ron's ears turned the same purple his face had been moments ago and he swallowed repeatedly as he stared at his hands.

'I asked after you, not by name of course,' he raised a hand to ward off any complaints Ron may have been about to express. 'And the madam directed me to a lovely redheaded young woman. Of course, when I spoke with the young lady myself, she refused to answer any of my questions, which made me all the more certain that she knew you,' the verdaant lifted his hand and waved it slightly to emphasize his point. 'But that didn't bring me any closer to actually *finding* you. I had only one hair left after the brothel and to be honest, I was not optimistic... But,' he threw his arms open wide, 'here we are.' Silversgleaming paused for a moment and when no one responded, he continued. 'It was a rather arduous process and one at which I nearly failed. So, as I said, it seems highly unlikely that there are many others with such skill and single-minded determination, especially since most of the world seems to believe you are dead.'

'Ron,' Brya's voice broke. It was the first time she'd spoken since they'd come inside. 'If he can find us, then Jade—'

'Jade does not wish to find you,' Silversgleaming interrupted.

'What?' Ron and Brya asked in unison.

'She knows that you are alive,' the verdaant said to Ron. He looked over his shoulder, again, at Brya, 'though she does not know that any of your family have survived.' He looked down at the table before continuing. 'She leaves you alive because she wishes you to experience the pain of continuing on without those you love.' Silversgleaming's voice was nearly a whisper now and there was something about the way he spoke that made LeiRain think he could relate to such pain. 'She wishes for you to live in sorrow and guilt.' A long silence passed as the four of them felt the impact of the verdaant's words.

'I guess,' Ron cleared his throat, voice cracking as he broke the silence. 'Only one question remains to be answered, then. Why would someone so powerful as you so desperately need *my* help?'

'My people, all of our peoples,' his eyes scanned each of them in turn, 'face a great threat.'

Ron burst into laughter. '*Your* people are threatened?' There was no humor in his eyes. 'One, just *one,* of your kind wiped out my entire clan. Verdaants are old and powerful and reclusive. Your settlements are infamously difficult to find and made nearly impenetrable by powerful wards. You are regarded as gods. *What* could possibly threaten *your* kind?'

Silvergleaming shifted in his seat and laced his fingers together on the table.

'You are familiar with the Royal Merchant Marine Company? And the affiliated group of human 'purists' known as the Royals?'

LeiRain held her breath through the long pause that followed.

'Yes,' Ron finally answered.

'Their xenophobia is spreading. They tell lies, create divides.' Silversgleaming sat forward in his small chair, leaning over the tabletop toward Ron. 'The Royals were once only informally affiliated with the company, but the original business owner has died and been replaced by his son, Ulrik Odro. He has more formally embraced the organization, offered to ... sponsor their pursuits.'

'I thought they just hated blends,' LeiRain said, tentatively, 'How does this threaten dwarves or ... deities?'

'I saw it myself when I went for supplies,' Brya broke in. She took a step toward the table, placing one hand on it while the other clung to the ax. 'The villages are becoming hostile to anyone who isn't human. The prices I paid for goods were higher than what the humans charged one another. Whether it's intentional or not, the limited resources available to non-humans has begun to cause them to mistrust each other. And not just blends. The solebloods are just as distrustful. It will only get worse.' She shook her head then stepped away from the table to lean against the wall once more.

'With more money behind their efforts, the Royals are recruiting more to their cause every day,' the verdaant explained. They become bolder in their dislike of other non-humans, just as your sister says. Just as I suspect you have seen for yourself.'

Ron had seen it. LeiRain recalled his warnings to Brya when they'd first arrived, how he'd spoken of his fears about the rising disregard for any who were not human.

'I suspect that they are intentionally sparking rivalries between different races, the likes of which have not been seen in hundreds of years. If there is conflict between us all, there will be no one to stand against them, no one to oppose their growing power. We will face another War of Sorrows.' Silvergleaming raised his eyebrows as he looked at Ron. He was waiting for a response from the dwarve. Ron crossed his arms over his chest and said nothing. 'Perhaps you don't understand,' the verdaant shook his head. 'You're so far removed from everything here. But it's getting worse. More and more conflicts arise as more and more people compete for the same resources. The Royals are turning us against one another just as it was before The King's Peace.'

As if the King's Peace ever applied to blends, LeiRain thought.

As if reading her mind, Silversgleaming said, 'it's not just the blends who are being mistreated and abused. Solebloods are turning on other solebloods as the Royals fan the flames of discord between races.' He sat back in his chair again, his long, slender fingers wrapping around the arm rests as if he might push himself to standing. The verdaant's eyes darted up to the low ceiling as he thought better of it. He folded his hands in his lap. 'My people isolate themselves and rarely deign to think about other beings. Nevertheless, we are touched by this discord. I feel the hostility toward other races growing within the verdaant. It used to be enough that our lands were warded and little attention was given to any who were seen to be encroaching on our territory. Though the wards remain as effective as ever, it is now the practice to slaughter those who come near uninvited. Hate spreads like a disease. If we do not act soon, if they are not stopped, the Royals will breed a hate that brings our world to war once again. No life, no piece of land, or sea, will be left untouched by such conflict. Peace is fragile, and it is breaking.'

LeiRain felt a heat building inside her. She sat back abruptly in her chair and crossed her arms. The motion drew the attention of the two men so she decided to speak her mind.

'I've read about the King's Peace,' LeiRain said, her

growing frustration making her sound more confident than she felt. 'But I have never *known* peace. Perhaps solebloods have,' she looked pointedly at Ron. She thought of Bren, how he could pass for human as long as no one saw the tips of his ears. 'It really only seems to matter what one looks like and I can't see how that's ever been a reasonable measure of worth.' She paused to draw breath. 'It seems to me that everybody except for *blends* were living *The King's Peace* until now. And even with this so-called peace, *I* have never witnessed a great deal of harmony between men of different races. In the many hours I spent watching people at the Harbor, I saw tolerance there and little more. So,' she unfolded her arms and gripped the edge of the table as she looked at Ron. 'Maybe we can all agree that The King's Peace has been a peace for the sole-bloods and nothing more?' LeiRain released her grip on the table and placed her hands in her lap.

Silver's face was unreadable but his eyes sparkled as they watched her. Ron sat back in his chair. He closed his eyes and stroked his beard with his left hand while his right still rested on the ax. Several seconds passed in this manner until, finally, he opened his eyes and leaned over the table. He looked at LeiRain and shook his head, slowly.

'I'm sorry, Demi. I... You're right and I'm sorry.' He shook his head once more.

LeiRain hadn't really planned her words and hadn't expected such raw vulnerability in Ron's reply. She couldn't bring herself to respond. The way he looked at her now, his brow furrowed and eyes sad, she felt like she was being seen by him for the first time. LeiRain swallowed the sob that was building up inside her and gave dwarve a nod of acknowledgement. Clearing her throat, she turned back to Silvers-gleaming.

'But *why* do you need *Ron*? You haven't really answered

that. Surely your people are powerful enough to stop such a war.'

'My people need to be moved to action. They do nothing, ignoring my pleas, dismissing the seriousness of the situation. They are so isolated, so far removed from the rest of the world, that they do not believe they can be touched by it. I need his help to find proof of the coming storm, to convince them that war is imminent.'

'Why would they listen to him?' LeiRain asked. 'He is surely not one to win the sympathy of your people when he lost his entire family to one of your kind.'

'It's because of my hate for them that he seeks me out,' they turned their heads to Ron as he spoke. 'Because I have no reason to warn them unless the situation is, indeed, dire.'

LeiRain turned to Silversgleaming to see how he would respond. He was nodding his head. 'Exactly,' he whispered.

'I don't trust you,' Ron went on. 'And I am not agreeing to help you. But,' LeiRain shifted in her seat as Ron spoke, 'I do agree that it is time someone took a stand against the Royals. I should have stood up for blends a long time ago. Now, I must take a stand for us all. I will need to think on what to do next.'

'Let me stay for the time being,' Silversgleaming said. 'I ask that you not send me away yet. Let me earn your trust. The only way to stop this now is to take on the Royals directly and you cannot do that alone.'

Ron stroked his beard again and studied the verdaant. 'I'll call you Silver, then. *Silversgleaming...* Too many syllables.' The verdaant nodded in acquiescence. 'I promise nothing, Forest God, but as you already know where we live, I will accept your presence here for the time being.'

'Thank you,' Silver replied.

'That can't be all there is,' LeiRain blurted out. There was something more to this that he wasn't saying. She felt it when their eyes met. 'What are you not telling us?' He held her gaze for what felt like a very long time before he finally replied.

'There's something ... off about all of it.' Silver shook his head. 'The younger Odro has never had a reputation as someone with a love for diversity, that much is true. But he was also not known to care a great deal about anything aside from the weight of his coin purse and how he might spend the whole of it in a night's diversions. He wasn't even a member of the Royals before he took over for his father. From the information I've gathered, it seems he was more likely to buy a round for everyone than to start a brawl. Yet he now commands one of the most violent organizations on land or sea.'

'He has more power, now, more wealth. Perhaps this has corrupted his heart,' Ron offered, sounding tentative.

'That's still not all,' LeiRain said. They had only just met Silver, and she wasn't sure how she could tell, but something in her just *knew* that he was still holding back. His eyes narrowed at her. He brought his hands to the table then placed them back in his lap, wiping his palms on his pant legs. It was as close as he'd come to fidgeting or displaying any signs of nervousness. Silver let out a loud sigh.

'Odro's father was found dead, burned alive in his bed.'

'And?' Ron chimed in. 'Fires happen all of the time. He was a bit old, wasn't he? Probably succumbed to the smoke before the flames even reached him.' Ron waved a dismissive hand.

'Nothing else was burned.' Silver swallowed. 'Only his body, and the linens where they touched his body. Everything else was intact, unmarred by flame.'

'How?' LeiRain's brown crinkled. Silver shook his head in response.

'When I learned of this, I asked my father how such a thing was possible. He is very old and powerful, and full of knowledge. I thought that he must know how such a thing could be done.'

'And did he?' Ron asked. 'This sounds like *old* magic.'

'Yes, but ... he would not speak of it to me. He dismissed it. He chastised me for concerning myself with the dealings of other beings. But I saw the recognition on his face when I described it to him. There was fear in his eyes. There is little that threatens my kind so fear is not something readily displayed by a verdaant, even less so by one as powerful as my father.'

'It is difficult to imagine a verdaant fearing much of anything,' LeiRain said.

'I find myself in agreement,' Silver replied. 'There is something more to this, a danger so great that even the most powerful beings walking this earth will not speak of it freely. I believe there is something behind this that goes well beyond the Royals. This mission will present great danger.'

Ron laid his hands out on the table, palms flat against the smooth wood. It was the first time he'd taken his hand off of the ax in Silver's presence. Silver looked down at the dwarve's thick, gnarled fingers, not missing the significance of the gesture.

'Well,' Ron grunted, 'you probably should have led with that.'

25

─────────

L et us get you set up in a room, then, if you're staying,' Brya said. Her voice was tight, and she, unlike Ron, still held her weapon.

'I can make myself comfortable outside,' Silver said, his eyes moving back and forth between Brya and Ron. She nodded, making no objection.

'It's quite cold when the sun goes down,' LeiRain pointed out, concerned despite her wariness of the verdaant. Even though the season was shifting to spring, there was still a bite to the air, especially when darkness fell.

'I will not be troubled by the cold,' he replied, looking between the dwarves rather than at LeiRain. 'Please excuse me as I see to my comfort.'

Silver pushed his chair back from the table and stood, his head slightly bowed to accommodate the low ceiling. LeiRain's chair was nearest to the door and she stood as he walked by, meaning to move out of the way so that he could more easily pass. Instead, her shoulder brushed his arm as she tried to push in her own chair. The contact made her heart race and the dormant pool of magic inside her rose up.

Her body stiffened but Silver seemed not to have noticed. He slipped out of the dwelling, closing the door behind him. The swell of power in LeiRain receded, and she nearly collapsed with the emptiness it left behind. She stood there for several seconds, clinging to the back of the chair for stability.

By the time her head had finally cleared, Brya was sitting at the table next to Ron. The two had their heads bowed toward one another and were talking in hushed tones. LeiRain felt her stomach rumble as she watched them. They had all missed lunch and it was now nearly time for LeiRain to begin making dinner. LeiRain slipped out the door without excusing herself, blinking as her eyes adjusted to the light outside. She stretched, her back stiff from sparring this morning and spending so much of the day sitting in a chair. She probably hadn't had enough to drink, either. Ron had warned her about the effects of dehydration on the body, how it could make the soreness worse, make her feel tired. There was water in her room, but LeiRain decided to walk to the mountain spring instead.

She thought of the way her magic had risen up when Silver brushed by and it crossed her mind briefly that she might be able to ask him about the loss of her power. She quickly dismissed the idea, reminding herself that he was not to be trusted. Lost in thought, LeiRain paid little attention to her surroundings. She was already kneeling at the stream, bending to cup some of the water in her hand, when she saw him.

Silver stood on the far side of the stream with his back to her. His arms were raised and... LeiRain gasped. Where a thin sapling had been just this morning there now stood a tall, thick tree. She could see where its roots had disrupted the soil and displaced clumps of grass as they widened and spread.

Silver was unmoving but before him, the tree continued to grow. It sprouted more branches than seemed natural and began to bend forward the limbs reached for the ground. There was a groaning sound as the tree grew and stretched and spread at an unnatural pace, the branches curving into a rounded shelter. As she watched, the boughs of the tree sprouted more offshots, and then wove through the skeleton of the dome. When Silver finally lowered his arms, the tree before him looked like a giant, upside down basket. He waved one hand, barely lifting it from his side, and the weave of branches in front of him parted slightly to make a kind of doorway.

'Amazing,' LeiRain whispered to herself.

'I do not think your friend would be much pleased to share a dwelling with me and even less so if I shared a dwelling with his family,' Silver spoke as he turned around to face her. He must have heard her exclamation.

Silver raised his hands and cupped his palms together. When he opened them again, a ball of blue light, a self-contained flame, floated in the space between them. LeiRain was at least eight feet away from him but even at this distance, she could feel warmth radiating from the light.

'How do you do that?' She asked, her eyes fixated on the blue flame. 'The... This fire... I thought that the verdaant commanded only living things, plants, the earth.' She gestured to the shelter he'd constructed for himself out of what had only recently been a sapling.

'It's fae light,' he replied.

'Fae?' LeiRain scrunched her face in confusion. 'Fairies, the fae... They have been extinct for hundreds of years.' She could see the pictures from her book, *Before the War*, with fae, mounted on dragons, fighting to end the turmoil between mortals. So little was known about them now that even artists dared not try to imagine their likeness. Fae faces were blurred in all the images she'd seen. But LeiRain knew they had been powerful, and they had sacrificed themselves for The King's Peace. It seemed like a terrible waste.

Silver tilted his head and looked her over. Once more, LeiRain felt bare under his gaze. Her breath hitched, and she broke eye contact before she could feel his power call to hers again. She bent down over the stream and finally took the drink of water she'd come for.

'You referred to my kind as deities earlier,' Silver said as she cupped the water, 'I think you are, perhaps, misinformed.'

'You're a verdaant, like my father,' she replied. 'But you're a forest deity instead of water—' He waved a hand in front of him, signaling her to stop. LeiRain let out a huff of air and crossed her arms.

'I am no deity, Rain, and neither is your father. The verdaant, the tempest, we are *fae*.'

'There are no fae anymore,' she said, her frustration growing. She took another mouthful of water in hopes of cooling her rising temper. She'd had little to eat or drink today, which made it easier than usual for anger to rise to the surface.

'That is an untruth that the fae have allowed to spread. You yourself are half-fae.'

'What are you talking about?' LeiRain pulled herself to her feet. The part of her that wanted to trust him was retreating and she wondered what game he was playing with her. 'I'm a demi-god.' She crossed her arms and shook her head. 'I'm... My father is a water god, you're a forest go—'

'No,' his reply was firm but his voice did not rise. 'Fae are very powerful, Rain, and power is frightening to those who do not have it. It must be explained, confined to terms that those without such power can comprehend. Mortals made us gods in their minds so that what we are and what we can do makes sense to them. We let them believe it. If people believe that you are extinct, they stop looking for you. If people believe you are immortal, they stop trying to kill you.' His tone sharpened and the calm demeanor he'd maintained all day was beginning to slip.

'We clung to this lie because of what we lost during the War of Sorrows. The fae gave so much to end a war they had no part in creating. Verdaant and tempest alike have no desire to meddle in the wars of mortals again, which is why it will take so much to bring my people to act in order to prevent one now.' He looked down as he said this, his face in a grimace of pain. When he spoke again, his voice was once more soft and musical. 'But I am no god. I am fae, and I am immortal only in that my life will be very long and it is very difficult to kill me. Same as you.'

She stood before him, shocked into silence. LeiRain's eyes blinked rapidly as she tried to make sense of all he'd just said. Riv had told her she would be very long-lived. She'd almost forgotten this in light of all that had happened since she left Corallis. Now, the immensity of immortality loomed before her.

She'd spent the first eleven years of her life not knowing who or what she was. As terrifying as her father had been, meeting him had been a relief. It had provided the answers to questions she'd been asking her mother for years. She'd been angry at her mother for withholding the truth of her heritage, then angry at Ron when she realized he'd known as well and failed to share this with her. But neither of them really knew what she was, or who she was. They only thought they did.

'You're still you, Rain.' Silver's voice drew her from her thoughts. 'You are a very powerful half-fae. I can feel the power in you.'

LeiRain felt her cheeks heat up. The connection had been mutual.

He nodded toward the fae light that was now floating, of its own accord, a few feet away from where she stood. 'You might learn one day to produce fae light of your own. Not all half-fae can, but I suspect that you have the ability.'

'You said...' she began as she recalled his first words to her, "When you first arrived, you said that my learning to fight with a sword and shield was *interesting*. Why? What is wrong with a daughter of tempest learning such things?'

'Nothing at all!' His eyes widened in a look of surprise. 'I did not mean to give offense.' He bowed his head slightly when he said this. 'I'm sorry if it seemed that way. I did not say it was wrong, only that it was interesting because it is so unnecessary. As I said, you are very powerful. I think you will find such weapons are only accessories once you've mastered your magic.'

'How—?' She thought of the water's silence in her mind, her failed efforts to command it. LeiRain's magic had lain dormant for months now, unwilling to rise to the surface when she called, but it had nearly spilled out of her in response to Silver. She wanted to ask for help, to confess to him that her magic seemed to have gone, but she held her tongue. Afterall, what did she really know about him? Certainly nothing that should inspire her to start sharing personal secrets. LeiRain had told no one outside of Corallis of her magic, nor the loss of it. Sharing such information would be a kind of intimacy she had never known.

'You're shivering,' he interrupted LeiRain before she could decide how to finish her sentence. She had grown cold, her fingers numb from cupping handfuls of icy water and the clearing now in shadow as the sun began to set. LeiRain took advantage of the change in conversation.

'I need to clean up and start dinner,' she announced. Without waiting for a response, LeiRain turned from him and walked away. Perhaps she was imagining it, but LeiRain thought she could feel his eyes on her as she went. She didn't allow herself to turn around and look. Inside her room, she leaned against the inside of the door and closed her eyes, ignoring the gentle tug of her magic as she shut Silver out.

26

———————

$\int$ he was sparring – but not with Ron. At first, she didn't recognize the figure in front of her. His features were obscured, but he was too tall and lean to be a dwarve. He lunged at her and his face came into focus; it was Ethan. He would have been handsome were it not for the scowl that twisted his features as he stabbed at LeiRain. She was fending him off, holding her own far better than she had thus far with Ron. Then, the smell of smoke caught her attention. As always, she ran from Ethan, scrambling to save her mother. She clawed at her magic to put out the fire. But, as always, her mother burned, and LeiRain felt her breath leave as Ethan's knife plunged into her stomach.

LeiRain jolted upright, clutching at her abdomen and gasping for air. Her brow was damp with rain drops – no, with sweat. She squeezed her eyes shut then opened them again, her heart still beating fast but her breathing slowing. LeiRain took in the details of her room, noting how the covers were tangled at the end of her bed. She had kicked them off in the middle of the night, restless and unable to sleep. That's how she'd ended up sitting by the fire, watching the flames dance.

And that's where she'd fallen asleep, by the fire, upright in a chair. She swore at the flames in the hearth. She was grateful for the warmth but the smell of it always wound its way into her dreams. Even when it didn't recall memories of the worst day of her life, the fire always reminded LeiRain of her mother. It reminded her of Alarra who always smelled like smoke and wore ash smudges the way some women wore rouge. Fire smelled like homesickness, fear, and regret. LeiRain's hands tightened on her stomach as she was overcome once more by a stabbing pain in her mid-section. She peeled off the blanket she had draped over her lap and stood. Even her legs were thick with sweat, her thighs sliding against each other as she took a few steps toward the ewer. LeiRain tugged her damp shift away from her stomach and off the back of her legs.

She filled a glass with water and drank it down before she turned back to the fire. The tan blanket she'd just discarded lay draped over the chair. A dark stain drew her eyes, deep red turning brown. LeiRain tugged up her shift and looked at her inner thighs, and now she understood that the pain in her stomach hadn't just been a part of the dream and it was not only sweat that dampened her clothing. Seeing her legs were streaked and smeared with rivulets of blood, she closed her eyes and swore again.

LeiRain knew that courses came monthly for most women, or at least they had for her mother. Brya had confirmed it was the same for her when she pulled LeiRain aside a month ago and asked if she needed anything for her "special time". In addition to offering clothes and pain medication, Brya had also expressed some concern that LeiRain had been on the mountain well beyond a month and had not yet bled. LeiRain had explained that her own courses only came a few times a year, normally every three months, though the dates weren't always exact. Sometimes she bled for only a day, sometimes she bled for almost two full weeks. The only consistant was that her courses were *always* painful.

Her bleedings had started when she was thirteen, and Alarra had shown her how to place a piece of linen in her undergarments to absorb the flow, but her mother had never offered her any solution for the pain. LeiRain had discovered on her own that a warm bath could sometimes help, but often the pain was so severe she couldn't manage to heat and carry the water. She'd been so surprised when Brya offered her a medicine for pain that she'd said *no* without thinking, and wished now that she hadn't. LeiRain had been on the mountain for almost six months now and this was her first course since she'd arrived. She hadn't really thought much of it, but when she reflected on those first few months, LeiRain recalled how little she'd eaten or slept and thought that perhaps her body had decided she was dealing with enough.

This was the longest she'd gone without a course before and if the pain in her stomach was any indication, it was going to be a particularly uncomfortable experience. She briefly considered going to Brya for that medicine now, but LeiRain decided against waking her in the wee hours of the morning. Alarra had worked at the forge through her own pains, so at the very least, LeiRain could make it until breakfast. But she did need to do something about the blood now. The only way to prevent staining would be to rinse it out with cold water before it could set into the fabric. With a heavy sigh, LeiRain pulled the soiled shift over her head and gathered up the blanket.

She cleaned herself off with the edge of the already-soiled blanket, slid on a pair of underwear and placed a thick rag in them to absorb further bleeding. She then dressed hastily in a worn pair of slacks and an overlarge tunic. She threw a cloak around her shoulders and stepped outside, certain that she had not slept more than a few hours. Cold wind stung her face and raised goosebumps on her arms as it blew over her sweat-damp skin. The moon was bright but it still took a moment for LeiRain's eyes to adjust to the dark clearing. There was no sign of dawn and the stars shone boldly in a black sky. Steeling herself against the cold, she marched purposefully toward the stream, stopping abruptly after only a few steps.

Silver. She'd forgotten about Silver. The deity. No, the *fae*, she corrected herself, had made his shelter only a few feet from the water. *Damn it*. It would be hard to rinse her things without waking him.

Despite her best efforts, LeiRain couldn't think of a way around it without letting the blood stain.

'Fuck it all,' she muttered to herself, and resumed her walk toward the stream. LeiRain moved as quietly as she could and, once there, knelt down slowly. She set the load of soiled clothes on the ground beside her, pulling out her shift first and rubbing the fabric together beneath the icy water. The blood had already begun to dry in places and it was proving difficult to remove.

Winter had come to a close and there hadn't been snowfall in weeks, but the last one had been heavy. Large mounds of white were still visible higher up on the mountain and as they melted, they ran into the stream. It was warm enough not to freeze over, but just barely. LeiRain worked the fabric hard between her fingers, which were fast becoming numb. *I should have been prepared for this*, she thought. She had always kept track before, having at least a general idea of when to expect her course. She usually bled somewhere within the first week of the year's quarter and until she'd fled to the mountain hide, she'd always been aware of the month and days without trying.

Like so many other things, the months and days had

ceased to matter in the wake of her mother's death. It suddenly struck LeiRain that she would also have the disadvantage of having lost track of the months when she was in Harbor. She had experienced only three days while the rest of the world had experienced six months. She would have to check with Brya tomorrow and see if they kept a calendar, or if she could at least tell her what day and month it was so that she could keep track from here on out.

'Rain,' the whisper came only a few inches from her ear and she nearly dropped the blanket into the stream. She hunched over her sodden linens. Silver was kneeling next to her, his body silhouetted by the moonlight.

'I'm sorry if I woke you.' She tried to hide her bloody shift from his view.

'I smell blood. Are you alright?'

She gritted her teeth.

'I'm fine.'

As if to prove her wrong, a painful cramp seized LeiRain's abdomen and she let out a small groan, her hand going protectively to her stomach. There was a long pause, long enough that she thought Silver had gone back to his shelter. The cramp faded, leaving a dull ache that shot straight through her abdomen and into her lower back. She was about to resume scrubbing when his voice came again, from the darkness beside her.

'Oh...' he said, 'I see.' She felt his heat next to her as he came closer and asked, 'Can I help?'

LeiRain froze, shocked by his offer. Even Ron, who she'd learned today was known to frequent brothels, appeared uneasy if she or Brya even hinted at a conversation about their courses. That this powerful being, this male that she had only a few hours ago believed to be a deity, would offer to help rinse her soiled linens...

'Thank you, but I'm fine,' she responded. LeiRain did not dare look at him, knowing that she would fall under Silver's spell if she met his gaze. It was difficult enough to withhold her trust from him right now without his magic drawing her in. She forced herself to imagine the slaughter of Ron's clan, to see in her mind the evidence of a verdaant's lethality. Still, something inside her was drawn to Silver, so she kept her eyes down.

'I hope you find rest tonight, Rain.' The warmth of him beside her disappeared.

She remained kneeling in the darkness, shivering as her numb hands worked in the stream. When, as best as she could tell in the moonlight, her clothes and blankets were clean, she carried the damp heap back into her dwelling and laid the articles out before the still smoldering fire. She curled up on the floor next to her drying laundry, relishing the heat as it soaked into her muscles and eased the cramping. Sleep eluded her for the rest of the night, but pain and desire to avoid another exchange with Silver eroded any motivation she had to practice with sword and shield.

LeiRain was already seated at the breakfast table when Silver entered to join the morning meal. He had not taken dinner with them the night before, perhaps letting them all adjust to his presence slowly. It must have been working because there was a bit less wariness on Brya's face this morning than yesterday. Ron made no remark when Silver slid a chair out and sat down at the table opposite LeiRain, though the dwarve did begin to chew his food slower and a bit more menacingly as he watched the guest. Rayand made no effort to disguise his stares. This was the closest he'd been allowed to the verdaant so far, and the boy swallowed spoonfuls of breakfast porridge without ever taking his eyes off of him. Silver slid his chair as far in toward the table as he could without knocking his knees.

'Good morning,' LeiRain said. She looked straight into his eyes, forbidding herself to fall into them this time. The second their gazes locked, LeiRain felt a small tug toward him as her magic responded to his. Just as she found herself about to slip into that strange connection, her insides cramped. She kept her eyes locked with Silver's, daring him to look at her differently after their late-night encounter, but the pain grounded her in her physical body.

After a few seconds, his magic no longer seemed to pull at her. The fae – she was slowly getting used to the idea that he was not a deity – looked back at her with a serene expression. There was no evidence of embarrassment or familiarity there. She took this as a silent agreement between the two of them to proceed as if the exchange had never taken place. LeiRain poured a bit of extra honey on her porridge, feeling relieved.

For the next several minutes, LeiRain focused on her food. She was licking excess honey off her spoon when she looked up to find Silver staring at her. His head was tilted very slightly to one side and one eyebrow was raised. He didn't smile but the corners of his mouth turned up minisculely and his eyes sparkled with amusement. LeiRain's cheeks and neck flushed warm and she knew they were turning lavender before his eyes. She set her spoon down and reached for her coffee, staring back at him over the rim of the mug. Her flush reached its peak and it was a struggle not to look away.

Their eyes were still locked when Silver took his first sip of coffee. He flinched at its bitterness, obviously struggling against the reflex to spit it out. LeiRain laughed, then coughed on her mouthful of drink. She tried to breathe through her nose long enough to keep from spitting out her own coffee as she watched his reaction with amusement. Silver broke eye contact with her as he looked down at the substance in his mug. He wore an expression of shocked betrayal. He scanned the room to see if the others had observed him. It seemed a miracle that both Brya and Ron were not watching the verdaant. The two were engaged in a hushed conversation over their own breakfasts. LeiRain had caught bits of an argument between them this morning. It sounded as though Ron had been urging Brya to leave, but that was all LeiRain had heard before they'd realized they were no longer alone. Given how engrossed they were in each other's whispers, she suspected they had picked up this topic again.

Rayand, too, had given up his watch on the verdaant. It seemed he had dropped a bit of biscuit into the near empty jar of honey and was now occupied with scraping it out. The pastry crumbled into smaller and smaller bits with each attempt the boy made to pull it free of the sticky substance. LeiRain watched him for a few seconds as his efforts to recover the biscuit deteriorated into eating spoonfuls of honey dotted with biscuit crumbles. She smiled to herself and then looked back at Silver.

When their eyes met again, she gave him a knowing smile. LeiRain made a show of pouring a bit of goat's milk into her own coffee before passing the pitcher across the table. Silver looked at the pitcher, then skeptically at his mug, and then back at LeiRain who was no longer trying to hide her mirth. He poured a generous amount of milk into his mug and pursed his lips thoughtfully before drinking. He did not recoil from it this time, though LeiRain noted that he still did not look pleased either. After another appraising sip, he nodded his thanks to her, one corner of his mouth finally turning up in a half-smile.

She had felt her face and neck blushing as they stared

each other down and had been happy to find that laughter cooled the apprehension between them. The look he gave her now, his silver eyes flashing with humor, reminded her of the warmth she'd heard in his voice the night before. *Can I help?* LeiRain's heart sped up as she thought of the encounter. Alone in the night with a powerful creature and her blood-stained bedclothes. Her abdomen cramped again. She winced and her smile faltered. Silver arched an eyebrow questioningly and LeiRain looked back down at her bowl, focusing on the last few bites of porridge.

When she dared sneak another glance his eyes were still on her. LeiRain noted that he was blushing too. His light green cheeks had taken on a bluish hue. Silver's smile was gone, but his face was not unkind. They remained locked in this silent exchange for several moments, the room around them fading from LeiRain's awareness, until Ron belched at the other end of the table, and whatever spell had overtaken them was broken.

''Scuse me,' the dwarve said, unselfconsciously. He wiped his mouth with his shirt sleeve and turned toward Silver.

'I think we'd better talk about a plan of some kind, Forest God.'

27

'S o,' Ron tugged on his beard, thoughtfully, 'If I agreed to trust what you're saying and go out of my way to help you, what exactly is your plan?'

Brya and Ray had just excused themselves to work in the garden. Although Ron had agreed that he and LeiRain would wash up everyone's breakfast dishes, they both still sat at the table with Silver.

'I would prefer you call me Silver.'

Interesting, LeiRain thought, *he doesn't admit that he is fae.* She had not told Ron about her conversation with Silver; how she'd learned that she was half-fae, not a demi-god after all. Now she wasn't certain that she would. It seemed to be some secret, meant to be kept between those who shared fae heritage.

What would Silver do in order to maintain this secret? She thought of the way power hummed between her and the verdaant whenever they locked eyes, and how she'd felt when her shoulder brushed against him. The sensation was exhilarating and also frightening. LeiRain had been wary of trusting

Silver and until now, hadn't considered the joy she might feel at being trusted *by him*.

'Okay then, *Silver*. That still doesn't answer my question.' Ron's words were laced with poison, but the fae went on, undeterred.

'Ulrek Odro...'

'The new owner of the Royal Merchant Marine Company, right?' LeiRain asked, asserting her presence in the conversation even as the two men stared each other down.

'Correct.' Silver went on, 'He has established himself on an island known as the Arborris Enclave. It was a kind of retreat for him before he had the responsibility of company owner-ship, but now it seems to have become the homeport for the Royal Merchant Marine fleet. Goods are warehoused there and...'

'How do you come about this information?' Ron asked gruffly.

To his credit, Silver nodded his head, accepting this skepti-cism. 'I did some intelligence gathering prior to finding you.'

Intelligence gathering sounded very clandestine to LeiRain. She leaned forward in her seat, waiting for Silver to tell them more. She studied the verdaant's face as he looked at Ron, but his expression was unreadable.

'What kind of intelligence gathering? How do you know you can trust these sources?' Ron spoke her own question aloud.

'To be perfectly frank' – the fairy cleared his throat – 'I have been eavesdropping.'

Ron blinked his surprise at Silver's candor. LeiRain's own eyes widened a bit in surprise. Given his formal demeanor, she had expected a more sophisticated approach.

'Verdaant have superior senses and sailors like to talk when they are in the bottle.' Silver shifted slightly in his seat.

'I visited a few coastal taverns and had only to sip ale for a few hours to gain a fair bit of information on the Royals, and Odro,' he cleared his throat and raised one eyebrow, 'and some rather unsettling and irrelevant details about the bedroom exploits of a great many seafarers.'

Ron, who was no stranger to taverns and surely knew the kind of conversation that Silver had endured, fought a smile. LeiRain had overheard similar talk on the docks, but was sure it was much more explicit after a few ales.

'Right then, Arborris Enclave, you were saying?'

'They have some goods warehoused there but, more importantly, it is where they now conduct all of their fleet maintenance and the majority of the record keeping. Once there, I hope to gain access to the business's records. They'll have a scribe, somewhere, to make copies of important contracts and correspondence. I believe that I'll be able to find some evidence of their disregard for non-human life, their ruthlessness. We can use this and' – he paused long enough to swallow – 'whatever else we find to persuade my kind to act before we are all at war with one another.'

'And how will you get access to these records? Surely, they've got some security, even if it isn't much.'

'Yes, well, that will be difficult to determine until we've reached the island. Unfortunately, the men who can be found frequenting low brow taverns generally aren't privy to that level of detail.'

'Fair enough.' Ron conceded. 'And what else is it that you think we might find?'

Silver looked away from him then. His stare was aimed in LeiRain's direction but his eyes were unfocused, as if they were seeing much further away. 'I don't know exactly. I think...' Silver trailed off.

LeiRain and Ron sat very still and waited for Silver to

return to them. After several seconds had passed, Ron grew impatient enough to speak.

'Silver!'

The verdaant twitched slightly. He looked back at Ron with a discernible frown on his face and his brows drawn together. He shook his head, slowly.

'I truly do not know, but I feel there is something more here. I believe perhaps there is a magic that we've never seen before.'

'What kind of magic?' LeiRain asked, leaning forward.

'There are rumors that new weapons are being forged, deadly things that can throw fire and pierce a man's body from great distances. I don't know how true these are, but it would explain why the Royal Merchant Marine Company has been so desperate to buy up mines and force people out of resource-rich territory.' He drew in a breath and held it for a few seconds before continuing. 'At the very least perhaps we can bring back one of these weapons, or even a diagram of the design. If we show this to my people, maybe it will be enough to draw them to action.'

Ron choked on his coffee.

'*We*?' His eyes were as round as saucers.

'As you pointed out just yesterday' – Silver's face was once again a mask of calm – 'your hate for my people will under-score the seriousness of the matter. I believe it will take drastic measures to move them to action. Your willingness to bring these concerns to them, to stand in their presence, will surely convince the verdaant that we must act.'

LeiRain's eyes darted back and forth between the two men.

'Just to be clear, not only do you wish for my help to acquire this item, but you're expecting me to present it to your people?' He thumped his chest with one hand. 'To make this case to *your kind?*' Ron's face had begun to turn a sickly shade of yellow-green.

'Yes, I think that is essential.' If Silver noticed the disdain in Ron's voice or the fear on his face, he gave no hint of it. 'They will see it as a mark of the severity of the situation, that someone with such hate for the verdaant is willing to accompany me in service of this mission.'

Hate and fear, LeiRain thought. That is what Ron would have to overcome in order to willingly visit the verdaant. His ability to do so might determine the future of the entire continent.

'I will go with you,' LeiRain interjected, hoping this would be a comfort. Ron didn't so much as look at her.

'The verdaant murdered my entire family, my clan. How is that any better than the Royals?'

Silver's face remained unlined but his hands came up to rest on the table and his fingers curled into the wood, his knuckles turning white.

'*The verdaant* did not murder your family. *One* verdaant perpetrated that crime. I will not defend the ethics of my fellow verdaants. I lament the low value they place on the lives of other beings and that only seems to be getting worse in the present circumstances. But Jade was an outcast before she murdered your clan, and she remained so afterward. She holds no place of power or sway with my people. My father on the other hand...' Silver looked down at where his fingertips were beginning to dig through the table's surface. He withdrew them from the tabletop and slid them into his lap. 'It is not easy to overlook such deficiencies, but for the greater good...'

'Greater good,' Ron scoffed. '*Deficiencies!*'

LeiRain knew that the two of them were wrestling for power, or at least Ron was. Silver was trying to find a way into

Ron's trust. The dwarve had good reason for his trepidation, but LeiRain was impatient with the growing tension. She examined Silver. There were no wrinkles in his brow, no frown to indicate concern or anger. But his eyes... The pools of silver in them moved like rippling water. LeiRain cleared her throat.

'What if we don't find a weapon? Or some other proof?' she asked.

Both men turned to face her. They looked surprised, as if the heated exchange had made them forget that she was there.

'I know what they do. *Who* they are.' She clenched her fists under the table. 'I want to stop them from hurting anyone else.' *The way I've been hurt*, she thought. 'But what if we don't find something we can bring back to the verdaant?'

'We must,' Silver replied.

LeiRain found herself relieved that he had not challenged the *we* in her statement. She'd had little sense of purpose since losing her mother. The thought of stopping the Royals and avenging her Alarra's death breathed new life into her.

'There has to be evidence somewhere. I heard that they were commissioning the weapons from a skilled smith in a small seaside village. I went to find her.'

LeiRain shivered. *Her*. Alarra was the only woman black-smith along the entire coast. Ron emitted a soft growl and she clasped her shaking hands together as Silver went on.

The fae cleared his throat. 'The uh... The brothel the tracking spell led me to was in the same village as the smith. She was already dead when I found her and the forge disman-tled. Whoever got there first saved me a great deal of work.'

The placid look he'd worn since their meeting remained in place as he said this, making LeiRain that much angrier. She disentangled her hands and slammed her fists on the table, making both of the men start with surprise. The fae's quick silver eyes shifted to hers and one silver eyebrow went up in question. LeiRain quaked with the tumult of feelings she was holding back. How many people had been hunting her mother? And how could Silver be so callous about her death. Unable to understand LeiRain's reaction, Silver returned his focus to Ron.

'I asked after the smith, as much as I could anyway, without arousing suspicion. The villagers were none-too-friend, but they said there was a red-headed dwarve that came to the forge often.' His voice grew quiet. 'They say that this dwarve was the one who killed her, so I thought that perhaps you already knew what the smith had been up to, that you had already known of the weapon and acted to stop the Royals.'

'*No*,' LeiRain hardly recognized her own voice. She stood, resting her palms on the table and leaning forward. 'She would *never* have agreed to make weapons for the Royals. *Never,*' she hissed.

Silver's eyes widened, realization dawning.

'You knew her,' Silver said, but his voice was nearly drowned out by Ron's.

'Alarra was a friend,' he growled. 'And she would never – I would *never*—' He leaned forward in his chair, his face a bright red.

'You're talking about my mother,' LeiRain went on, not waiting for Ron to finish his sentence. She glared at Silver and he studied her in return. How could she have ever felt drawn to him?

The verdaant held up his hands in a placating gesture.

'I have made an error,' he said. 'It was just that ... she was human.' The rapid blinking of his eyes was the only outward sign of his discomfort. 'I didn't know and I assumed—'

'That she was a Royal? That just because she was human, she sympathized with them?' LeiRain looked between Silver and her shaking fists as she said this.

'Well,' the verdaant looked briefly at his lap. He swallowed, throat bobbing as he did so, then looked up to meet her gaze once more. 'Yes.'

LeiRain waited for his apology or for him to justify his assumptions. He only stared at her, his *yes* still echoing in her ears.

'So perhaps your information isn't quite as reliable as you think,' Ron broke in. His face was still red, the veins in his neck standing out, but he leaned back in his chair.

'Perhaps not,' Silver conceded, pulling his eyes away for LeiRain's to meet the dwarve's. 'But that does not change the fact that we must find this weapon, some proof of it, or some other tangible thing to convince my people to act.' His eyes moved back and forth between Ron and LeiRain, now, and she did her best to make her eyes into daggers. 'If not,' Silver continued, 'we will find ourselves persuading the verdaant to halt a war, rather than prevent one. Odro is known to be somewhat fastidious in his record keeping; it seems to be a bit of a joke amongst his employees, the degree to which they are required to track their actions, their expenses, the reports they have to submit. If nothing else, perhaps we can bring back documentation of what they are doing or the weapon they are building. There *must* be something on that island that will speak to the extent of their corruption.'

'I can tell you, she refused them,' Ron replied. 'The Royals approached Alarra. Several times in fact. But she would not create such a weapon for such men.' He shook his head. 'And whatever it was, it was so vile that she would not speak of it, even to me.'

Silver sighed and stared into the distance, thinking. LeiRain looked down at the table, studying the grains in the wood. She recalled the vulgar exchange her mother had with Ethan. It was difficult for her to accept that there had been so much more, and that Ron had been privy to this information when her mother hadn't shared any of it with her.

'Demi,' Ron broke in, his voice gentle, 'wouldn't you prefer to stay with Brya? You've been through so much already.'

'I'm going,' she said. If half of what Silver told them was true, LeiRain knew that they must act. Plus, after hearing what he'd thought of her mother, she couldn't leave it to the verdaant to address the problem. 'Whether you are or not.' She turned her dagger eyes on Ron as she said this.

'I think you will be of great value,' Silver said. 'Especially on a sea journey.'

Ron let out a sigh and shot a glare at Silver. He folded his hands over his long beard.

'And yet,' Ron said, his voice cracking slightly, and his brow creased, 'you need *me* to make this journey worthwhile.'

28

Sparring was going no better today than it had the day before. LeiRain found her mind overtaken by internal noise that did nothing to aid her in fending off Ron's onslaught. He moved slowly and deliberately, giving her a chance to pick up on his tells and anticipate his actions. Still, she failed to repel his strikes or land any blows of her own.

LeiRain did not know where Silver had disappeared to after breakfast but she was glad that he was not there to watch. She felt pride when Silver said that she would be of use to the mission and worried that he might change his mind if he saw her now.

'Did you see how I held my wrist straight there, Demi?' Ron kept his voice bright, sensing her frustration. 'You don't want to bend your wrist ~ if you keep it straight, you have the power of your whole arm behind the move. See?' He demonstrated, swinging his blade in the air with a force that sent a breeze over LeiRain's face. 'If your wrist and arm are aligned and you twist at the waist, you've got your entire torso powering the strike. Not only does the bent wrist make it more likely that you'll be injured, it makes your strike a lot less effective.'

She listened to Ron's correction and felt her face heat with anger. She hadn't meant to bend her wrist. Hadn't even realized she was. Ron went on instructing, not realizing that she could no longer hear him. Tendrils of her hair fluttered as his blade sliced through the air once more. *I'm never going to get this*, she thought. Seething, LeiRain pushed her shield over her shoulder and grabbed the hilt of her sword with both hands. She raised it in front of her, blade pointing down, and shoved it into the ground. She felt a satisfying crunch as it broke through the soil. There was a jolt in her arms as the ground resisted and she gave in to its force. LeiRain released her hold on the hilt, not caring that the blade hadn't pierced the soil deeply enough to remain upright. It toppled over as soon as she took her hands away.

She stood, panting, looking at her fallen sword. Ron had taught LeiRain to show care for her weapons. Even though the blade was made of sorcerer's steel and wouldn't dull, he'd encouraged her to treat her it with the utmost respect. She waited for him to scold her, but that wasn't his way. He only looked at LeiRain with one eyebrow raised questioningly as he waited for her to recover.

'And, uh,' he tugged on his beard, 'don't forget to pivot—' Her glare brought Ron's words to a halt before he could say, *on the ball of your foot*.

'I'm taking a break,' she said, turning to walk away. Anger coursed through her limbs as she headed toward the far side of the clearing.

LeiRain made her way toward the mountain spring. She could hear it before she saw it, bubbling with melted snow. The days were getting longer. Flower buds were beginning to open and bloom around the clearing. The mountain top snow would be gone soon. Pulling the guige over her head, LeiRain let her shield fall to the ground. It settled on the grass beside her feet with a heavy *thunk*. She sat next to it and stared at the water. Jagged pieces along the rockface caused tiny rivulets of water to diverge from the main body of the spring. LeiRain watched as their paths took them in different directions before ultimately bringing them back to rejoin the wider body of water.

'You are angry.' The voice came from only a few feet behind her. LeiRain gave a tiny squeak of surprise before turning to glare at Silver.

'For gods' sakes, you've got to stop sneaking up on me like that.'

'I apologize,' he said, sounding sincere. 'I am naturally light of foot. I don't mean to startle you.' He paused as one corner of his mouth twitched. Was he amused by this? LeiRain narrowed her eyes at him but the mask of serenity had already fallen over Silver's face once more. 'The sparring is not going well.'

It wasn't a question.

'No,' she stared ahead at the water.

'Your anger runs deeper than that.'

LeiRain stilled, holding her breath.

'I am intimately familiar with such anger,' he said, seeming once again to know her thoughts, 'and the pain that feeds this monster.'

LeiRain slumped forward as she exhaled, letting the tension fall off of her shoulders. What could he know of her anger, her pain?

'Would you like to be left alone?'

She opened her mouth to say *yes* but quickly closed it

without replying. *Did* she want to be left alone? She didn't know *how* to be around someone else while sorting through turmoil. LeiRain felt like she ought to be alone, but disliked the thought of him leaving. She decided to answer honestly.

'I don't know.'

Silver acknowledged this statement with a throaty *hmm.*

'Then,' he said, with a hint of humor, 'I will stay, but I will try not to be *too* here.'

Despite her dark mood, a small laugh escaped LeiRain's lips. She looked over her shoulder at him. He now sat cross-legged on the ground where he had been standing.

'What does that even mean?'

'I shall strive to be as exactly present as you need me to be, here but unoppressive in my *hereness.*'

She smiled at him and turned back around. She appreciated his offer to stay, that he wasn't pressing her to talk about what was wrong. Paradoxically, the fact that he did not expect her to open up to him made LeiRain wish to do so.

'My birthday is in a few days,' she forced the words out. She'd asked Brya for a calendar so that she could track her courses. LeiRain had known that her birthday was drawing near, but she hadn't realized just how near.

Silver remained silent, but she could feel him sitting there behind her.

'A year ago, on the eve of my majority, I spoke to my mother for the last time.' She swallowed, her throat suddenly feeling tight, 'And ... I was a shit.'

A long silence followed and LeiRain waited in trepidation.

'I see,' Silver replied. 'Your mother, *the blacksmith.*'

LeiRain's shoulders drew up toward her ears as she recalled the way Silver had spoken of Alarra before he'd known she was her mother.

'I would not have killed her,' Silver offered. 'I only meant that the forge—' His swallow was audible, 'If I'd found evidence that she was making weapons for the Royals, I would have had to destroy the forge.'

'Oh,' LeiRain said, breathily.

'I have seen enough death,' Silver continued, 'to want to avoid it whenever possible.'

LeiRain could not see him, her eyes downcast, but she could hear something new in his voice. Thus far, his words had mirrored the serenity on his face. Not now. He sounded like a man who was remembering, like someone pressing on a bruise.

'My words must have hurt you very much,' he went on. 'I'm sorry for them.'

LeiRain sighed and responded with a 'hmm.' She couldn't bring herself to say that it was okay, to say anything that meant she was accepting his apology.

'And I'm sorry that I made assumptions about her, simply because she was human.'

LeiRain blinked, looking at the water as she absorbed his words. She couldn't remember hearing such sincerity before, not in an apology. Alarra certainly hadn't been one for heartfelt apologies. The grass whispered as Silver shifted.

'I accept your apology,' LeiRain murmured, the words running together slightly. She was surprised at how good it felt to say them. A few moments of easy silence passed.

'Do you want to talk about it?' Silver asked.

She reached out and ran her fingertips over the top of the water. The cool stream was a stark contrast to the warm sun on the back of her hand. 'I don't know,' she replied, watching the water divert around her fingers.

'Loss is complicated by the fact that those we love, and

who love us, are also the ones we hurt most often. And they are the ones who most often hurt us.'

LeiRain nodded. Tears pooled in her eyes. She had never thought of it this way, but the truth of his words resonated with her. The two of them sat like this for a long time before she began to feel her anger ebb. As the emotions dispersed, her mind cleared and she remembered that she had left Ron standing on his own on the other side of the clearing. She should get back to her training.

'Thank you,' LeiRain said as she stood.

'You're very welcome, Rain.' His mercurial eyes bore into hers as he smiled. He had a look of genuine care on his face. LeiRain allowed herself to meet his gaze, this time ready when his power surged up to meet hers. She felt heady as her own magic stretched toward him. It was a relief to know that her magic was still there, even if she couldn't use it. When it met with Silver's, LeiRain could have sworn that the mountain stream grew louder and the nearby trees shuddered though there was no wind.

Silver's magic was gentle where it intertwined with hers, though LeiRain could sense that it was *very* strong. His magic felt sticky and sweet, like honey on her fingertips. Like a golden summer sky after she emerged from the ocean. It felt new but also nostalgic.

What might her magic feel like to him? She wondered what Silver was experiencing right now. He seemed just as taken in by their synergy. He leaned toward her, shoulders back and body rigid. LeiRain inched closer to him.

'I need to get back to training,' she said, breathlessly.

'Yes,' Silver nodded.

Neither of them moved away. Finally, LeiRain forced her eyes away from his. She kept her eyes averted from Silver as she bent to scoop up her discarded shield. Eye contact broken, the magic that had coiled around them withdrew. A shiver ran through LeiRain's body as she felt her magic curl back up inside her and go quiet. It felt like having the blankets pulled off of her on a cold winter's morning.

She didn't dare look back at him as she turned and walked briskly toward where she'd left Ron. The thought of those warm blankets taunted her, nudged her to turn back and meet the verdaant's gaze once more. She wanted to find that heat again – to feel her magic, alive and loud, pressed up against and entwined with his. LeiRain's heart stuttered. *I shouldn't let him get so close, see so much of me.* What had he done so far to prove himself trustworthy besides not killing any of them? Then again, it was difficult for LeiRain to imagine someone whose magic felt like *that* could possibly be untrustworthy.

Her mood was much improved when she resumed training. Her form was better, her steps lighter, her errors less frequent. She'd never spoken so candidly to anyone before, and she hadn't expected it to cause so much *feeling*. Speaking the words aloud made them more real, more painful, and harder to push away and ignore. She had not spoken of what had happened, of her feelings about it, since they'd left Harbor Village. Ron hadn't pressed her and she was certain he'd warned Brya off of doing so as well. LeiRain had been grateful for their lack of interest, but now she wondered if perhaps the silence had done her a disservice.

And when the magic rose up inside her and Silver's came to meet it... It was the most intimate thing she had ever experienced.

~

I t was a quiet night, the mood at dinner mellow. Ron had spent his afternoon hunting and had carried home a large deer, which he then spent the early evening cleaning and butchering. Brya and Ray had been tilling the garden, their faces flushed and brows furrowed with effort. Her own work was not much better; it was her turn to do the laundry today. She'd grown hot standing over the boiling water and her arms were tired from the work of stirring and then withdrawing the waterlogged fabrics. Silver had offered to help the dwarves with the gardening, assuring them that he could make the task much easier, but Brya was still wary of the verdaant and adamantly refused his assistance. Silver had slid out of view down the rough mountain pass afterwards. LeiRain did not know where he went but he hadn't returned until dinner. When he did, he seemed just as subdued by his day's work as the rest of them.

After months of wielding a sword, LeiRain's arms were corded with lean muscle and her endurance had improved significantly. Still, she ached from the day of chores. The motion she used with the paddle required slightly different muscles than those she was accustomed to working with her weapons. And it felt like the wooden instrument met more resistance with each load of washing. By the afternoon, she'd grown weary enough to wonder about her magic. The work would have been much easier if she didn't have to exert herself stirring. It had been months since she'd tried to connect with the water. Each failure had been more painful than the last and, after a while, it didn't seem worth the disappointment. Thanks to whatever it was that existed between her and Silver, LeiRain knew that the magic was still there. She just needed to draw it out. Hopefully, she pulled the laundry bat from the wash basin, closed her eyes, and felt for the water with her mind. Nothing. She felt no stirring, no tendrils of magic she could grab on to. LeiRain resumed her work with the paddle, disappointment making the chore seem much more arduous than it had before.

Silver had emerged in the clearing just as LeiRain was taking down the last of the sun-dried laundry. The two of them set the table together in silence as Brya chopped vegetables. Brya waited for Ron to finish cleaning his kill before she finished dinner so that she could throw some bits of venison into their stew. Wildlife had been sparse in the winter and this was the first time they'd had fresh meat in months. By the time dinner was ready, the sun had begun to set and the kitchen was growing dim. There was no conversation, their usual banter lost to the eager shoveling of food from bowl to mouth. They were all ready for a second helping within a few minutes of sitting down, except for Silver who was eating his stew with great care.

LeiRain stole glances at the verdaant as he painstakingly removed pieces of venison from his bowl. Silver examined each spoonful before he put it in his mouth and whenever he found a piece of meat, stealthily placed it in his napkin. Nobody else seemed to notice and LeiRain said nothing, not wanting to draw anyone's attention. They often snacked on salted meats during the day and LeiRain tried to recall whether or not she'd seen the fae eat any of it. She could not.

The rest of the table finished their second helping of dinner with waning enthusiasm as appetites were satisfied and fatigue took over. Once his hunger was sated, Ray's eyes began to close intermittently, his head bobbing over the empty bowl before him. Eventually, the boy's spoon fell from his slack hand and clattered onto the table. This signaled an end to the meal and Brya shooed her son off to bed. Ron excused himself shortly thereafter.

'I'll wash the dishes,' Silver said as Brya began to stack the bowls in the sink. LeiRain was still poking a spoon at her last few bites of stew. Her stomach was full, but she kept eating, finding the flavorful meal to be a comfort after such a long day. Brya eyed Silver warily with slumped shoulders and drowsy, hooded eyes.

'Alright then,' Brya said, running a hand over her face. She winced as her other hand pressed into the small of her back. 'See you in the morning.' She disappeared down the hall, feet shuffling.

Silver slipped his napkin from the table as he stood, picked up his bowl and carried it to the basin. Had LeiRain not seen him picking the meat from his dinner, she probably wouldn't have noticed him shaking the cloth empty over the waste bin. Silver looked up and caught LeiRain staring at him. Before her magic could respond, he averted his eyes and continued with the work of cleaning up.

'Verdaant do not eat animals,' he said softly, his eyes focused on the dish he was scrubbing.

'Oh,' LeiRain replied, dumbly.

'Plants grow at our will,' he continued, moving on to another bowl. 'So we have enough food without taking the life of another.' He *had* offered to help with the gardening, LeiRain recalled. 'But I did not wish to offend.'

'I'm sure Brya would understand,' LeiRain replied, softly. 'Does it bother you?' She asked. 'When others eat meat?'

He stared into the sink for several seconds before answering. 'It would please me to see the world in such peace that no man or woman was forced to take another life to survive. We may yet reach such an ideal, but I understand that this is not the world we live in today, and I do not judge others for seeing to their own survival.'

LeiRain finished her stew during this brief exchange,

though she left a few chunks of venison in her bowl untouched. She'd never hunted herself, and had never before thought of the life that was taken to put such food on her plate. She brought her bowl to the waste bin and deposited the meat before setting her dish next to the sink.

'Thank you,' she said as Silver continued cleaning. He nodded in response but kept his eyes on the dishes.

29

LeiRain slipped out of the kitchen into the cool dusk air. Sparring and drills always made her mind work just as hard as the rest of her body. Laundry washing, however, had allowed her mind to wander. Although her body felt heavy with fatigue, LeiRain's mind was alive with thoughts; sleep was a far off thing. She walked back to her dwelling and knelt in front of the fire, now little more than a few glowing embers after a day of neglect. Gently, LeiRain coaxed the flames back into existence before sitting down on the hearth rug and pulling the pins out of her hair. Strands fell in loose coils over her shoulders and down her back. Her curls had grown softer in the absence of salt water and she ran her fingers through them easily, unraveling what remained of her braids as she went. She massaged her scalp, enjoying the release of tension after a day with her hair up. LeiRain's eyes fell closed with pleasure.

Just as she was beginning to think she might be able to fall asleep, there was a loud pop that made her eyes shoot open and her heart race. She scanned the room, eyes darting to every shadow, before she realized that it was just the fire. She watched the flames dance and the shadows move with each flicker. LeiRain had built this fire, and now it had turned on her, pulling her back into memories of her mother's death. The smell of her home burning as she followed Ron through thick woods, the callous laughter of men receding into the distance. LeiRain had to get out of this room. Each crackle of the burning logs made the knot in her stomach grow tighter. Abruptly, she stood, draped a short cloak over her shoulders and walked toward the door with haste.

The door snicked shut cleanly behind her and LeiRain stood looking at a sky full of bright stars. Dusk seemed to have disappeared during the short time she'd been inside, though the night was cloudless and well-lit by stars and a large moon. Something about the night sky reminded LeiRain of the deep ocean, fathomless and cold. She imagined wading into the pool of blackness, deeper and deeper, until it swallowed her entirely. Her heart sped up as she remembered what that had felt like... The ocean coming up to meet her, her body descending slowly until she was submerged and all that surrounded her was water. LeiRain ached for the taste of salt water and the smell of brine. Perhaps her magic worked better in salt water and that was why it had not responded to her attempts to wield it here on the mountain. If salt water was the key, she just needed to get closer...

LeiRain let her awareness expand beyond her visible surroundings. She honed in on that extra sense, the one that told her where water began and where it ended. She could sense ponds, lakes, the stream nearby... LeiRain reached further. *There it is.* Her heart fluttered. She could almost taste the salt, feel the brine on her skin. It was a distant presence but she could feel its uneven edges stretch inland from time to time, an inlet not quite so far as the broader sea. It was probably brackish, a mixture of both salt and freshwater, but that was still more familiar than the fresh water she had here. LeiRain felt herself flush with excitement as she looked around the clearing. The doors were all closed, the light of the fire flickering through the kitchen window growing dim. A similar, though dimmer, glow showed through the window of her own dwelling and that of Ron's. The sun had only just set and the inlet didn't feel *so* far away – she could surely make it back before the others woke in the morning.

LeiRain crept to the edge of the clearing and began to work her way down the side of the mountain. The large moon and bright stars made it easier for her to traverse the difficult terrain, but she still found herself stumbling every few steps. In the daylight, she was always careful to put her feet exactly where Brya or Ron's had been. Now that she was on her own, LeiRain seemed to find every loose rock and protruding root. She could probably walk more gracefully if she moved at a slower place, but LeiRain was driven by an eagerness to feel the salt water again.

A few hours into her journey, she realized that she'd failed to bring any drinking water with her. The cold air made her throat feel scratchy and she'd begun to sweat with the exertion of nearly running down the mountain. LeiRain shook off her irritation at this oversight as she reminded herself of all the smaller bodies of freshwater she'd felt between her and the inlet. She'd find drinkable water soon enough. She just had to press on. But her process slowed when she reached the lower portion of the mountain. Its base and the flat land surrounding it were all covered with densely growing trees and brush.

LeiRain hadn't been this far away from the mountain hide since she'd arrived in the late fall and had forgotten how long it took her and Ron to make their way through these woods. The trees were filled with the sounds of chittering creatures and swaying branches. The dark shape of an owl flew so near that the tip of its wings nearly brushed her face. She caught the scent of fresh-turned earth when the bird's talons raked the soil, grabbing its prey. The trees blocked most of the terrestrial light so LeiRain had nothing to navigate with now save her connection to the water. She swallowed painfully, again wishing she'd brought something to drink, and tried to feel her way through the flora.

The further away she moved from the mountain's base, the darker it became until she was relying entirely on sound and the feel of bark under her palms to make her way through the woods without stumbling. Her head was constantly whipping around at the sound of a cracking branch or whisper of shifting leaves, but she could see almost nothing. Her long, loose hair caught on branches and the bark of trees. She wished that she'd left it in a braid. LeiRain initially moved with purpose and determination, powered by hope and longing, but now she began to sag under the weight of regret.

I've made a terrible mistake, she thought. Though the water might be only a few miles away, the miles were hard and slow. Even if she turned around now, the best she could hope for was to make it back to the hide before the others woke. How could she have been so stupid? So impulsive? It was the same way she had behaved on the eve of her majority, a year ago today. LeiRain felt a tightness in her chest. Her mother had died because of her impulsivity and selfishness and she had learned nothing from it. Her breaths were short and strained. She sniffled and swiped at her nose with a sleeve as tears began to burn behind her eyes. Sobs pressed against the inside of her throat as she tried to choke them off. LeiRain hated the way anger sometimes made her want to cry. Despite her best efforts, a groan escaped her lips.

'What was that?' A man's voice said.

LeiRain froze. Anger receded as her every sense focused on identifying the direction from which the voice had come.

'Just an animal,' someone replied.

LeiRain willed herself to be invisible, standing so still that she dared not even breathe.

'Sounded big,' the first voice replied after a long silence. She heard the scrape of a blade being drawn.

'Maybe a mountain lion,' the other voice sounded worried. LeiRain heard them draw another blade, 'You sure this is the direction the verdaant went?'

Was he talking about Silver? LeiRain couldn't hold her breath any longer. She tried to breathe with slow, shallow sips of air. No movement, no sound.

'No, but this is the best lead we have.' She heard the man swallow. Then, in a loud whisper he said, 'You don't think it's him, do you?' His voice quivered a little as he asked.

She heard the murmur of disturbed brush as one of the men pushed his way closer to her.

'Only one way to be sure.' His voice was closing in on her.

LeiRain's heart was beating so forcefully that she worried they would hear it. Slowly, carefully, LeiRain reached for the pommel of her sword. Her hand met with empty space. She remembered now, seeing her sword and shield leaning against the wall as she left her room, the opal reflecting the orange firelight. *How could she have been so foolish?* LeiRain had never commanded the water without the aid of her shield, so even if she had made it to the inlet, the trip was futile. What could she do now? If she ran, the men would hear her. Even if she got away from them, LeiRain would be leading the men straight to Ron's family. Straight to Silver, the verdaant these men must be searching for.

Something stirred in the brush on her left side and the man closest to her grunted. LeiRain heard a blade thunk into a nearby tree trunk as he swung blindly at whatever had agitated the shrubs. She sucked in a breath, the noise covered up by the sound of more branches rustling off to her left.

'What is that? Where's it going?'

'I think it's circling around us!'

LeiRain shuddered in relief as the men's footfalls moved heavily away from her. They crashed loudly through the foliage and she wondered how they could move so quickly through the dense woods. Slowly, she stood a little straighter, preparing to move quietly back in the direction from which she had come. Even if the men didn't find her, there *had* been something loud crashing through the woods. LeiRain had no weapon to defend herself against that or anything else lurking in the dark.

She turned to head back up the mountain. LeiRain took one long stride before halting, finding herself mere inches away from a muscled chest. She inhaled sharply and brought her hands up defensively before she realized it was Silver that stood before her. She swallowed back a cry of surprise. Despite her best efforts, LeiRain fell into the fae, unable to halt her momentum in time. Her cold fingers came into contact with his warm chest and she tried to push him away, but Silver's fingers were already wrapped tightly around her biceps.

Her eyes went up to his face. It was too dark to discern his expression, but LeiRain could tell that he wasn't looking at her. Silver was watching the men retreat, his eyes like glowing pools of molten metal. His tall figure looked menacing in the dark, and as she stared at him, the burning light in his eyes began to illuminate the rest of his features. There was nothing serene about his expression, now. The sharp angles of his face looked like they had been carved from wood and brought to life, a sentient embodiment of the forest, vengeful and deadly.

Silver's usually soft demeanor made it easy to forget how dangerous he was, but LeiRain clearly saw the ruthlessness with which Silver could wield his power. It frightened her, especially now that she was here alone with him, but it also made the magic inside her hum with pleasure.

After several seconds, Silver's head dipped down toward hers. LeiRain felt his hair brush against her cheek and she struggled to breathe, fearful of being alone with him and so far from Ron, without a weapon.

'I've led them away, but they will return.' Silver's voice slid through the night like the whisper of leaves, his warm breath tickling her neck. Heat grew in LeiRain's core. 'We must leave.'

Slowly, she withdrew her hands from where they rested against the flat of Silver's chest. Light-headed from all of the shallow breathing, LeiRain let herself suck in a lungful of air. She felt her breasts brush against his chest as she did so. There was something fresh about the way he smelled, like basil and lavender. His grip on her arms loosened slightly as he tugged her forward toward the mountain. She pulled back, resisting him.

'Where are you taking me?'

'Back to where you came from,' he said, confusion apparent in his voice.

'To ... the mountain?'

'Of course,' one of his hands dropped away from her. 'But we must go now, Rain.'

She let him lead her with the hand that remained on her arm. The path ahead of them seemed much smoother than it had on her way down and it took LeiRain a while to realize that this was because Silver was causing the tree roots and brush to bend out of the way.

'That was you,' she said. 'You made the trees rustle so that those men would follow them away from me.'

Silver didn't reply. LeiRain's voice was hoarse from the cold night air. She swallowed, trying to clear her throat but it made no difference. Without warning, Silver came to a stop. His hand on her arm was all that kept LeiRain from falling forward. She was shivering, as much from fear as from the cold. Why had he followed her and had he been so nearby this entire time? Something cool and smooth was pressed into her hand.

'Drink.'

It was a waterskin. LeiRain hesitated for only a moment, her thirst far outweighing any suspicions she harbored. She wiped her mouth with her sleeve when she was done and passed the skin back to him.

'You followed me.' It was barely a whisper, but there was an accusation in her voice. LeiRain's hands balled into fists at her sides in a vain effort to hide how much they shook. Her fingers itched for the pommel of her sword, not that it would do her much good against a verdaant. Several seconds passed where he did not reply. It was difficult to make out his expression in the dark, but he seemed to avoid looking her in the eyes. It made him seem almost sheepish, which caused LeiRain to take a step back in surprise. At the suddenness of the movement, Silver's head snapped up but he made no effort to restrain her.

'Why? What are you going to do to me?'

His molten eyes met hers.

'*Do* with you?' He shook his head. 'Rain, I saw you walk away from the safety of the hide with no weapons, no water, and hardly enough clothing against the elements.' He was right. Now that they had been standing still for a few minutes, LeiRain's hands and feet had gone numb with cold. LeiRain felt herself drawn in by those eyes and everything behind them. Her heart sped up once more and heat rose to her cheeks, although the purple blush of her skin would be invisible in the ink-black night. LeiRain felt her magic waking, stirring in response to the fae's, but before it could rise up, he looked away from her. 'I had to be sure...' Several uncomfortable seconds of silence filled the space between them. He turned abruptly and began walking up the mountain again.

'Be sure of *what?*' LeiRain followed close on his heels. He didn't answer for a few seconds, long enough that she thought he was ignoring the question. He stopped again and LeiRain halted behind him, grabbing a nearby tree to maintain her balance.

'I had to be sure that no harm came to you.' His voice was low and husky as he said this.

LeiRain's breath caught. Silver resumed walking but it was several seconds before she followed. LeiRain had a feeling in her stomach like she was falling. The way she did when a wave picked her up and carried her into shore. It was both exhilarating and a bit terrifying. She tried not to think too hard about what it meant.

'We'd best hurry if you want your nighttime foray to go unnoticed by the others,' he said over his shoulder.

Soon, the trees around them grew thin and Silver no longer had to move the brush from their path. The ground grew steeper. Just as LeiRain was bending to climb up on all fours, Silver turned and offered her his hand. She hesitated for a moment before putting her hand in his. His fingers were warm as they curled around her wrist and he pulled her over one of the more difficult patches of terrain. LeiRain remembered how he'd smelled her blood and wondered if his senses were heightened enough to hear her heart speed up at the skin-to-skin contact. If they were, he gave no hint of it. They paused one more time before cresting the final rock scramble.

'Can I ask what exactly you were doing?' Silver looked at her with an eyebrow raised.

LeiRain looked at the ground, too embarrassed to meet his eyes, and wrapped her arms around herself.

'I...' She had no idea how to explain herself without sounding ridiculous. 'Before, when I was near the ocean, I had magic.' LeiRain bit at the dry skin on her lower lip. 'I haven't been able to use it since—' *Since I saw my mother murdered.* 'Since I came here. I thought maybe it was only the salt water I could control, that if I were closer to the ocean, maybe...' LeiRain let the sentence trail off. 'Do you think they will come back? I think... I think they were looking for you.'

Silver sighed. 'They *might*, but I don't think they will. I don't think they would have ever gotten so near me if I hadn't been following you.'

'I'm sorry,' she whispered. 'I didn't mean to– I just– please don't tell anyone. I didn't think about the hide and everyone else's safety.' She rubbed her tired eyes. 'I just wanted to find my magic again.'

Silence followed this declaration and, eventually, she forced herself to look up at his face. The sky was lightening and the warm orange tones of the rising sun were reflected in his smooth, silver strands. He extended a hand toward LeiRain, brushing her cheek lightly with his fingers as he reached for her hair. To her surprise, she felt a light tug on her scalp. Silver pulled his hand away. He held up a surprisingly large twig. The sadness disappeared from his face, replaced by his usual mask of calm. It happened so quickly that LeiRain wondered if she'd imagined the whole thing.

'You've got quite a large bit of forest clinging to your hair,' he said, his voice giving away no particular emotion. 'You'll want to do a thorough job of brushing it all out before break-fast. Ron might not notice, but I suspect that Brya will. It won't matter that I've kept your secret if you sit down at the table looking like *that*.'

The ghost of a smile passed over his lips before he took a few easy steps up the last climb and disappeared from sight. LeiRain scrambled after him but by the time she stood in the clearing, Silver was nowhere to be seen.

30

LeiRain slunk into the kitchen after tidying herself up, hopeful that nobody else had noticed last night's foray or realized that today was her birthday. Silver slid into the room gracefully and sat across from her, his demeanor giving nothing away of her misadventure from the night before. Desperate for the energy boost, LeiRain finished her coffee more quickly than usual and stared into the bottom of the empty mug, longing for a second cup. Given the rise in Royal presence, they were rationing supplies to avoid any extra trips into the villages, so she tried to content herself with an extra serving of porridge instead. LeiRain sat down after refilling her bowl and blinked in confusion at the full mug that sat in front of her chair.

Silver tapped his fingers lightly on the table, and she looked up at him. One corner of his mouth curved up slightly, and he *winked*. She was almost as surprised by this playful gesture as she was by his generosity. LeiRain nodded and mouthed *thank you* before sitting down to enjoy the coffee he had given her.

After breakfast, LeiRain forced herself to run through a

few sword drills, mostly to avoid suspicion. The dark circles under her eyes were a constant now, but she'd seen herself in the mirror this morning and knew that she looked a bit paler than usual. Brya had narrowed her eyes at LeiRain when she'd come to breakfast, but had made no comment. After lunch, they all took to their various chores and LeiRain did her best to avoid Brya's gaze as they both dug up root vegetables in the garden. By the time they sat down to dinner, LeiRain felt as if she'd fallen down the mountain and then been trampled by goats. Her body was sore in a way she hadn't experienced for months and her head throbbed with the need for sleep. She rubbed at her temples between spoonfuls of dinner.

'Headache?' Brya asked.

LeiRain nodded in response.

'I've got just the thing.'

LeiRain didn't argue when, a few minutes later, Brya set a small tablet down in front of her. It gave off a pungent odor that was evident even before she picked it up.

'Put it in your mouth and chew,' Brya commanded.

LeiRain wrinkled her nose as she obeyed, working her jaw frantically so that she could be done with it as soon as possible. After she'd swallowed, Brya offered her a cup of sweet smelling tea. LeiRain accepted, swishing the drink around her mouth to rid herself of the pill's bitter taste. The pain receded as she finished the rest of her dinner and was soon replaced by a thick drowsiness.

'You'd best go lay down now. We'll handle the clean up,' Brya said. She brushed a gentle hand against LeiRain's cheek, and LeiRain found herself leaning into it slightly, the drowsiness of the tea making it hard to resist the motherly gesture.

'Alright,' LeiRain said through a yawn. She left the table and stumbled to her room, just managing to change into bed clothes before she collapsed face down on the mattress.

. . .

W hen LeiRain woke, her headache was gone and the sun had set. Though the heaviness of exhaustion still weighed down her limbs, her mind was clear enough to begin worrying. She found herself pacing the room in a frenzy, twisting her hands together as she tried to push away unwanted memories. The relief she'd felt in confiding to Silver the day before had faded, and once again she was alone with regret and a sadness so deep that it soured her insides. Still in her bedclothes, LeiRain felt nauseated and claustrophobic.

She plucked her sword and shield from where they lay on the hearth rug and stomped toward the door. With a shuddering breath, she stepped out into the moonlight. LeiRain stood there for several seconds taking desperate lungfuls of mountain air. She had expected the briskness to enliven her, had hoped it would relieve the nausea she now felt. But the night air did nothing to ward off troubling thoughts or the growing feeling of sickness. The cold burned her lungs and, with little warning, she found herself heaving up the contents of her stomach.

LeiRain's eyes watered and her abdomen ached with the force of her retching, which continued until there was seemingly nothing left to be ejected from her stomach. She walked with bare feet toward the sound of running water, only half conscious of her direction as something deep and instinctual tugged her forward. When she reached the water's edge, LeiRain let herself collapse on the ground. Her sword rested beside her without its sheath. LeiRain let one edge of the freshly polished shield rest against the ground in front of her. She made it lean toward her at an angle so that she could set her forehead against the cold, hard edge. She released a long, slow breath. Her stomach seized, threateningly, and then relaxed. LeiRain took a few more deliberate breaths, willing her heart to slow its thundering and the sickness to recede. The nausea abated. Relieved, she lay down her shield and knelt over the stream, collecting water in her hands so that she could rinse out her mouth. As she spat, LeiRain heard a rustling sound nearby and then the clearing of a throat.

'That is one way to purge yourself of feelings,' Silver said.

She felt the corner of her mouth quirk up in a half-smile as she realized that he had intentionally made noise on his approach. She wanted to thank him, but was afraid to open her mouth lest she vomit again.

'Memories?' he asked, simply.

She nodded her head.

'Can I ... is there anything I can get you?'

She shook her head. 'Could you just be unoppressive in your hereness, again?' She whispered.

'Of course.' He stepped over the stream and sat across from her as she sat back and brought her knees to her chest.

'I *wish* I could get rid of my anger so easily,' she said, and meant it. 'It's just so present, all of the time.' Even before she'd lost her mother, LeiRain had carried around so much anger.

'I sense that you keep it at the ready, to don like armor when your soul feels too bare.'

She flinched. Was she so easy to read? Or...

'Can fae read minds?' she asked, her voice full of suspicion. Had he been privy to all of their thoughts this entire time?

He laughed, then his face became serious.

'No, but I have walked a parallel path to yours, I think. I know how to wear anger to cover my grief and shame like a second, much-thicker skin. I know how to cover up the uglier things with it.'

'Isn't anger itself ugly?'

Her response was reflexive and it was only after she'd said it that LeiRain wondered if she'd missed an invitation to ask Silver about his past. He always seemed so even keel and unaffected, it was difficult to imagine Silver warring with something like shame or grief. It was even more difficult to imagine him feeling genuinely angry.

'It can be ugly, but sometimes it's all we have to hold ourselves together.'

Yes, that's exactly what anger had done for her. It had shored her up, given her strength when she wanted to crumble.

'It won't work forever, Rain. Not if you want to be happy again.'

Aside from those few days in Corallis, the memories of which were now tinged with regret, LeiRain wasn't sure she'd ever been happy.

'Or,' he continued, 'if you ever want to wield your magic again.'

LeiRain had been listening to him while staring at the moving water. Now, her eyes snapped to his face. She felt nausea roll over her once more and she clutched at her stomach.

'What does...?' Her heart beat so loudly now that she struggled to hear her own thoughts, to find the words she was looking for. 'Why does it get in the way of my magic?'

'Elemental magic obeys not because you force it to, but because it wants to. It is a part of you, the water, the wind—'

'The wind?' LeiRain fisted the thin fabric of her shift just over her stomach. She swallowed back the bile that was rising in her throat.

'Yes, surely. Perhaps your connection with the water is

stronger, but I feel the power you possess, and I believe the wind will answer your call as well.'

She looked at the stream, leaning her body toward it without thinking. Their eyes remained locked, but her free hand slid across the grass until her fingers were only inches from the water. LeiRain shook her head, frowning.

'The water won't even respond to me now.'

'These feelings stand between you and the elements, just as they stand between you and those who care for you.'

She looked at him and he looked back with sad eyes.

'When you push these feelings away, and cover them up with anger, you push away everything else, too. You cut yourself off from hurt, but you also cut yourself off from happiness, joy, love ... and magic.'

LeiRain felt sick again and cringed, breaking eye contact. Sweat ran down her temples despite the cold. Determined not to throw up, she reached a hand into the stream, splashed water on her face and held her hand over her eyes until the nausea passed. She then dipped both her hands in the stream and ran them through her hair before winding it into a tight braid. For a few minutes, the wet on her face and the damp hair felt refreshing but it didn't take long for LeiRain to start shivering.

Silver stood and offered her a hand. 'Here, let's go warm up.'

She shook her head, keeping her eyes on the water.

'No, I don't want to go inside. I don't want to be by the fire. It reminds me...' she trailed off, but he seemed to catch her meaning.

'I'll use fae light, but at least come and get out of the wind.'

She took his hand and let him lead her into the shelter he'd made for himself. Inside, he motioned for her to sit, and she watched in silence as he moved the soil with a few sweeps of his hand, creating a small hole in the ground between them. She didn't understand Silver's purpose until he created a ball of warm fae light and placed it in the hole. With another wave of his hand, the soil smoothed over the fae light, and LeiRain began to feel the ground beneath her warm. He did this twice more, burying orbs of light throughout the enclosure until warmth emanated from the ground. LeiRain hadn't realized how cold she was until her feet and hands began to thaw. She allowed her body to uncoil as the chill receded and now sat with her legs splayed out in front of her, leaning back on her palms.

'I killed my brother,' Silver said, breaking a long silence.

Her eyes raked over his body as she brought them up to his face. LeiRain watched him, examining his features. She was careful to avoid eye contact, knowing the breathless rush that came with falling into his gaze. He was frowning and his brows were drawn together. A tiny muscle jumped in his jaw as he clenched his teeth. LeiRain did not know what to say or how to respond.

'At least that is what I believed for a very long time.'

She shook her head, struggling to imagine such a thing. She had found the verdaant to be unexpectedly kind and reminded herself now that he was equal in power to her father. Her father, she had gathered, had murdered her grand-parents and left her mother living in fear. Perhaps Alarra had once believed her father to be kind too.

'Therris was thirty years my senior.'

Silver, an immortal, was probably much older than he looked if there could be a thirty-year age gap between siblings.

'I looked up to him very much. He was an advocate for those less powerful than the fae, and this did not endear him to the traditionalists in verdaant society. Most of my kind,' he said, looking up from the ground and into her eyes, 'believe fae to be superior beings, worthy of more consideration than other sentients who are shorter lived.' LeiRain swallowed and tried to summon the strength to break eye contact. 'Therris believed that we should not live in such isolation from others and spoke often of the benefits we might experience by integrating with other races.'

His eyes slipped away from her face and looked back down at the ground again.

'My parents – no, my *father* did not agree, though they humored him for quite a while. Until he decided to take a non-fae lover.'

'Just to prove a point?' LeiRain asked, carefully.

'No, I – I don't think so now, but maybe I did then.' Silver sounded thoughtful. 'Now, I believe that he truly loved Rhoon. She was of mixed heritage…'

'A blend,' LeiRain offered.

'Yes. Her mother was a pixie and her father was of undetermined heritage himself. When our parents learned of the relationship and Therris's plans to mate with her, my father felt that the indulgence had gone too far. He and a number of more senior verdaant planned to kill Rhoon, thinking that this would rid them of the problem. They recruited me to their cause, though I did not know at the time that they planned to kill her, only that they planned to spirit her away. To separate them.

'They told me that it was for her safety, as well as his, and filled my head with fear. My father spoke of how dangerous it was to mix the blood of fae with that of mortals; expressed concern over Rhoon's fate should she become pregnant with my brother's offspring. The others spoke of how important it was that Therris mate with one of our kind, emphasizing the low birth rates among verdaants and the importance of continuing our line.'

'Was there any truth to this?' LeiRain was reminded of the water elves and the infrequency with which they bore children.

'Some,' he said, and when their eyes met this time, his brimmed with unshed tears. LeiRain felt an unexpected tenderness, a desire to comfort him. She made no move to do so, but her magic reached for him, tenderly brushing against his power. Silver's breath hitched slightly but he went on.

'Verdaants have a very low birth rate. Some mates attempt for centuries without producing offspring. But the danger of *crossbreeding*, as my father put it, is entirely false. He simply did not want the *shame* of such a grandchild.

'I didn't see this at the time, and the elders made me feel quite important by involving me in their plan. My job was to lace my brother's drink with a kind of poison – the only substance known to slow a verdaant's healing; the ash of foxglove.'

'The *flower?*' LeiRain hadn't meant to interrupt but surprise had overtaken her self-control. She watched Silver's throat bob as he swallowed.

'I should not tell you this, but for reasons unknown to me, I trust you deeply,' he stared directly into her eyes now. 'But yes. It's such a threat to our kind that verdaant have buried fields of the flower, smothering them in dirt so that they cannot spread and even their remains cannot be burned.'

His eyes swept over her, resting on her mouth for a long moment before meeting her gaze once more. LeiRain no longer tried to resist eye contact.

'Rain, you must not—' Was that fear in his eyes? 'I don't know why I told you—'

'I won't tell anyone,' she said, cutting him off. LeiRain did not understand why he had entrusted her with this precious information anymore than she understood her own feelings of tenderness for him. But she knew she would keep his secret.

'Thank you,' his words were soft, barely audible. LeiRain felt the familiar hum of energy between them before he turned away once more and continued:

'Ash of foxglove does not only slow our healing. It also strips us of magic for a time. My father made it my job to slip some ash into Therris's drink. He said... He said it was only so that they could weaken him. It was meant to disable him just long enough to take Rhoon away. My father told me that he would explain to her the dangers of a relationship with a verdaant. He said that he was certain my brother had not done so and that he was doing her a great favor. I was told that he would take Rhoon somewhere she could live out her years safely, far away from my brother, far away from our people.' His hands clenched into fists.

LeiRain thought of her own father, who clearly had no qualms with impregnating a human. But perhaps he had rejected LeiRain for the same reasons that Silver's father rejected the idea of Therris and Rhoon. Perhaps he felt she was unworthy of his attention because she was not wholly tempest. Did her father believe LeiRain was unable to survive the world in which he lived? She had never given much thought to the grandparents on her father's side, but now she wondered if her own father had a family who disapproved of his dalliances with a human.

'I was the only one—' Silver seemed to be struggling to get his words out now. 'The only one that he trusted, so I was the only one who could get close enough to him. He knew they disapproved, understood better than I did what was at stake. So, I gave him the drink and told my father once it was done.'

'I wasn't there when they came for her, but my brother could hardly put up a fight, his powers stripped away by the poison I had given him. They didn't *take her away* as they had promised. They killed her. Murdered Rhoon right before my brother's eyes. My father thought that this would rid Therris of his ideas about integration. Instead, it broke him. The female he loved was dead by the hands of his kin, and he must have known at that point that I had betrayed him as well. With the foxglove still in his system, he stabbed himself in the heart with the same knife my father had used to cut his lover's throat.'

One of her first thoughts was that the verdaant sounded remarkably like Royals in their disdain for otherness, but she knew that Silver must already be painfully aware of this. Ron had certainly taken every opportunity to point this out.

'Thank you for telling me this,' she said. 'For trusting me with ... all of it.'

'I wanted you to know.' His voice was a whisper. 'To understand that you do not have to live in your pain and regret forever. I've had to learn to forgive myself for the role that I played, for the things that a young, foolish version of me did. I'm not the same person as I was then, and you, too, are more than your mistakes – whatever they might be.'

LeiRain let the words settle over her. Her mind was usually quick to swat away hopeful sentiments, but Silver had been so open and vulnerable with her that she couldn't bring herself to reply with a snide remark. The adrenaline that had coursed through her when she fled her room began to fade away. Without it, LeiRain was left feeling groggy and weak.

She shifted her weight between her hands before deciding to lean back on her elbows, and from there it was only a small shift to lay back fully, prone on the fae-light-warmed grass. She rested her hands over her abdomen, which was already feeling sore from the heaving. She did not want to fall asleep, afraid of what dreams may come, but felt the fatigue winning out as her eyelids fluttered.

'Silver,' his name came out as a whisper. 'How old are you?'

If she hadn't been so tired she might not have asked, but her exhaustion was like wine in the way it erased her inhibitions. The words slipped from her easily. He laughed softly.

'Eighty-seven. Still young for a verdaant.'

'Eighty-seven,' she repeated before drifting off.

31

LeiRain opened her eyes to bright rays of sunlight piercing through the branches overhead. It took her a few seconds to remember where she was, where she'd fallen asleep. It was a mystery to LeiRain how she'd slept so soundly. If she'd dreamed last night, she didn't remember any of it and for that she was grateful. But as consciousness crept in, she began to process the reality of her situation. LeiRain was normally up well before the sun so Ron was probably waiting for her outside. This made LeiRain bolt upright, pulling her legs beneath her to stand but before she could do much else, a wave of dizziness overtook her. LeiRain swore and clutched a hand to her head.

'You sat up a bit too quickly, I think,' Silver said from nearby.

She turned her still-spinning head in his direction and saw him kneeling there, shirtless, holding a cup out toward her. 'Water,' he said, pushing the container into her hand. Still in a crouch, LeiRain took the cup from him and drank until it was empty. She remained where she was, with her knees bent, bottom only inches off the ground, waiting for her head to clear. At first, she kept her eyes downcast, but without meaning to, her gaze trailed up Silver's body, taking in his taut stomach and smooth, hard chest. Her eyes came up to his face as she finally stood.

'If I don't hurry, Ron will be waiting for me.' She hoped that Silver would understand what that implied, the awkwardness she would feel if Ron saw her leaving here in nothing but her shift.

'He is already waiting,' Silver replied. He gave her an apologetic smile.

'Shit,' she whispered. *Shit shit shit.* 'How long?'

'Maybe a half hour.'

She turned toward the arch of parted branches that marked the doorway.

'Rain, wait,' he warned. She spun back around to face him. 'You threw up your entire dinner last night, and then some.'

With this reminder, LeiRain became aware of the bitter taste in her mouth. She swallowed, her mouth dry despite the water, and felt her face twist in disgust. Her hand twitched, wanting to cover the lower half of her face. She knew it was too late to matter. With such keen senses, Silver must have already smelled her rancid breath. He stood up now and took a few steps toward her, closing the distance between them. She forced herself not to flinch away.

'I think you should eat something before you do anything else,' he said. Silver extended his hand to her, a small bowl resting on his palm.

'I got this for you before you woke up.'

LeiRain stared at the bowl. Her stomach ached with emptiness but she was afraid to eat something after having been so sick. She also worried about Ron, what she would say to him when he saw her. Part of her wanted to forgo breakfast just to get the confrontation over with. Silver took another step forward. He was so close to her now that the bowl nearly touched her collar bone. Finally, she accepted his offer. She ate slowly, taking small bites of the bread, mushy from being soaked in goat's milk. Silver produced a pitcher from behind him and refilled her water cup as she ate. LeiRain finished the modest meal and downed another glass. With that little bit of food in her stomach, she already felt better; the world was less fuzzy and her mind clearer.

As the fog of sleep and sickness left her, LeiRain looked down at herself and let out a heavy sigh. If her nightclothes were immodest in the moonlight, they were scandalous in the morning sunshine. Fresh, morning air made its way up her shift and her nipples, which were clearly visible through the pale fabric, perked in response. LeiRain looked back at Silver. Warmth rushed to her neck and cheeks and she knew her skin was flushing purple. The rush of it made LeiRain feel light-headed again and she swayed slightly. Silver's eyes flicked down to her breasts then quickly back to her face. She was surprised to see a similar flush overtake him as he reached out and gripped her arm to steady her. But the fae was the least of LeiRain's concerns. What would Ron think? Silver withdrew his hand after LeiRain had ceased swaying. His tunic and cloak both lay neatly on the ground and he picked up the latter, holding it out to LeiRain.

She squeaked a thanks as she draped the cloak around her shoulders. There would be no hiding the fact that she was in her bed clothes, but at least there would be something left for the imagination if she couldn't sneak past Ron. LeiRain held the cloak closed with a fist, swallowed a thick lump in her throat and stepped outside.

Any hope she'd had of passing unseen vanished when she spotted Ron perched on a boulder near her door. The dwarve held a steaming mug of coffee in one hand whilst the other rested lightly on the handle of his ax. There was no way for her to get into her rooms without him seeing but she couldn't hide here all day in her shift. LeiRain paused, recalling that she'd brought her weapons with her last night. Where was her sword and shield? She scanned the clearing and saw no sign of them. Just as LeiRain was about to turn back and ask Silver, Ron caught sight of her. It took him a few seconds to register what he was seeing but when he did, his eyes widened with shock and he choked on the sip of coffee he'd just tried to swallow.

Determined to feel no shame, LeiRain walked confidently toward the door to her room. She and Silver had done nothing wrong. They hadn't laid together, just slept near each other, and even if it had been something more, LeiRain was free to lay with whomever she pleased. She was an adult. Twenty now, a full year past her majority. At least for anyone who hadn't spent half the year in a time-warded, underwater city. Ron had no right to interfere or to judge. *Especially*, she thought, *since he himself visits brothels*. Her thoughts became less brave as she drew closer to him, but she refused to let anything but confidence show on her face. LeiRain's eyes looked straight forward and she forced her chin to remain up and her shoulders back, even though her hands shook inside the cloak. She clutched it more tightly to hide this from Ron.

The dwarve said nothing other than a mumbled *good morning* as she passed. LeiRain wasn't sure if she was relieved at this or disappointed. He'd never been one to nag, but she had an uncomfortable feeling that he would revisit this with her sooner or later. She suspected that only shock kept him from saying something just now. She slid past him and into her dwelling and was relieved to see that both sword and shield were inside, propped against the wall near the door. The shield was well-shined and her sword had been returned to its sheath. Silver must have stowed them for her after she'd drifted off.

'Be with you in just a minute,' she called to Ron, before latching the door behind her.

LeiRain put on proper clothes and washed her face with a basin of cool water and a small piece of soap. She rubbed a mixture of charcoal, salt and mint leaves over her teeth and tongue before using a small brush to clean them. She had to do this twice to get the foul taste out of her mouth. When she finished, the water in her basin was cloudy. There was no sink in her room so she would have to dump it outside later. Finally, LeiRain brushed and rebraided her hair then walked toward the door. She picked up her weapons without giving herself time to think about what waited for her outside.

'You'll want to do a few drills to warm up first,' Ron suggested. He seemed to have gotten over his shock and was now acting as if nothing unusual had transpired. It was a dance with which LeiRain was intimately familiar.

They moved routinely through the rest of the morning's training without so much as acknowledging the less than ordinary start to the day. When Silver walked past them just before breakfast, both LeiRain and Ron ignored him entirely. LeiRain began to think that Ron might not address the awkwardness from that morning at all, which suited her just fine. As soon as the verdaant's tall figure disappeared into the kitchen, Ron waved off her attempt at another round of sparring.

'Nah,' he said, 'It's time to eat. You've done well this morning.'

LeiRain gave him a genuine smile. She *had* done well this morning, despite the rough start. The night of dreamless sleep had been good for her. There was also something invigorating about being entrusted with Silver's secrets, even if she felt a tiny bit guilty for keeping them from Ron.

'You're doing that more these days,' Ron said. LeiRain watched him from the corner of her eye as she sheathed her sword.

'Doing what?'

'Smiling.'

'Am I?' she asked.

She tried to sound unmoved, but it was now clear that Ron's earlier hesitance to confront her had been strategic. He had wanted to make sure that Silver, with his heightened senses, was out of hearing range before initiating this conversation.

'You know you are,' Ron replied. 'And I'm glad of it, Rain.'

She looked at him, frowning, unnerved by his genuineness.

'You are?'

'Of course I am, Demi,' he said, sliding back into using his old nickname for her.

The extent of his caring was plainly visible on his face. Her heart clenched and LeiRain blinked back tears. Ron had been a family friend for as long as she could remember. She saw now that this friendship had grown into something more. Even though Ron had been careful not to broach any sensitive topics with her, not to push LeiRain into sharing her grief, he had been there for her always. What she had interpreted as emotional distance was actually deep care and respect.

'Thank you,' her voice cracked as she said this. She turned to hurry inside. The conversation had crossed over into that uncomfortable territory of soft feelings.

'Of course,' came his reply from behind her, 'But be careful there.'

She stopped in her tracks at the warning in his voice.

'Careful of what?' she asked, her hand hovering over the door handle. Anger began to slide over the top of all the things she'd been feeling.

'He's not your healing.'

LeiRain spun around to face Ron.

'I never said he was,' she spat. All of the affection that she had felt just moments ago disappeared.

'I know you didn't but...'

'But what?'

'Demi, I...'

'Don't call me that,' she snapped back. She felt angry at being mistaken for a demi-god, even though it had been her choice not to share the truth of the fae with him.

'Rain... I'm just saying that you've lost a great deal. Even before – your mother left something to be desired in raising you...'

'What do you know about my mother?'

'A great deal more than you might think, De—... Rain. I knew Alarra for a long time and she didn't have an easy childhood, so it's not surprising that she struggled...'

'You know nothing of my mother. You came and you went. You were nothing more than a customer.' She knew the words were false even as they fell from her mouth. 'My mother raised me well enough,' she said. 'And I don't need to take relationship advice, *healing* advice,' she swallowed, preparing for her final blow, 'from someone who failed to protect his own family and buries his troubles in alehouses and the sheets of brothels.'

Ron closed his mouth and his face went white. LeiRain held his injured gaze for a few seconds before she stalked off toward the kitchen, not sparing him a backward glance.

The door closed behind her and she knew by the looks on their faces that Brya, Rayand, and Silver must have all heard her shouting. She painted a smile on her face as she pulled out a chair. Brya set a bowl of hot porridge in front of her without speaking. Silver passed a steaming carafe of coffee. LeiRain took it gratefully, inhaling deeply as she filled her mug. She focused on the honey she drizzled into her bowl when she heard the door open behind her. No one said a word as Ron came in and sat down.

The only sound to be heard over the meal was the thunk and shuffle of earthenware on the table. LeiRain glanced up briefly to see Silver watching her with concern and she quickly looked away. As the silence stretched and LeiRain's temper cooled, even the generous helping of honey could not prevent her porridge from tasting like ash in her mouth.

32

———————

In the days that followed LeiRain's outburst, a quiet understanding settled between her and Ron. They maintained a delicate peace that depended on the willingness of all five parties to behave as though nothing had happened. This was second nature to LeiRain, but there were times when she thought that it was not so easy for Ron – pauses in training when she thought he might be struggling to find the right words. But they always rolled back into sparring without anything being spoken.

And there was the drinking. Rain had seen Ron drunk on several occasions during his respites in Harbor Village, but since they'd been with Brya and Rayand, he drank sparingly. Since the fight, he'd been downing a heavy glass of ale or mead with dinner and even after lunch if they were done training for the day. She hadn't witnessed him drunk and stumbling the way he had been when leaving taverns in the village, but he'd been emerging from his dwelling much later in the mornings with dark circles under his eyes, and he smelled like a distillery whenever he sweated. Every time

LeiRain saw him like this, something clenched in her gut and she averted her gaze.

She was responsible for his state, but couldn't bring herself to apologize. LeiRain knew that he'd been right about her mother, and about Silver. While there was something between her and the verdaant that made her insides sing, it couldn't relieve LeiRain of the heaviness she'd carried since leaving Harbor. LeiRain had thought that Ron did her a favor by never talking about her loss, never asking her about her feelings. Now, she felt resentful that he hadn't done so. Until he'd suspected her of consorting with Silver, Ron had been content to let LeiRain wrestle these demons on her own. Instead of telling him how she felt, she'd gone on the offensive and wounded him. It had been a cheap shot, mentioning the brothel. LeiRain regretted it, but couldn't figure out how to take the words back. Even more galling was the realization that this proved Ron's point about her upbringing. Alarra had never really demonstrated an apology and had left LeiRain with a deficit in relationship-mending skills.

Over the few days following the encounter with Ron, LeiRain had also shied away from Silver. They continued to exchange glances over the kitchen table, but he hadn't made an appearance during any of her early morning solo warm-ups, and she had gone out of her way to avoid the running water where they always seemed to meet. Even as she kept her head turned away from his shelter, LeiRain felt pulled in that direction. She told herself it was just the call of the water but eventually, she began to accept that she was drawn intensely to Silver. After three days of nothing but coy glances, LeiRain planted herself on the ground in front of the stream – as near to his shelter as she could get without being able to peer in through the open arch.

She sat toward the climbing face of the mountain,

watching for Silver's approach in her peripheral vision. She saw him before he could make a warning rustle of leaves and she turned to face the fae as he approached. She was getting used to the idea that he was fae: an immortal but not an indestructible god. It made him seem more ... like her. Flawed, tired and somehow persevering.

Silver's face wore the usual mask of calm and, when he smiled at her, LeiRain couldn't stop herself from smiling back. Her mind flashed back to when she'd stood before him in nothing but her shift. LeiRain wondered how clearly he'd been able to see her curves as morning light cut through the thin cloth. The thought made heat rush to her face. Dropping her smile, LeiRain bit her lower lip and turned her face to the side in a vain attempt to hide the telltale flush of purple on her cheeks. When she dared look back at him, Silver's own cheeks were darkened with a hint of blue.

She pursed her lips, delighted by his blush, heat rushing to other parts of her body now. He sat beside her, his shoulder nearly brushing hers, as they both looked up at the mountain. LeiRain felt the cool rush of water to her right, and the presence of Silver to her left. She shifted her weight slightly to get more comfortable and let out a huff of surprise as her thigh came into contact with his. He was so *close*. LeiRain tried to dredge up feelings of suspicion and doubt, to recall the fear she'd once experienced in his presence, anything to keep some kind of wall between her and this man that Ron distrusted. But her body and her magic betrayed her in their desire to be near him.

'I should have woken you sooner,' Silver said. She glanced sideways at him. He was frowning slightly. 'I didn't think about... I just thought perhaps you do not often sleep so well. It seemed unkind to wake you, but now I see that it was unkind to let you sleep.'

'No, it's fine. Ron's just' – she motioned toward Ron's private quarters – 'protective of me, I think. And really, that was the best I've slept in a long time.'

'There's something about the warmth of fae light that soothes.'

'And you,' she said, the words tumbling out of her mouth before she could stop them. LeiRain drew her knees to her chest and wrapped her arms around them. She rushed to change the subject before he could reply.

'How long ago was– did your brother die?'

She had just barely stopped herself from saying *was your brother murdered,* knowing that Silver had struggled with feeling responsible for his brother's death.

'Forty-some years ago.' There was no hesitation in his reply, so perhaps he did not find the question inappropriate. 'We don't track time the way mortals do, but I know I was a few years shy of fifty when it happened. The age at which verdaant are considered fully adult.'

'How long did it take you to move on?'

'Forty-some years.'

She turned her head and looked at him, her eyebrows raised in surprise and confusion. He lifted one corner of his mouth, amused at her expression, and nodded his head in acknowledgment.

'I don't know if you ever really *move on*. I certainly haven't. I think it's more like ... moving *through*. Everyday, I have to move through the pain and loss again, but every day the journey gets a bit easier. Or at least most days it's easier. Some-times,' he looked up toward where the mountain disappeared into the clouds, 'it feels just as raw as it did the day I lost him. But I think what you're asking is how long it took me to heal enough that I could live again.'

That was exactly what she was asking. LeiRain could feel

the desperation in her eyes, in the way her breathing hitched. This was what she wanted to know.

'I took maybe ten years to move through the feelings that cut me off from others, to feel the emptiness in me start to fill back up. And to find my way back to my magic.'

'Ten years?' LeiRain thought she might cry. Would she spend the next ten years with this hollow ache in her chest? It seemed unfathomable.

'I don't think it *has* to take that long,' Silver replied. 'I think it took that long for me because I was holding myself back.'

'How?' LeiRain thought she might already know the answer.

'I ran from it,' he said. 'I avoided the thoughts, the feelings, the memories as much as I could. I had to stop avoiding it. I had to face these things and sift through them.'

His answer sat heavily on her chest, restricting her breathing. Unconsciously, LeiRain brought one hand up and pressed it between her breasts. Her heart beat furiously into her palm.

'I wasn't letting myself feel. I was hiding away all of those soft spots underneath anger. I was so angry, at myself, at my father, the older fae who tricked me into thinking I was doing the right thing for my brother. I had to stop letting that anger hide my pain and face the mess underneath. You have to take the armor off, Rain.' He shifted and the fabric of his tunic brushed against her arm.

Just the thought of facing that vulnerability made LeiRain want to retreat, to withdraw from the world.

'I know,' he said, gesturing to the protective posture she'd taken on. LeiRain was coiled in on herself, her arms wrapped so tightly around her legs that they were beginning to go numb. 'Trust me, I know. But it really is better in the long run.'

LeiRain's fingers clinched her biceps hard enough to bruise. The physical pain seemed to ground her in the present. It prevented her from slipping into the awful memories that Silver was suggesting she face.

'I don't know how to do anything else,' she whispered against her knees.

As she said this, LeiRain thought of what Ron had been trying to tell her the other day; how her mother had perhaps not done the best job raising her. It suddenly occurred to LeiRain that Alarra had not known how to do these things for herself. For the first time, she felt sadness rather than anger when she thought of Alarra's shortcomings as a mother. The guilt she felt for speaking to Ron so harshly became more acute.

'It's what my mother did,' LeiRain admitted. 'She pushed things away, hid behind her strength.' She sucked in a sharp breath, shocked by her own candidness. There was a rush of fear as she revealed the soft underbelly of her hurt, but also a kind of relief at the unburdening. 'It worked for so long, for so many things. I don't know what it looks like to face those feelings.' She choked on a sob. 'And I don't really think I've been truly happy before in my life.'

She paused and took a few steadying breaths. Silver did not speak, did not move. He simply waited.

'I hated my village, and I hated my mother for making us stay.'

Anger creeped back in. At herself for speaking these words out loud. At Ron for making her question Alarra's parenting, even if he was right. At her mother for not being the mother that Brya was for Rayand. She looked to Silver and let her wrath shift to him.

Who was *he*, a near stranger, to tell LeiRain that everything she had learned about navigating hardship was wrong? Who was *he* to make her feel?

Silver sensed her internal struggle. Moving slowly, carefully, he reached over and placed a hand on one of hers. His warm fingers rested tentatively on hers, as if he were afraid that she might yank her hand away any second. Her arm tensed, and LeiRain did think about pulling away, but then she looked into Silver's eyes. The fire that raged in her sputtered out as she fell into his magic's embrace. The anger was replaced with a different kind of fire, and LeiRain began to lean into his touch.

A companion, she thought as she melted under his gaze. *I have a friend*. Something warmed in her chest at the realization that Ron was a friend too. Even Brya and Rayand had become friends. For the first time, LeiRain saw how unhelpful it was to push those who cared for her away.

'I – how am I supposed to do this?' She sputtered. 'I don't know how to just go around… feeling things.'

How did she now carve a different path? LeiRain wanted to be strong, but she did not want to be hard. Her mother must have been so lonely, just as lonely as LeiRain had been in Harbor. Silver's voice broke into her thoughts.

'Just a moment ago, were you feeling angry?' He asked.

Her jaw tightened as she answered.

'Yes.'

'What else did you feel?'

'Just anger,' she said, shaking her head and squinting her eyes in confusion. Silver said nothing, but looked at her skeptically. LeiRain took a few more seconds to consider and realized that there had been something there beneath the anger. There had been a *lot* hidden behind her emotional armor.

'Your childhood sounds lonely,' Silver said, redirecting her.

Her hands kneaded her biceps as she sat there, feeling everything. The hollow space in her chest ached as if it were brand new. Her sadness was a physical pain and it was everywhere in her body, inescapable. Emotions rushed at her so quickly that she could barely identify them all. There was the familiar anger, but also loneliness, bitterness, and so much sadness that LeiRain thought she might choke on it. There was guilt, not just for the way she had behaved toward her mother but for questioning Alarra's parenting, when her mother wasn't there to defend herself. And for hurting Ron. LeiRain's mind pulled her back to that day, that moment when she saw her mother's throat split open under Ethan's knife. Words tumbled out of her.

'I left and I didn't tell her. It was only three days. I *thought* it was only three days. But when I came back, six months had passed. And when I got home...'

LeiRain shivered with the intensity of the memory. Her palms were sweating, and bile rose in her throat. She could see Alarra, her head pulled back, neck craning. It was more like reliving it than remembering. LeiRain looked at Silver, pleading in her eyes, and though she could clearly see him there, she could also see the flash of sunlight off of Ethan's blade.

'There were so many of them. I didn't know what to do.'

Silver's fingers closed around LeiRain's as she watched Alarra fight and kick against her captors. She squeezed her eyes shut, willing the images away, but the scene continued to play out behind her eyelids. This is why she did not let herself think about these things, feel these things. This was why she had not spoken of them to anyone since leaving Harbor Village. The nightmares were bad enough, she did not want to spend her days reliving this hell.

33

_____

She was sobbing now. It was beyond her control, and each breath she took was a strained effort to bring air into her lungs. She sensed Silver taking her hand away from her arm, prying her fingers free. She squeezed his hand mercilessly and still, he did not withdraw.

LeiRain's other hand released its grip on her bicep and clutched a fistful of the fae's tunic. She could feel the seams of his shirt giving way in her grip but continued to cling to him. Silver reached up and slid his fingers over the back of her hand. LeiRain expected him to pull his shirt free of her grip. Instead, he rested his fingers gently atop her knuckles. LeiRain gave herself permission to fall apart, knowing that in this moment, his embrace would hold the pieces together. She was crying so hard that she could barely see as she tried to wheeze out an explanation.

'I ... watched them...' she gasped. That was all she could get out before her words were lost to sobs.

LeiRain did not try to speak again for a very long time, not until she had cried so much that she felt wrung out, with no tears left to shed. Her eyes stung, her head ached, and an overwhelming fatigue settled over her. The memories, which had been so vivid and overpowering, had eventually receded on their own. Sniffling, she peeled herself away from Silver. LeiRain looked at where she'd clung to his blouse and felt her stomach flutter with embarrassment. There was a hand-sized patch of tunic in the middle of his chest that was wrinkled and damp with sweat from her palm. His breast was splotched with her fallen tears. She slid her fingers out of his and scooted away from him, wrapping her arms around herself once more.

'I'm sorry,' she said, her voice raspy.

'I wish you weren't,' Silver replied. LeiRain looked at him through her swollen eyelids. 'I'm glad I could be here and sit with you,' he explained. 'No one should have to go through this alone. Like I did.'

She looked away.

'It might help if you talked about it more.'

LeiRain faced him again, too exhausted to be indignant at this suggestion.

'I don't talk about it at all,' she replied, her voice small and flat. 'I just tried...' She hiccuped as her lungs tried to reestablish a rhythm. 'And look at what happened.'

'It will help,' he said, nodding. 'And it will get easier.'

'All I did was think about it,' she replied, 'and you saw what became of me just now.'

'LeiRain,' Silver shifted until he was in front of her and their eyes were locked. 'That is because you hide it away most of the time. It's like...'

He paused, his face pensive as he searched for the right words.

'It's like trying to hold back an ocean wave. It will force its way through eventually, one way or another. It will be much easier on you, much less painful, if you let it happen gradually.

If you would just—' He shook his head. 'Just let it out, some-times, instead of holding it back, it will become more bearable.'

It's a good analogy, she thought. LeiRain's whole body ached from the force of her emotions crashing into her.

'The only way out,' Silver continued, 'is through. You have to face these things, Rain. Or the storm inside you will grow, as will your loneliness. If you continue to hide this part of your-self away, you will never again connect with your magic. You will never fully connect with anyone or anything. You deserve a better life than that.' His hands gave hers a light squeeze. 'Do you understand?'

She shook her head, frowning.

'How can I deserve better after the way I treated her? How can I just keep going, enjoy things, while she is dead? I should have stopped them ... or it should have been me.'

Still hoarse from the crying, her voice cracked on the last word.

'Could you really have done something to stop them?'

She knew the answer, but she didn't want to say it out loud. He raised an eyebrow in question.

'No,' she shook her head. 'I don't think so. There were too many and—' She shrugged. 'There were just too many. But I could have given myself over. They were there for me. I heard them say so.'

'Can you be certain that giving yourself over would have prevented her death?'

LeiRain opened her mouth to say *yes,* but stopped herself.

'Certain?' she asked.

Silver remained silent, one of his thumbs tracing delicate circles on the back of her hand.

'Maybe not,' she admitted.

There was freedom in this, in the realization that she was

not entirely responsible for her mother's fate. Even if LeiRain had turned herself in, Ethan might have still killed Alarra. Her mother had refused to make their weapons, but she was privy to the design and would have posed a risk to the Royals if left alive. LeiRain also began to question her assumption that Alarra would have fled the village if only she hadn't been waiting for the return of her prodigal daughter. They had endured so much in Harbor and, still, her mother had insisted they stay. There was no way to know for certain, but LeiRain gave herself permission to believe that this might not be her fault either. Tears pricked her dry eyes again.

'May I hold you?' Silver asked.

LeiRain responded by burying her face in his chest, further soaking his soiled and wrinkled tunic with her tears and snot. He wrapped his arms around her and LeiRain focused on the rise and fall of his breathing. She tried to match her breaths to his, letting his herb garden scent calm her. Silver wove one hand into her hair as he clutched her to his chest. His other hand rested against her lower back, fingers curling around her hip.

She'd never been held like this before. Bren's touch, while tender, had always been filled with lust. Their closeness had been enjoyable, but purely physical. This was much more intimate. She'd tried to keep her distance from Silver, to withhold her trust. But it had been a losing battle. Something deep inside LeiRain was drawn to the verdaant and in this moment, nothing seemed more natural than resting in his arms.

They stayed like this for a long time. Her sobs gradually came to an end, spacing themselves out until she was finally breathing with slow regularity. LeiRain felt her weight shift as Silver laid back on the grass pulling her with him, her face still pressed into his chest.

She was still in Silver's arms when the bright sun gave way

to the softer tones of dusk. LeiRain's body felt tired and wrung out as she settled comfortably into the crook of Silver's arm. A bone-deep fatigue began to overtake her. LeiRain blinked lazily, her lashes brushing against the cloth of Silver's tunic. She was on the threshold between wakefulness and sleep when his voice brought her back. Her eyes fluttered open.

'Reach out for your magic,' he whispered. LeiRain ignored him and let her eyes fall closed once more.

'Rain?'

'Mmm?' This was all she could manage as a reply.

'Just reach for it, you don't have to do anything else.'

Later, LeiRain thought as she drifted in and out of wakefulness. When she didn't reply, Silver wiggled the arm that was holding her to his chest. She groaned in response.

'Just see what it feels like right now.'

LeiRain felt a light tug from somewhere inside her as Silver's magic tried to coax her into cooperating. The tug was taunting, teasing, piquing her interest while refusing to do all of the work. The gentle nudge was effective. LeiRain reached out on her own, searching for her magic. She sensed it there, keeping its distance. Silver's magic withdrew as she searched for a hold on hers. LeiRain felt the emptiness where his power had been and tried harder to find her own so that she could reestablish their connection. She kept reaching, reaching... but it did not respond. Then, just as LeiRain was about to give up and give in to fatigue, magic slid into her grasping mental fingers. LeiRain let it brush against her, reveling in the sensation and asking nothing of it. The magic rose up and wrapped itself around her, cocooning LeiRain until it was as if she were one with the water. Silver's magic reappeared then, mixing in with her own as it wrapped itself around her. She sighed and sank further into his chest where, swathed in love and safety, she fell asleep.

34

LeiRain opened her eyes to find thin strips of sunlight stretched across the hardwood floor.

She jolted out of bed, surprised and confused at having slept so soundly and so late into the morning. And also at having woken in her own bed. The last thing she remembered was being wrapped in Silver's arms. She'd cried so hard, so much, that it had wiped her of strength and energy. Her cheeks warmed as she thought of the way he had held her. She shook it off, telling herself that he'd held her like that only because they both knew the same pain.

She fumbled a bit while getting dressed. The residual fog of sleep and her efforts to rush made LeiRain's fingers clumsy as she did up the ties on the front of her slacks. Ron would likely be waiting, but at least this time she would be appropriately dressed. Her body was unaccustomed to so much deep sleep and LeiRain thought she might not wake fully until she'd had some coffee. Just as she tugged the tunic over her head, flashes of her dream from the night before began to play in her mind. Not a nightmare this time, but an actual dream. A pleasant one, even. LeiRain closed her eyes and strained to recall the details. She could remember how it had felt when she reached out for her magic and found it opening to her embrace. It was a comfort, and recollecting the dream made her long to be near water.

The smell of cooked oats filled the air when she stepped out of her private rooms. Ron was not waiting for her; perhaps it wasn't as late as she had thought. The sun had begun to rise just a bit earlier each day and set slightly later each night as they moved deeper into Spring. Perhaps, LeiRain worried, Ron was sleeping even later today, his head still throbbing with the alcohol he'd consumed the night before. Still, neither of them had spoken of their argument. Neither of them had apologized and things had not slid back into place as they always had after she'd argued with her mother. Alarra had been good at pretending that a conflict had never happened. Ron tried to do the same, but was failing miserably. He wasn't himself, and LeiRain knew that she was partly to blame. *I'll apologize the next time we're alone*, she told herself.

LeiRain finished buckling her sword belt and hefted her shield onto an arm before walking toward the spring. She shook off her thoughts of Ron and their strained relationship, and let herself be drawn to the water. The stream bubbled loudly as the sun melted the last of the snow. A cool breeze emanated from the ripples, sweeping toward her off the top of the water as she approached and making her shiver. Silver was nowhere to be seen, and she felt a mixture of relief and disappointment.

LeiRain hadn't made it to her bed of her own accord; she knew that much. The fae must have carried and placed her there. Did he not wish to spend the night with her curled against him, or had he been concerned about the embarrassment she'd suffered before, when Ron had found her leaving his shelter in the early morning? They had crossed some divide last night, some line that marked a new level of inti-macy. She did not know what it meant, but was sure it was something from which she could not turn back.

The water drew her attention. It felt... familiar this morn-ing. Her dream began to feel more like a memory.

Water magic responded to her touch, wrapped around her; they became so entwined that it was impossible to tell where she ended and the water began.

Even before her mother's death, she had not experienced such an intense connection with the water. She could vaguely recall the feel of Silver's chest beneath her, the warmth of his arms around her, and she knew for certain that she hadn't been clutching her shield.

She gripped her shield now as she sat before the chilly water. LeiRain concentrated on the rippling surface. She reached out with her mind, extending her mental fingers toward the mountain stream. A smile spread across her face, so wide that she felt her dry lips start to crack; the water was responding to her touch.

Icy tendrils lapped against her mind. LeiRain didn't grab for it, didn't command it, just basked in the feeling. It was as if a heavy curtain had hung between her and her magic, and all of the tears and confessions the night before had swept it open. It was still there. LeiRain could feel its heaviness draped around the edges of the connection, but for now, the curtain remained parted and magic thrummed through her entire body. Her connection was different with this freshwater than it had been with the ocean, but not any less. This water felt lighter and cooler, but no more difficult to wield.

'Oy.' LeiRain jumped at the sound of Brya's voice. Her eyes flew open and the caress of magic slid abruptly out of reach. She turned to see the dwarve standing on the threshold of the kitchen, shading her eyes with one hand as she squinted against the morning sun. 'Come eat while it's hot!'

The door thunked shut behind Brya before LeiRain could reply. She let out a long, emptying breath and sent a mental *thank you* to the water before turning and making her to the warm kitchen.

To LeiRain's surprise, she found both Silver and Ron already seated at the table. Silver had never before gone early to breakfast, and she wondered if he had done so to prevent the others from suspecting he was responsible for her late start. LeiRain was almost certain now that Silver had carried her to bed so that he could save her further embarrassment. The fae looked at her when she walked in, and LeiRain responded with a subtle smile. She hoped that her eyes communicated gratitude. One corner of his mouth quirked upwards in response, and he gave her a barely noticeable nod.

LeiRain ate cheerily. Her good mood must have been contagious, as Silver's face glowed with uncharacteristic warmth. His usual lack of expression was replaced with an air of genuine amiability as he looked around the table at the others. The fae even gave Ray a smile and a wink as he passed the goat's milk. Ron, on the other hand, sat grimly at the other end with his head bowed over a steaming cup of coffee. He nudged his porridge bowl away, and Brya glared in response. LeiRain narrowed her eyes, looking carefully at Ron in the dim light of the kitchen.

He looked *awful*. His hair, usually pulled back in a tight braid, fell wild around his face and over his shoulders. Ron's normally ruddy skin was unnaturally pale, and he held his eyes half closed. His lips were pressed together tightly and turned down at the corners. His beard was a ratted mess, unbraided and sticking out from his face in all directions as if he'd slept on his face for part of the night.

'You need to eat.' Brya sat, scooting the bowl of cooling porridge back toward her brother-in-law.

Ron grunted in annoyance but didn't argue. Brya caught LeiRain's eye then, and LeiRain knew that the look of concern on her own face must have matched what the dwarve was feeling. Ron usually bristled at being told what to do and he'd never shied away from bantering. His drinking must really be getting out of hand. Brya filled a large cup with water and sat it in front of him.

'Drink,' she said.

Ron set his coffee down and complied without argument. He drained the cup and then his mug of coffee. Brya refilled both without being asked, and Ron had emptied both vessels a second time before LeiRain had finished her porridge. Looking somewhat healthier now that he was hydrated, Ron began poking at his porridge, which had cooled and was now congealing. He lifted small, timid clumps of it from bowl to mouth, scowling when he caught LeiRain watching. She looked away.

Out of respect for Ron's hangover, breakfast conversation was kept to a minimum. LeiRain reflected on her encounter with the water as she savored the bracing bitterness of her morning drink. They were taking turns at the small wash basin, clearing the table and rinsing out their bowls when LeiRain was startled by a loud whooshing sound just outside the kitchen window.

35

'Arrows,' Ron growled, looking more awake now than he had all throughout breakfast. For that matter, he looked more awake than he had in days.

Brya grabbed Rayand by the arm. The boy looked up at his mother with wide-eyed confusion. Brya motioned him toward the back of the living space where the walls, made of mountain stone, would better protect him. Ray's eyes narrowed, the serious look on his face making him seem suddenly much older than he was. He pulled his arm out of Brya's and picked up his small ax from where it had been resting by the fire. His fingers flexed on the weapon's handle.

'Hide,' Brya said. She pointed toward the back of the dwelling again. 'Be ready to fight or flee.'

'I'm old enough. I don't need to hide,' Ray replied. He took a step toward the door.

'You're not of age *yet*,' Ron growled without looking back at the boy.

LeiRain pulled her own sword from its sheath as she edged around the table to stand behind Ron. Her eyes flicked back and forth between where Silver stood at the door and where Ray stood in front of the fire.

Ray's jaw flexed as he gritted his teeth and turned away. Brya watched him go, unbothered by the scowl on his face. When Ray disappeared into the dark hallway, Brya stepped toward the wash basin. She reached below it and pulled a large ax and a thick, iron shield out from under the sink. Brya then pressed up against the wall near LeiRain, who was holding her blade close to her body. The space was too tight to pull the shield over her shoulder but her fingers itched to tug on the guige. *You've been training for this*, she told herself, but still LeiRain's legs shook and her palms were becoming slick with sweat.

Silver pressed against the door this whole time, listening, waiting. His hand, which had been resting on the doorknob, turned slightly. He cracked the door open a hair's breadth. LeiRain could only just make out a thin sliver of daylight, but Silver's fae senses would detect more.

'Fire,' he said, turning back to them.

His gaze went first to Brya, then LeiRain. When their eyes met, she felt a gentle tug as their magic entwined. Silver blinked, his face giving away nothing of this intimacy, and his eyes moved to Ron who had slid his helmet on. He hadn't worn it since they'd been on the mountain, in his sanctuary. Unused and recently polished, light gleamed off of it as he nodded his head at Silver. The fae turned back toward the door. LeiRain could feel her pulse pounding as one second passed, then two... Silver threw the door open.

The thunk of arrows grew louder and LeiRain jumped when she heard another thunk against the side of the house. Silver and Ron both rushed out the door. LeiRain followed, sliding the shield over her chest as soon as she was clear of the doorway, with

Brya close on her heels. Brya pushed past LeiRain and ran forward to flank her brother-in-law. The three of them, Ron, Silver and Brya, yelled to one another. There was a roaring in LeiRain's ears that made it impossible to understand what they were saying. She watched arrows, their tips aflame, arc overhead before hitting the house. Only a few had managed to plant themselves into the wooden face of the structure. At least two arrows lay on the ground in front of the dwelling, the grass beneath them scorched. One *had* met its mark and bright orange flames crawled up the wall nearest the garden. The smell of smoke was quickly becoming overwhelming and the crackle of flames drowned out the voices of her companions as LeiRain stood frozen in place.

The sword drooped in her hand and the shield would have fallen to the ground if it hadn't been held to her with the guige. She forced herself to look away from the fire, but even as she did so, memory threatened to overtake her. LeiRain could hear her own ragged breathing as she tried to absorb the scene around them. Silver seemed to be taking the brunt of their attack as bolt after bolt flew at him. A translucent wall of blue fae light glowed in front of him as he walked toward the hidden archers. An arrow, its fire sputtering out in the air, hit the magical shield and bounced off. Another followed, this one still alight, and LeiRain shrieked as she watched it hit Silver's fae light and continue its trajectory, piercing his shield to land at his feet. Her head spun as she scanned the clearing. Weapons flew at Ron and Brya as well, though none of these were aflame. LeiRain took a step forward, legs shaking, as she watched Brya bat an arrow away with her shield. The two dwarves moved forward with confidence and purpose, inching their way closer to the attackers. The sun was still rising behind the archers, making it difficult to determine where the arrows originated. She wanted to be helpful, wanted to provide cover for Silver as the onslaught continued, but they fired so rapidly that she could only identify the general area from which they came. Most of them bounced off the blue fae light, but LeiRain felt her shoulders tense everytime an arrow pierced Silver's magic.

There was a loud crack behind her and LeiRain looked over her shoulder to see a portion of the roof starting to give way to fire. Her head snapped back and forth between the dwarves and the house. Neither Ron nor Brya seemed to notice the spreading blaze as they focused on their advance. Would the stone walls be enough to protect Rayand? If the fire continued at this rate he would surely be overcome by the smoke. LeiRain had to do something.

As she looked at the house, the small sapling in front of it began to grow. The thin branches quickly thickened and sprang upward, reaching for the sky before bending back toward the roof. LeiRain could hear the tree groan and feel the ground vibrate as the plant stretched its bows and extended its roots with unnatural rapidity.

LeiRain looked at Silver to her left, and watched his eyes dart back and forth between his shield of fae light and the former sapling. Another bolt penetrated his shield, but he didn't seem to notice. LeiRain lunged forward clumsily knowing she was too late to block it, but still desperate to make herself useful. She wasn't fast enough, her movements not sharp enough to respond to the attack. Silver continued to move forward with one hand held out to maintain the shield, while the other stretched toward the house.

When she glanced at the house again, green leaves sprang from the tree's branches. The tree covered the flames in thick clumps of greenery as it continued to grow and spread. The moist leaves popped with heat and thick coils of white smoke rose up as the flames were smothered. She worried about Rayand. The fire was mostly out and Silver had turned his focus entirely toward the attackers. The blue light of his shield now flickered each time it was struck and his face looked strained. His energy was waning, and he could spare no more thought for the burning roof.

LeiRain saw her opportunity. She could do something. She could fix this. Opening her mind, she called to the water, pleading her case and asking for its aid. She held her breath for several seconds, awaiting the response. At first, there was nothing and LeiRain's heart began to sink. *Please*, she thought. *I need you*. Then, she felt it. LeiRain felt the water rise up to meet her, felt it answering her summons. She took a deep breath and pulled the water toward her. It was coming, moving with her will.

A searing pain shot through LeiRain's right arm, breaking her concentration. Blood ran from her bicep to her elbow where an arrow had grazed her and taken a piece of flesh. The pain was a blessing. It distracted LeiRain from her insecurities and when she renewed her focus and called on the water again, it responded immediately. Streams of it danced through the air over her head as she guided the water to the smoking leaves. It poured over the house in a torrent, the roof sizzling as she doused the remaining flames.

'Rain!'

Focused on her magic, LeiRain had lost all situational awareness. She spun around in time to see Silver dive in front of her. His shield stretched out ahead of him to cover LeiRain as he moved. Two arrows came whistling through the air, aimed at LeiRain's chest. One ricocheted off the fae light but the other broke through. She held her breath, but the magic shield disrupted the arrow's course and it whizzed past her thigh before landing in the grass. LeiRain's own shield had slipped from her hand and hung unhelpfully near her left hip. Her sword, she now realized, had slid from her fingers and lay on the ground beside her. LeiRain knelt to pick it up, shield now held in front of her chest. She rose with the weapon in hand and squinted against the sun. The attackers were hiding just behind some of the large boulders at the top of the rock scuttle, their silhouettes visible briefly each time they took aim. They'd chosen the time and angle of attack well; backlit by the sun, they were nearly impossible to target.

Ron was pushing his way closer to them, his heavy shield protecting most of his body. The dwarve was deadly with an ax, but would have to be very close to effectively strike with it. Brya stalked forward as well. She took a position just behind Ron where she was protected by both her own shield and the stocky figure of her brother-in-law. If the archers somehow managed to take Ron down, Brya would be right there to take his place. LeiRain watched the two of them, her mind reeling. They both looked at home in a warrior's stance, shields before them, axes ready. They moved around each other like it was a dance and LeiRain wished that she knew the steps.

'Fire at the green one,' one of the men shouted.

LeiRain flinched as another flaming arrow pierced Silver's shield, missing him by only a few inches. The arrow landed near her feet and she took a moment to study it. The weapon had a small, sharpened tip, which she expected but behind this was an ovular metal cage, stuffed with blackened cloth that smelled like pitch. The oddest thing she noticed was the strand of flowers that wrapped around the outside of the metal cage. They were wound tightly around the metal, all the way down to the arrow's piercing tip. The first arrow had sputtered out when it hit the grass but even so, the strand of flowers were already withered and burnt.

'I *said* the *green one*,' a shout came from the man furthest to the left.

'I've got other problems over here,' one of his companions growled in reply. Ron and Brya were closing in on him.

LeiRain heard a grunt and the clatter of sliding rocks. That was followed by the sound of a sword being unsheathed as one of the attackers discarded his bow for a melee weapon.

The man stood, blade drawn, and Ron charged forward with a guttural cry. Brya followed him, her own shout sending chills up LeiRain's spine. Steel met steel. Sunlight flashed off blades. Ron moved with a grace and swiftness that she'd never seen before and realized, for the first time, just how much he held back with her in sparring. LeiRain brought up her own sword and readied herself for action, though she still stood several feet away from the fighting. She took small, shuffling steps forward and looked for an opening, forcing her numb hands to maintain a hold on her weapons. Still, she watched, unsure of herself. It was all happening so fast. This was nothing like sparring, this was not what she had expected.

LeiRain caught a blur of movement in her peripheral vision as one of the men darted into view. Instead of stepping into the confrontation as his companion had done, this man turned and ran, skittering out of view down the path.

'Go,' Ron shouted and Brya obeyed.

She moved with a litheness that didn't seem possible for such a brawny woman. Rocks scattered with each of her footfalls as she pursued the runner. He was fast, but Brya knew the mountain. The man would not make it.

Silver was still moving forward, closing in on his own quarry. Though it wavered, he kept his shield in place as he made his way to the remaining archer. LeiRain took another few steps forward and her attention jumped between Ron and Silver.

Silver let his shield drop just as the man stood. The archer reached for the blade at his hip. Unbothered by this, Silver raised a hand and drew on his magic. LeiRain moved closer, her curiosity overpowering the fear that had held her in place.

She watched as thorny vines wrapped themselves around the man's legs. He slashed at them, frantically, his blade cutting through his own flesh as much as the vines. Still, the thorns continued their advance. In his desperation, he dropped the weapon and began pulling at the plants with his hands. The man cried out as thorns tore open the flesh of his palms but he continued to grip and yank them until his own blood coated him from fingertips to wrist. Still, the thorns outpaced him and began to work their way up his thighs, around his hips.

From behind her, LeiRain heard a soft, wet sound and then a thud. Her head swiveled and she saw Ron standing over a body. It lay limp, resting on the same boulder the man had been using for cover only moments before. His arms were splayed wide and his right leg bent at an unnatural angle. The handle of Ron's ax rested against his shoulder and crimson dripped from the sorcerer's steel as he studied his enemy. LeiRain's stomach roiled, the breakfast she'd just eaten threatening to come back up.

She looked away from Ron and back to Silver, whose quarry had stopped struggling. The man was on his knees now, his breath coming in quick, gasping sobs. His chest and shoulders were held back by the tension in the vines and his chin tilted slightly upward so that he looked at the sky. Briars had wrapped themselves around his torso and crawled up his neck, the sharp tips of thorns leaving pink scratch marks as they slid over his pale skin. Vines shot up from the soil and wrapped around his wrists and forearms, bringing an end to his attempts to free himself. He tried to move his head and, in response, the vines began to constrict around his throat. Tiny pricks of blood appeared just below his Adam's apple.

As she watched, Brya reappeared, coming up the path behind the restrained man. Her blouse was partially untucked from her skirt and her hair had come out of its bun and hung in wild tangles down her back. She barely glanced at the captive as she walked by and paused only when she reached the clearing. Brya took a few deep breaths as she pulled a dishrag from one of her skirt pockets. She ran the cloth over her blade until it was clean again, then used it to wipe the blood stain from her fingers. Tucking the rag back in her pocket, Brya nodded to Ron and walked purposefully toward the house to check on her son.

Rayand would be fine. The fire was out and the roof only smoked lightly now. Surely, the back rooms were deep enough and the fire put out early enough that Ray wouldn't have succumbed to smoke. LeiRain adjusted the grip on her weapons as the feeling slowly came back to her fingertips. She tried to release some of the tension she'd been holding but her body continued to shake with unspent energy.

'Good,' Ron said, coming to stand beside her. 'You've kept yours alive.' He looked thoughtfully at Silver's captive. The man was sobbing now, his eyes closed. ''Fraid mine fought back a bit hard and I, uh... Well, he won't be able to answer any questions.'

LeiRain swallowed as she looked past Ron to the slain body, laid out in the sun. This was the second time that she had witnessed death, and her reaction had been much the same as the first. Frozen, terror-stricken. The dead man's eyes stared blankly up at the blue sky overhead. She was grateful that it was the stranger who lay lifeless and not her friends. Why had she even bothered to train if this was how she would respond in a fight? What was the point if she still couldn't protect those she cared for?

Ron and Silver moved together toward the sole survivor.

The vines around his throat loosened noticeably and trails of blood ran down the man's neck as some of the thorns withdrew from his skin. He took in an audible breath, though it caught in his chest when the vines around his torso refused to give way.

'Please,' he exhaled, looking at them as best he could out of the corner of his eye. He was still unable to turn his head without tearing more of his own flesh. 'Please, let me go.'

'Are there more of you?' Silver asked.

His voice was cold, dangerous. It was not the voice of the man who had held LeiRain last night while she cried. It was the voice of a dangerous and powerful being, an immortal. For the first time since he'd first arrived at the mountain hide, Silver truly reminded LeiRain of her father.

'Just the three of us ... *please.*'

Ron and Silver appeared unmoved by his pleas.

'We weren't expecting ... so many ... we just came ... for the verdaant.'

'Ah,' Silver nodded, looking at the ground. Ron glared at the fae.

'Who are you and why did you come for him?' Ron asked.

'I'm Tomlin,' the man gasped out.

'Fuck's sake, who cares what your *name* is? That's obviously not what I meant.'

LeiRain had never seen Ron like this before. His anger made her afraid to interject, but she did so, anyway.

'They're Royals,' she said.

It was difficult to make out Tomlin's blue arm band with his clothing and skin so torn and bloodied. So LeiRain pointed, instead, to the dead man strewn across the boulder.

'Look,' she commanded. The men followed her outstretched arm. A large swath of royal blue was still visible on the left arm of the fallen man, though it was turning a dark purple as blood seeped into it.

'Of course,' Silver snarled.

A shadow fell over his face and Tomlin began to wheeze. LeiRain looked at the captive and saw that the brambles were tightening around his throat again.

'Please,' he wheezed, 'I was just following orders.'

The vines stilled.

'You swore an oath,' Silver asked, 'to the Royals?'

'Yes,' the man whispered.

'I see. So you were honor-bound to obey their leadership?'

'Yes,' he gasped. Tomlin could barely speak now, but hope flashed briefly over his face.

'Please, I had no choice,' he added.

Silver nodded as if he understood. He leaned in close and whispered into the man's ear. 'There is no honor in an oath sworn out of fear and hatred.'

The man's face paled. He knew then that there would be no mercy.

'There is *always* a choice,' Silver words were clipped and his eyes narrowed.

The vines once again began to tighten around Tomlin's neck, thorns disappearing as they sunk into his flesh. His eyes bulged as he struggled to take in air. LeiRain looked away, unable to watch. She didn't want to see what Silver was capable of.

She heard a wet crunch and then a thump as the body hit the ground. LeiRain looked up, then, and saw the man's corpse slumped over in the dirt. His neck was broken, his head turned at an impossible angle. There was a splatter of blood on the rock in front of him where his skull must have hit when the vines retreated from his body. LeiRain's throat burned and she swallowed back bile.

'I'm sorry,' Silver said.

At first LeiRain thought that he was speaking to her, apologizing for the violence she'd just witnessed. When she looked at him, his eyes trailed after Ron as the dwarve stomped off toward the house.

'I do not know how they followed me,' Silver said, sounding both remorseful and astonished. 'It is no easy thing to track a verdaant.'

'Gather your things,' Ron called over his shoulder. 'We leave before nightfall.'

'Was it me?' LeiRain asked. 'Was it– did I lead them here the other night?' She whispered to Silver as Ron made off toward the house.

He didn't acknowledge her, but instead turned back to the man he'd just killed. He knelt down where Tomlin had taken cover and picked up the small flint box the man had used to set his arrows afire.

There were only a few arrows remaining in the quiver that hung from the dead man's belt. Silver slid one out and examined it. He looked at the small, metal cage behind the tip. LeiRain moved closer to him and sheathed her sword. She resisted the urge to place her hand on his back. Silver handled the arrow delicately, turning it over in his fingers. He brushed the flower petals against his palm, and that's when LeiRain realized what they were, the flowers. It was foxglove.

'Ron,' Silver said loudly. The dwarve had just shut the door behind him and it creaked back open. Silver didn't wait for him to answer. 'Come look.'

Ron made no effort to hide his annoyance as he stomped across the clearing.

'What *now,* Forest God.'

Silver's jaw tightened at the use of the distasteful nickname but he did not correct him.

'He was telling the truth,' Silver said. He turned toward Ron. 'They came for me.'

'I thought you said you weren't followed,' Ron growled. 'And how do you know they were here for *you*? There are plenty that would like to see me dead.'

LeiRain felt her cheeks heat with shame and she opened her mouth to confess to Ron, to tell him that she'd ventured out alone, in the dark, and run into men in the woods. Sensing what she was about to do, Silver gave her a warning glare.

'Because of this,' Silver said, not giving LeiRain a chance to speak. He held up one of the arrows and pointed to the flower that wrapped around it. 'This is foxglove.' Ron looked unimpressed. 'And the ash of foxglove is the only thing that can seriously injure or kill a verdaant.'

Ron narrowed his eyes at Silver. 'And here I thought gods were unkillable.'

'Perhaps gods are.' Silver pursed his lips and inhaled deeply. His hands were shaking where he held the arrow, and the fae stole a brief glance at LeiRain before refocusing on the dwarve. LeiRain reached inside herself and latched onto her magic, sending a gentle wave of it to wash over Silver. His hands stilled. Ron's arms were crossed and his face stern as he listened. 'But I am fae, and fae *can* be killed.'

36

R on's eyes were wide and blinking rapidly. He didn't respond for several seconds.

'The *fae?*' He sounded incredulous.

'Yes.' Silver placed a hand on his chest. 'The fae live.'

'But the War of Sorrows—'

'Nearly wiped us all out. That's why our continued existence is a well kept secret. As is our vulnerability. People do not try to kill that which they believe to be unkillable.' Silver raised one eyebrow as he waited for Ron's reply.

'I— What—' Ron stammered, 'Why in the gods' names would you tell *me*, then?'

'I thought it was time you knew, Ronland the Red. Let this be a mark of the trust I have given you. How you use this information is out of my control. Regardless, I suggest we leave here with haste. We cannot know if there will be more.'

Silver's eyes slid briefly over LeiRain, though not long enough for her to feel the sizzle of their magic connecting. The verdaant then focused on the purple and white flower petals that wound around the arrowhead, bringing them close to his face as he examined them. He sighed and let the arrow drop from his hand and onto the ground.

LeiRain fought the urge to take his hand in hers. She was certain that it was her own rash actions that had brought these men to the mountain hide, and it was her fault that Silver's life had been put in such danger. Now, Silver was forced to share his people's most guarded secret in order to protect her, and maintain the relationship he had begun to build with Ron.

Silver drew himself up and stood before the dwarve, his tall frame casting a shadow over him. 'Are we not allies?' He asked, his voice soft and questioning.

Ron considered him for a moment, then nodded his head and said, somberly, 'I suppose we are.' There was a subtle note of surprise in his voice. He cleared his throat and turned to LeiRain. 'Pack your things, but pack light. Come to the main house when you're ready.'

She had very few things to gather since she'd come to the mountain with only the clothes on her back, her sword and her shield. Brya had made some clothing for her over the last several months and she packed these tightly in a burlap satchel. LeiRain had last used the bag to carry root vegetables from the garden to the kitchen so she did her best to shake the dirt from it before packing. There were probably still bits of soil clinging to the inside, but that was a trivial problem given the events of the day.

In her private rooms, she massaged the handle of her shield, reaching out to the water. LeiRain was unsure if it would respond at such a distance and without the urgency she'd found during battle. Her stomach fluttered with excitement and gratitude when she was met with its cool embrace. The magic was a comfort and it helped fortify her before she joined the others and left the mountain hide.

So much had shaken her today: her own response to the

threat of combat, the coldness in Silver's eyes as he dispatched a life. She had come to trust the fae and to long for his company. Now, she wondered if she was following the same path as her mother. She'd seen a different side of him when he stood before the fallen archer. Perhaps Silver was not so different from her father, Caspian, the tempest who had murdered her grandparents and left her mother living in fear. LeiRain recalled the savage look on Silver's face as he interrogated the Royal, the way his lip curled and his jaw twitched. But then she remembered the softness of his embrace and how tenderly he'd held her the night before. She heard the vulnerability in his voice when he revealed the truth of his nature to Ron. *Are we not allies?* LeiRain groaned as she ran a hand over her face.

Reluctantly, she released her hold on the water and picked up the satchel. She closed the door to her rooms behind her, sad to be leaving this place where she'd found some semblance of safety and love. LeiRain walked to where she knew the others were gathered in Brya and Rayand's quarters and found them all there, waiting in silence. Silver stood with no visible belongings, bent slightly at the shoulders so that his head did not brush the ceiling. Both Rayand and Brya clutched heavily-loaded canvas bags that rested on the table. Ron had a small satchel like LeiRain's draped over his body.

'Ready then?' Ron asked her, and she nodded her reply.

'Is there another route?' Silver's voice was soft and tentative. There was no sign of the battle-hardened fae she'd seen earlier this morning. They would not want to traverse the same path on which the ambush had arrived, LeiRain realized, lest there be more attackers lying in wait. But there was no other trail, as far as she knew, and LeiRain worried that they would have to traverse the steep and thickly wooded slopes of the mountain.

'There is,' Brya said, exchanging a knowing glance with her brother-in-law.

'Come,' Ron motioned for them to follow. 'I'll show you just how gifted a forger your mother was, Rain.'

She frowned in confusion but followed behind him as they left the coziness of the kitchen behind for good.

T hey stood before a gray, stony rockface. LeiRain saw no discernable path either up or down from this angle and fidgeted with the strap of her bag as she waited for Ron to explain what they were doing here.

'Dwarves,' he said, 'have held these mountains for centuries. We have multiple hides, and we *always* have a back-up plan.' He smiled at LeiRain, the first time he had done so since their altercation almost a week ago. Her stomach clenched as she realized that she still hadn't apologized for her behavior.

Brya stepped forward and held out her ax. She slid the blade into a crevice among the rocks and kept it there. Rain and Silver watched, the verdaant's face reflecting her own confusion. There was silence, save for the shuffling of Rayand's impatient feet. The two adult dwarves continued to stare at the smooth stone.

Several seconds passed, and LeiRain was about to ask for an explanation when she heard a loud *click*. The stone wall in front of them jumped out a few inches. LeiRain reflexively took a step backward and bumped into Silver. One of her shoulders bounced off of his chest but she was so fascinated by the shifting rock that she barely noticed.

Ron winked at LeiRain as he spun his ax around in a

dramatic flourish. 'Not just a weapon,' he said, 'each one is a key.'

LeiRain's eyes went wide as she took a step toward Brya who withdrew her ax from the crevice. The rock jumped out a bit further as she did so and LeiRain caught a whiff of musty air leaking from the opening. Ron brought his weapon up to his face, focusing briefly on the sharp edge before passing it to Leirain.

'*My mother* did this?'

He nodded. 'She wasn't the original forger,' he said, 'but your mother knew how to cast these weapons and enchant them. Such blades are usually forged and mended by dwarven iron workers, but when our clan was wiped out, so were they. Alarra is the only person I trusted with such work, and she did not disappoint.'

LeiRain examined the blade, recalling the day Ron had dumped the shattered pieces of it on the earth before her mother's forge. She felt the familiar ache of loss, accompanied by a hollowness beneath her breastbone. LeiRain watched her reflection in the well-polished steel as she passed the weapon back to Ron and pressed her hands to her chest where grief was a physical pain. What else had Alarra hidden from her all of these years? What more did Ron know of her mother that he hadn't yet revealed? LeiRain wanted to ask him, but not in front of the others. And besides, the day was advancing. It had already been more than an hour since they put down the Royal attack. It was time to leave.

Ron kept the ax in hand as he squeezed through the narrow opening in the mountain face. Once they were all through, Brya and Ron placed their weapons in similar keyholes along the inside wall and the stone shut with a loud, grinding sound. LeiRain swallowed, her chest tight as she felt several feet of hard rock slide into place between her and the mountain spring, between her and the ocean.

The only light inside was a small sliver of sunshine that seeped through a thin crack between the mountain and the edges of the stone doorway. Ron removed his ax from the wall and strapped it to his belt. When Brya followed suit, the rock clanked shut, becoming one with the mountain face. The golden strand of afternoon sun was blotted out entirely and LeiRain gasped involuntarily at the utter darkness.

She jumped when something grazed her, but when LeiRain caught the smell of lavender and basil, she knew that it was Silver. His warm hand rested reassuringly on her shoulder as the space before them lit up with the soft, blue of fae light. Rather than a single burning orb, Silver had lit the way forward with small patches of cerulean fire. They bounced in the air like glowing insects, sweeping away the darkness as they fluttered. LeiRain turned to thank him but stopped short, taken aback by Silver's appearance. His face was still in shadow and his eyes glowed like silver flames. It forced Leirain to recall the raging storm she'd seen in her father's eyes so many years ago, and her earlier misgivings about the fae returned.

'Much obliged, Forest God,' Ron said. There was a smirk in his voice as he used the nickname to gode Silver.

LeiRain felt the fae stiffen beside her but he said nothing as Ron pushed past them.

'Are you all planning to stand there for the rest of the day?' Ron kept walking as he said this, his footsteps echoing off the walls of the cave. Brya and Rayand moved forward and LeiRain followed them with Silving bringing up the rear. The path had twisted in different directions as they progressed and, within an hour, she had no idea which direction they were facing. Brya and Ron stepped confidently, and so she trusted them to know the way. When the tunnels were wide enough, the two adult dwarves walked side-by-side, murmuring and Rayand would drop back to walk next to LeiRain. Silver maintained his position, alone and in the rear, regardless of the space available.

After a few hours, the adrenaline of flight receded and fatigue began to set in. LeiRain's eyelids felt heavy, her tired feet stumbled more often and she longed for her bed. She was beginning to appreciate the vastness of these tunnels as the one they traversed became wider, the ceiling higher. Eventually, it opened into a large chamber. She hadn't realized how stuffy the air had been until a cool breeze hit her face. The space was an intersection for several other tunnels and LeiRain slumped against the wall in relief when Ron declared that they would be resting here for the night. She pulled the strap of her satchel over her head and let it drop to the ground.

They were in a chamber roughly as large as Brya's kitchen. At the far side of the chamber were three different tunnel openings branching off in various directions. LeiRain settled herself in the middle of the room, Silver between her and the tunnel from which they'd just emerged, and the dwarves between her and the trio of new tunnels. There was something comforting about having a solid wall to her back rather than yawning darkness. The blackness of the unexplored tunnels reminded LeiRain of the drop-off and, involuntarily, she thought of the sheel. She recalled its rancid smell, yellowed teeth and the oily sheen of its skin. She cast a glance at the tunnels behind Brya and Ron and wondered what else might be lurking in the dark.

Somewhere unseen, small droplets of water made a noise as they fell into a pool. *Plunk*. The sound echoed off the stone. *Plunk*. She could smell the water, feel it nearby. It was unlike anything she'd encountered before. It didn't have the refreshing brine of salt water, nor the crispy cleanliness of the mountain spring. *Plunk plunk.* It smelled like clothes that had been left too long in a damp pile, the scent of mold forever lingering in their fibers. LeiRain wondered if the smell would follow them when they left the cave, if the scent of mildew and dust would ever leave her hair.*Plunk.* Her eyes closed and her breathing slowed as her head sank into the satchel she was using as a pillow.

～

'We can go on our own,' Brya said as she handed a water skin to Rayand. LeiRain, lost in her morning ablutions, had missed the first part of the conversation.

'I know ya can, but I'd prefer ya didn't,' Ron replied.

She gave him a warm, knowing smile.

'I can see ye' will regardless of my preference,' he conceded.

Brya and Rayand were headed to another mountain hide, leaving Ron, Silver and LeiRain to carry out the mission of infiltrating the Royals.

'Where exactly are *we* going?' Silver asked.

His voice was soft and tentative. He was obviously reluctant to interrupt their conversation, but Brya and Ron had been at it since LeiRain woke.

'Brya and Ray will make their way to another settlement.'

He glanced warily at Silver, daring him to question this. It was bad enough that the verdant had found Ron's mountain hide. It was almost unthinkable that Ron would give the verdant knowledge of other clan settlements.

'*We*,' the dwarve gestured with one hand at himself, Silver and LeiRain, 'will hide somewhere along the coast until I can book us passage to the Arborris Enclave,' Ron went on.

Ron and Brya seemed to have finally settled their disagreement and the group of them sat and ate breakfast. They consumed the fresh food first, finishing off the venison that Brya had packed in wax-coated paper, splitting a loaf of bread. LeiRain savored the softness of it, knowing that the bread they ate tomorrow would be turning stale. Silver had condensed the tiny balls of fae light into four palm-sized, blue blazes. He spaced them evenly around the cavern so that their light touched everything in the space and their heat reflected off the walls. Still, the stone floor was cold and hard and LeiRain was almost as happy to rise from it as she had been to lay down the night before.

LeiRain ate quietly. She'd fallen asleep quickly the night before but woke early, thinking of her failings in the previous day's battle. She saw herself standing there, frozen with fear and indecision. Afraid of waking the others, LeiRain layed there, staring at the blue glow of fae light as she toyed with the end of her braid and listened to her heart drumming in her chest. She fretted over whether she'd be able to respond differently in the future and tried to imagine possible scenarios and how she might handle them. The events of the day replayed for her over and over again as she pictured herself chasing down a retreating archer or holding the point of her sword to one of the men's throats.

Time felt strange here without the sun or the moon to signal its passage. Lost in her thoughts, she was surprised to realize that Ron's heavy snores, which had been echoing off the chamber walls all night, had ceased. She could hear him shuffling about, gathering up his things. He walked off down one of the tunnels to empty his bladder and the others began to stir too. LeiRain tried not to groan as she sat up, bone-tired and sore from laying on hard stone.

After they'd finished breakfast, thd began to repack what little they carried with them. Brya came to kneel by LeiRain where she was tucking a cloak back into her satchell. Brya set her own bag down on the ground in front of them and gingerly withdrew several small, opaque vials. She held them out to LeiRain.

'Here, take these,' she said, pressing them into LeiRain's palm.

LeiRain stared back at her, confused. 'Wha—'

'They stop your courses or keep you from getting with child if you take them after—' Brya whispered.

'Sssh,' LeiRain held a finger up to her lips. She looked over her shoulder and watched Silver packing up his cloak. There was no sign that he was listening, but with his superior senses, LeiRain had no doubt that he had overheard.

LeiRain wasn't unfamiliar with such things. She took something like this whenever she lay with Bren. She shook her head and pushed the vials back to Brya.

'I don't need these.'

The dwarve shoved them back at her with surprising force. 'No woman ever needs them, until she does.' She cast a glance across the space to where Silver sat talking to Rayand. 'My boy is the best thing to ever happen to me, but pregnancy is hard and mothering is harder. Take this. It's your freedom.'

LeiRain felt her face and neck grow warm and was grateful for the dim lighting that would hide her flush. Their whispers would be as audible to Silver as if they were shouting at each other from across the room.

'I brewed these for you, days ago. Just take them. Use them if you like. If nothing else, they'll ease the pains.'

LeiRain felt her eyes burn with unshed tears as she

resisted the urge to bury her face in Brya's hair and hug her tightly. Her fingers wrapped around the bottles and she placed them carefully in her satchel.

'Thank you,' she said, her voice cracking. Without warning, Brya threw her arms around LeiRain. The tears she'd thus far been able to hold back began to fall. She blinked them away, quickly, as Brya pulled back and looked at her.

'Take care of yourself, Rain,' Brya said with a sniffle. LeiRain saw a damp track running down one of the dwarve's cheeks. The dwarve smoothed down a piece of LeiRain's hair before moving on to hug her brother-in-law.

37

Goodbyes were brief. Ron did not seem much inclined toward sentimentality and Silver stood on the periphery, quietly averting his eyes. When Rayand wrapped his arms around LeiRain, he squeezed her so tightly that she thought he may have cracked one of her ribs. She took shallow breaths, enduring the pain because she couldn't bring herself to pull away before he was ready.

Brya and Rayand turned down one of the dark tunnels and set off, disappearing into the black with no fae light to guide them. LeiRain, Ron and Silver turned down another. The trio walked in relative silence, the sound of shuffling feet echoing off the tunnel walls. Silence had been comfortable when there had been five of them. Now that it was only LeiRain, Silver and Ron, it felt oppressive.

LeiRain wrestled with her thoughts as she trudged on between the two men. She couldn't help but worry that they judged her harshly for the way she'd frozen in the midst of combat. Her shame was so tangible that it felt like a fourth set of footsteps following along the tunnel. All of that time spent training, all of the time that Ron had dedicated to teaching her, nearly every day for months, and LeiRain had failed to use any of it when the opportunity had come. That heavy curtain in her mind, the one that had drawn back to let her reconnect with her magic, was beginning to slide closed again. She could feel it settling over her emotions, the shadows creeping slowly over her mind as the curtain glided into place.

Ron led them through the vast network of tunnels, fae light bobbing a few feet in front of him as he went. His steps were sure, but LeiRain could see the drudgery of their travels wearing on him. Or, perhaps it was disappointment in her? The dwarve's shoulders became gradually more slumped and his pace slowed. Meanwhile, Silver walked behind LeiRain, distant enough that she could not feel the warmth radiating from his body, but close enough that she could still sometimes hear his breaths. LeiRain wondered what the fae was thinking, and if he, too, worried about her performance during the skirmish. He'd been the one to say that she might be very useful on this venture. Was he regretting that now? Did he see her as a liability? As they continued their march, LeiRain worked herself up over her failure, telling herself stories about what Ron and Silver were thinking and convincing herself that she was a disappointment.

She waited for one of them to say something, to bring up their concerns. The longer they walked, the more her imagination built up their disapproval and she longed for one of them to call her out on her cowardice. She told herself that it was only a matter of time before they confronted her, and the suspense of waiting was nearly unbearable.

When Ron finally did speak, LeiRain responded without actually hearing his words.

'I'm sorry!' she yelled. Her voice echoed down the tunnel.

Embarrassed, she halted with a suddenness that put Silver's grace and reflexes to the test. He just barely missed slamming into her, stepping to the side at the last minute to avoid the collision. Ron slowed and looked over his shoulder, his brows knit in confusion.

'What in gods' names for?' he asked.

'I didn't help, I... I froze... After all my training...'

Ron waved a hand in the air, dismissing her concerns.

'De— Rain... You didn't do anything wrong. You kept your head enough to put out the fires. I've never seen you do that before– didn't even know that you could!'

She stared at him, blinking rapidly to fight back tears. The shadows that had been growing over in her mind slowed their creep.

'Training's one thing,' Ron went on. 'Battle is another. You get used to it but the first time's a shock.'

'Everything was moving so fast and I just stood there.' She shook her head. 'I didn't know what to do.'

It was just like when they murdered my mother, she thought.

'It happens to a lot of folks – happened to me, even. Damn near lost my head to a longsword in my first scuffle. Lucky for me, another clansman had the wherewithal to shove me to the ground before I could take too much damage.'

'Really?'

She found it hard to imagine Ronland the Red standing confused in the heat of battle. He'd been so confident, so unafraid.

'I wouldn't lie to you.'

'It was the same for me,' Silver said, stepping forward into the blue glow. 'Though violence starts at a young age for verdaant.' He looked at the ground as he said this.

'Don't let it get into your head, Rain,' Ron said as he placed a hand on her shoulder. 'There were only three of them, anyway. Nothing we couldn't handle. I still trust you with my back.'

Ron's eyes were soft as he gripped her shoulder. LeiRain could hear apology in his words and knew that he was trying to build a bridge back to the friendship they'd had before their argument. It was her turn to apologize. She *needed* to apologize. LeiRain thought about doing it now. *I'm sorry. I didn't mean it. I was angry and it was wrong.* That's all she had to say. He had clearly already forgiven her so there was little to lose. But they weren't alone. LeiRain couldn't bring herself to speak the words where Silver could overhear them. Ron's fingers gave her shoulder a light squeeze before he spoke again.

'You're young yet, Rain, and inexperienced in violence. I don't look forward to you growing more world-weary, but I know you'll come through when it counts. You're brave and strong. *Just like your mother.*'

He tilted his head to the side and winked at her. LeiRain nodded, believing him. She was like her mother, in both good ways and bad.

'Now, I asked ya if you wanted to have a snack.'

It didn't take long for LeiRain to lose track of time inside the mountain. Fae light banished the darkness, but it gave no clues as to whether it was night or day. Its glow had been a comfort initially, but now the blue haze seemed eerie and disorienting. The tunnels began to feel cramped to LeiRain, monotonous and suffocating. The path became narrower as they moved further away from the central chamber and

LeiRain could stretch out her arms and put a hand on either side of the cavern. She longed for sunlight and open spaces and for the smell and feel of moving water. Moisture in the cave was abundant, but it was stagnant and the damp stone felt slimy under her fingertips.

When they finally reached the end of their tunnel and stood facing another solid wall of mountain rock, LeiRain's heart sped up. She was eager to be out of the mountain and at the same time, afraid of what awaited them on the other side. She held her breath as Ron placed his ax in the keyhole.

Nothing happened at first and LeiRain's throat tightened. What if they couldn't get out? Would they have to turn around and go back, spending another series of days and nights inside this stone prison? Her mouth went dry and she reached for her water skin. LeiRain's hands shook so hard when she brought it to her lips that she spilled as much water down the front of her tunic as she managed to swallow.

Before her anxiety could reach a crescendo, the rock shifted and a thin breeze lifted the loose strands of hair around her face. She inhaled the scent of a spring dusk. LeiRain imagined that they would exit to the blinding light of day and had looked forward to the warmth of the sun on her face. Instead of sunlight, the cool illumination of a partially shaded moon shone through the fissure. LeiRain could see a sweep of orange across the horizon as the day said its final farewell.

The stone door refused to move further outward, presenting much more resistance than the entrance through which they had come. Ron swore and moved his ax in and out of the magical lock, but nothing more happened. He threw his shoulder against the rock and still it did not shift. Silver came to his aid and they worked together to create an opening large enough to allow for their exit. There was no more room for LeiRain to stand beside them and push, so she stood watching as the men's boots scraped the floor in their attempt to move a mountain.

Slowly, the rock inched forward. Ron grunted with the effort. Silver remained silent beside him, but LeiRain could see muscles bulge beneath his tunic. After several long minutes of this, during which LeiRain was cut off from the fresh, outside air by the mass of the male bodies, there was enough space for each of them to slide out of the tunnel. On the other side of the door, Ron lifted his ax and slid it into another crevice. The door slid firmly shut, sending up a puff of dust as it sealed itself so tightly that LeiRain couldn't find the seams despite knowing where they were. The bulbs of fae light hovering around Silver's head winked out.

LeiRain stepped forward and stumbled, not seeing the small tree that had fallen across her path. Now that she had noticed it, she saw that it grew from the base of the rock the men had just worked so hard to move. Their efforts to open the door had ripped the sapling from the earth and now it sat crooked on top of a clump of grass, a thick twist of roots protruding from the ground. It had clearly been a long time since anyone had used this entrance.

Silver stood in front of the felled tree, one palm held open over its rootstock. LeiRain watched as it began to stand straighter and the dislodged roots worked their way back into the soil. She'd seen Silver work his magic before, but this was the first time she'd really *felt* it. Her body vibrated with his power, and her magic hummed a response. As they sank, the roots pulled the trunk straighter and straighter until the tree was fully righted. When he had finished, the earth around the base of the sapling was all loose soil. Silver's palms hovered over the bare earth and bright green grass began to pop up through the clumps. The grass grew until it was thick enough to cover all traces of their exit. LeiRain wrapped her arms around herself, as the buzz of Silver's magic faded away. She felt cold and empty now that it was gone.

Still, it was good to be free of the tunnels. She breathed in greedily, lungs hungry for the fresh air. LeiRain stretched her arms wide, something that hadn't been possible for the last few days, and drank in the fresh scent of lilac as she brushed her fingers over the tiny, fragrant blossoms. The ocean wasn't visible from this distance, at least not in the faint moonlight, but the smell was unmistakable. Her skin dimpled as the tiny hairs on her arms and the back of her neck rose. The salty tang of ocean water and bait fish felt like home to LeiRain and her magic sensed the stretch and recoil of waves rolling up onto the beach and then back to sea.

LeiRain's mind was flooded with grief and longing and she worked to shove these things into the back of her mind so that she could continue to enjoy the moment. Meanwhile, Silver stood nearby with his arms held aloft. His power ran through her again as the lush greenery expanded and twisted at his command, creating a shelter much like the one he had made for himself on the mountain.

They bedded down inside the canopy he had created and Silver thickened the branches around them so that they would be entirely hidden from the outside. Overhead, he left wide gaps in between the tree limbs so that they could still see swaths of star-lit sky. She knew that this was intentional and tried to catch Silver's gaze to smile at him in thanks, but he stared at his hands, eyes unfocused.

Laying down, LeiRain rejoiced at the feel of grass pricking her bare skin. It might not be as comfortable as a mattress, but it was a welcome bed after several nights of sleeping on stone.

Silver came back to himself and, noticing the chill in the air, buried fae light in the soil beneath them. LeiRain relaxed into the soft earth and let her eyes fall closed. An owl hooted in the distance and a light breeze rustled the leaves. Somewhere nearby, there was the soft buzz of nighttime insects. Warm and free for the first time in days, sleep quickly overtook her.

38

A thin sheet of blue and platinum shimmered on the horizon. Even with the bright sun, the ocean was just barely visible from where they'd exited the tunnels but LeiRain had no doubt that it was there. She felt each wave as it crashed ashore like the gentle brush of fingertips on the back of her neck. The nearby sea and the sun on her face soothed LeiRain even as she took the last gulp of water from her waterskin.

'It's a bit of a walk to freshwater,' Ron said apologetically.

LeiRain hung the flask back on her hip and gripped her shield. She broadened her awareness, letting her mind pick up on all the sources of water nearby. She recalled the mountain stream and how differently the water felt when compared to that of the ocean. LeiRain searched for something with the crispness of melted snow.

Her senses pulled in a thousand different directions at once. LeiRain felt the water stored inside lush green leaves and tiny pools of morning dew that had not yet evaporated. For a brief moment, she was entirely overwhelmed by the sensation and started to pull away from her magic. She stopped herself from recoiling, took a deep breath and let it out very slowly. Some of the tension left her shoulders as she exhaled. Little by little, she tuned out the pieces of information that weren't useful and narrowed her focus on the collections of water that held the most promise. *There!* She could feel something large and deep nearby, moving slowly but not stagnant.

'There *is* fresh water nearby!' She opened her eyes and blinked, surprised at her success. Less than a week ago she had struggled just to connect with the water. Now, that connection came easily. 'I can feel it.' Her mouth broadened into a smile as she said this.

'Lead the way, then' Ron said as he smiled back at her.

LeiRain paced around the grass, trying to get a better sense of where the water lay. She shook her head and let out a frustrated sigh. There was no sign of a stream anywhere but her magic told her it was *right here*. She walked back and forth, back and forth, trying to pinpoint the location of the water. It was cool and dark when her mind met with it, quiet and untouched.

'I'm sorry,' she said, shaking her head. 'I must be wrong. I thought –' She looked down at her feet where the water ought to be. 'Oh!' LeiRain laughed as she realized what should have been obvious from the beginning. 'Groundwater,' she exclaimed. Her eyes met Silver's and magic thrummed between them. He smiled back at her, amused by her joy.

'Alright then, Demi,' Ron said, smiling at her. 'Good to know but not sure how we'll get to it.'

He didn't seem to notice that he'd slipped back into using her old nickname and she didn't correct him, glad that the tension between them had lifted over the last few days. Her smile faltered a bit when she remembered her own unspoken apology, but finding drinking water was a more urgent concern.

'I can help with that,' Silver said, softly.

The fae took a knee beside LeiRain and held his hand open a few inches above the ground. The earth beneath his palm began to part, the grass peeling away and dirt rolling itself into several small piles until there was a gaping hole, at least a foot wide and twice as deep. LeiRain leaned forward, admiring Silver's handywork. While the dirt that had been moved thus far was dry and crumbling, the soil at the bottom of the hole was damp and rich in color.

'Can you help?' Silver asked, looking up at her.

She nodded and knelt beside him. Her leg brushed against his and she felt a surge of his power join with her own.

'See if you can draw the water up.' LeiRain felt the caress of his breath on her neck when he spoke. She took in another steadying breath and forced herself to focus as she exhaled. Shield still in hand, she opened up the place in her mind where the connection to the water felt strongest. She stared down into the make-shift well, but her focus was inward. Her mind grazed the water and it rose to meet her. LeiRain projected a feeling of want, asking the water to continue rising, to draw itself out of the soil. She sighed with relief when she felt the water obey. The hole filled quickly as moisture rang itself from the dirt, but LeiRain frowned when she saw that she'd produced a pool of dark gray water, swirled with debris.

'Uh, not quite drinkable. Sorry—' As she was speaking, she felt the thrum of Silver's magic beside her. The murky well stirred and, as LeiRain watched, the water turned from a gray-brown to something more opaque. Bits of earth and plant matter pulled to the edges of the hole and melded back into the soil. Eventually, the water was clean and clear, the bottom of the hole easily visible. Still Silver's magic pulsed.

She looked at him, observing the concentration on his face, his half closed eyes and his lips drawn tight. There was something sensual about those heavy-lidded eyes. LeiRain thought of the way she'd let the water see her desires and knew that Silver must be doing the same with his own magic. She imagined what it might feel like to have Silver look at her in such a way, to be the object of his desire. Without meaning to, she sent a jolt of her own magic vibrating back through whatever it was that stretched between them. Silver's eyes widened in response, but the surprise disappeared from his face almost instantly and his focus was back on the ground in front of him. LeiRain looked down at the water they had drawn together. A thick tree root coiled around the edges of the well, keeping the soil at bay. Silver cupped his hands and filled them. Sunlight sparkled off the water's surface as he brought it to his lips.

They filled their waterskins and ate a modest breakfast of dried fruit before Ron departed for the nearest village. They would need sea passage to the Arborris Enclave and Ron thought that he might have a useful connection in a nearby port town. Ships came and went and the schedules often changed due to weather and shipping demands, so they couldn't guess at how long it might take him to arrange the travel. Ron would have to go immediately, and alone, to make arrangements. LeiRain and Silver were too conspicuous to accompany the dwarve – especially Silver, since he had clearly been trailed before.

With Ron gone, the two of them sat quietly in the early morning sun, left with little to do while they waited for their friend to return. LeiRain had laid her cloak over the thick grass and sat there quietly, watching the distant shimmer of the ocean far below. Silver sat nearby on his own cloak. She could hear him chewing as he finished the last of his breakfast. Neither of them spoke for a long time. The twitter of birds and buzzing of insects filled in some of the silence. Once the sun had fully risen, LeiRain felt something shift and the silence between them became awkward. She fidgeted with the end of her braid and shifted her weight where she sat. They hadn't spoken about what had passed between them while they were finding the water, or about what passed between them every time their eyes met.

She was staring at the ends of her hair now, working up the courage to speak. The last time they had been alone with each other had been one of the most intimate experiences of LeiRain's life. It felt like a line had been crossed in that encounter and there was no going back. If she asked him about their magic, the connection between them, that would cross yet another line. The thought alone made LeiRain feel naked. She laid back on her cloak with a sigh and tried to focus on the clouds, on the bits of pollen that floated by in the breeze.

'You feel your magic again.' Silver's statement broke the silence.

She bit her lower lip thoughtfully before replying.

'I do,' she said, 'Did you—' She took a steadying breath. 'Was it like that for you?'

He looked at her for a moment and she thought perhaps he'd missed her meaning so she added, 'When your brother died. Was your magic silent and then just suddenly loud again?' It was the best she could do to put it into words. Of course, her magic hadn't been entirely silent, especially after Silver had come into her life.

'It still is, sometimes.' His voice was low and breathy. She could hear the pain in it. 'But not as often anymore. I have mostly forgiven myself.'

LeiRain could feel the warmth of his body, only a few feet away, and ached to be in his arms. Briefly, she considered getting up and going to him, but quickly recoiled from the thought. What if he did not want to be close to her the way that she wanted to be close to him?

What she felt for him, the connection they seemed to have, went beyond anything she'd ever experienced. But as much as she longed for Silver's touch, she also feared it. Feared showing him any more of herself than he had already seen. Ron's words rang in her ears.

He's not your healing.

What had Ron meant by that? Was it wrong to take so much comfort in Silver's presence? These questions swirled about in her mind and LeiRain let the silence between the two of them stretch.

'It's not quiet now, Rain.' His voice was almost a song as he said this. She let her braid fall from her fingers. LeiRain swallowed her nervousness and slowly brought her eyes up to meet his. 'It *sings*.'

LeiRain felt the breath rush out of her lungs as his magic slammed into hers. Her head tilted back slightly as she sucked in more air. A small groan escaped her lips. Desire warred with embarrassment. One corner of Silver's mouth curled up and a low growl came from his throat.

'What is this?' LeiRain asked in a whisper, her eyes never leaving his.

'I believe,' his voice gravelly and baritone, 'that this is *magicae canentis*.'

LeiRain smiled and, as she did so, another pulse of Silver's magic raced toward her. She shuddered with the pleasure of it. 'I have no idea what that means,' she replied with a laugh.

'Magic that sings. It happens sometimes, two people find that their magic compliments each other. It can happen between anyone, but often it is,' his throat bobbed as he swallowed, 'between lovers.' That's exactly what it felt like. Her magic rose up to meet his, vibrating through them both with a melody of their own making.

'But you're not sure?'

'I'm *sure*.' His eyes narrowed on the last word. 'I've just – I've never felt it before. The descriptions hardly seem to do it justice.'

'You've never felt it before?'

His eyes stayed locked on hers as he shook his head. 'No,' he whispered. LeiRain suddenly became aware of how close they were to each other. They'd both inched forward off of their cloaks and onto the grass. 'It is a very rare thing,' his eyes left Leirain's and ran down her body. His eyes slowly worked their way back up to her face and she warmed all over when his eyes lingered on her mouth. He reached out a hand and ran his fingers lightly down her braid, moving still closer. He lifted one of her hands from her lap and held it between his, his thumb sliding back and forth over her wrist in a gentle caress. Their magic continued to twist and thrum.

'Rain,' his eyes narrowed as he said her name. His voice had lost its huskiness. 'This feels so natural.' She shook her head, agreeing emphatically and ignoring the hint of sorrow in his voice. 'But my father is dangerous. The *verdaant* are dangerous.'

Silver's magic began to pull away as he spoke. It withdrew slowly, just as his hands pulled away, tracing her palm with his fingertips before he let her hand drop back into her lap. Her own magic drooped it coiled itself back into her chest.

LeiRain squeezed her eyes shut for several seconds. She reminded herself of Caspian, her father. Of the storm in his eyes. She recalled the way Alarra had clutched a young LeiRain to her chest as her father disappeared into the ocean. Her mother, never one to show affection, holding her as if she'd almost been lost. Her mother, strong and fearless, refusing to leave Harbor because of him, her father, *a fae*. When LeiRain opened her eyes again, she met Silver's with a cool gaze. He was watching her, his brow furrowed and wariness in his eyes.

'I think I'll go look for berries or root vegetables,' she declared as if the last few minutes had never happened. 'I'd like to have something to eat for lunch that isn't dried.' LeiRain forced an artificial lightness into her voice as she stood. She dusted off her trousers and shook out her cloak.

39

LeiRain had meant to excuse herself to hunt for berries, but she hadn't thought about how easy such a task would be for a man who could make them grow with the wave of a hand. Instead of escaping the awkwardness between them by heading into the brush alone, LeiRain found herself accompanied by Silver who seemed quite cheerful about helping her locate wild sustenance.

'Tell me about your village,' he insisted as he held his satchel beneath a cluster of berries and willed them to drop off the branch. They fell with a light *plunk* onto the berries he'd already gathered.

'There really isn't much to say,' she replied. Magic stirred in her as Silver wielded his, but LeiRain held it in check.

'Do you have friends there?'

'One,' LeiRain said, but then she saw Bren standing in the clearing, eyes wide, while her mother's throat was slit. 'I *did* have one,' she amended.

'I'm sorry,' Silver said. She felt him turn toward her but LeiRain kept her eyes on the fruit she was picking. 'Is he...'

'Dead?' LeiRain studied her berry-stained fingers. The

dark red beneath her nails could almost be mistaken for blood. 'To me he is.'

Silver did not reply to this but LeiRain felt his eyes burning into the back of her neck for several seconds before he turned back to his work. Her stomach twisted with guilt at the way she had so blatantly sabotaged his efforts to start a conversation.

'It was very dull,' she offered. 'And it was very human. The entire village was human, except for me, so there weren't many people offering to be my friend.'

'There were none like you?' Silver asked. 'Not even—' He was silent for a few seconds. When he spoke, his voice was much softer. 'Not even your mother?'

'Not even my mother,' she said. 'My father is tempest, my mother was just an ironworker.' LeiRain remembered Ron's ax, how it had literally parted stone for them. 'Maybe not *just,*' she added. 'My mother could enchant sorcerer's steel. But that's not something the villagers could see just by looking at her.'

'No, they wouldn't,' he replied.

For several minutes, there was no sound besides the rustling of leaves and the gentle plop of berries falling on top of one another.

'Where did you grow up?' LeiRain had wondered this. Silver had been such a mystery to them all, giving away so little about himself, aside from his heartache over his brother.

'The Green Court.' His voice was hard as he said this.

'I've never heard of it,' LeiRain turned to look at him but it was his turn to avoid eye contact. His focus remained on the nearly empty berry bush in front of him. 'Where is it?' She asked when seconds went by without a reply.

'Inland.' She watched a muscle in his jaw flex as he gritted his teeth. 'It moves so it's not really possible to say exactly where.'

LeiRain could tell by the muscle and veins standing out in his neck and the rigid set of his shoulders that this was not a comfortable topic for him, but she was too fascinated to let it go.

'How do you find your way home?'

He turned to look at her now. A cold chill ran down her spine when Silver met her stare. His platinum eyes, normally full of light and mist, were clouded over.

'The Green Court calls to me. It's always there. The tug, the pull to return. But I will never again call it home.' He looked back at the berry bush. 'If we take any more, I will have to force it to regrow them.'

LeiRain looked into the satchel she was holding. It had become rather heavy, so full that the berries on the bottom might start to be crushed if she kept adding more.

'I think we have plenty,' she said.

Silver waved a hand in front of the bush and caused it to sprout a few new clusters of berries anyway. 'So it's not too obvious that anyone was here,' he said.

LeiRain shuddered. It hadn't occurred to her that they were still in danger of being found or followed. Not after they'd spent a few days trekking through the inside of a mountain. When they returned to the clearing, she felt vulnerable in the openness. A long silence passed between them as they ate from the satchels.

LeiRain was somewhat disappointed by the bitterness of the berries. It wasn't intolerable and was still better than their dried rations, but she had imagined something more akin to the blueberries she'd grown up eating. She struggled to relax now, the fear of being found causing her head to whip around every time the wind rustled the leaves. The third or fourth time she did this, Silver made a soft noise in his throat that caused LeiRain to look at him. There was concern on his face.

'I had thought—' LeiRain swallowed and took a deep breath before continuing. 'I mean, after going through the mountain, it didn't seem likely that anyone would be following us. Not until you made the point about the berries...' She looked away as she trailed off, embarrassed by her naivety. Several seconds passed before Silver responded.

'I suppose it is much less likely now,' he said, his tone conceding. 'Perhaps it is just that old habits,' he gestured to himself, 'die hard. I have never stopped watching my back, not since I lost Therris.'

LeiRain shook her head. 'That sounds exhausting.'

To her surprise, Silver laughed. His face creased with smile lines and his eyes glittered.

'What?' She asked. Surprised and unsure, her cheeks went hot with embarrassment.

'It's just ... you're right. But it never would have occured to me to describe it that way.'

The flush in LeiRain's cheeks turned from embarrassment into hunger as his smile spread wide across his face. She'd never seen him smile quite like that before, never seen him so relaxed and transparent. If Silver was beautiful when his face was serene, he was divine when his smile reached his eyes. LeiRain smiled back at him briefly before nervously sucking at her fingers in a vain attempt to eliminate the berry stains. Silver's eyes slid down to her lips as she did this. They lingered there, his silver irises smoldering. LeiRain responded by leaning closer to him and returning the gaze, examining his lips. She imagined the press of them against her own, the feather lightness of them as they trailed down her jaw, her neck, the low collar of her shirt.

She tried to remind herself of the warnings that he had

given her. *The* verdaant *are dangerous.* LeiRain reminded herself how badly she wanted to avoid making the same mistakes her mother had made. But still she imagined Silver's thin fingers peeling her blouse down over her shoulder, his kisses sliding still lower – LeiRain felt a surge of power, her magic rising. *Yes.* She moved a few inches closer to him, sliding over the grass. *Yes yes*, her magic urged her on. LeiRain was certain that he could smell her arousal, her want. Silver swallowed audibly. Slowly, he began to lean toward her. They were so close. LeiRain's heart was pounding, her lips anticipating his.

Silver's head turned away. LeiRain's magic gave an anguished cry as its demands went unheeded. The smile had left his face entirely and it was suddenly easier to understand his earlier warning. He *looked* dangerous. Silver cleared his throat, the noise startling her. The hardness had passed from his face and the Silver she knew, the serene forest fae, looked back at her.

'I umm—' She'd never heard him stumble over his words before. He cleared his throat again as he pulled something from the inside of his tunic. It was a weathered piece of parchment, folded over several times. 'I can't show you exactly where the Green Court is because it's always moving,' he said as he unfolded the paper. 'But I can show you generally where it resides on The Continent.'

Silver laid the paper on the grass between them, smoothing it out with his hands. His fingers were clean, no trace of the berry juice that had soaked into LeiRain's, as they swept over the map. LeiRain had seen maps before, in some of her books, but none so detailed. One of her history books, *Before the War*, had featured a large map of The Continent just inside the cover. The cities, especially those near the heart of the human kingdom, had been drawn in great detail but the space between them was almost entirely blank – the author had not cared to include any of the smaller villages, forests or lakes in his depiction.

Silver set the map down so that the Southern edge was closest to LeiRain. It had clearly been drawn by someone with an appreciation for her art. There were small villages dotted along the coast, their names written in tiny calligraphic letters. She found Harbor Village on the map and was surprised to see how close it was to other coastal villages – the tip of her thumb could cover both Harbor and the nearest settlement. It was strange to see it this way, just a small piece of a larger world. Harbor had felt like the entire world to her for so long.

Many more villages dotted the map, separated by large stretches of trees, with the King's palace located in the center. Much of The Continent appeared to be covered by thick forests, which were drawn with such precision that LeiRain could make out some of the individual leaves on the vast, uneven rows of trees. 'This,' he said, sweeping his hand over a large area of hand-drawn trees very far from the coast, 'is generally where you can find the verdaant.'

'Is the Green Court an actual court?' LeiRain asked. 'I mean, do they have a king? Like the humans do?'

Silver stiffened at this and LeiRain glanced up from the map. There was no sign of distress on his face but his body was rigid and he took a few seconds to respond. She turned back to the drawing.

'Yes,' he said. There was hesitation in his voice. 'They have a king. He is ruthless. More dangerous than any other verdaant I've ever encountered.'

'So you've met him? The King?'

When he answered, his voice was so quiet that it was nearly lost to the breeze. 'Yes.'

LeiRain leaned over the map again, feeling a flutter of excitement at being so close to him.

'So,' her voice wavered slightly and she swallowed to clear her throat, 'where did you look for Ron before you finally found us?'

'That's a bit of a winding tale,' he shifted his position so that he was sitting next to her.

'We don't have much else to do,' LeiRain replied. She kept her eyes on the piece of parchment, willing herself not to think of other things they might do to pass the time.

'I suppose we don't,' he said, LeiRain watched him out of the corner of her eye, catching the hint of a smile on his face as he replied.

Silver dragged his finger over the map, his skin making a quiet *shush* as it slid against the parchment. He traced a path that led from the Green Court, or the approximate location of it, anyway, to a seaside village directly to the west of the thick forest.

'I began here,' he said, 'finding the cloak at a local shop. Then,' his finger slid along the western coast of The Continent, 'I stopped here.' His throat rumbled with subtle laughter. 'This is where I encountered the feral cat.'

LeiRain laughed with him but kept her eyes down.

Silver continued to trace his way up the coast in a northerly direction, leaning into LeiRain as he did so. By the time his finger came to rest on Harbor Village, his shoulder was pressed against her. Her mood shifted slightly as she stared at the tiny dot of the village next to Silver's finger. LeiRain could feel the pull of magicae canentis. It pulsed between them, objecting when she began to draw away. She'd meant to lighten the topic with her question, but thinking of her village, of Silver arriving there to find her mother's remains and the wreckage of their burned home—

'I'm sorry,' she said, shifting her feet beneath her to stand. 'I think, I need to …' *To what?* She asked herself. *To not think about her mother? To not be so near Silver?* 'do some sword drills. I haven't done any for days.' This was true enough. They made their way through the cave with haste and there'd been no energy or time left for sparring at the end of each travel day, and even if there had been, the space was far too cramped.

'Of course,' Silver said, his voice even. She watched him fold up the map again and stow it in his tunic, but turned away just as he hooked up at her and made eye contact.

She spent the rest of the daylight hours drilling. When nightfall came, LeiRain was too tired to worry over the strain between them. It was better for everyone if she kept her feelings on a tether. There was no reason to think that she would ever see Silver again after they completed this mission and she could still remember the piercing heartbreak she'd felt when things had ended with Bren. She didn't want to do that to herself again. There was also a haunting sense of foreboding when she remembered her father.

Surely, Caspian had not always been so fierce and frightening. Her mother would have never involved herself with such a creature. Perhaps her father had been just as charming and serene as Silver appeared now, until he had what he wanted. LeiRain could not let herself fall into the same trap. She owed Alarra more than that. Even if she and Silver must be physically near one another for the time being, it was best that she kept her heart tucked away from the verdaant, safely out of reach.

Silver cocooned them in tightly knit branches, the fae light buried beneath them, and they lay down. LeiRain rested stiffly on her cloak for what felt like a very long time. Silver was only a few feet away and it would be obvious that she was restless if she tossed and turned, so LeiRain forced herself to stare blankly at the moonlight seeping in through the leaves overhead, her hands clutched together on her stomach. To make things worse, the night had grown cold. Even with the fae light radiating heat from beneath her, LeiRain still shivered. She wrapped the edges of her cloak around herself, but as soon as she began drifting off to sleep, the cloak slipped out of her fingers and the cold air woke her.

After what must have been hours, LeiRain gave up on sleep entirely and was instead trying to count the vast swath of stars overhead when Silver's hand slid across her stomach. He'd closed the distance between them silently. Neither of them said a word, and LeiRain did not resist as he pulled her onto her side and tucked himself around her. For several minutes, she leaned stiffly against his chest, heart pounding, his hand resting on her abdomen. She could feel his breath on her neck and the heat from his palm seeped through her tunic. Eventually, her heart slowed and she relaxed into him. Though there was still a part of her mind that warned LeiRain against this closeness, she decided it would be okay to let Silver care for her. Just one more time. With their combined body heat, it wasn't long before LeiRain was thoroughly thawed and overcome with drowsiness. She spent her dreams walking through herb gardens in the warm sunshine.

LeiRain woke up in the morning with Silver's cloak draped over her, in addition to her own. Despite this, she could feel the absence of him in the cold against her back. The grass beneath her seemed to be running out of heat as well and she wondered how long fae light glowed if left on its own. The morning was unusually cold for the season, much like the night had been, and LeiRain could feel a storm inching toward them. She had always known when a big storm was coming. Incoming rain felt like something brushing gently against her skin, feather light, just barely noticeable but there nonetheless. A storm, though, that was different. It was like lightning crawling beneath her skin. It was bright and energizing. With a storm rolling in, LeiRain didn't long for morning coffee. She already hummed with borrowed energy. The storm was close.

LeiRain ducked through the hole in the woven branches with Silver's cloak draped neatly over her arm. She was a bit surprised when she didn't immediately see the fae, but remembered his caution the day before and didn't dare call his name. She left his cloak folded on the ground and went to another patch of woods, far from where they slept, to relieve herself. When she returned to the clearing a few minutes later, there was still no sign of Silver. LeiRain paced back and forth, her feet flattening patches of grass as she made a path around their drinking well. It wasn't all nerves at Silver's absence. It was just so difficult to remain still when she could feel the storm's energy lighting up her veins. Wind groaned through the trees, the only sound LeiRain could hear. Even the birds were quiet this morning.

'Good morning,' LeiRain jolted, surprised. She turned to see Silver holding a bulging satchel. Seeing her eyes drift to it, he said, 'Thought you might enjoy a bit more fresh food before we're stuck eating hardtack for a while.'

He'd gone to get more berries. If he'd offered her more last night, LeiRain would have turned them down. She'd eaten so many the night before that her stomach had ached. But she was hungry this morning and the berries did sound good, though this time she'd also nibble on some of their dried stores to avoid upsetting her stomach again. She pulled the satchel out of his hands and passed him his cloak. Silver raised an eyebrow at her.

'It's going to storm,' she said.

'Ah,' he nodded. 'I thought there was going to be rain.'

'Not rain, a *storm*,' she clarified. 'Can you make the shelter thicker? I can redirect the water but I don't know how long I can keep that up.'

'Of course,' he replied and followed her into the shelter.

LeiRain began to pick at the berries as the branches around them grew thick. Where bits of gray morning light still worked their way in overhead, smaller limbs sprouted and wove their way through. Silver paused for a moment to create a few floating orbs of fae light as the natural light overhead disappeared entirely. He sat down beside her and took a handful of berries from the pile on top of the open satchel. Before he could finish the fruit in his palm, there was a crack of thunder and loud tap of raindrops pelting their shelter.

Relief and euphoria flooded LeiRain as the storm settled overhead. The excess energy that had been pulsing through her body slipped away as if it were going home, rejoining the storm. It was only the anticipation that was uncomfortable. The release when a storm finally arrived was pure pleasure. She groaned and her eyes partially closed.

LeiRain didn't dare let herself look at Silver. She could feel his eyes on her almost the same way she'd felt the storm approaching. It was electric. If their eyes locked now and their magic entwined, LeiRain didn't think there was anything she could do to stop herself from becoming his. Her chest heaved with a deep breath as she thought about the ecstasy of his touch. Parts of her body swelled in anticipation. LeiRain wished desperately for privacy so that she could touch herself, relieve some of this pressure. But there was no privacy to be had, so she laid down and listened to the rain with her eyes closed, pretending that her body wasn't on the edge of release.

40

LeiRain was relieved when Ron returned the next morning. His presence served as a buffer between her and the verdaant. Somehow, a company of three felt like it offered her greater privacy than being alone with Silver. The two of them had spent most of the previous day and evening in silence as thunder sounded overhead and rain pelted the outside of the shelter. She'd fallen asleep early and dreamt of kisses trailing down her body, her fingers knotted in Silver's hair. When the rain had slowed and they'd gone to refill their water skins in the early morning, she let her hand brush lightly against his. It was the first time they had touched since the day before, and even though their gazes didn't lock, LeiRain could feel her magic giving away all of her secrets. It thrummed with her desire and swelled with arousal when his magic responded in kind.

At the touch of their hands, Silver had gone unnaturally still. LeiRain had finally looked up and the fae stared into her with such intensity that his eyes looked like pools of silver flames. He knew. She saw him read her magic's message. His own power telegraphed his understanding and the mutuality

371

of the desire. Now that he was aware of her body's secrets, the aching for him intensified. They leaned over the well, their faces only inches apart... LeiRain's breath still caught on the memory. Somehow, she'd resisted the urge to lean in, to kiss him.

She remembered his words from a few days ago, his warning about verdaants. LeiRain thought of the power she'd seen him wield, the way his eyes burned differently when he'd killed that Royal. She recalled the way he'd turned his head when they'd been on the cusp of kissing a few days before. LeiRain held herself back, not certain what she feared more, that he might reject her advance or that he might embrace it. Silver had cleared his throat, and parted his lips. LeiRain wondered if he'd been about to ask if he could kiss her. In a world where most men took what they wanted, Silver always asked. This earth-wielding fae before her would take nothing from LeiRain without her permission. She watched him lick his lips, a hungry expression on his face. But LeiRain would never know what Silver had been about to say because, just as her name passed his lips, footsteps crunched nearby and Ron bellowed out a greeting.

The dwarve had returned much sooner than they'd expected, having found them passage on a vessel called The Mad Return. He knew the captain well, having chartered with Dearvian before. As a shifter, Dearvian was sympathetic to their cause.

'The atmosphere's not so friendly, though,' Ron told them, describing his brief stay in the village. 'It was tense, at best. Most of the town is segregated now. Blends and any other non-humans have been forced into a rundown excuse for an inn. Even the innkeeper looked like he didn't want to be there, but he was a blend himself so at least I got a fair price on the room. Everywhere else in town, non-humans are paying *at least* double for their purchases. And that's if a vendor will even sell to them in the first place!' He paused to take a drink of water. It had started raining again and Ron was practically yelling to be heard over the storm. 'I have to tell you, there wasn't any love lost between the non-humans either. Everybody seems to be fighting for their piece of the world.' He shook his head. 'Saw two scuffles break out in the inn on the first night. Started taking meals in my room after that.'

Just as Silver had predicted, the violence perpetrated by the Royals had led to increased animosity between virtually everyone.

'You can't sit within six feet of a member of another race without them side-eyeing you. And to top it off, they've been commandeering ships.'

'The Royals?' LeiRain asked, aghast.

'In some parts of the ocean, yes. And anyone who's challenged them hasn't survived to tell the tale. Either the humans are all supporting the Royals or too scared to speak out. Everyone else is too divided to fight back.'

Silver's face was glum as he listened. He took no satisfaction in being right.

'We'll have to stick to the shadows tonight,' Ron said.

'We're going tonight?' LeiRain asked. 'It's not going to stop raining until tomorrow morning.'

'Aye,' Ron nodded slowly. 'It'll be better in the rain, safer for us. Not many people out and starting trouble. Of course, the way will be slippery, but once we're in town it will be easier to pass through and board the ship unnoticed. All the busiest places are along the waterfront.' LeiRain nodded. The best business was always along the waterfront. 'Nobody will think a thing of it if we all have our hoods pulled over our faces since it's going to be pissing rain the entire time.'

It took them most of the day to make it to the edge of the

village. They stayed hidden in the thick trees until nightfall. The three of them had been able to follow a trodden path down the mountain for a good portion of the trip, but much of that was slippery rock and then squelching mud as they'd gotten to lower elevations. Ron had made them diverge from the path a few miles outside of the village so that they weren't spotted too early. Even peeking through the thick trees, LeiRain could tell that the village was similar to Harbor in size and layout. Quiet residential streets turned into cobble-stone roads the closer they got to the water.

It grew dark early, the sun having never really been given a chance to shine through the storm clouds. They crept out of the woods as close to the harbor as possible so as to avoid traversing any more of the village than necessary. Rain pelted their heads and rolled down their cloaks in great streams. LeiRain had to restrain herself from redirecting the rivulets of water that trickled over the edge of her hood and onto her face. There weren't many people out, but someone might notice a stranger with the power to redirect the rain, so she tolerated the cold trickle.

A warm glow emanated from tavern windows, and LeiRain's stomach rumbled when the smell of cooked meats and vegetables wafted toward them. She could hear the clink of dishware and the clank of mugs coming together as toasts were made, just barely audible over the patter of rain on cobblestones. The heavy storm that assailed their silent party contrasted sharply with the merriment emanating from the pub, making their walk feel somber. LeiRain tried to sink further into the hood of her cloak.

Ron directed them to the far end of the harbor where a medium-sized ship was moored to the last pier. She had to squint to make out the faded and peeling letters that spelled *The Mad Return* across the bow. Boards had been laid down midship so that the crew could come and go this evening. They walked up the rickety, make-shift brow.

The vessel was dark save for a warm yellow light that glowed in the windows of what must have been the captain's cabin. They saw no one save a single member of the ship's company who sat on the deck, snoring, with his back against a barrel at the top of the brow. He startled awake at the noise of them stepping aboard. At first glance, the sailor looked like a human, but LeiRain saw his eyes flash green when the light hit them. He was huddled beneath a cloak with a large-brimmed hat protecting his face from the rain and LeiRain couldn't help but wonder what other inhuman features hid beneath the cloak.

She thought that she caught the scent of body odor and rum wafting off of the sailor when he said something inaudible to Ron. She couldn't be sure because whatever she smelled was quickly masked by the scent of briny water and damp wood. Harbor's smell. A wave of unexpected homesickness for Harbor Village crashed into LeiRain. It wasn't a longing for the village, exactly, but a pang of grief at having lost the simplicity of life in her youth. Though she wasn't a fan of venturing into strange waters at night, LeiRain had to fight the urge to dive overboard. She missed the feel of ocean water, the texture, the smell, the taste. The rain falling on the water's surface, sending splashes of ocean spray into the air, only made her ache more deeply for the water's touch.

Ron shushed the blend sailor and spoke in a quiet and hurried manner. The sailor nodded, rubbing sleep from his eyes, and pointed toward a darkened set of stairs near where they stood on the starboard side of the ship. The dwarve gave the sailor a coin for his discretion and motioned for LeiRain and Silver to follow him down the stairs.

They took careful steps, feeling their way in the dark.

LeiRain inhaled the scent of ocean and rain as deeply as she could before they descended beyond its reach. The glow of fae light would have been helpful, but they had gone to great pains to make their entrance as unnoteworthy as possible. They couldn't risk the attention it might draw. But once they'd made their way to the bottom of the staircase, absolute blackness swallowed them and there was no choice but to draw on Silver's power then.

He held out his hand and produced a small, blue flame, no bigger than a gold piece. It hovered in front of them, revealing a second stairwell, which they followed to a cargo hold and a partially opened door opposite the stairs. Silver nudged the door further open with his foot and it swung back to reveal a small cabin containing three cots and a cast iron bucket that would serve as a chamber pot. The bedding on the cots was minimal. The sheets were dingy and probably supposed to be white, but looked like a light gray in the blue illumination. The wool blankets were threadbare and dark. It was impossible to tell their exact color in this lighting, but they were probably brown or gray, and LeiRain could tell just from looking at them that they were scratchy. The bedding and everything else in the space did at least look clean and the smell of lye told LeiRain that the room had been recently scrubbed. Something scurried out of sight in the back corner of the space as she scanned it, the creature's feet scratching the wood planks as it went. LeiRain shuddered.

'Home for the next few weeks,' Ron said. 'With the currents this time of year and the winds, Captain Dearvian thinks it'll take seven days minimum to make it to the Arborris Enclave. More if the weather turns foul.'

He pulled his hood back and stepped into the cabin. 'Said it might be a bit quicker if the winds are on our side. You know, he thinks tempest can control wind as well as water.'

Ron looked at LeiRain. 'Any chance you've been holding out on us?'

She blinked, making an effort not to wrinkle her nose at the musty smell, only partially masked by the scent of lye, that permeated the space. Silver had told her that he believed she could control wind as well as water. She vaguely remembered Riv saying something about tempest offspring shaping and shifting wind as well. But she had only just rediscovered her connection to the water, and even that required the use of the enchanted stone on her shield.

She shook her head and smiled apologetically.

Despite the smell and the sound of rodents scratching about in the dark corners, LeiRain was thankful for the opportunity to rest her legs as she peeled the wet cloak from her back. There were hooks on the wall and she placed her cloak on one of these before sitting on a cot. LeiRain slid off her boots and laid back. The surface beneath her was almost as hard as the ground and definitely as lumpy. Still, she was soothed by the closeness of the water. Her eyes closed easily. When she opened them again, the floor was rocking gently beneath her and she let it lull her back to sleep.

41

L eiRain sat up drowsily, clutching at her spinning head as her stomach flipped. The deck rocked beneath them, bobbing up and down rather than rocking gently as it had in the night. Each time the vessel dipped into a wave, her stomach fluttered with the drop. When she tried to focus across the room, she felt off kilter and dizzy. LeiRain realized for the first time that the waves felt very different aboard a ship than they did from beneath. She had fallen asleep without eating the night before, and suspected that this further contributed to the dizziness she was experiencing. LeiRain had noted the smell of lye last night, but this morning the room smelled sour which only made her nausea worse. She picked up her bag and was quietly rooting through it when someone knocked on the door.

'Who is it?' Ron's reply sounded angry, The knock had woken him up.

'Breakfast, sir,' came the timid voice of a young male.

Ron grunted in approval, seeming somewhat cheered by this news.

'Come in, then.' He sat up on his cot.

'Um, sir,' there was a quaver in the young man's voice. 'I can't open the door. My hands are full and...'

Ron rose and swung the door open before the boy could finish his explanation. A pale young sailor stood in the narrow hallway, struggling to hold up a heavily laden silver tray. His face was still round with the last vestiges of youth and his frame was thin for his considerable height. LeiRain could smell ocean spray in the fresh air that wafted down the stairwell and into their dank quarters. But she also caught the scent of black tea and looked eagerly at the large, tarnished teapot in the center of the tray. The boy's throat bobbed when Ron snatched the tray from him. Ron, still half-asleep, seemed oblivious to the effect he was having on the boy. He set the tray down on the floor between the cots and kicked the door shut behind him, right in the frightened young man's face.

'Thank you, boy,' he yelled through the door, 'We'll return it to the galley when we're done.'

The boy's shuffling footsteps moved away up the stairs. LeiRain unstacked the cups that were sitting next to it and began to pour the dark, hot liquid. She would have preferred coffee, but the mildly bitter black tea was a comfort nevertheless. LeiRain sipped gingerly from the steaming cup. The tea was not as sharp and strong as she had expected – either steeped from too few leaves or ones that had gone stale. She set it aside to cool and reached for one of the bowls of porridge. Silver passed her the one he'd just picked up. LeiRain gave him a polite nod of thanks, meeting his eyes so briefly that her magic didn't have time to stir in response.

She watched Ron fish through his satchel as she ate. He seemed especially irritable this morning and as she looked at him, she noticed a sickly green hue to his normally flushed countenance. Clearly not finding what he was looking for, Ron let out a frustrated growl before turning out the contents of his sack onto the floor. He snatched up a large clay bottle before it could roll away from him. *Alcohol?*

LeiRain winced with guilt as she realized she had *still* not apologized to him for the things she had said. She hadn't seen him drink since their last night at the homestead and had thought that perhaps he had managed to forget their unfortunate exchange of words. Ron uncorked the bottle, took a single gulp, and then replaced the stopper. Almost immediately, his skin pinked and his disposition improved. LeiRain took her first sip of tea and promised herself that she would get Ron alone long enough to tell him how sorry she was.

LeiRain stared at the closed door while they finished their breakfast. She longed for the fresh air, remembering the salty breeze that had wafted in through the open door when their food had been dropped off. Her stomach now full, the dizziness abated and she threw back the rest of her weak tea. She had to grip one of the support beams for balance as she stood and announced that she would be going topside.

'Are you alright?' Ron looked at her with concern. 'You look ... a bit gray,' indicating that her blue skin had paled.

'I just...' she closed her eyes and swallowed hard, realizing that the dizziness was gone but her stomach was still churning, 'I need some fresh air, I think.'

'I don't know if you should be going up there by yourself with the boat rocking like this.' Ron narrowed his eyes.

'I'll go with her,' Silver chimed in.

'I can *breathe* underwater, you know,' she said, rolling her eyes at their concern. All the same, she accepted the steady arm that Silver offered her.

She clung to him until they reached the stairs and then shifted her grip to the railing. LeiRain was instantly flooded with relief when she crested the final set of steps. Warm beams of sunlight and a fresh ocean breeze greeted her.

LeiRain stepped out of the shadows and onto the main deck, which was flooded with activity. She continued to stumble under the ship's movement and pressed her hand against the nearest bulkhead to maintain her balance. In the water, she'd move with the rise and fall of the waves, but the ship was unyielding. Onboard, she was subjected to a world that tilted sharply from side to side. As soon as she had the rhythm of it, they would fall into a lull and the pattern of rocking would change. At least her stomach was settled enough now that she no longer worried her breakfast would make a reappearance.

'Are you seasick?' Silver asked. He sounded almost incredulous. When she glanced back at him, he was smirking.

'I'm the daughter of *tempest*,' she said. 'I'm not *seasick*.' LeiRain made the mistake of rolling her eyes at this and a fresh wave of nausea washed over her. She swallowed. 'I've been in the sea many times and I've *never* felt sick before.' Her mouth twisted in annoyance as she looked at the deck. 'I'm maybe just a little *boat sick*,' she conceded.

'Hmmm, boat sick.' A half smile appeared on his handsome face. 'That's a new one.'

'I'm usually beneath the waves,' she clarified. 'Moving through the water on a boat feels wrong. It's unnatural.'

'Ah,' he nodded. 'Well, I'm sure you're a very capable swimmer, but that would make the journey much longer and quite perilous for those of us who require air.'

She smiled back at him, happy to feel some of the ease returning to their interactions.

She recalled one of their earlier conversations from back at the mountain hide and Ron's question from the night before. 'Do you really believe that I might be able to control the winds?' She asked.

'It is possible that you possess the ability to do that, and more.' He answered. Silver looked out over the waves,

381

squinting against the glint of sunlight on the blue expanse. 'Fae came to be known as deities because of their expansive power. Tempest can control the water, the wind, and the skies. There's no way to know where your powers end without pushing their limits.' He looked at her and said, 'I can tell you for certain that you have not even come close to reaching the limits of yours.'

She recalled the skies the day her father had left her standing on the beach with her mother. A sunny morning had quickly turned dark and gray, and a thick, unnatural fog had rolled in, blotting out the sun. She shook off the memory. She'd only been able to control the water with the aid of her shield, and even that seemed tentative. To control the wind and the skies... It seemed too remote a possibility to entertain.

'How are you feeling?' He asked, sensing her pensiveness.

'Better,' she replied. 'Fine, now that I can see the sky, and breathe in fresh, ocean air.'

'Good. I'm not sure that Ron can spare any of his tincture.' She raised an eyebrow in question.

'The bottle he drank from this morning was for his sea sickness.'

'Sea sickness?'

'By gods, how hard did you sleep last night?' A quiet laugh escaped Silver's lips. Even with the dizziness, his smile made her toes curl. 'And to think only a few weeks ago you had trouble sleeping at all! The poor man started retching as soon as the ship left the pier.'

That's why it smelled so foul when she woke. She recalled how the color had returned to his cheeks once he'd drunk from that bottle. LeiRain felt badly for having thought the worst of him, assuming that it was alcohol. She looked back at the stairs she'd just come up. Ron was alone in their quarters right now. As much as she didn't want to go back into the stuffy sourness of the room, she couldn't let the apology wait any longer.

'I'll be right back.' She turned away from Silver, away from the open ocean and fresh air, and walked towards the stairs. She stumbled as the vessel rocked, widening her stance just in time to keep herself from falling.

'I can come with you—'

'I'll be right back,' she said with finality. 'Wait here.' LeiRain hurried down the steps, taking two at a time. The ship rolled and she nearly missed the last step entirely. *Thank the gods for the handrail,* she thought. She kept her hand against the wall for support as she made her way to their room. She knocked on the door lightly once she got there, cracking it open slightly before speaking. She didn't want to rob Ron of much-needed sleep just for the sake of her own conscience.

'*Ron?*' She whispered into the room.

'Demi? What are you doing? Come on in.'

She slipped through the door and closed it behind her. A dim lantern lit the room just enough for her to see how poorly Ron looked. He sat on his cot and leaned back against the bulkhead.

'You don't look well,' she said as she came to sit across from him on her own cot.

'I feel even worse.' He replied. To her surprise, he laughed. 'I'll be alright, Demi. Happens every time and never stopped me from getting where I needed to go. Just have to conserve my tincture. I have two bottles, but one of them leaked in my bag.' The work *leaked* came out like a snarl. His eyes narrowed at her. 'But that's not why you're back down here, giving up fresh air to smell my sick. What's going on?'

She looked down at her hands, which sat on her lap, fingers entwined. LeiRain took a deep breath to steady herself but quickly realized this was a mistake. She pushed the air out in a huff, determined not to let Ron see her wince at the smell. When she looked up at him again, Ron had leaned forward on his cot. His elbows rested on his knees and he looked at her with a furrowed brow. She had his full attention. LeiRain felt her palms grow slick with sweat.

'I said horrible things to you and I'm sorry.' The words came out in a rush. Ron shook his head in confusion. She repeated herself, slower this time. 'I said horrible things to you.' Her hands were shaking now. 'I'm sorry. I'm really sorry, Ron. I didn't mean them.'

His eyes softened and she thought there was a subtle smile underneath his heavy beard.

'Ah, Demi, I hope you haven't been beating yourself up. I know you didn't mean it. I forgave you a long time ago.' She let out a shaky breath as he went on. ''Sides, your mother has said way worse to me, and she definitely meant it.'

LeiRain couldn't help herself. She laughed.

'I'm sorry,' she said through a mouthful of giggles.

'Don't be,' Ron replied. 'Somebody's got to be brave enough to tell off Ronland the Red.' He chuckled and a belch escaped. Ron threw a hand over his mouth. 'You'd better go enjoy that fresh air,' he said from behind his hand as he reached for the chamber pot. 'Thank you, though. Your mother never learned how to do the apologizing part.'

LeiRain would have given him a hug if he hadn't so clearly been about to heave into a bucket. She stood and rushed from the room, shutting the door behind herself just as Ron lost his breakfast. She bounced up the steps, finding it easier to move with the sway of the ship now that she no longer felt weighed down by guilt. She blinked at the sun as she emerged. Silver was right where she had left him.

'How is he?' He asked as LeiRain approached.

LeiRain shook her head. 'Don't see why he bothered to eat

breakfast,' she replied. 'He said he's having to ration his tincture because the other bottle spilled out. I'm not sure how long just the one bottle can last him.'

If she could control the wind, she could ensure they reached the islands quickly. Was that power buried somewhere, deep within her?

'Let's hope the winds carry us swiftly.' Silver replied.

There was genuine concern in his voice, and LeiRain was reminded of the gentleness with which he'd held her after she had been sick. She wanted to reach out now and take his hand in hers, but she resisted the urge, clasping the ship's railing instead. She thought of her father, of the power that Silver insisted roiled within her. It struck LeiRain that she must have only seen a small fraction of Silver's power as a verdaant. He may have been gentle with her once, but she had seen him kill, and had heard the ice in his voice when he spoke of how violent his childhood had been. Even if he did want her the way she wanted him, she could not escape the fear that he would turn out to be too much like her father.

42

C losing her eyes, LeiRain took a deep, slow breath and centered her attention on the air moving in and out of her lungs. It was humid and tasted like salt water and sun. Steadied and focused, she began to reach out with her mind, probing for her connection with the water. LeiRain did not have to look far. The water now moved toward her with enthusiasm whenever her mind reached for it. Her sweaty fingers fought to maintain purchase on the handle of her shield as she pulled from the stone's power to focus her magic.

There, she thought. *I think I have it.* LeiRain opened her eyes and watched the water dance before her, tiny beads of sea spray flitting about her head like insects. She smiled and let the droplets fall, leaving damp spots on her clothing.

'Lunch?'

Captain Dearvian's broad shoulders cast a shadow on the deck as he held out a bowl of stew in one hand and an orange in the other. Fair-skinned, and handsome, he looked entirely too young to be a ship's captain. Pieces of his black, short-cropped hair fought to free themselves from under the wide-brimmed hat that he wore whenever he was on deck. His cheeks were pink from the sun and it looked like a perpetual flush on his delicate skin. Lean and muscled, Dearvia walked about the ship with a lithe step. His jaw was wide and rounded but his cheekbones high and sharp. There was something about the way his mouth always turned down slightly when he wasn't smiling that reminded LeiRain of a cat. But he could have passed for human if it weren't for his eyes – the golden irises and slitted, feline pupils.

LeiRain had seen ship's captains interact with their crew and dockhands many times in Harbor, but she'd never seen one as level-headed and kind as Dearvian. Though he remained strict with his men, she had never heard him resort to insults and there had been no physical punishments since they'd come onboard. In Harbor, it hadn't been uncommon to see men leaving ship with blood seeping through the backs of their shirts; many captains used the whip to keep their crew in line. Not Dearvian, at least not as far as LeiRain could see. But then, his crew seemed to respect him so much that, thus far on their journey, there had been no need for the administration of discipline. The Captain looked past LeiRain to the horizon, his pupils narrowing to tiny, vertical slashes in the sun. There was an air of mystery about him, but Ron trusted Dearvian and so did his men, and therefore so did LeiRain.

She smiled and accepted the offering of food he held out to her.

'The ship's captain delivering my noon meal? To what do I owe this honor?'

'The honor is mine,' he replied, with a bow.

Warmth spread through her belly as he rose from his bow with a broad and dashing smile.

All of LeiRain's pants now had extra pockets, thanks to Brya, so she stuffed the orange that Dearvian gave her into one of them and sat on the deck near the bow of the ship. She held the bowl of stewed root vegetables he'd offered in one hand and scooped large spoonfuls into her mouth with the other. There was little variety in their diet at sea and LeiRain had offered to help cook, in part out of a selfish desire to create something more flavorful. There were plenty of times in Harbor when the market had slim pickings and she'd had to get creative with dinner. LeiRain was certain that she could make something more enticing than the mushy gruel they ate every day. But Dearvian's eyes had grown wide and he'd shaken his head at her request to help.

The ship's cook would be very offended at the offer, he told her. *You'd best not repeat it if you want to continue to get the same rations as everyone else.* So, though the vegetables were over-cooked and bland, she ate the stew with appreciation, or at least resignation. LeiRain brushed a damp tendril of hair from her face. It had grown wet with a steady misting of salt water that came off the bow. Between the dampness and the wind, she knew her hair was frizzing its way out of its formerly neat braid, but the seaspray was cool and refreshing in the humidity. It was also much easier to eat up here than in their cabin, which now reeked of bile.

The captain sat down gracefully beside her. It was an unusually informal gesture for the captain of a ship, LeiRain thought. Yet as he sat crossed-legged on the deck, Dearvian somehow made the pose seem dignified. The two of them stared at the dark clouds in the distance, visible signs of an oncoming storm, not that LeiRain needed to see it to know it was coming. Even if there hadn't been a cloud in the sky, the storm ran through her veins. It wouldn't be a terribly powerful storm, she knew, but the weather's energy roiled inside her. A storm would mean rough waters and unpredictable winds, which translated into a longer journey and a very sick Ron. When LeiRain had warned them of the approaching weather,

Ron had taken to rationing his tincture even more strictly. *I need to be strong when we arrive*, he'd explained, *so I'll save more for the last few days of the journey.* It made good sense, but did not make it any easier to sleep below decks, near a bucket of vomit.

Dearvian growled at the clouds. Something about him reminded LeiRain of a more mature Bren, if she allowed herself to forget that her former lover had been complicit in her mother's murder. Nothing between her and the Captain came close to what she felt for Silver, but she let the flirtation play out. It was a piece of normalcy that she'd previously been denied. Ron had assured her, or rather *warned* her, that Dearvian flirted with everything that moved so she wasn't concerned about leading him on. It simply felt *good* to be treated as though she were desirable, something she'd never experienced in Harbor. It was a simple pleasure to feel as though she were no less than any other woman. And LeiRain didn't mind thinking that it made Silver a bit jealous, too, even if he'd shown no such signs.

'Did Ron ever tell you about the time he nearly got my ship blown to pieces?'

'No,' LeiRain said through laughter.

'Well, he chartered The Mad Return for a job. I don't remember what it was – retrieving some lost item of value for some wealthy sod who was too cowardly to do it himself, or some such things. Anyway, he's *certain* it's on this island that's supposed to still be populated with dragons.'

'*Dragons?*' LeiRain had been staring off at the horizon alongside Dearvian. Now she turned and watched him, hanging on each word.

'Right, but just wait.' He shook his head. 'It's somewhat on our way to the next delivery of goods so I offer him a discounted price for the charter. Of course, I was younger and a relatively new captain.' He looked at LeiRain and winked, making her cheeks warm to a purple flush. 'I did not yet know Ronland the Red quite so well. So, off we went on this little adventure. We get to the island. No dragons.' He held out his hands and raised his eyebrows comically. A snort of laughter escaped LeiRain. 'So that was a relief.'

'So what almost destroyed the ship?'

'Well,' Dearvian laughed, 'it turns out that the reason the island had the reputation of housing a community of dragons was because it was covered in active volcanoes!' LeiRain gasped and Dearvian shook his head. 'That's not even the worst of it. The volcanoes weren't all *on* the island. Some of them were *underwater*.'

'I didn't know that was even possible!' LeiRain was almost as fascinated by this as she had been by the prospect of dragons.

'Yes, it's quite possible. And quite dangerous. One of them erupted not fifty feet from where I had been about to drop anchor. Had we been fifty feet further to port, you and I wouldn't be having this conversation right now. As it was, the blast sent a wall of waves crashing down on us. We went spinning out to sea and the torrent nearly tore off our main mast! Of course, our friend Ron was already on shore by that time. He'd taken a small boat in by himself. By the time all of my men were accounted for and repairs were done, Ron was way overdue. In typical Ronland fashion, though, the mission had taken him two days longer than he'd planned so he'd only been waiting a day by the time our sails were visible to him. I absolutely refused to bring my ship so near those shores again; I couldn't risk the crew! So Ronland had to paddle his way out to us.' He laughed, then looked at Rain and said, 'it was a good two hours off shore and I don't feel a bit guilty about it. He was knackered by the time he made it back and I don't think he made a penny off of that mission by the time he'd paid for all of the damages.'

The two of them laughed. LeiRain knew that Dearvian must be much older than he appeared to have so many harrowing tales of adventure in common with Ron. She wondered if shifters aged slower than other beings, but thought it rude to ask. She enjoyed his company too much to risk offense.

LeiRain glanced at him as he watched the horizon. Dearvian's hair was perfectly black, not a single gray strand visible. And even though he spent endless hours squinting into the sun, there were barely any lines around his eyes to show it. He'd been keeping her entertained throughout the journey by sharing tales of a younger Ron, from the years before *Ronland the Red* had become infamous. Perhaps she could ask Ron how old Dearvian was, and how quickly shifters aged.

'We'll have to go around,' Dearvian said, shaking his head in disappointment at the blackening horizon.

Going around meant it would take them still longer to get to the Arborris Enclave, and it meant that his ship would be at an increased risk of seizure by Royals. Dearvian had managed to avoid the Royals thus far by primarily sticking to routes that he knew were far from their preferred shipping lanes. Deviating from their planned course would put them all in more danger. Ron would have to make his one bottle of medicine last even longer. If he was this ill on the tincture, LeiRain worried about what would happen when he ran out.

'Was he always so prone to seasickness?' LeiRain asked as she pulled the orange from her pocket and began peeling.

'As long as I've known him,' Dearvian said with a laugh, 'though I've never seen him without an adequate supply of medicine. You must have left in quite a hurry.'

They had, and the local apothecary in the port where

they'd found Dearvian was a staunch Royal. Ron hadn't thought it worth the risk.

Soft footsteps padded on the deck behind them, and LeiRain knew without looking that it was Silver. She threw the last of the orange peel over the side of the ship and shifted her weight to stand. The flirtatious banter that she enjoyed with Dearvian felt shameful when Silver was there. Her stomach twisted as she wondered how much he'd seen of the jovial exchange. LeiRain was also ashamed at how much she hoped Dearvian's presence would frustrate Silver. She knew that her own world would be turned upside down if she had to watch the fae flirt with another woman. LeiRain didn't dare look directly at him, to draw his eye contact and the attention of his magic. Instead, she watched him from the corner of her eye, looking for any evidence of disappointment or jealousy. Frustratingly, Silver's demeanor was as serene as always. Disappointed, LeiRain excused herself.

If she and Silver had been left alone for long enough, LeiRain knew that they would have done things, said things, that they couldn't take back. Or at least, she would have. This realization had made her draw back from him a bit and she couldn't tell if Silver was relieved at this or if he was just doing an incredible job of respecting her boundaries. Things remained cordial and easy between them, as long as they kept their conversations short and the topics light, and, more often than not, their eyes averted. She gave the verdaant a friendly but impersonal smile, letting her eyes rise only to his collarbone, before she went to the scullery to fetch broth for Ron. She could feel Silver watching her as she left, but he did not follow.

S he handed a cup of warm broth to Ron and fought the reflex to cover her nose with her hand. The small space reeked of his sweat and the various contents of his stomach over the last few days. He looked pitiful: his normally ruddy skin was sallow, the flesh under his eyes now purple from lack of sleep. His stocky frame had grown thinner and his shirt hung loose on his shoulders. Ron had taken to sleeping in the back corner of their quarters. His cloak and satchel were tucked into the corner behind him to prop him up and his shoulders brushed the walls on either side of him. His legs were splayed out in front at the moment, the blanket from his cot in a pile on his lap. It didn't look very comfortable to LeiRain, but Ron said it was where he felt 'the least dizzy' in the space. He thanked her weakly as he accepted the cup of broth. Despite her own queasiness at the conditions, she sat down to keep her friend company for a while.

'There's a storm on the horizon,' she said. 'Dearvian says we'll have to go around.'

'Dearvian, huh?' Ron laughed, feebly. 'Didn't take you long to get on a first name basis.'

'He's your friend,' LeiRain retorted, feeling defensive.

'That he is, and I know what kind of man he is too. Not a bad one, mind you, but not the kind to trust around a sister or a daughter ... or a wife or girlfriend for that matter.'

'I'm none of those to you.' LeiRain shrugged, feigning indifference. She wanted him to object to this. She'd started to wonder if her relationship with Ron wasn't a bit like what someone might have with a father, or at least a much older brother. Ron didn't object, but LeiRain thought she saw a brief flash of hurt in his dulled eyes.

'What about Silver?' he asked, surprising her.

He let the question hang in the air, watching her face

closely for a reaction. There was a tightness in LeiRain's chest that made it difficult to reply.

'What about him?' she finally managed.

She tried to keep the emotion from her face but her heart sped up.

'You tell me, Rain.' He winked at her and laughed softly.

He was being careful with his words, both of them recalling what had happened the last time they'd discussed this. She shook her head.

'Nothing. There's nothing there.'

'I don't believe that. I see the way you look at each other.'

Something fluttered in her chest. Was it really possible that Silver's desire matched her own? That there was more there than lust? What had Ron seen?

'It doesn't matter,' she said as much to herself as to Ron. 'He is a verdaant. I will not make the same mistakes my mother made.'

'Demi,' he said, before pausing and holding a hand up in the air. LeiRain saw his stomach tighten, and his body go rigid as he leaned over the bucket, but nothing came out. He was fighting to keep down the cup of broth she'd just given him. Ron pushed the bucket away by a few inches and brought his head back to rest against the wall. His face was red with exertion and there was sweat on his brow. He forced his breathing to slow and swallowed the bile in his throat. His eyes were watered from the effort. 'Demi, you are not your mother. She was a very different woman—'

'I know you don't think she was the best parent,' LeiRain interrupted. She'd only just apologized a few days ago for the way she'd spoken to him. Everything he'd said about her mother had been true, but she'd been too angry and defensive to hear it. Despite herself, LeiRain found the same wall coming up now.

'No, listen. Alarra...'

'I don't need you to tell me about my mother's feelings,' LeiRain said. She stood to leave, fists clenched at her sides, the muscles in her jaw jumping as she ground her teeth.

'Rain,' Ron called. Her hand was on the doorknob.

'Rain!'

Something flew past her and hit the door with a thud, causing her to flinch and throw her hands over her face. A mangy boot rested on the deck before her. Surprise and incredulity distracted LeiRain from the outrage that had been building. She turned to look back at Ron. The dwarve was holding the boot's mate in his hand.

'You threw a shoe at me,' she said. She shook her head and gestured with her arms in a *what the hell* manner.

'Not at *you*,' he clarified with a glower. 'At the door. I need you to listen to me, and I'm not in the right state to go chasing after you if you storm out.'

She eyed him warily. He kept the boot at the ready until she walked back to her cot and sat down.

'First, let me explain myself.'

'You don't have to explain anything to me, Ron.' She was determined not to insult him this time, regardless of what he said.

'No, I do. I want to, but you need to shut up for a minute and listen for gods' sakes.'

LeiRain blinked dumbly and pursed her lips. Ron had never spoken to her like this before.

He continued when it was apparent that she planned to stay and hear him out. 'You remember when Silver said he used a locator spell? That he ended up at a, um...'

'A brothel?' She volunteered.

His cheeks had just been returning to their sickly pallor when the words made him blush.

'Yes,' he carried on, shaking off the apparent discomfort. 'But it's not what you think.' He raised a hand to shush her before she could again object to an explanation. 'I had a wife and a daughter, Rain. Before Jade.'

'Oh.' It was all that she could get out.

LeiRain was reminded in that moment of how very little she knew about Ron's past before the slaughter of his clan. She'd read plenty of stories about him, but those were always of his exploits and nothing of the life he had made for himself, his home. She realized with a feeling of hollowness in her stomach that she had never bothered to ask. Ron had told her about Jade, about how his brother had died to save his wife and child. He had shared so much and she'd been too caught up in her own story to even consider that there might be more to his.

'Loralie was my daughter's name. Her mother was Vala. Loralie would be a bit older than you now, if she'd lived.' He paused and heaved into the bucket in front of him. LeiRain looked away until he'd finished and wiped the saliva from his chin. So much for the broth.

'Sorry,' he said, gesturing to the bucket. 'One of the children I saved, a girl who'd been abused by Jade's lover... She was so young. And she looked—' He swallowed. 'She looked just like my Loralie. Same bright red hair. Same mischievous smile. Her name is Riva and I found her a good home. *I* thought it was a good home. And I left. If I hadn't lost my own daughter, I never would have gone back. With Loralie one, Riva felt like the closest thing I had to her. So I decided to check in on the girl and when I went back for a visit, she'd left the home and gone to work at the local brothel. In Harbor. She still works there now, I imagine.'

'Whenever I have time between jobs, I go there to visit. Pay for the whole night with her, just to keep away the other men.

I buy her food and we talk and I try to persuade her that she doesn't have to live that way. She doesn't have to sell herself; I'd make sure she was taken care of. I offered to let her come live with Brya and Ray. She had given me hope, a reason to keep going and I thought that through her, I could heal, and recover from my losses. When I'm around her, I don't feel like I have to drown out the bad thoughts with drink. But despite everything, Riva resents me. Last time I saw her, she told me that I make it worse – make her feel ashamed of what she's become. I'm not ashamed of her,' he said, shaking his head. 'I just want her to be happy, and safe. If she is then– well, it doesn't matter because she told me she wanted me to leave and never come back. It broke my heart all over again.'

'Ron, I'm so sorry.' LeiRain's voice was barely a whisper. She wondered for the first time what might have become of her if Ron and Brya hadn't taken her in. She could probably have made her way by selling off whatever she found beneath Harbor waters, but she would have had to find a new home. She couldn't have stayed in Harbor. And it wasn't like she found something valuable every day. Sometimes, weeks went by without her earning more than a few copper pieces off of what she'd pulled from the sand. Would she have turned to selling her flesh? Would she have found safety and happiness in it? It would certainly earn a more consistent wage than selling off water-logged trash. LeiRain's chest warmed with gratitude at everything Ron had done for her.

'I don't want that to happen to you, Rain. I want you to heal full and well, not patch yourself up with that verdaant or with anyone else ... and for gods' sakes, not Dearvian.'

She nodded. Tears stung the back of her eyes.

'But I also don't want you to shut Silver out, to shut me out. *That* you got from your mother. And I know what you're thinking. I saw the fear in your eyes when you watched Silver with that Royal back at the mountain, but it was that man's life or all of ours. I killed just the same as he did and you haven't given me so much as a second glance. Silver isn't your father anymore than you're your mother. That forest fae could have taken anything he wanted from us, but he hasn't. He's *asked* for everything when he could have demanded, and waited for me to agree to this venture on my own. He has power, but he knows restraint.'

Ron hadn't been there that day with Caspian. He hadn't seen the rolling storm clouds in her father's eyes. He didn't know it was Caspian who had kept them bound to the village that hated her. 'But he—' She tried to interject.

'He killed him,' Ron interrupted. 'I would have if he hadn't. There was no way we could have left one of them alive. Not after they'd seen us all together and had managed to track him to us. I'll also say this: I'm not a big fan of your father's, but I was ready to shake his hand when he did off with your grandfather.'

LeiRain's mouth dropped open and she stared at him in shock.

'He – your grandfather wasn't a good man. He beat your mother black and blue every other week and wouldn't hear of her learning a trade when he thought he could sell her off as a wife. All she was to your grandfather was an opportunity for improved social standing through marriage, in that sorry little village. I wasn't there when it happened, but I can tell you that your father had good reason to rid the world of that man.'

She let this new information sink in. Ron had said before that Alarra hadn't had an easy life, but she'd never imagined this. She'd never considered that her father might have been protecting her mother when he killed her grandparents.

'But, what about my grandmother?' she asked.

'That happened a few weeks later, and I don't know why

he did it, but I can tell you that your grandmother knew full well your father was abusing Alarra. She looked the other way and she was happy to let your grandfather sell your mother off to the highest bidder. If your father hadn't done away with them both, your parents would have had her marry Ethan Prospus.' *The man who had killed her.* 'Once they were gone, Alarra was free to make her own decisions. Of course, you couldn't say a word against your grandparents to your mother. She wouldn't have it, even though they caused her enough pain that she refused to use their surname. In case you ever wondered why your mother never gave you a family name.'

'Why didn't you tell me this before?' she asked. She often wondered about the lack of a surname, but it was another one of those questions her mother had refused to answer. Jokingly, Alarra had always said she could call herself *LeiRain, Daughter of Alarra, Enchantress of Steel.* LeiRain had never found it funny.

'Larra didn't want you to know.'

'Then why tell me now?'

'Because I think your mother intended you to be ignorant to ensure your happiness, not to prevent it. Don't think you're making old mistakes in trusting Silver. He's good, better than your father for sure. I've seen how he can make you laugh and smile. But you had healing to do before you even lost your mother, because I know she didn't teach you how to love properly. Don't push him away just to avoid the mistakes Alarra made, but know that it—' He turned suddenly and retched into the bucket. LeiRain's own stomach lurched in response and she swallowed back bile. When he caught his breath, he continued. 'Know that it won't be easy because you'll have to stop running from all those things that make you so uncomfortable. Oh *gods*.'

Ron heaved and the sound he made caused LeiRain to gag

too. Nothing came up this time, but she needed to get out of this space, to get fresh air. He saw the look on her face and shooed her away.

'That's all the wisdom I can spare for today,' he said, face green.

He closed his eyes and laid his head back against the balled up cloak.

43

LeiRain left Ron and went topside, taking in the fresh air and everything he'd just told her. Her head was spinning, and not just from the rocking of the boat. LeiRain could still feel the energetic buzz of an impending storm, but the sensation was fading as Dearvian steered them out of the storm's path. But that nervous energy, along with the rush of so many thoughts and emotions made LeiRain feel like she might burst. Her stomach ached and her arms itched to swing a sword. She thought about retrieving her sword and shield from where she'd left them below, but the deck around her was cluttered with sailors going about their work. And since they were trying to skirt around the edges of the storm, the seas had become less calm and the ship rocked violently every few minutes.

Silver was standing at the bow, looking meditative as he watched the white water slide off the hull. His hair flashed silver-white in the afternoon sun. She imagined running her fingers through those strands, looking into his eyes, telling him more about her past and why she hurt so much. For the first time, the thought of talking about her past, sharing her pain with someone, seemed like it might unburden her rather than re-wound.

LeiRain was brought back from her reverie by the loud cry of a sailor up in the crow's nest, the large perch near the top of the main mast and the best place to get an unobstructed view of the horizon. Set just aft of the ship's center, it was the highest point on the vessel. The sails were pulled taut, full of wind. Of course, the sailor on watch up there always had a long-range looking glass with him as well, so he could see much further than the naked eye. Or at least much further than most people could, fae notwithstanding.

She walked toward Silver, coming to stand beside him at the bow. She watched him as he scanned the horizon for whatever the lookout had spotted. LeiRain took a sweeping, if somewhat futile, glance and spotted nothing. Silver, on the other hand, had his superior vision fixed on a point that was forward off the starboard bow. She was about to ask him what he saw when Captain Dearvian appeared next to him, leaning forward as he looked through a brass telescope. Dearvian passed the scope off to a nearby crewman. Without looking away from the horizon, he held out his hand to receive another instrument from the sailor, this one looking a bit like several tiny telescopes attached to a seamster's ruler.

'What is that?' LeiRain asked.

The Captain flashed her a charming smile but kept his eyes on his work.

'It's a sextant,' he replied, adjusting his hold as he looked through one of its multiple scopes. 'We use it to measure distances and angles. There is another ship out there and I'd like to know if she is heading toward us, away from us, or if we both just happen to be heading to the same place.'

'Can you see their flag?' Silver asked.

The captain lowered the sextant and looked at the fae, his expression grim.

'No, but I'll check her course again in a bit. I think she's heading toward us, but I hope I'm wrong.' Silver and LeiRain exchanged a worried glance.

'If they are headed for us, or the Arborris Enclave, they'll have to go 'round the storm, just like we will. We'll see how closely they follow when we shift our course.'

He rubbed a hand over the stubble on his face. LeiRain knew that she could simply throw herself overboard if the Royals succeeded in taking the ship. Riv had told her that she could call to them from anywhere in the same body of water and they would help. She could call them and ask to go back to Corallis. She had an escape route, but what about her friends? Dearvian would surely be slaughtered if the Royals pressed the ship into their service. There was no way of hiding that he was a blend once you were close enough to look him in the eye.

LeiRain was certain that Silver could fend for himself on land, but he relied heavily on the earth to do his bidding in a fight. How would he defend himself so far at sea? And Ron was far too ill to be of any use right now. She scanned the faces of the crew as they bustled about the deck. Many of them were blends.

'We will run into the Royals sooner or later, even if that ship doesn't fly under their flag. We are heading straight for their fleet headquarters, after all,' Dearvian said coolly.

He turned and handed the sextant back to the crew member who restored it to its case. Then, the Captain walked swiftly toward midships without casting a second glance at LeiRain and Silver. He was shouting orders as he went and sailors began running about the deck to carry them out.

LeiRain looked down. She was clutching the wood railing

so tightly that her knuckles had gone white. One of Silver's hands rested on the guardrail only a few inches from hers. LeiRain searched herself for the courage to close the distance. She wanted to feel his touch, to be closer to him, but all she could do was stare at the small space between their hands. She forced herself to look up and jumped slightly when she saw Silver watching her. His bright eyes scanned her face, the fae's expression giving away nothing of his thoughts.

As she gazed back at the verdaant, LeiRain wanted very badly to tell him all that Ron had revealed to her. She wanted him to know what she now did about her grandparents, her father. She wanted to tell him the rest of her own story, how she'd gone to Corallis and found her magic for the first time. How she had unknowingly abandoned her mother for six months. She wanted to rid herself of these secrets.

'I...' She swallowed and looked away, her eyes coming to rest on the water. It was several long seconds before she could bring herself to look back up. When she finally did, LeiRain found that bravery had left her. 'I'm going to tell Ron to take more of his tincture. I know we won't reach the Enclave for a while, but the seas will be bad if we're tacking around a storm.'

He gave her a critical look, his forehead creasing. He knew that's not what she'd been about to say and he was thinking of challenging her on this. LeiRain could feel the magic begin to vibrate between them, pulling her in. She wasn't ready. Even though she wanted to tell him everything, she didn't know how. So LeiRain gave him an awkward smile and abruptly turned and walked away. She made her way downstairs toward Ron. Although it hadn't been her original intent, LeiRain decided that there was likely some merit in coercing dwarve to take a larger helping of his tincture. The seas were going to get very rough as they outmaneuvered the storm, and if the Royals did manage to overtake them, Ron would need to be in top form.

It was quiet on deck as a large, silver moon rose over the night sky. Only the few crewmen on watch remained nearby, the night being the most dangerous time to be above decks. The dark made it nearly impossible to find and recover anyone who fell overboard. But LeiRain could not drown and the sea was the calmest she'd seen it since they had first set sail. A perfect replica of the moon shone back over the surface of the water, only occasionally disturbed by a ripple of the current.

LeiRain leaned over the railing and watched glowing figures dance playfully beneath the surface. 'Glittering Seas,' the Captain had called it. Sailors believed that tiny fae-like creatures came out to play in the waters at night. The radiance of their fae light made the normally hidden play of dolphins visible, causing them to leave bright, blue streaks in their wake beneath the water's surface. Whatever the cause, the effect was dazzling. She watched the sea creatures move gracefully through the ship's wake and smiled each time one of them broke the surface in a joyful leap. Glowing tendrils also ran off the bow of the ship as The Mad Return cut through the water at speed. LeiRain felt her shoulders relax and the tension in her jaw soften as the beauty of the ocean made her temporarily forget all that weighed on her.

'Remarkable,' Silver said, sliding out of the dark to stand beside her.

'I've never seen anything like it before,' she replied, with a sigh.

Silver said nothing in response. When she looked up, his eyes were on the water. LeiRain's own gaze slid back to the ocean and its dancing lights. She kept her eyes on the Glittering Sea, even when Silver moved closer. His arm brushed against hers where it rested on the railing and LeiRain's heartbeat quickened. Silver was so close now that she could smell him, his fresh forest scent mingling with the tang of salt water.

'Absolutely breathtaking,' he said, and she finally let herself look at him again. Silver was not watching the Glittering Seas this time. He was looking at her. LeiRain felt a fire spark in her core as their eyes met, her magic pulsing in time with her heart. The moonlight reflected in his eyes, making them even more dazzling than the fae-like glow illuminating the dark waters. He took yet another step toward her. LeiRain's breath hitched as she turned her entire body to face him.

'May I?' he asked, bringing a hand up to her cheek. LeiRain remembered Ron's words, that Silver was powerful enough to take whatever he wanted from them, yet he always asked. Never took anything she didn't want to give. LeiRain could not find the breath to whisper a reply, so she simply nodded. Silver closed the remaining distance between them. He brushed his fingers over her cheek and cupped the back of her neck, pressing his palm against it so that her head tilted upward slightly. The nearness of him and intensity of his gaze made a deep want pulse between the apex of LeiRain's thighs. Silver's other hand reached behind her and came to rest on her lower back, pulling her even tighter against him. It was all she could do to keep from groaning.

He gave a throaty 'Hmmm' as she watched his eyes roam over her mouth. 'May I?' he asked once again. LeiRain opened her mouth to reply, to say yes...

L eiRain woke with a thud as she was thrown violently from her cot and into the bulkhead. For a fleeting moment, she recalled the warmth of Silver's hands on her back, her neck, the closeness of his mouth to hers ... but as the ship rocked beneath her, memories of the dream receded. What was happening? How long had she been asleep? She tried to shake off her confusion and the pain of the impact.

The ship shuddered and tilted before LeiRain could collect herself. Her cot tipped over on top of her and she let out a cry as the other two cots came sliding in her direction. The force of their impact took her breath away momentarily. She was pinned down, a hard wall against her back and the weight of three cots pressing into her chest, making it hard to breathe. She swallowed down panic. The pain she felt was sharp and urgent as the edge of her cot's metal frame jammed into her leg. She felt the rip as it tore through her trousers and then the sting as it bit into her shin.

LeiRain wriggled, managing to pull one arm free and relieve some of the pressure on her chest. She allowed herself the luxury of a deep breath before she continued working to free herself. She had almost inched her way out from beneath the cots when the ship shuddered again. The bedding and everything else in the room, including LeiRain, slid across the deck and slammed into the opposite bulkhead. She grunted as her hip met with a hard surface. What was happening?

Fingers digging into the deck planks, LeiRain pulled herself from the pile of cots. She felt the tear in her pants expand as she did so. She winced as she scrambled to her feet and discovered a deep gash in her thigh to match the one on her calf. Her left shoulder throbbed from where it had impacted the wall. *I have to get out of here*, she thought, pushing through the pain. LeiRain kept her stance wide for balance, gritting her teeth through the agony of her injuries as she made her way across the shifting deck. The door to their quarters was open. She'd left it that way in an attempt to rid the space of the smell of vomit. Now, it swung back and forth with the ship's movement, threatening to slam shut.

Panicked voices were audible from the weather decks.

Cautiously, she made her way across the room, bracing herself against the wall and the support beam. The ship began to shudder again and the floor leveled off. Taking advantage of this, she rushed to the door and into the stairwell, a hand on either bulkhead as the ship continued to rock.

The voices grew louder and more urgent as she climbed the steps. Had they sailed into the storm afterall? As she reached the top of the stairs, she could see men rushing by. Some looked fearful, but most looked stern-faced and determined. Captain Dearvian's confident and unwavering voice could be heard above them all as he shouted orders. A tall figure appeared at the top of the stairwell. Even with his face in shadow, she knew immediately that it was Silver.

'Rain,' he sounded relieved, 'you're alright.'

'What's happening?'

The sky behind him was light blue, no sign of foul weather. It wasn't a storm that rocked them.

Silver's posture made gooseflesh break out over LeiRain's arms and back. Something was very wrong. He took a few steps down and she could make out his features more easily now. 'We're being attacked. Several men have already gone overboard.' She swallowed, trying not to think about the lives already lost.

'I – I need my shield.'

She cursed herself. How could she have not thought of that before she clamored out of the small space? LeiRain turned to their cabin. The door still swayed back and forth. Staggering, she entered the room, doing her best to hurry despite the shifting vessel beneath her feet. There was no time to waste. If she was fast enough, perhaps she could save some of the sailors' lives. Her shield lay in the back corner. She covered the distance in only a few, stumbling steps. She strapped it to her back with the guige and started to make her way out of the room. She needed to reach the weather decks as quickly as possible.

The ship swayed again and LeiRain fought to keep herself upright. The weight of her shield threw off the delicate balance she had been maintaining, even as she grabbed for the nearest support beam. She had hoped to find Silver's steady arm waiting for her, but he had of course gone back upstairs to aid the ship. LeiRain wobbled and hit the floor with a heavy thud, her hip striking first, then her already injured shoulder. She cried out, overcome by the sudden sharpness of the pain.

The vessel tilted again as she began to sit up, and it sent her sliding to the back of the room, hands grasping ineffectually at the smooth wooden planks. Just as she was about to slam into the wall, there was another shudder and the ship leaned the other way. The force of it threw LeiRain forward and she tumbled through the doorway and into the passageway. She skidded into the stairwell, stumbling into the bulkhead as soon as she tried to stand. She heard the door to their quarters slam shut behind her. Gripping the handrail, LeiRain pushed the pain out of her mind and pulled herself up the stairs. This ship would *not* go down without a fight.

44

Leirain staggered out of the stairwell and onto the main deck. Sailors scurried about, feverishly manning lines in an attempt to adjust the sails. LeiRain forced herself to take in the whole scene, despite the glaring sun. On the uppermost deck of the ship, a wide-eyed crewman fought to maintain control of the helm, his muscular arms taut and face slick with sweat as he held the rudder steady. Captain Dearvian stood back a few feet from the helmsman, barking orders. The ship groaned and shook. LeiRain grabbed onto a coil of rope that hung from a nearby hook, barely managing to stay upright. She had to figure out where the damage was. She couldn't let the ship sink.

'How the fuck are they able to fire on us from such a distance?' LeiRain heard Dearvian say before he pointed at one of the crew members. 'No, you, Gabriel – see that the cannons are fully ready. They may yet come in range of our weapons.'

Ron and Silver stood on the port side of the ship. Ron was between the upper and main decks, clinging to the stair railing with both hands, ax strapped to his belt. His face was pale, but not the sickly green color it had been a few days ago. He wore his chainmail over his travel clothes in preparation for a boarding. Ron's jaw was set and his body coiled, ready to spring. The ship that was hurling cannons at them was still too far away for Ron's combat skills to be of any use. Silver stood on the main deck near the dwarve, his stance wide, expertly balanced. LeiRain let go of the rope and threw herself toward the two men. Her friends stood on the port side of the ship as it listed heavily to starboard. LeiRain had to fight gravity to reach them, seizing netting, lines and any other handholds she could find to pull herself along. Her feet slipped out from under her as the ship bobbed with the impact of another cannonball and LeiRain just managed to grab onto an eyelet before she could be thrown across the deck. Ron and Silver were only a few feet from where she'd come up the stairs, but it felt like it was taking an eternity to stumble her way toward them.

'What is happening?'

She followed Silver's gaze to a large vessel on their port side. The solid blue of the Royal Merchant Marine flag was now clearly visible. When she'd gone to rest, the ship had still been no more than a speck on the horizon, discernible only through the telescope or Silver's impressive vision. How long had she been asleep? The attackers seemed to have covered at least a day's distance while she'd been below decks.

'That ship is moving impossibly fast,' Ron explained over the noise on deck. 'They shouldn't be in range yet, but they just started firing on us.'

Ron pointed to a missing section of railing toward the bow of the ship. LeiRain's eyes grew wide and a weight dropped into her stomach. The Royal weapons were tearing the ship apart.

'Their weapons must be something new, or maybe,

enchanted, but I can't imagine who with such power would aid the Royals.' Ron yelled. She could hear the tightness in his voice, and the confusion, even over the clatter around them.

An enormous *boom* came from nearby, followed by a loud *crack*. Then LeiRain heard the sound of rushing water as the ocean poured into the ship where a cannonball had found its mark. She instinctively raised her hands to cover her ears but quickly replaced them on the railing to prevent herself from being flung away from her friends. A deep groan emanated from the hull of The Mad Return. LeiRain felt her ears pop with the change in pressure as the ship began to suck in water at an alarming rate. The deck beneath her strained as the ocean tried to pry the boards apart.

'Fuck it all.' The Captain rushed by her to lean over the edge of the ship and survey the damage. 'They have the son of tempest on board, I swear it. I can see him clear as day in the 'scope.' LeiRain shook her head in disbelief. She couldn't imagine anyone like her helping the Royals. But even as she opened her mouth to say as much to Dearvian, she realized that she could *feel* it. LeiRain hadn't recognized the sensation before, when she was just learning her magic in Corallis. Everything was new and strange and exciting then. But now she knew what she was sensing was tempest magic. It was different from Riv's but still somehow familiar. She squinted into the distance as she pried the information from her memory. *Eaton.*

'Impossible,' Ron shook his head, still bracing with both hands. He leaned forward over the port side to get a better look. As if he might be able to make out the son of tempest with the naked eye, Ron squinted at the vessel.

'I see him too,' Silver said, confirming the Captain's assertion.

'Why in the gods' names would a blend help an organization that hates them?' Ron growled.

Captain Dearvian swore at the Royal vessel. It was still safely out of range of any weapons aboard The Mad Return. 'I saw him,' he said, narrowing his cat-like eyes. 'I don't know why he would help them, but I saw him in the 'scope before they began firing. He must be commanding the wind, carrying their cannon balls further, filling their sails so that they close on us with unnatural speed.'

That's what made the magic feel so strange – it was wind magic, not water. But it was definitely Eaton, one of the tempest offspring she met while in Corallis. She kept this to herself, unable to make sense of the realization.

Dearvian turned to LeiRain. 'Can you do what your kinsman is doing? Can you fill our sails? Aid our weapons?'

'No.' She shook her head. Her stomach felt sick with the shame of being unable to help in that way. She hated that there was a son of tempest aiding the other ship, and hated even more that she was not as powerful as he was. LeiRain felt responsible for the disappointment in Dearvian's eyes. 'But I can perhaps save your men who've gone overboard, keep them from drowning.'

He shook his head, but his eyes brightened a bit.

'No – stop the water filling the hole in my ship, if you can. There's no use in saving a drowning man just to put him back on a sinking ship.'

'I'll do it,' she said, not feeling quite as confident as she sounded. But whether she believed she could or not, LeiRain knew that she *must* save the ship.

. . .

H er eyes struggled to adjust to the darkness as she made her way through the bowels of the ship. Footsteps thundered overhead. Cargo and various pieces of gear could be heard sliding, scraping the deck above her as the vessel's center of balance shifted. The air was warmer down here, stuffy and smelling of mold. After the stairs from the main deck, she had tried a few doors before finding the one that led to another ladder well into the main cargo hold. The weight of her shield made balance more difficult, but she had no hope of keeping the ship afloat without the aid of the amplifying stone. The ship continued to rock and shudder as she made her way down the last ladder. Her shoulders strained as she tried to hold onto the ladder while being thrown from side to side. Once she was halfway down, LeiRain jumped and splashed into thigh-deep water.

She yelped at the cold that bit into her legs and the sting of salt water seeping into her wounds. It was a stark contrast to the thick muggy air that made her skin sticky. Water was gushing through a submerged hole, but she could easily identify its location by the current pushing her away from the bulkhead. She braced herself against a support beam near the center of the room and pulled the shield from her back, holding it tightly in one hand while clasping the beam with the other.

Closing her eyes, her mind reached for the water. Her knees nearly buckled beneath her as she made contact with it. LeiRain had never tried to embrace or command so much of it at once and the joining, which normally felt like a clasping of hands, now came with breathtaking force. She fought to remain standing. Her grip on the support beam slipped and LeiRain fell backwards, splashing into the cold water. She nearly lost her grip on the shield as well, but she was still holding it when she hauled herself back up. LeiRain tried to shake off the doubt that plagued her. Her friends were depending on her. The *ship* was depending on her. But even as the water rose, she was being swallowed by feelings of inadequacy, guilt, and shame. What if she failed?

If the ship sank, she would survive, but her friends and the crew would not. She forced her mind to focus on the water pushing its way into the ship, into her mind. She felt the water resist her will and press, press, press on her mind. Press its way into the ship. LeiRain began to push back. The water acknowledged her, not shying away from her rough touch, but not giving in, either. Her heart beat so fast she thought it might burst, but she refused to give up. LeiRain tightened her grip on the handhold of her shield just as she squeezed her eyes shut and grabbed at the water, wrestling against it with her mind.

The ship groaned and listed slightly more to port and LeiRain noticed that the rushing water now reached her waist. A chill ran through her as the icy sensation climbed up her midsection. Her eyes shot open as she scanned the room. The space was thoroughly flooded now, some of the lighter cargo bobbing along on the water's surface. The task before her was immense, overwhelming.

I can't do this. I'm not strong enough to stop it.

The adrenaline that coursed through her was reminiscent of the moments before she'd lost her mother. Though ice water sloshed around her, LeiRain saw only a pool of her mother's blood and the rising smoke of a burning homestead.

Focus lost, debris swept LeiRain's feet out from under her. She fell back into the water once more, slipping below the surface. Bits of loose cargo knocked into her with bruising force as she struggled to regain her bearings.

LeiRain was so close to giving up, to letting the shield drop from her hand. Then she remembered Ron, and heard his voice in her head. *Don't let your mother's death have been in vain.* She saw Alarra, then, standing over her forge. Burn scars stretching over sweat-slicked skin, auburn hair coming loose from a plait as her mother swung a hammer. She remembered the look of stubborn defiance on her mothers face, even as Ethan held a knife to her throat. *It won't be in vain*, LeiRain thought.

With a burst of determination, she forced herself to surface, clawing her way up the support beam. Water rushed in with such force that it threatened to throw her off her feet once more. LeiRain inched around the beam until she could feel the crush of water pressing her back into it.

I am the daughter of Alarra, bender of steel and weaver of enchantments. I am a daughter of tempest.

She closed her eyes again and reached out with her mind, ignoring the cold water that kept rising around her.

I am a descendant of the fae. Power runs through my veins.

This time she was prepared for the force of connecting with so much water, and she welcomed it. She let the edges of her mind blur so that the line between where she ended and the water began was unclear. She whispered her will to the ocean, asking it not only to stop pushing its way into the vessel, but to change its nature entirely.

The water hesitated, as if it were thinking over her proposal, and then she felt it start to respond. The water ocean outside of the ship changed its course, redistributing the pressure.

I am the daughter of Alarra, bender of steel and weaver of enchantments. I am the daughter of Caspian.

LeiRain felt her magic surge as her father's name echoed in her mind. A stillness fell in the cargo hold as the ocean ceased to rush in through the damaged hull.

Power runs through my veins.

The brief silence was replaced by the deafening sound of water pushing its way out through the tear in the hull as the ocean bent to her will.

45

LeiRain laughed despite her exhaustion. The ankle-deep water was winding its way up the bulkhead and out the gaping hole. It was not just bending to her will, it was *bowing* to it. She could see daylight peeking in from the shattered bulkhead. The footsteps of a crewman could be heard rushing down the ladder. He was coming to patch the ship. *Thank the gods*, LeiRain thought.

She did not know how much longer she would be able to hold the connection. It felt more natural, more a part of her than ever before, but her body was sagging as everything she had poured into the magic. There was little left to buoy her up as water drained from the space and LeiRain's legs began to quiver. She leaned heavily against the beam. She saw the crewman coming down the ladder and strained to recall his name. *Tamer.* She'd only spoken to him once before. He seemed to keep to himself, head down as he carried out what-ever tasks were assigned to him. Tamer had the large wooden plug in one hand, ready to patch the hole. She hoped it would hold long enough to get them to port where more thorough repairs might be completed.

Tamer dropped into the space, landing in front of LeiRain with a splash. He gave her a brief nod, eyes widening slightly as he took in her exhaustion. His long hair, having slipped from its plait, hung in shaggy curtains around his face. The little bit of his cheeks she could see through his dark beard were flushed as he set himself to the task of repairing the hole. He dropped to one knee and pushed a wooden plug into the damaged bulkhead, using the force of his body. Then, he pulled a mallet from his belt to tap it more securely into place. LeiRain watched as he lifted his arm and swung, her magic straining to hold the water back on the other side. Just as the mallet came down against the plug, there was a deafening *crack*. The ship shuddered violently and LeiRain hit the floor on her knees. Her jaw snapped shut with the impact, teeth cutting into her cheeks. The coppery taste of blood filled her mouth. At first, LeiRain thought that Tamer had swung the mallet too hard, but then she felt the force of roiling ocean water and knew. The ship had been struck again. LeiRain's hold on her magic shattered.

Water abruptly reversed its flow and began to push back into the space. It moved with such force that large wooden shards tore away from the edges of the hole, widening it. Sunlight now shone through another hole only a few feet away from the first. LeiRain heard a cannonball roll across the deck as the ship began to list back to port. Water poured in from both of the holes. She tried to stand as she scanned the room for Tamer, but the pain in her knees was excruciating and her thigh had begun to bleed again. The space began to flood rapidly. A stack of heavily loaded crates crashed down on LeiRain just as she spotted the crewman face down in the rising water. She struggled against the weight, trying to pull herself out from under the crates. If she could just wriggle free, perhaps she could still save Tamer. *If he's not already dead*, she thought. A rush of ocean sent flotsam across the room at impressive speed, driving tiny wooden splinters into LeiRain's skin. She screamed into the water as they slid into her flesh. Something large smashed into her skull, cutting off her screams. Searing pain burned behind her eyelids and then darkness overtook her.

There was darkness all around when LeiRain opened her eyes again. And it was quiet. She could hear scraping and thumping, but underwater, it sounded muffled and far away. There was no longer the sound of gushing water; it took her a moment to realize that this was because the space was fully flooded. She could feel it, could sense that the water had taken over the room.

LeiRain tried to move, fighting the cold that seeped into her bones. A terrible pain shot up her neck and into her head as she strained against a hard pressure on her chest. She was still pinned beneath the cargo. The wooden crates were somewhat buoyant in the water, but they were loaded with cargo. It was so heavy on her chest that LeiRain was certain other crates had toppled over and were likely sitting on this one. She had to get out of here. She had to make sure her friends were safe.

LeiRain pushed against the crate, both with her body and her magic. It was hard to tell which of the two felt weaker. Her limbs were quivering with exhaustion and her magic responded sluggishly. She could only lift the crate a few inches before other cargo forced the weight back down on her. She looked from side to side but could make out very little. There was no sunlight coming in through the damaged hull anymore. The ship must have listed so far that the torn hull was fully submerged. She couldn't see Tamer but she hoped that he had somehow gotten out of the space before it had flooded entirely. LeiRain knew that he probably hadn't.

Each time LeiRain lifted the crate, she squirmed a bit before giving in to the weight. Gradually, she was shimmying her way out from beneath the pile of cargo. She lifted, scooted her body a few inches, then rested with the weight of the box pressing down on her again. She winced each time she had to let the weight resettle on top of her.

Progress was slow and LeiRain struggled to keep her panic in check. She wasn't afraid for herself – she could go down with the ship and still survive. She was afraid for her friends, for Dearvian and his crew. She kept at it. Lift. Shimmy. Rest. She had only one leg pinned beneath the crates now, so close to being free. With a final, desperate shove, LeiRain lifted the crate. She jerked, twisting her legs sideways. Red flashed before her eyes as her knees protested the movement. Ignoring her battered knees, she pushed off the nearest bulkhead with her feet, screaming as she did so. The crates came crashing down where her body had been only seconds before. She placed a hand on her temple, willing her head to stop spinning. She panted with exhaustion, but at least she was free.

LeiRain felt around in the darkness. She could make out only dim shadows and none looked like her shield. She ran her hands along the deck and in between piles of debris. Her fingers were numbed by the iciness of the ocean water, which made it difficult to discern what she was touching. Splinters worked their way into her hands as they passed over jagged bits of hull and shattered crates. LeiRain began to think that she might never find her shield, fumbling in the dark like this. But when her hands ran over it, she recognized it immediately. Her magic was still tired and threadbare, but the enchanted shield hummed at her touch. It called to her, a sensation that broke through the numbness. It offered to lend her its power.

It was wedged between a toppled cargo box and the bulkhead. LeiRain swore when she tugged on the weapon and it failed to move. The smooth sorcerer's steel slipped through her fingers over and over again. She wouldn't be able to retrieve it with physical strength. LeiRain placed her hands against the shield and let it pour magic into her. It focused what little magic she had left, rallying the sliver of power that remained inside her. With a mental tug, the boxes pinning the shield to the bulkhead slipped to one side and she pulled the shield free. Wasting no time, she strapped it to her back and began to work her way through the debris.

The ship was no longer completely upright and debris floated in all directions. The effect was so disorienting that she nearly lost track of where the deck was, confusing it with a bulkhead. She found the corner of the room and reached out with her magic to locate the holes in the ship's hull, where it linked with the ocean. She let this serve as her anchor. Oriented to the room, again, she swam through the water along the floor until she wrapped a hand around a ladder rung.

Most of the ladder was submerged but she could still use it to pull herself upward. Head throbbing and muscles burning, she climbed, one rung at a time. Just as she was about to pull her face from the water, she felt a sharp sting in her right thigh. LeiRain nearly lost her grip on the ladder as she cried out.

She reached down with one hand. Her fingertips tapped gently against her leg as she fumbled to find the source of the pain. She screamed again when her hand brushed against a piece of wood. A large splinter had found the gash in her thigh and pierced it further. The jagged wood now jutted out from her leg, firmly implanted in the exposed muscle. The shard was large, at least two inches wide and it had gone at least as deep into her already torn flesh. LeiRain resisted the urge to rip the thing out of her leg. In the dark she was more likely to make the wound worse.

She climbed up the ladder by another rung and whimpered. The wood sticking from her leg met with resistance as she tried to pull herself from the water. It was risky to remove the splinter, but now it seemed just as risky to leave it in. If she moved too quickly, if it caught on something, it could tear her leg wide open. With tears in her eyes and hands shaking, LeiRain reached out for the wood shard. Gripping it tightly, she yanked the shard from her leg. Her howl of pain echoed through the bowels of the ship.

The edges of LeiRain's vision grew dark and she felt her consciousness trying to slip away again. With a guttural scream, she hauled herself upward. Her body hit the deck with a thud. She saw stars behind her eyelids. It would be so much easier to succumb to her wounds. Every inch of her was on fire with pain. But LeiRain fought to stay awake. She was free of the flooded compartment now and her friends waited somewhere above.

Palms pressed flat against the wall, LeiRain pulled herself to her feet. Sharp pain shot through her knees. Her thigh throbbed, blood pulsing from the wound with each step. LeiRain stumbled and tried to find something to grip with her hands. The ship was listing so far to port that the floor tilted dramatically. She managed a slow limp, her body leaning at an odd angle. The lanterns had all gone out, but a thin stream of sunlight was visible at the far end of the corridor. She shuffled her way toward the light. The stairwell was not as well lit as it ought to have been. The midday sun should have been streaming down, but the lean of the ship had angled the stairwell away from the sky.

She moved slowly and painfully, but with more confidence now that she could see where she was placing her foot each time she limped forward. When she emerged at the top of the stairs, the bright light sent bursts of pain through her aching skull. Heart pounding, she looked for her friends. Crew members rushed back and forth. A group of men pulled lines and called out commands as they adjusted the sails. If they could catch the wind, they might still escape. Men dropped over the side in rope harnesses, wearing belts that were laden with tools as they worked furiously to save the ship. If they didn't repair some of the damage soon, the vessel would be lost.

Ron was helping a harnessed sailor lower himself over the side of the ship, slowly releasing more slack on a rope that was secured to an iron bit on the deck. Silver was even closer to the ship's rails, leaning forward with a look of total concentration on his face. She knew that he must be using magic, but couldn't tell what exactly he was doing. Relief flooded LeiRain, even while cannons continued to splash in the nearby water; her friends were still alive. The air was filled with the smell of sweat and smoke but she saw no fire. A large streak of something that looked a lot like blood was smeared over several planks beneath her feet. Every once in a while, a coppery tang mixed in with the smell of gunpowder and salt water.

The Captain looked like a mad man. His wide-brimmed hat was gone, revealing a tangle of dark hair. His jacket had been discarded and his sleeves were pulled up above his elbows. Dearvian waved his arms dramatically as he directed the crewmen. There was a gash several inches long on his right cheek. It had bled down the side of his face and into the collar of his shirt, but the wound looked superficial. He saw LeiRain. His eyes shone golden in the sun as they searched her face for answers. He was looking for hope. LeiRain shook her head as she mouthed an apology. Dearvian's face fell. His shoulders sagged. At least, she thought that's what she had seen. But a second later, the Captain had broken eye contact with her and was directing his men with just as much confidence as he had before.

'You bought us time, Rain,' the Captain called to her, looking over his shoulder. He pointed skyward. 'We're adjusting the sails,' he said. 'They've lost all wind. The son of tempest is making it so we cannot run.'

He looked to the attacking vessel, which now sailed menacingly off their port side.

'They're not even firing at us anymore, just waiting for us to sink! We're too far from land. They've shattered half our lifeboats and anyone who takes the ones that remain will be easy targets.' LeiRain's heart sank. Her friends might be alive now, but for how much longer? She watched the blood smear over Dearvian's chin as he wiped his face with the back of his hand.

He swallowed, bringing his confession to an end. Dearvian's knuckles had sprouted long, sharp claws and his eyes became those of a predator. She swallowed nervously as thin white fangs appeared, pressing against his lower lip. For one brief moment, she thought that the fierceness of his stare was directed at her.

'I'm sorry,' LeiRain said. Her voice was a rasp. 'What can I do?'

But he didn't hear her. He turned his predatory gaze on his men and began demanding updates on the status of repairs. LeiRain watched him, dumbly. She looked around at the crewmen. She saw no place where she could help. What she had to offer was her magic and that had already failed. A loud boom interrupted LeiRain's thoughts. Her ears buzzed and voices around her sounded distant though she was surrounded by crewmen. The enormous *crack* that followed could be felt as much as heard. The ship jolted as the smaller of the two masts groaned and cracked.

LeiRain watched the mast sway. Time seemed to slow as it wobbled in place. She could predict its path – it would land on or near Ron and Silver. Her chest was tight with panic. She could not move fast enough to save anyone from what was about to happen, especially not with her damaged leg. Her feet slid out beneath her and only her grip on the nearby rail kept LeiRain for sliding across the deck. She watched in horror as the mast tilted too far, so far that it could not wobble back into place. The large wooden beam came crashing down, the attached sail billowing behind it.

Large splinters flew outward from where the mast split and she brought her shield up to cover her face. Her own scream sounded muffled as wooden shards embedded themselves in her right side, some too small to be pulled out by hand. She clutched her rib where tiny bits of wood had pierced her tunic and buried themselves in her skin. Instinct made her curl in on herself defensively, but this only drove the splinters further into her skin. She pulled a larger shard from one of her biceps. LeiRain discarded the bloody fragment and looked back up just in time to see the fallen mast strike the deck. It came down on Silver. She shouted and took a few stumbling steps toward him. The terror of watching him disappear over the side of the ship was worse than any physical pain LeiRain had endured thus far.

The vessel sank down several more feet on the sport side, the weight furthering their list as the broken mast dangled. LeiRain lost her footing and slid, loose lines slipping through her frantic fingers. She caught hold of a bit and wrapped herself around the cold iron.

She searched for Ron but her eyes caught on a wild looking creature, part man, part panther, clinging to the remaining mast. The Captain had begun to shift. Dearvian's large, taloned paws gripped the wood, holding him steady. Shining black fur, the same color as his hair, sprouted from his sleeves. He still wore the face of a man but his glare looked feral as he assessed his surroundings. Feline eyes flashed back and forth as he watched his crew members clinging to lines, dangling over the edge of the ship, desperately holding on. His long black tail flicked from side to side in an agitated manner.

A slack line dangled over the edge where Ron had been standing moments ago but LeiRain saw no sign of him. She recalled the chainmail he'd been wearing and her search became more frantic. She looked down at the water and saw wood fragments floating next to slack pieces of rope. The dingy white fabric of the sail draped in the water, obscuring much of her view, while the mast itself remained partially aboard the vessel, caught on the remnants of the rails.

I have to find them.

She unclipped her shield from the guige and let it go. The solid piece of sorcerer's steel slid across the deck, over the ship's edge and into the water. LeiRain uncoiled from the mooring bit she'd been clasping and followed the same course.

46

Leirain plunged through the water's surface, sinking into the debris-crowded ocean. Shredded bits of the ship obstructed her vision as she pushed her way through the detritus, searching for her friends. There were flailing limbs all around her, their churning making the water hazy. LeiRain scrambled around a sinking barrel and swam directly into a body. The man rolled over with the current and as he turned to face her, LeiRain recognized Tamer. She froze momentarily, staring into his unblinking eyes. His long hair and wispy beard swayed in the water. LeiRain shook her head clear, forcing herself to focus on those she might still save. The dead could be mourned later. Her gut churning with anxiety, LeiRain continued to search.

The ocean was so deep here that it felt bottomless. LeiRain dove, searching through the fallen bodies and shattered pieces of The Mad Return that were now lost to the sea. Her body ached in ways she hadn't even known was possible, some of her injuries throbbing while others sent intermittent jolts of hot pain up through an arm or a leg. Still, LeiRain weaved her way through the churn of fallen objects. She worked to contain the panic that propelled her through the water. The muffled boom of cannon fire could be heard from somewhere overhead, and *The Mad Return* was coming apart so quickly that the hull's creaks and groans echoed hauntingly around her.

She felt a mixture of relief and despair when she spotted Ron. He was still conscious, thrashing and tangled in the line he'd been holding onto when thrown overboard. He still wore his chainmail and now struggled against the weight of it. While the rope restricted him, it was also the only thing that had kept Ron from sinking like a stone, its other end still tethered somewhere to the ship above. She had almost reached him when she was thrown back by a rush of water as the mast crashed between them, missing her by only a few inches

LeiRain shoved her way around it, pushing the billowing fabric of the sail out of her path as she made for the dwarve. His arms no longer fought to get his head above the water. The stream of bubbles coming from his nose and mouth had slowed to a trickle. By the time she reached him, Ron's body had gone entirely slack. LeiRain struggled to push him toward the surface. The armor was heavy. She was tired. She was in pain. Still, LeiRain kept pushing. *I won't lose you too*, she thought. Progress was slow, but little by little she made her way to the surface with the dwarve.

LeiRain grabbed the line that was still tied to the bit on the ship's weather deck and heaved with one arm, gripping Ron as best she could with the other. Time ... she was running out of time. How long had he been without air now? She still had to find Silver.

As she kicked toward the surface with Ron in her arms, a flash of platinum caught her eye. She turned to look and saw Silver. His eyes were closed and the verdaant's hair had come loose from its binding, waving freely as he drifted limply. He disappeared from view as the heavy fabric of the mast settled between them.

Water rushed from her lungs as LeiRain screamed in frustration. She pushed against the weight of Ron's body, now trying to nudge him toward the surface from below. She had to hurry. But it was useless. LeiRain could push past the pain, but her torn muscles and bleeding cuts still held her back. Her legs barely responded when she tried to swim to the surface. A stream of red ran from her thigh, coming faster each time she kicked.

LeiRain looked past her feet into the darkness below, hoping for a glimpse of her shield. She regretted sending it overboard ahead of her. She let out another scream and it resonated through the water, full of desperation and despair. She shoved Ron again, his body refusing to move closer to the surface.

A bright light flashed in front of her. LeiRain suddenly found herself staring into the face of a water elf. His skin was blue and mottled with green and LeiRain noted a dark, pink scar on his chin. She looked into his black eyes and found her own panicked face reflected in them. He held something out to LeiRain; her shield. She looked at Ron's paling face and gave the dwarve one last push upward before letting him go and taking hold of the shield. With another flash of light, the elf disappeared.

Though her mind was heavy with fatigue, she forced herself to focus, to reach out to the water. It responded to her call, moving Ron toward the surface much more quickly than she could have done herself. The water elf reappeared next to Ron and looped an arm around him, tugging the dwarve toward a large piece of wood that floated nearby. Ron must have maintained some fragment of consciousness after all because he began kicking his feet and grabbing for the floating debris as soon as his body met the surface. Knowing he was safe, LeiRain turned her full attention back to Silver.

She fought through the sail, the fabric impeding her view and her progress. LeiRain's head pulsed with each heartbeat. All the noise of battle faded as she focused on finding Silver. He *had* to survive. Shoving her way past the billowing white fabric, LeiRain was surprised to find two more water elves. They were working to free one of Silver's legs, which was entangled in a set of lines still knotted to the mast. A male elf held Silver by his limp arms while his female companion used the sharpened edge of a seashell to cut through the rope that held him. Finally the line snapped, untethering him from the sinking mast. The elves immediately sped toward the surface with him, LeiRain following close behind as she directed the water to speed their ascent.

Silver's body broke the surface and the elves held him aloft. They remained submerged beneath his limp form as LeiRain broke through beside him, and they helped her slide his body onto a large piece of hull debris. She watched him intently, waiting for him to resume breathing. LeiRain could feel the tendrils of grief ripping another hole in her center as she waited for the rise and fall of his chest. His normally emerald skin was drained of color and she found herself desperate to see his cheeks flush blue once more.

'Please.' She said to the still form.

LeiRain reached toward Silver's neck and placed her fingertips just below his jaw. She could feel no pulse. Her throat tightened as she tried to hold back a sob. Not another loss. *Not Silver.*

'Please,' she said once more, grabbing hold of his cold fingers. '*Don't leave me.*'

The water beside her erupted. LeiRain gasped as one of the elves who had helped carry Silver burst through the water.

His face shimmered blue-green in the sunlight and the gills on his neck expanded and contracted frantically as he struggled to speak.

'Pull –' the elf's voice was raspy and thin, 'the water...' His gills flared wide, revealing the dark red flesh within. 'From his lungs.' He made a gasping sound, '*Demi-god.*' The last word came out as a wheeze just before he plunged back into the water where he could breathe.

Pull the water from his lungs... Yes! What was drowning but water in places that it shouldn't be? LeiRain focused on pulling together the remnants of her exhausted magic. With one hand, she clasped the debris on which Silver rested and gripped her shield tightly with the other.

LeiRain closed her eyes, focusing, calling on her magic. She let the water feel her pain and fear. She let it feel her love for Silver, and the way his magic called to her own. She asked the water to remove itself from his lungs and return to the ocean from where it had come. It was difficult with so much water around her. She'd never before attempted to use her magic with such precision. Slowly at first and then faster, water began to stream from Silver's nose and mouth. It ran down his neck and poured onto the wooden planks beneath him before finding its way back into the ocean. LeiRain felt herself smile as the water drained away. She watched Silver's chest, hopeful and eager to see it rise with his breath. But before that could happen, LeiRain felt the smallest bit of resistance from the water.

I'm supposed to be here, it told her. *Take too much of me, and he will die.* She stopped focusing on Silver's breathing for a moment, and did her best to truly listen to her magic. LeiRain didn't just *hear* the water, she felt it. If she took anymore, his lungs would whither. With a *thank you* to the water, she let her magic go.

Silver's chest remained still. She reached up and gripped his shoulder, shaking it lightly. LeiRain felt her own breathing stop as she waited. She'd been too late. Fingers curling into his shoulder, LeiRain whimpered.

'I can't lose you,' she cried, shaking him.

Silver's eyes shot open. He began coughing, violently. He leaned onto his side and vomited a mouthful of ocean water. LeiRain sucked in a relieved breath as she watched him take his own frantic gulps of air. The grief that had been closing disappeared.

She let go of the tension that had coiled in her body. This last bit of magic had taken everything LeiRain had left. Her body, *her soul*, was heavy with exhaustion. Silver's eyes met hers and she felt her lips curl up in a smile. Her vision narrowed to only his face and she interlaced her fingers with his even as her eyes closed and she slipped below the water's surface.

47

LeiRain covered her face with her arm. Even with her eyes closed, the light shining through her eyelids was painfully bright. Her head ached and her eyes were dry and swollen. Everything from the waist down felt bruised and sore. Her physical discomfort was so complete that it took LeiRain a moment to realize that the hollow pang in her stomach was hunger. She groaned as her midsection rumbled. The only time she'd felt anything close to this was when she'd encountered the sheel and used her magic for the first time. She recognized it as the ravenous aftermath of extreme magic use and healing and the realization brought back memories of the battle. The need for food was so powerful it made LeiRain open her eyes.

She tilted her head away from the sunlight and held up a hand to shield her eyes. She blinked at the sandpaper dryness of them and tried to clear the blurriness in her vision. Though the warm sun felt good on her skin, the light that reflected off the sand made it nearly impossible for her to fully protect her tender eyes.

There were people moving across the beach, figures made

indistinct by the hazy glare. One of them came to kneel in front of her. A shadow fell over LeiRain's face as the figure blocked out the sun. Backlit, it was difficult to discern his features, but at least she was able to open her eyes a bit wider as they blocked some of the sun.

'Here,' the figure said in a gentle but masculine voice. A familiar voice, but one that LeiRain couldn't yet place. He handed her a cup. She gratefully accepted the fresh water, suddenly realizing just how thirsty she was. Her throat had the same sandpaper feeling as the inside of her eyelids. LeiRain emptied the cup quickly. The water was cool and seemed to wipe away some of the rawness in her throat. She felt a pang of regret at not drinking it more slowly, savoring the coolness of it.

'I'll get you some more,' the man said. Where did she know that voice from? 'But I'm sure you're hungry too, so eat this and I'll be right back.'

The figure stood, removing the shadow that he had cast over her and suddenly exposing LeiRain to the bright light again. Her eyes shut automatically against the sun as it hit her face. After several seconds, she could feel her eyes adjusting and began to slowly crack them open. A piece of fruit rested in front of her, a swatch of fabric beneath it. The fruit was almost the same color as the sand and speckled with small black spots. *Longing fruit*! Now she realized why that voice was so familiar. LeiRain's head jerked up as she scanned the beach for the man who'd gone to get her more water. Her vision blurred and she winced at the stab of pain in her skull. All she could make out were hazy silhouettes.

LeiRain bit into the fruit, eyes still scanning the broad expanse. She expected the taste of suncakes, which is what the longing fruit had tasted like when she first ate it in Corallis, and was surprised to find her mouth filled with the flavors of honeyed porridge. As if the fruit were transporting her through space and time, the flavor made LeiRain feel as though she were sitting at Brya's table again, surrounded by friends. Suncakes were delightful, but the taste of honeyed porridge carried a warmth of feeling that the delicate pastries never would. She took another bite, letting the longing fruit take her back to the comfort of life in the mountains.

Her friends. LeiRain jolted into an upright position. She clutched her head, the sand in front of her wobbling as she was overcome by dizziness. She remembered more details now: the sudden assault on The Mad Return, the on-rush of water she couldn't stop, Silver and Ron disappearing over-board. LeiRain took a few steadying breaths. Where were her friends? Had they made it ashore? Did the ship survive?

Her caregiver returned with a fresh cup of water. As he approached, LeiRain forced herself to stare past the burning sun to make out his features. His skin was a light blue, just like her own. He had broad, muscular shoulders and a narrow waist. His steps were just a little awkward, like he was unac-customed to moving on land. He turned his head slightly to speak to a passerby. The handsome profile was unmistakable. Riv.

He held out the full cup. She took it from him, her slender fingers brushing against his as she pulled it from his grip. LeiRain drank the water before speaking. This was partly because of her extreme thirst, and partly because she wanted to buy herself some time. She remembered the tension between them in Coral-lis, how she'd admired him. How she'd hoped to return and make a life in Corallis, maybe a life with Riv, even while she watched him pine for Cordelia. *Cordelia*. Was the beautiful daughter of tempest here? LeiRain resisted the urge to scan the beach for her.

'I'm sorry I didn't come back,' she said to him. Her voice

was raspy, despite the water. Riv sat back on the sand and crossed his legs. He shook his head. His cropped hair had dried into blue-green waves. LeiRain's hand twitched as she fought the urge to touch those waves. She reminded herself of Silver's smooth locks, the scent of basil and lavender that wafted from them. Her desire to reach toward Riv waned.

'I told you,' he said, with a sad smile. 'I knew you wouldn't come back.' He looked at her tenderly. His eyes slid from her face to her body and then back. 'But it's alright.'

'Why didn't you tell me?' LeiRain asked. She felt anger begin to burn in her belly. 'That so much time was passing? If I had left earlier—' Her voice trailed off. Maybe things would have been different, she thought, but maybe not.

'I *did* tell you,' Riv replied. 'I told you that time moves differently in Corallis.'

'You could have been more *specific*.' LeiRain's words were sharp. She made no effort to hide her annoyance at his coyness.

'If I had told you more, you would have left sooner and I would have had even less time with you.'

The corner of his mouth quirked up into the half-smile she'd seen so often in Corallis. He brushed a piece of hair out of her face.

'You seem different,' He said. There was a hungry look in his eyes as he scanned her body again. LeiRain's cheeks heated under his gaze. She turned away. Had he looked at her like in Corallis? No, she was sure he hadn't. LeiRain *was* different now. She was no longer alone in the world. She was stronger, physically and mentally.

'Where's Cordelia?' She asked. Partly because she wondered if the girl cared enough to come to her aid, and partly because she wanted to know if something had changed between Cordelia and Riv that might explain the interest he now showed in her.

'Cordelia?' Riv pulled a face. It contorted his handsome features into something distinctly less pleasing to the eye. 'She never leaves Corallis. Especially not when there might be danger.'

LeiRain thought about the way Riv had coaxed her into staying a bit longer in the warded city. He'd convinced her that just a few more days wouldn't matter. If she had returned to Harbor Village sooner, she could have told her mother what she'd found in Corallis. Maybe she could have assuaged her mother's worries and freed Alarra to move on.

Her anger flared, briefly. She'd looked at Riv so admiringly then, and he must have seen it in her eyes. He'd known he could convince her to stay. LeiRain drew in a breath and as she exhaled, her anger receded. What was the point? It would not bring her mother back and even if he had told LeiRain how much time was passing on land, if she had returned earlier, could she be sure that her mother would have left Harbor? No.

'Are my friends well?' she asked? 'The verdaant and the dwarve?'

'They are both well, as are most of the crew.' He shook his head, 'Save the few who drowned before we arrived.'

'How did you know to come?'

She didn't know exactly where Corallis was located, but imagined that it was much closer to The Continent than where they had been sailing.

'Orca heard your cry.'

'My cry? I didn't...' Her voice trailed off.

She *had* called out, had screamed in frustration and despair.

'The water elves have repaid the life debt they owe you,' Riv said. 'With significant interest,' he gestured toward the crew members scattered across the beach. 'The vessel will not be easy to repair, but we saved what we could.'

She scanned the waters for *The Mad Return. Something* sat in the waters offshore, but she didn't at first recognize it. There was so little left of the vessel that she had mistaken it for an awkwardly shaped rock jutting from the shallows. There was the vague shape of a hull, but most of it had been torn away. The bowels of the vessel were now exposed to daylight. There were crewmen working around it, dislodging bits of cargo that had somehow remained in the holds, searching through the wreckage for anything useful that might be salvaged.

'Where are we?'

'I am told this is the Arborris Enclave,' he replied. 'It was not the closest piece of land, but it was where the ship's captain requested we take you.'

So Dearvian had survived as well. And they had reached their destination.

'What about the Royals? The other ship that was attacking us?'

'Eaton ran out of energy at almost the same time that you did and the other vessel fled as soon as they no longer had the advantage.'

'Eaton.' *That's right.* 'Why would Eaton help the Royals?'

'Eaton ... he ... and Pearl,' he swallowed hard before continuing. 'We hadn't seen either of them for weeks. Corallis weeks,' he clarified.

LeiRain pursed her lips at this reference to Corallis time. Riv looked sheepish under her glare.

'Why would he help them?' LeiRain asked once more. Though she'd only met Eaton once, there was something about him aiding the Royals that felt deeply offensive, almost personal to her. It was a betrayal.

'He is my friend,' Riv replied. It was a statement, but there was a note of questioning in his voice. 'The two of us grew up together in Corallis. When I saw his face today—' Riv's brows knit together and tears pooled in his eyes. 'He looked pained, sad, and afraid. If it were just himself he had to think of, I don't think the Royals could coerce him..' His eyes narrowed, gaze sharpening as he looked at LeiRain. 'The Royals must have Pearl.'

She tried to take this in. It had never occurred to her that the Royals would manipulate blends in this way. Eaton would be nothing more than a tool to them. Riv's eyes seemed to look through her now. They both sat silently with the heaviness of what he had said. LeiRain didn't want to say this aloud, but if Eaton couldn't be freed from the Royals then he would have to be eliminated. He was too powerful a weapon. She shuddered at the thought, hating that it had even occurred to her. If they did have Pearl and were forcing Eaton's hand, then he was innocent. He didn't deserve to die. And yet, with him, the Royals might control the seas. Her heart sank at the hopelessness of the situation.

'We will wait.' Riv's words startled LeiRain out of her reverie. 'The elves cannot come ashore. They don't survive long on land. But we will wait nearby.' Riv swallowed and frowned. LeiRain's stomach knotted as she waited for his next words.

'Your ship cannot return to sea without our help. We saved many lives for you today, Rain.' He paused, searching her eyes. 'We want you and your friends to find Pearl and bring her back to us so that we can free Eaton. It's a fair exchange.'

LeiRain considered this. When she spoke, her voice was little more than a whisper.

'And what if she is no longer alive?' LeiRain asked. Riv nodded, as if he had expected this question.

'Even that knowledge will free Eaton. If he has no one to

protect—' His voice trailed off. If Eaton was only working for the Royals because he feared for his mate's life, then news of her death would free him to turn on his captors. As much as she dreaded the idea of Eaton being forced to serve the Royals, she hoped that Riv was right. Because if Eaton wasn't being coerced then the alternative was that he had chosen this path. 'Okay,' LeiRain said. She placed her hand on top of Riv's. 'I will do what I can.'

Their mission had been to find evidence that could persuade the verdaant to view the Royals as a real threat. She shouldn't make such promises before speaking with Ron and Silver but when she looked at Riv's face, she couldn't help herself.

'We'll find her,' she said. 'We will free them. Both of them.'

Some of the strain on Riv's face disappeared and his mouth shifted from a frown to a subtle smirk.

'Learn any new magic tricks since our last lesson?' he asked.

LeiRain smirked back at him. 'A few,' she replied.

48

S *ilver.*
   It was good to see Riv again after all this time, but she needed to see the fae. She needed to hear his voice, see him alive and well.

LeiRain had come so close to losing him. Her memories were sharpening and as her mind replayed those moments she spent waiting for Silver's chest to rise again ... Now that LeiRain understood what she felt for him, she had to tell Silver. Even if those feelings weren't returned. She stayed with Riv for a long while, not wanting to be rude to the friend who had just done so much for her, but her distraction was apparent. There was hurt behind Riv's smile when they parted, which made LeiRain wonder if she'd misjudged his feelings for Cordelia. LeiRain wasn't sure if she truly hoped for more than friendship, or if he just missed the way she'd doted on him in Corallis.

When Riv left, she started looking for Silver. None of the crew seemed to know where he had gone. LeiRain had to settle for finding Ron who was helping the sailors salvage supplies from the wreckage. She called his name when she saw him, but only a quiet rasp escaped her lips. Somehow, Ron heard her anyway. A smile spread over his face as the dwarve turned to face her. He dropped the barrel he'd been holding and walked swiftly toward her. When he reached her, Ron wrapped his arms around her and hugged LeiRain tightly. She sank into his embrace. He smelled like pine, a scent she'd come to associate with the mountain, and sun. And he hugged her like he meant it.

'I know you saved me,' he said, pulling back and looking at her. 'Gods damn heavy armor. Should have brought my light armor but we left in such a hurry.'

She smiled back at him.

'It wasn't me,' she said. 'The elves are to thank.'

'And who do we have to thank for the elves' appearance?' He winked at her. He looked better than he had in days, despite the near drowning. His cheeks were ruddy once more, and though he had clearly lost weight during the long days of sea sickness, he seemed solid and sure of himself with both feet planted on dry ground.

'He went off scouting the woods on his own,' Ron said, reading her well enough to know that she was looking for Silver. 'Careful if you go after him, Rain. We know this side of the island is populated, but we don't know if they're friendly or if we'll find more Royals.'

She nodded and turned to make her way to the tree line.

She was twenty feet or so into the thick brush when she lost sight of the beach. Despite the midday sun, it was dark. The only thing that told her how to find her way back was the thin ribbons of golden light that still managed to leak through the branches. LeiRain could still smell the sea water and brine, but now also the scent of rich soil and green things. It was cooler now that she was shaded from the sun, and the air seemed unnaturally still with the foliage blocking most of the sea breeze. The trees here were different from what she was used to, their bark smooth with large, fat leaves that fanned out from the top of their trunks. Giant ferns, some reaching as high as her waist, impeded her progress as she walked.

With each step, her heart seemed to beat a little harder in her chest. Her fingers itched for the pommel of her sword. The landscape was vastly different from that of the mountain, but the stillness and darkness reminded LeiRain of the night she'd so foolishly ventured out on her own. If Silver hadn't shown up, if he hadn't been following her – LeiRain didn't want to think about what might have happened. She swallowed, her throat tight with fear. She didn't want to walk further into the dark. She was determined not to make the same mistake twice. Just as LeiRain was about to turn around and wait for Silver on the beach, he slid from the shadows only a few inches away from her. A single, thick fern separated them. They peered at each other over the long fronds. Her breath caught as she felt the intensity of his gaze. Her magic caught fire in her core.

'There you are,' she said, lamely. All of her confidence and determination seemed to bleed out into the darkness. Her eyes ran over him in the dim light. He was safe, alive. There were no marks of injury on his handsome features, though there were dark smudges under his eyes that suggested fatigue. LeiRain watched the muscles in his throat jump as he swallowed. Magic swirled inside her, thirsting to drink him in.

'I'm glad you are well,' he replied. He tilted his head to the side, his eyes searching her face for something.

'Me too,' she said, then thought to clarify, 'I mean, I am also glad that you are well. I thought you might die.' She coughed. 'I thought you had died.' Why had she thought it was a good idea to come looking for him? What was she going to say? Now that he stood before her hardy and breathing,

LeiRain's words caught in her throat. Magic flexed inside her, as though it might push the words out.

'I – I just wanted to see that you were okay. For myself. They said you were okay, but—' LeiRain shook her head.

With a wave of his hand, the fronds of the fern between them bowed. Silver stepped over them, closing the gap between their bodies. He did not touch her, but came within a hair's breadth, never taking his eyes off her face. *Magicae canentis.* She felt it humming between them now, *magic that sings.* Her breath hitched, feeling the chords of their music vibrate through her body.

'I might have died were it not for you. If you had not pulled the water out of my lungs' – her cheeks burned as embarrassment washed over her – 'yes, the water elf told me what you did,' he said in response to her blush. 'If you had not done that for me, I would not have survived.' *Immortal, not indestructible.* 'Thank you.'

'It was nothing,' she said, breathily, backing away from him.

Her entire body flushed and, standing this close to him, she felt an ache between her thighs. LeiRain felt the desire to press her mouth against his, an impulse that she had always been able to ignore and push away. Until now. All of the intimate moments between them pressed in on her. If she gave in to her feelings, there would be no going back. Not for her.

'It was not nothing. I saw what it took from you. Thank you,' Silver replied.

He did not follow her, but he did not move away either.

'You're welcome,' she said, half calling it over her shoulder as she turned to head back to the beach.

She couldn't do it, couldn't tell him how she felt. It was too much, too scary. She halted as ferns rapidly unfurled their leaves and grew tall, blocking her path. LeiRain didn't turn around, but she could feel him there, watching her. Could feel the song of his magic vibrating through her body.

'LeiRain,' he said, sounding as desperate as she felt, 'please don't leave me.' They were the same words she'd whispered to Silver when she thought he was dying.

LeiRain allowed a small bit of hope to flare in her chest as she turned to face him again. She tried to find her confidence. She thought of his pale face and unmoving chest, silver hair plastered wet to his cheeks as he lay lifeless. Something in her chest cracked at the memory. *Tell him. Tell him. Tell him.* Her magic was insistent.

'You're holding something back,' he said. He reached out to her but pulled his hand away before he made contact. Silver's eyes were liquid pools of light that dimmed as he spoke. 'You have been for days, I think. I – I saw the way that the half-fae looked after you, the way he looked at you ... is that it? You have feelings for him?' His voice was soft and quivering.

'Riv?' she said, surprised. 'I don't feel that way for him.' *Tell him.* 'Not the way I feel for *you.*'

Silver's eyes blazed with swirling light. He had to be able to hear her heart pounding, smell her arousal. She took a step closer to him, erasing the distance she'd created when she tried to walk away. His face, always so serene, looked feral. His magic, which he must have been holding at bay, now jolted through her body like lightning. She let go of her own restraint and allowed her magic to answer in kind. Silver's lips parted and he groaned. He *groaned*. LeiRain's knees went weak and it was all she could do to remain standing. Silver moved closer to her too, and reached up to lace his fingers through the loose coils of her hair. The muscles in her stomach tightened and LeiRain bit her bottom lip. Tentatively, as if he waited for her to pull back or push him away, Silver brought his face closer to hers. Their lips brushed lightly.

'Rain,' he breathed, against her mouth. She sighed with longing and pressed her lips to his. She kissed him greedily with no gentleness. Her magic swelled as it pressed into his.

LeiRain fisted handfuls of his tunic as she drew their bodies closer. His mouth left hers and began a trail of kisses down her cheek, her neck, her collarbone. She pulled at her own tunic and his hands slid from her hips up her torso, taking the fabric with them, pulling it over her head. The cloth she'd used to wrap her chest hung somewhat slack after having been soaked in sea water and dried on her body. Silver hooked one finger under the fabric and tugged. The cloth uncoiled itself with this gentle suggestion. LeiRain reached down and further loosened it until the wrapping fell into a pile on the forest floor. Silver pulled off his own shirt. Their bodies pressed together, skin against skin, and all LeiRain could think was that she wanted *more.* Silver scooped her feet out from under her, cradling her to his chest before laying her on the ground.

He planted a hand on either side of her head as he leaned over. She ran her fingers down his muscular chest, stopping just above his pants. The fae's eyes closed as he gasped. LeiRain let out an involuntary whimper, hating the distance between their bodies. At this, his eyes flew open, burning with intensity, and he brought his mouth to hers again.

He resumed his trail of kisses, which, unhindered by her blouse this time, continued all the way down to where her trousers fastened. She kicked off her boots as he worked on the ties, lifting her hips so that the pants slid off easily. His warm, wet lips continued to trail down her body and she groaned with pleasure as they brushed along her inner thigh.

His silver hair somehow caught bits of light in the darkness and, as it tickled her skin, goosebumps followed in its wake.

The ferns surrounding them unfurled and grew, reaching unnatural heights as Silver kissed his way back to her mouth. LeiRain wound her fingers through his silken hair, holding him there.

'I've never been this close to someone,' she said, surprising herself.

'This is your first time?' he asked, his eyes widened in surprise.

'Oh, no. I've... I've been with a man before. But you've seen me, you've seen who I am like no one else. And this ... *magi-cae ca-nen-tis,*' she fumbled through the pronunciation. 'It makes this feel so different. More.'

There was wonder in her voice as she realized the truth of this. Bren had been good to her. Had always made sure that the experience was just as pleasurable for her as it was for him, but this felt so much better. The ache she felt for Silver went deeper than lust. This was not a temporary escape into pleasure, but a joining of two souls. He pulled back from her slightly, and she froze. For a brief moment, LeiRain feared that he was bringing an end to this intimate encounter. But he had pulled back only to be able to look into her eyes. A growl came from somewhere deep in his throat.

'It is the same for me, Rain. Just touching you. Looking into your eyes.' He paused and ran a finger down her torso from the curve of her breast to the curve of her hip. He pressed his magic against hers and she felt it in the depths of her soul. LeiRain's back arched in response. 'It's like being known for the first time.'

Their mouths met again, and she opened her legs for him. He sank into her. She pulled at his shoulders, wanting to feel all of his body on hers. He laughed softly as he pressed against her, covering her body with his own. He moved slowly inside her and a groan escaped her lips as Silver went deeper. He kissed her jaw, her throat. He stilled for a moment as he planted a kiss on her neck just below her ear.

'I love you, Rain. All of me,' at this she felt the rolling caress of his magic, 'is yours.'

He started to move inside her again but stopped when LeiRain reached up and grabbed his face. With one hand on either cheek, she pulled his eyes to hers. She knew the silver flames burning there were for her as she said, 'And I love you, Silversgleaming.'

LeiRain felt a shiver run through Silver's body. Her fingers dug into Silver's muscled back. The ferns grew thicker and curved over their heads, leaving them in utter darkness for a few seconds before a ball of fae light blazed into existence above them.

'I am yours, Silver,' LeiRain whispered between gasps. 'Entirely yours,' and she let her magic writhe against his. The fae light above them pulsed in time with the movement of their bodies, nearly exploding with blue fire as the two of them reached their climax together.

49

The crew huddled together in small clusters on the beach. The humidity had dropped considerably after the sunset, and there was a cool breeze sweeping in from the ocean. They relied on the combined warmth of their bodies to keep away the night chill. They didn't dare start a fire for fear of being discovered. The vessel that had attacked them had most likely been headed to the main harbor on the other side of the island, which was at least thirty miles away. This side of the island was populated, Dearvian explained, and it had a reputation as a bit of a vacation destination for seafarers. They had discussed the merits of asking the locals for help, shelter or food. But they couldn't be certain that this side of the island was safe from Royal influence.

At Silver's suggestion, the shivering clusters of crew members drew closer to the trees. Here they could benefit from the shelter of the ferns. The leaves grew thick and tall, forming a circular barrier around each group of men. Silver grew the ferns around himself and his friends last. Once they were hidden behind the tall fronds he produced a ball of fae light and buried it in the sand. LeiRain, Silver, Dearvian and

Ron sat, bringing themselves in closer contact with the warm sand as they discussed the way forward. LeiRain fought off a blush as the fronds overhead swayed with the breeze. Her core heated, thinking of how similarly the fronds had swayed with the movement of her and Silver's bodies just hours before. She shivered with pleasure as she felt the ghost of his lips trail down her skin. There was a gentle pulse of power from Silver, a subtle surge of magic that told LeiRain he was having similar thoughts.

'There is a village, maybe three miles from here, along the coast,' Silver recounted, based on his day's reconnaissance. He'd walked the edge of the island, hidden inside the trees, as the crewmen bandaged up the wounded and worked to salvage whatever they could from the wreckage of The Mad Return. It had been a long day for everyone. 'The forest is passable, though not easily. But I can help with that. The brush will still slow us down, but it will provide cover that the coast lacks.'

Ron nodded in agreement as Dearvian cleared his throat.

'I have a responsibility to the crew,' he said. Dearvian took turns making eye contact with each of them. His cat-like eyes were the only remaining vestige of the fierce feline she had seen clinging to the mast earlier that day.

'My first priority must be repairing the ship and ensuring the safety of my charges. While I believe your cause is a worthy one, it is my responsibility to think about their welfare first. I cannot order them to accompany you or go with you myself. I will stay here with them so that I may continue to lead them. However, if some wish to volunteer, *and they likely will*, I will permit it. I am truly sorry but that is the best I can do.'

LeiRain looked at Ron and Silver. Their faces were solemn. The old scar on Ron's face contrasted starkly with the paleness of his skin in the fae-light. Ron looked tired, his eyelids drooping slightly, but he nodded his understanding to the Captain. Silver sat next to her with the stillness of a fae. His chin dipped slightly in acknowledgment of Dearvian's words. LeiRain found herself looking back at the Captain with similar solemnity. None of them could object.

The Captain went on. 'I have a friend on this side of the island called Galban. He is a blend so he will be no friend to the Royals. The settlement is known as Beachspire. The local tavern, The Speared Sheel, is his, and has been for many years. You should seek him out first, and see what he can tell you about the rest of the Arborris Enclave. He is well-placed to know the settlement's business.

'I want to go,' LeiRain said. She saw Ron stiffen and waited for his objection. None came. For so long, this was what she had wanted; to see the world. Experience it. These were not ideal circumstances, but that didn't shift her desires.

'We must go tonight,' Silver said. LeiRain started. It hadn't occurred to her that they would need to leave so immediately. Silver continued. 'We should go while little is known about The Mad Return and her crew. Surely, someone will see evidence of our presence, or wreckage from our vessel at the very least. And we don't know what relationship the locals have with the Royals, so it's best that we reach the village before any word can make it from the other side of the island.'

'I agree,' Ron said, speaking for the first time. 'But we all need some rest.' LeiRain tried to decide if she was still tired. She'd slept for the better part of the day, but she'd also used an immense amount of magic. LeiRain stole a glance at Silver. He still had those dark smudges beneath his eyes. It was the only sign of his fatigue and may have been invisible to anyone who did not know him so well, but she noticed. He'd been using his magic before he'd fallen overboard, and then he'd *nearly died*. Surely he, too, could use some rest. 'If we run into any trouble, we'll want to be fresh,' Ron finished.

One side of the frond circle parted under Silver's command and Captain Dearvian stepped away, heading toward the mass of his crew. LeiRain could hear snores coming from some of the other shelters while laughter and the rumble of men's voices floated out from others. The crew seemed to be in good spirits, despite the day's hardships. Sailors were a resilient breed, LeiRain realized. Unwillingly, she thought of Bren. She wondered where he was now, what hardships he had endured since they last met. Did he regret his role in her mother's death? Had he continued to pass for human or had the Royals sniffed him out?

The thoughts stirred up a mixture of emotions in her. Anger, hurt, and maybe a bit of pity for him. She hadn't been able to see it before, so blinded by her own desperation, but ever since she'd known him, Bren had lived in constant fear of being found out. The thought almost made LeiRain feel grateful that she was so different. There was no *passing as a human* for a girl with blue skin, so she'd never been tempted to hide what or who she really was.

Ron stood and LeiRain saw him look longingly at a barrel of ale the sailors had tapped. They'd been able to recover little of their stores from the wreckage, but two barrels of the stuff had made it safely ashore. With LeiRain and Silver's abilities, they did not have to fret over finding fresh water, but they would need to find sustenance on the island, ideally without disturbing the nearby inhabitants. She watched the dwarve's eyes harden as he looked away from the barrel. Ron cleared his throat and headed off in the opposite direction, away from the ale and the merriment that surrounded it. He had not, to LeiRain's knowledge, taken a single sip of alcohol since the day the Royals attacked their mountain hide.

LeiRain shifted as though she might also stand, then paused. Where did she have to go? What did she have to do but rest and wait? LeiRain let herself settle back onto the warm sand as she found herself alone with Silver inside the tented leaves. The fronds closed up around them again and her eyes slid to meet his. Silver sat with his hands draped casually over his knees, his eyes flickering like stars in the blue light as he looked at her hungrily. With fae swiftness, he slid over the sand to be closer to her. LeiRain thrilled at the nearness and pressed the side of her body against his. Silver gently tugged one of her legs over his lap as his warm fingers pressed into the back of her neck, pulling her mouth to his. LeiRain felt her magic flicker in response and grabbed tightly onto his tunic. They kissed long and deep, their magic and LeiRain's body vibrating with the connection. She released her grip on his shirt and slid her hands beneath it, dragging her fingertips up the skin of his back. LeiRain pushed the tunic up as she went, one hand drifting over his taut abdomen. Silver shivered and groaned as her fingertips ran over his navel. LeiRain moved to pull the top over his head but the fae pulled back slightly, sighing. He placed his hands on hers and gently lifted them out from under his shirt.

'You need rest, Rain.'

Silver's voice was somber but the corners of his mouth turned up slightly. He brought her hands up to his lips and pressed hot kisses to the back of them.

'I slept half the day,' she said, leaning in to kiss his neck.

A part of her feared that this wasn't real. What would happen to them when they finished this mission, when he returned to the people who had murdered his brother's lover because she was not verdaant? LeiRain knew that his people were dangerous, she remembered Silver's warnings. It just wasn't enough to keep her away from him anymore. She wanted as much of Silver as she could have, while she could have him. She wanted to reinforce the solidity of their connection.

'Because you needed the rest, and you need more still. You pushed your limits today, and your body paid the price. Trust me, you need rest.'

He pulled her to him and laid them both down on the warm sand. Her back pressed into his chest as he wrapped his arms tightly around her. LeiRain's head rested on Silver's bicep, while his arm curled around her. She remembered the night they'd spent together by the mountain spring, when she'd let herself be vulnerable. LeiRain had never dreamt of anything like the connection she had with Silver. Until now, she would have spent her life settling for so much less. She shivered at the memory, at how cold and alone she had felt before she met him. How alone she might have been if she'd never left Harbor and experienced the warmth of friendship and family with Brya, Ron and Ray. She thought of what she'd had with Bren compared to the soul fire that burned between her and Silver. LeiRain had been through so much, and had felt so much pain. But if she hadn't, she might never have known the pleasure of being seen. LeiRain thought of the pleasure of this vulnerability and shivered again. Mistaking it for a chill, Silver held her tighter.

LeiRain ground her hips into him and felt Silver's growl vibrate through her body, felt him harden. She reached behind her, fingers dipping into the waist of his trousers. Silver brushed her hand away. LeiRain looked over her shoulder at him. When their eyes locked, he sent a bolt of magic into her, making her entire body tingle and her core heat. LeiRain gasped at the sensation, arching her back. A quiet laugh rumbled in Silver's chest.

He reached up with the arm that rested beneath her,

squeezing her back to his chest as he cupped her breast. His other hand pushed past hers as he ran his fingertips over her stomach. She gasped.

'I see there will be no rest until you are satisfied,' Silver purred into her ear.

Before LeiRain could respond, his hand slid past her waistband. His fingers were warm, his touch light as he stroked her. LeiRain was surprised by the intensity of her own arousal. She panted and writhed against him. He laughed, breathily. She let her own hand trail down her stomach and over his arm. She let it rest on top of his, wanting more. Still, his touch remained featherlight. He kissed the back of her neck, still stroking.

Gently, he caressed her, fingers brushing back and forth. Slowly, rhythmically. LeiRain felt the pressure building up inside her. She squeezed his hand, tried to press him against her. Silver held firm, his fingers maintaining their light touch. LeiRain groaned again, half in pleasure and half in frustration. Just as she was about to beg him for more, his magic dove into her as Silver continued his delicate caress. The hand on her breast squeezed ever so slightly. LeiRain felt the piercing presence of his magic inside of her and her own magic latched on to it, squeezing itself around it. Back arching, LeiRain let out a final groan as she succumbed to the pleasure.

Her body collapsed against him, all the tension drained away. Silver continued his gentle stroking as she lay panting. LeiRain pulled her hand away from his and reached back once more, feeling her way down his stomach and to his groin. Silver's fingers stilled. He withdrew his hand from between her legs and wrapped his fingers around her wrist. He pulled her hand from his pants and twined his fingers in hers before bringing her palm to rest against her chest.

'Sleep, Rain,' he whispered. She felt a soft, warm kiss just beneath her ear. 'We'll have time for that later. Now, *rest.*'

Cocooned in the warmth of his arms, her muscles deliciously limp, LeiRain had to concede that her eyelids did feel quite heavy. Her breathing slowed as she gave into the fatigue. She felt Silver press another kiss to her neck and his breath against her cheek as he whispered something. She strained to make out the words as consciousness slipped away from her. *I love you*. LeiRain breathed in Silver's herb garden scent and let the smell of lavender and basil lull her to sleep.

50

'Rain, it's time.'

LeiRain opened her eyes and battled confusion for a few seconds before remembering where she was. The sand beneath her was still warm but starting to cool. Silver relaxed his hold on her, as if he knew how much harder it was for her to wake up while in his arms. He placed a gentle kiss on her neck before he withdrew. He stood, motioning for her to follow as he left the shelter of the ferns. LeiRain felt a chill where his body had been. She stretched and finger-combed her hair before re-braiding it, tightly. Brushing the sleep from her eyes, she stood and followed Silver.

It was nearly midnight according to Dearvian's water-damaged pocket watch, and most of the men were sleeping save for those few who were on watch. Silver stood with a small group of men huddled near the forest's edge, outside the protective cover of ferns. LeiRain's stomach flitted nervously as she joined them. Ron passed her some gamey, dried meat and a water skin. LeiRain bit into the meat despite a lack of appetite. It tasted better than she had expected, savory even, and she was pleasantly surprised to find her stomach calmer once it was full. The sound of the men chewing and swallowing was audible in between the crashing of waves against the shore. She drank deeply before passing the skin back to Ron.

'I will lead the way.' Silver's eyes shone brightly in the moonlight. 'I can clear a path for you. The woods are dense enough that we can walk by fae light, at least until we near the edge of the village – Beachspire – but take care to step lightly. Can any of you see your way in the dark?'

One man raised his hand tentatively. The crewman was bundled in a high-necked shirt and a wide-brimmed hat that was pulled down low. Not much of his face was visible, but his eyes were brightly glowing green orbs, clearly visible in the darkness of night. It was the man who'd been sleeping at the brow when they'd first come on board. The crewman's eyes were not human, but they didn't look feline like Dearvian's either. The sailor was one of three men from the crew who had volunteered to cross the woods into Beachspire with Ron, Silver and LeiRain. Two of them were blends. One was human. Dearvian had given them the description of his friend Galban, a thick-muscled, gray-skinned blend who they should expect to find behind the bar.

'You,' Silver said, looking at the green-eyed blend, 'will bring up the rear. Keep an eye on things from behind.'

Ron cleared his throat. He stood on the periphery of the circle with his arms crossed over his chainmail-laden chest. The moonlight glinted off his helmet, though not as brightly as it might if it weren't so tarnished. Salt water was not kind to metal and Ron's armor was worse for the wear after their sea journey and his near drowning. It was difficult to tell in the dark but LeiRain thought she could feel the dwarve looking at her. They hadn't really spoken since she and Silver had—

'Let's move,' Ron said, cutting off LeiRain's thoughts.

Silver walked ahead of them into the pitch-black forest with LeiRain following directly behind. She stepped forward gingerly, her hands held in front in search of obstacles, but after a few steps the forest floor began to glow faintly with blue fae light. She paused to watch the tangled brambles and thick fern leaves withdraw, creating a clear path ahead. LeiRain heard the rustle behind them as the foliage wound back into place, leaving no trace of their passage.

The beach had become chilly after sunset. The sand was cool to the touch and a cold breeze came in off the water. But among the trees, there was little wind and the air felt thick with humidity. Clasping her shield, LeiRain brushed her mental fingers through the air and felt the heaviness of water. She welcomed it at first but the damp warmth of the woods began to feel stifling as their pace quickened. She wiped sweat from her brow and licked her sunburnt lips. LeiRain wished she had brought her own water skin. Silver was too far away for her to whisper for the one he carried.

At Ron's suggestion, the group spread out as they made their way through the woods. Walking too close together, he said, would make them more vulnerable to ambush. Silver had seen no sign of others in the woods when he'd explored earlier, though he had not gone all the way to the edge of the forest so they proceeded with extreme caution. It took them nearly three hours to make their way to the edge of the trees that lined the small settlement of Beachspire, the place that Dearvian had described as a *haven of rest and relaxation for weary sea-farers*.

When they finally regrouped near the edge of the village, LeiRain was so relieved to be able to quench her thirst with Silver's water skin that she temporarily forgot to be nervous about entering the settlement. She recognized Ron's footsteps and quiet grunts as he pushed his way through the men to stand beside her. LeiRain continued to drink deeply from the water skin as they stood in near darkness. The treetops were thick enough to block the moonlight and Silver let the fae light die as they neared Beachspire to avoid detection.

LeiRain handed the water skin back to Silver. Her stomach tightened as she peered out at the village from inside the tree-line. Ron put his hands on her shoulders and gave a light, reassuring squeeze.

'I'll be right here if ya need me, Demi. If something doesn't feel right, just leave.'

Ron was nervous, too. She had barely been out of his sight since they had fled Harbor Village. Now she would be walking into the unknown without him. Dearvian had warned against entering Beachspire with weapons and armor, explaining that it would be out of place in the peaceful enclave. Ron would be recognized instantly if he entered without his helmet, his bright red beard and distinctive scar giving him away. The sailors had all visited Beachspire numerous times in the past, so they would also be recognized.

There was some merit to having them go into town first – Beachspire often played host to sailors. But all of the men had crewed on The Mad Return long enough for their association with the ship to be well-known. If this side of the island was under Royal influence, it would be too risky to send in crewmen belonging to a ship the Royals had tried to sink. That left LeiRain and Silver. The verdaant was rather conspicuous, but everyone agreed that LeiRain should not venture into the tavern alone – especially if she must leave her sword and shield behind.

It had to be near three in the morning now, and they hoped that the revelry at The Speared Sheel would be winding down. They wanted to talk to Galban alone, and discreetly.

'It will be fine,' LeiRain reached up and squeezed one of Ron's hands where it remained on her shoulder. 'We'll be in and out quickly and carefully.'

'Here.' Silver handed her a fistful of heavy coins. 'In the unlikely event that we are separated, you should have the means necessary to buy yourself out of trouble.'

She opened her coin purse and dropped the gold inside. They clanked against the few coins she already had. She cinched the bag shut and let herself grow accustomed to the increased weight on her belt. It was nothing compared to the weight of the sword she was used to carrying – that she wished she was carrying now.

The rest of the party dispersed along the edge of the woods while Rain and Silver stepped out into the unkempt grass, making their way to a well-worn footpath and then the slightly broader streets of the village. It was an exceptionally small settlement. A few low flames flickered dimly in lanterns along the two main roads. One, LeiRain could see, was dotted with small huts and stone houses. They were modest, but built from materials that could withstand the constant assault of salt water.

Silver paused, staring into the dark corners of the village. LeiRain strained her eyes in an effort to see what he was seeing. He pulled her close and pointed to a slash of white between two of the small homes. LeiRain shook her head, unable to discern what she was looking at in the light of fading lanterns. Silver directed her gaze to something similar between two of the homes on the other side of the street.

LeiRain gasped with surprise. 'Tents?' she whispered.

'I believe so,' he said somberly. Tents so near the waterfront – one heavy storm and they would be torn to pieces.

The two of them kept to the residential street until the sounds of revelry emanating from a structure on the waterside made them pause. They cut between two small houses to get to the street nearest the dock. There, they found the source of the noise. Two flickering oil lamps, slightly brighter than the ones on the back street, lit the paving stones outside a tavern situated directly across from the docks.

LeiRain scanned the waterfront and exchanged a concerned look with Silver. There were no ships moored in the harbor, yet the noise emanating from the tavern and the scattered tents indicated a much larger population than they had expected to find. She took in the front of the tavern.

There was no sign hanging over the entrance, but a large skeleton was mounted to the front of the building. It had to be at least ten feet long. A shiver ran up LeiRain's spine as her fingers came up to trace the raised scar on her bicep. She gazed at the long, slender shape and spindly, clawed appendages of a sheel. A spear jutted out from its ribs, embedded in the underside of the spine.

So ... this is how the tavern had gotten its name.

Silver reached out and took one of her hands. He gave it a light squeeze and then brought it to his lips, kissing LeiRain's fingers lightly before dropping her hand and gesturing toward the door. She fought the urge to reach back out for his hand as they walked up the stone steps and Silver pushed the door open.

A thin, smoky haze wafted out to greet them, followed by the smell of stale drink, freshly roasted meat, and the tang of body odor. LeiRain stepped into the warmly lit space, looking back over her shoulder to reassure herself that Silver was following.

'I'll get refreshments, you find seats?' he asked.

She nodded and feigned a smile, willing herself to be brave.

LeiRain pulled her attention away from Silver and

scanned the room. She took in her surroundings with wonder, making an effort not to let her mouth fall open. Never before had she seen so many different races existing seamlessly, peacefully, anywhere, let alone in such a small space. Non-human visitors in Harbor had always been tolerated because the local businesses depended on them, but it would have been a stretch to say they were welcome. The residents of Beachspire, on the other hand, seemed not to notice the differences between them.

A group of dwarves, joined by a few human males, sat around several tables on the far-right side of the room, guffawing at each other's jokes. One dwarve lay with his head down on the table, a hand still wrapped around the handle of a large mug. Two of his compatriots were laughing as they separated strands of hair from his beard and tied them in knots to strands of hair from his head. In the same group, another dwarve stood on the table, singing loudly and inco-herently. The space around them was littered with empty mugs. A half-shifter barmaid struggled to collect them, her bushy fox tail swishing behind her with agitation, as the dwarves harassed her for more drink.

Closer to the center of the room, a group in brown cloaks sat hunched over bowls. They ate without utensils, burying their faces in the dinnerware and lifting their heads as they chewed, open-mouthed. They sat with their hoods drawn up, hiding most of their faces, but brown and green-scaled snouts protruded from the dark fabric and LeiRain could see bits of food drop from their mouths as they chewed with small, sharp teeth. Scaly, clawed hands wrapped around their bowls and similarly clawed feet protruded from the bottom of their cloaks. Along the floor, thick, spiny tails peaked out from the bottom of their robes.

She struggled not to stare as she made her way to a small

table near the back wall, but as she walked by with her eyes diverted, they met unexpectedly with those of a violet-skinned woman. She was seated with a group of three other blends as they played some sort of card game, but the woman held LeiRain's gaze intently for several seconds.

The blend's cheeks were flushed with what LeiRain could only assume was drink. Thick, black hair fell over her shoulders and down her back in waves. Curved horns protruded from either side of her head, just behind her hairline. They were a rich brown in color and reflected the light as though they had been polished. She winked one wide, dark eye at LeiRain before returning her gaze to the table. A pretty, petite woman wearing a barmaid's smock squeezed onto the chair beside the blend, running her fingers through the woman's dark hair as the two of them shared a brief kiss. The barmaid was dark-skinned with short-cropped, tightly coiled hair and a set of tiny wings that fluttered contentedly. *Half-pixie*, she thought.

A flush crept up her neck and into her cheeks as she pulled her eyes away and focused on finding a seat. Anyone showing such a public display would have faced serious consequences in Harbor and, as far as she knew, the rest of The Continent. Seeing that kiss, however chaste, made her feel as though she'd just intruded on some private moment. LeiRain had never thought much of it before – her liaisons with Bren had always been in secret so there was no such thing as public affection in her world. But as she stole another glance at the two women, she wondered why the rest of the world couldn't be this way. There was a warmth between the people in this village that she'd never seen. Whatever else might be happening on this island, LeiRain was growing to appreciate Beachspire.

She weaved her way to an open table, wondering what it

might have been like to grow up here. A place where women could sit across the table from men and gamble without being in a whore house. A world where lovers didn't have to hide their affections and differences did not mean an end to civility. Harbor couldn't even blame the Royals for its condition. The village had been an intolerant place long before the organization had come to be. LeiRain slid into a chair at the table along the back wall.

'I thought you might still be hungry.' LeiRain jumped as Silver appeared before her with a bowl of stewed meat in one hand. With his other hand, he set down two large mugs full of a sudsy drink. Liquid sloshed over the rims and onto the table as it wobbled beneath their weight.

Steam wafted off the stew in front of her and LeiRain's stomach rumbled. She grabbed the spoon protruding from the bowl and eagerly scooped up a mouthful. It was so hot that it burned her tongue slightly, but she kept chewing. The meat was well seasoned and not oversalted, as many of the meals had been on ship. She tried to pick out the flavors. She recognized garlic, oregano, and something else – a unique spice that she had never tasted before. It gave the meat a sharp aftertaste and made her realize just how terribly bland their food had been over the last few weeks.

'We should be careful with our words here,' Silver murmured. 'I did not see anyone who met Galban's description at the bar. If we can't find him, I think we should at least inquire with someone about traveling to the other side of the island.' He took a small pull from his mug and casually scanned the room.

LeiRain nodded and then went back to shoveling food, surprised at her own hunger. Silver downed the rest of his drink and glanced at LeiRain's nearly full mug. She pushed it toward him in offering, happy for an excuse not to finish the bitter beverage.

'No, no.' He shook his head and nudged the cup back toward her before looking over his shoulder and raising a hand. Moments later, a curvy barmaid with light gray skin appeared beside their table. Her tall, pointed ears were covered in soft-looking gray fur and LeiRain could see a slender gray tail swishing around the floor below the hem of her skirt. Shifter offspring.

'Will you have another?' The woman asked, reaching to clear the empty mug off the table. Silver turned a charming smile on the barmaid, and even though she knew why he was doing it, LeiRain felt a fire spark in her chest. As if he knew what she was thinking, Silver sent a soft pulse of magic into her core. *Don't be jealous*, it said. *I'm yours.* The barmaid's pale cheeks and the skin beneath her fur blushed red.

Silver placed a hand on top of the barmaid's where hers rested on the empty glass. 'Yes, thank you … what is your name?'

LeiRain tried not to focus on where Silver's hand rested. Instead, she let her magic mix with his. *I'm yours*, Silver's magic said. *I know*, LeiRain's magic replied.

'Talia,' she answered. She pressed her lips together briefly, but ultimately failed to hold back a giggle.

Silver slowly removed his hand from hers and she lifted the mug, absently clutching it to her chest. 'Anything else I can get you?'

'Talia,' he said, keeping his eyes and dazzling smile on her. LeiRain, despite her dislike for this encounter, was impressed. Silver's imperturbable countenance had never suggested he could act so convincingly. 'We were hoping you could tell us how to get transport to the other side of the island. Our ship was meant to port there but…'

COURTNEY POLLMAN-TURNER

The blush left the barmaid's cheeks, her gray skin turning almost white.

'We don't go there,' she said before Silver could finish his sentence.

His charming smile didn't falter. 'I'm so sorry, have I offended—?'

'I'll be right back with your drink,' she said, interrupting him.

'Of course, Talia, and thank you so much for the information...' She was turning to walk away before he had even finished his sentence.

Silver looked back at LeiRain and she absently took a swig of the ale, wincing at the sourness. LeiRain set the drink down abruptly. She was glad that the barmaid had fled, but felt a twinge of guilt realizing that they hadn't got the information they needed.

'I haven't seen any Royals here,' she said, 'and the way everyone is getting along – blends, dwarves...' She made a sweeping motion with her arm. 'Whatever those things are' – she tilted her head toward the scaly humanoids in cloaks – 'I've never seen anything like it.'

She remembered what he had said when he'd first appeared, that the hate that was spreading would eventually lead to all-out war.

'Do you think—' She paused, hoping that she was wrong and things weren't this bleak. 'Is it possible that *all* of the non-humans live on this side of the island? Those tents that we saw ... it's like they have nowhere else to go.' She went on. 'Judging from the crowd at this late hour, the area is far more popu-lated than it is meant to be. The tents, the crowds ... and there are no ships. It's like a refugee camp.'

How many of the beings in this room had been displaced by the Royals? She thought of the increasing hostility described by both Brya and Ron, the violence that should have moved her mother to flee. LeiRain poked at the layer of stew that was growing cold in the bottom of her bowl, unsure what they should do next. She was torn from her reverie by a loud scream.

51

———

The crowd of patrons who had been milling about between tables quickly cleared. LeiRain turned to see a small figure pressed against the wall. He stood only a foot or so high, but his shoulders were wide and his body thick. His blond beard was closely trimmed and furious dark eyes glared out from beneath the brim of his small hat. A gnome. He gnashed his teeth, grunting in pain as he looked up at his right hand, which was pinned to the wood panel behind him. From where she sat, LeiRain saw that a tiny blade had gone through the palm of his hand and sunk into the wall. Blood ran from his palm down his arm, staining his white shirt and dripping slowly onto the baseboards. On the floor near the growing puddle of blood lay a coin purse, tightly cinched with leather straps. LeiRain gasped when she saw it. She recognized the worn spot on one side, and the way the leather string was knotted. She felt along her belt to confirm what she suspected. The purse was hers.

The tavern had gone so quiet that the splash of blood droplets became audible. LeiRain held her breath as she looked around the crowded pub. The table of dwarves was still, their faces serious, all signs of jocularity gone. The lizard-like figures peered out from beneath their hoods, beady eyes closely examining LeiRain and Silver. *Every* patron and barmaid now stared in their direction. *So much for being discreet.* She felt her palms begin to sweat. They'd seen no one fitting Dearvian's description of Galban, the one Beachspire resident that Dearvian could vouch for. Even if the villagers weren't owned by the Royals, there was no guarantee that they would be friendly to their cause. LeiRain forced herself to let out a breath and willed her heart to beat at a reasonable pace. She felt the gentle brush of Silver's magic and could sense his own trepidation even as he tried to comfort her.

LeiRain's eyes fell upon the violet woman and their gaze met once more. This time, the woman held her stare for several long seconds. Her dark eyes searched LeiRain, an amethyst fire burning in them. The woman leaned toward her partner, whispering something in the smaller woman's ear. The half-pixie slid off the edge of the chair, allowing room for her partner to swing her legs to the side and stand. LeiRain watched the woman come to her full height, standing almost as tall as Silver. She tossed her head to one side, sending a curtain of hair black over her shoulder as she put a hand on the swell of her hips.

'Nothing to see here.' She smiled as she spoke and ran her gaze over the crowd, 'Go back to your revels.' She commanded them with confidence and the crowd obeyed. Just as suddenly as the disruption had silenced the crowd, lively chatter resumed. The dwarve standing on the table picked up his song again, while his companions threw chunks of bread at him and drank from their foaming mugs. The hooded lizard men bowed their heads over their bowls once more. The half-pixie slid back onto the chair that the purple-skinned blend had just vacated, and the human man across from her began to shuffle cards.

LeiRain and Silver now sat in stunned silence, a thrum of magic filling the air between them. She could hear the grunts of the gnome behind her as he struggled to pull the knife from his palm. The blend sashayed toward them, her hips swaying in her worn leather pants. But the woman's attention was focused entirely on the gnome as her eyes narrowed. A long, thin and furless tail that had not been visible while she was seated now swished behind her, giving away her irritation. She knelt behind LeiRain's chair, bringing her face close to that of the gnome's. From where she kneeled, the blend's glossy brown horns were at eye level with LeiRain.

'I'm going to remove this blade,' the blend whispered, 'And you're going to clean it off for me. Then,' she tilted her head to the side, 'you're going to leave and not come back. I do not tolerate thieving in my establishment.'

Her establishment? LeiRain looked back to Silver whose brow arched in response. *What happened to Galban?*

'Understood?' The blend asked.

The gnome gulped as he looked up at the woman. His face was red with pain and dripping with sweat. He nodded stiffly as he brought his free hand away from the knife. He let out a cry of pain as the blend yanked the blade from his palm. She flipped the blade over and offered it to him. Tentatively, the gnome took it from her and grasped it in his uninjured hand. He wiped the blade along his tan linen pants, leaving thick streaks of his own blood behind on his thigh. He passed it back to her and then went skittering out of the bar. The violet-skinned woman slid the knife back into a leather strap on her bicep and picked up the coin purse.

· · ·

'I'm Anya,' she said, turning to face LeiRain and Silver. She offered them a smooth smile. 'I apologize for that,' she said, setting the coin purse down on the table. I hope that this won't dissuade you from visiting The Speared Sheel in the future.'

LeiRain stared dumbly at the purse. She hoped that Silver would be better at thinking on his feet.

'You must be new to the island.' She smirked. 'Word to the wise: be more careful.' LeiRain thought she detected wariness in the woman's eyes but the mask of untroubled confidence slid back over her beautiful features.

'Let me know if I can be of any further service to you. Your next round of drinks is on the house.'

She winked at them and turned. The dark waves of her hair swinging as Anya walked back to her own table.

LeiRain exchanged a worried glance with Silver. This was a small village; everyone would know of their presence by the time the sun rose. LeiRain picked up her tepid ale and swirled the mug in front of her face. The sour smell of fermentation wafted up from the disturbed glass and LeiRain cringed, setting it back down and pushing it away from herself by a few inches. She couldn't help but feel that this was her fault. It had been her coin purse that the gnome had stolen. She picked at the wooden table, puzzling out their next move. LeiRain wanted to flee and return to the safety of the dark woods. But they would only draw more attention if they stood to leave now. Besides, they didn't yet possess the information they'd come to collect. Though with Anya claiming this as her establishment, it seemed unlikely that they would find Galban.

A barmaid materialized beside the table just as LeiRain was about to apologize for not keeping better track of her coin purse. It was a different barmaid before. This girl was curvy with short-cropped blond hair and looked, on the surface at least, to be human. She held a glass of ale so large that she was forced to grip it with both hands.

'On the house,' she said, not meeting either of their eyes. 'Courtesy of Mistress Anya.' She set the mug down in front of Silver who pushed away from the table slightly to avoid the slosh of liquid splashing out of the cup. He thanked her, but the barmaid scurried away before she could hear him.

LeiRain prodded his magic with her own. *Be careful.* Silver frowned at the mug as he prodded back. *I know.* His lips pressed together tightly and his nostrils flared as he took in the scent of the beverage. It didn't *look* poisoned, but it was better safe than sorry. Neither LeiRain nor Silver took another sip, but they stayed silently huddled over their beverages for what felt like an eternity. Finally, some of the tables in the tavern began to empty and revelers started to slowly file out the door. Anya's table cleared out, though cards were still scattered over the surface next to empty mugs. Silver nodded to the door and they made their exit, scanning the room as they went.

The majority of the dwarves who remained were now collapsed from drunkenness. The vaguely reptilian creatures hidden beneath their clothes were nowhere to be seen. Anya had disappeared as well. Still, they saw no sign of Galban.

'That was weird,' LeiRain whispered as she and Silver walked arm and arm back to their escorts.

'Agreed,' Silver replied.

Ron and the crewmen were still waiting in the tree line. He looked relieved at the sight of them. He opened his mouth to speak, but Silver held a finger up to his lips, and motioned for them to move further into the trees. Once they were at least a good twenty feet into the woods, the group assembled in a tight circle. Silver brushed his hands over branches that thickened around them, dampening any sound they might make.

'Through no fault of our own,' Silver said, 'We drew far more attention than is ideal.' His eyes stayed on LeiRain as he said this, already knowing that she would blame herself. 'As best we can tell, this village is full to bursting with relocated beings. Most non-human, but some humans too. The humans that were present did not appear to have any affiliation with the Royals or their ideology.'

'No blue arm bands,' LeiRain added, tapping one of her biceps.

The crewman with the glowing blue eyes let out a relieved sigh.

'But,' Silver went on, 'I do not think that they are in a position to give us aid. The resources here are overburdened as it is and these beings do not appear to maintain contact with the other side of the island.' Silver paused and LeiRain took this opportunity to jump in.

'And we didn't see any sign of Galban.' She felt the sailors begin to fidget. 'There is a female blend who said she owns the tavern. Her name is Anya, purple skin, dark brown horns. Does anyone know of her?'

She looked between the crewmen. Two of their faces were screwed up in surprised confusion and they shook their heads. But the man with the glowing blue eyes spoke.

'I'm not sure,' he said, 'but there *was* a girl the last time I was here – she was young, mind you. Not old enough to manage a bar. Probably shouldn't have even been in one but Galban had her managing the till. She had purple skin and dark hair, and I *think* she had horns. But that was a long time ago so I'm not sure..'

'Interesting,' Silver replied. 'We shouldn't discuss it any further here. We shouldn't linger.'

They were still well-hidden in the trees, but Silver's eyes flashed in the dark as he scanned their surroundings. Apparently satisfied that they were alone, the fae flicked his wrist and the plant life around them thinned out, repositioning itself. With another flick, tree after tree lifted or bent its branches to allow the group to pass deeper into the woods. Despite the clear path, LeiRain found herself tripping over her own feet, her hands scraping against bark as she caught herself. The effects of her nap on the beach had worn off and fatigue was getting the better of her. LeiRain was relieved when she began to hear the distant crash of waves. It meant they were almost back to where the others were camping. She imagined curling up with Silver, fae light warming the sand beneath them. Her eyes fluttered and she missed a step, crashing into the brush.

Silver hissed. LeiRain started to mumble an apology.

'No,' he whispered. 'Quiet! Get down.' He motioned with one hand for her to duck as he lowered his own stance.

LeiRain froze. Her sleepiness evaporated, her entire body becoming alert. She held her breath and listened. The others must have been doing the same thing; the woods were silent. She listened intently for a sign of ... anything, but could hear only the distant waves and the sound of her own heart beating. With his superior senses, Silver could hear what she and the others could not. His bright silver eyes scanned the woods around them, his head tilted to one side. LeiRain was just close enough to see his brows pull together in concentration. His body was taut, alert.

LeiRain felt the quiet of the woods close in on her. She willed her heart to beat less loudly but it continued to thunder in her ears. She thought of her mother, how the Royals had come for her. LeiRain's hand shook as she brought it to rest on the pommel of her sword. If they took her now, Alarra would have died for nothing. None of them dared move. LeiRain felt a surge of energy as her body prepared for whatever hid in the dark. She would not go down without a fight.

The leaves overhead rustled slightly in the ocean breeze and nighttime insects chirped all around them – nothing out of the ordinary. LeiRain wanted to ask Silver what he had heard, but she swallowed back her words and remained silent. Silver flinched and a second later, a large figure dropped from the branches, landing directly in his path. Silver's hands were up, palms held out as he prepared to work his magic on the forest. Whoever this was, they'd picked the worst place possible to start a fight with a verdaant. Silver's magic buzzed around her as he snapped his shield of fae light into place. It glowed faintly, stretched thin to cover as many of them as possible. She saw the flash of a blade in the dark figure's hand and drew her own sword.

'Immortal,' the figure said. The voice was female, familiar. 'Why are you here? What do you want with the Royals?'

When Silver replied, his voice was melodic but there was still a cold edge to it that made LeiRain glad he was on her side. 'Put down the weapon and we can speak as friends, Anya.'

Anya. The woman from the pub.

'I'll ask just this once more, Silversgleaming; what is your purpose here?'

'I am no friend to the Royals. I – we search for them only to stop the spread of their corruption, to limit their power.'

'Why come now?' Anya asked. 'The Royals have been here for many years and no one has come to aid us.' She'd barely made a sound when she dropped from above and her footsteps were silent as she began to circle Silver. The hilt of

LeiRain's sword grew warm in her grip. Anya was trying to work her way behind Silver's shield, or between him and the other members of the group. LeiRain shifted her weight subtly as she watched Anya prowl. Silver was trying to avoid a fight, but LeiRain was determined to act before this stranger could get the upper hand.

'We did not know you were in need of aid,' Silver said, his voice softening. 'At least, not any more than those on The Continent. I began this journey nearly a year ago, and I came much too late. It took me many years to recognize the extent of the poison they bring and to overcome the complacency to which my kind have fallen victim.'

There was a long pause.

'I will come with you to your camp,' Anya finally replied. The blade of her knife disappeared into its sheath. 'And we will discuss the details of our alliance.' LeiRain heard a few sighs of relief from members of her party and her own muscles relaxed slightly. She sheathed her sword.

Anya fell into step beside Silver, their footfalls equally light. The woman's posture had relaxed slightly, and she trusted them enough to turn her back to most of their group. LeiRain could feel an excitement emanating from the men around her, an eagerness to know what this blend had to share with them. The group reached the edge of the wood not long after this encounter. Anya had been patient enough to wait and see where they were going, but smart enough to stop them before they could reach the security of their camp. Ron sent one of the crew members off to wake Dearvian – he would need to be a part of this conversation.

'He has a right to know that we've brought a stranger into our midst,' Ron said.

And that there was no sign of Galban, LeiRain thought.

478

52

Once the shifter captain had joined them, he dismissed the crewmen to their rest. They left reluctantly, curious about what would come from the conversation with Anya but respecting their leader too much to press. LeiRain could see a set of glowing blue orbs cast glances back at them as the men walked away. Silver weaved together foliage that offered both privacy and protection from the cool winds rolling in off the water. Blue light flickered to life in his palm, illuminating everyone's faces and casting shadows on the sand and the walls of the enclosure.

Anya seemed to have some ability to see in the dark, just like Dearvian and Silver. She looked at the Captain where he sat across from her watching Anya's face, his yellow eyes reflecting back the light. Silver set the blue flame down on the sand between them.

'And who is this?' Dearvian asked. His eyelids were heavy with recent sleep, but he was awake enough to be wary. His brows pulled together and he gazed with intensity at Anya. 'What of Galban?' His voice was raspy but there was authority in it.

Anya cocked her head to the side and looked at him, searchingly. 'What business is it of yours, shifter?'

There was a dangerous heat in Anya's gaze, the flicker of blue flame in her irises. If Dearvian saw it, if it frightened him, he gave no indication.

'Galban is a friend. I would like to know,' he growled, 'whether or not your gains are ill-gotten before we move forward in discussing our ... situation.'

Anya raised a dark eyebrow. 'A friend?' she asked, sounding skeptical. 'When did you last see him?'

Dearvian did react this time. Just a tiny hint of something, guilt maybe, flashed across his face before his cool mask was restored. 'It has been six years since I've visited the Arborris Enclave. Last I was here, I had just taken command of The Mad Return.' There was a bit of sadness in his voice.

LeiRain had not thought of what he must have sacrificed for the sake of captaining a ship, caring for his crew and making a reasonable living.

'Galban *was* your friend,' Anya replied. 'He is dead.' Her voice did not waver but unshed tears pooled in her eyes. The blend quickly blinked them away. 'He left the bar to me.'

'How?' Dearvian was shaking his head. 'When?'

'Two years ago.'

Her answers were short and Dearvian grew frustrated. 'How did he die?'

'The Royals used to come to this side of the island to get away, relax. But as their numbers grew, as the company's wealth multiplied, they became bolder, more aggressive. They started demanding things they weren't entitled to.' Anya stared down at her hands, studying her palms for a few moments before she continued. 'He was a father to me. I spent many years in the possession of traffickers. Galban bought my freedom when I was eight and raised me like his own after that..'

LeiRain's stomach churned. *Trafficked* could only mean one thing.

'Two years ago, some of the Royals thought they might take liberties with me.' Anya glanced scathingly at LeiRain, seeming to sense and disapprove of her sympathy. 'I can defend myself,' she said, lifting her chin, 'but with rather significant consequences.'

Anya reached out and broke off a thick frond from a nearby fern then looked back at the circle of faces. LeiRain tilted her head to the side, unsure what the woman was about to do. Anya gripped the frond with her right hand and held it out in front of her as her fingers quickly began to glow a deep crimson. LeiRain covered her mouth with the back of her hand as smoke rose from Anya's fist and the air around them filled with the smell of fire. The frond, still clutched in Anya's hand, blazed with blue flame and then the fire flickered out almost as quickly as it had flared up. It left nothing but a pile of ashes and when Anya tipped those into the sand, her hand was unscathed.

Only Silver looked unsurprised. LeiRain recalled how Silver had recognized the power in her, had known it was there before she even knew herself. He must have already sensed what Anya was capable of. Dearvian and Ron both wore looks of mixed shock and fear. *Fire.* This was not a power that LeiRain had seen before. She'd never even heard of such a power. She thought of how the former Royal leader was rumored to have been found dead, burned in his sleep, only his person showing marks of the flame. She wondered if Silver and Ron were considering the same thing.

'But,' Anya spoke again, disrupting her thoughts, 'Galban never stopped being protective of me, even after I learned to take care of myself. He stepped in instead of letting me handle it myself, and they killed him.'

The owner of The Speared Sheel shifted in the sand before she went on with her story. 'There were three of them, three Royals that came for me. I had been working behind the bar, but they followed me when I took my break.' Anya's voice was cool and smooth as she spoke. Only her eyes gave away her sadness.

'Gods.' Dearvian let out a gasp. 'I remember you. You were that small, timid thing behind the bar! Always cloaked, never speaking.'

She nodded.

'The Royals offered to pay me, but I do not want to work in that trade. They wouldn't take *no* for an answer. When they tried to take what they wanted by force, I defended myself. More of them came. Galban tried to fight them off.' Anya brushed a hand over her eyes, wiping away the tears before they could fall. 'He took a few down, too. There were others who joined him, who defended me and who took the opportunity to defend their loved ones who had suffered similarly under the hand of these men. But still *more* men came until, finally, there were too many.' Anya refocused on her immediate surroundings. She looked between each of them, her gaze naked and pained. 'With the distraction of the mob, I was able to slip away. Galban told me to run, and so I did. When I came, I found his body, and several others, lying cold near one of the piers.'

LeiRain opened her mouth to say something. Anya's pain was not unlike hers. The Royals had taken her parent, too. But she remembered the warning glare she'd received earlier and decided to keep her mouth shut. Instead, she met Anya's eyes. *I know your pain. I see you,* she tried to say with a look. Anya studied her for a moment and her gaze softened. Her shoulders rose and fell with a deep breath, then Anya's posture changed. She sat up straighter, lifted her chin, and LeiRain watched all traces of vulnerability and sadness disappear from the woman's face. The confident, intimidating tavern owner was back.

'We buried our dead,' Anya went on. 'And that's when we began putting up wards. I was going through Galban's things afterward and found that he'd already put my name on the deed to The Speared Sheel. I wanted to leave, to get away from here, but by then it was already impossible to get past the Royal ships. Knowing that he wanted me to have the tavern – it complicates things. It's become the place where we all gather now, those of us who lived here before and those who have been forced to stay since the Royals have prevented anyone from leaving.'

'If Beachspire is warded,' Silver asked, 'how is it that we came to be here?'

Anya's pursed her lips. 'The wards are failing.'

'We clearly cannot get off the island, either,' Dearvian said softly, 'with my ship in pieces and crew still recovering. Why are you telling us all of this?' Anya nodded her understanding at Dearvian but turned to look at Silver.

'You are verdaant.' She shifted her attention to his right. Ron sat quietly beside the fae with his helmet tucked into his lap. The scar that cut across his face looked dark purple in the fae light. 'And you,' she said to Ron, as she explored his scar and glowing red hair, 'are Ronland the Red. I do not know what gifts the rest of you may or may not possess, but I know that you want something from the other side of the island and you need my help to get there. Well, I want something from the other side of the island, too.'

I f the current state of the Arborris Enclave was a measure of what would happen on The Continent if Royals were allowed to continue their current course, Silver was right to fear the worst. Anya filled them in on all that had happened in the last few years, how they had targeted the blends at first, but then began to oppress all non-humans. Anyone who was not a Royal or a Royal sympathizer had been forced off the other side of the island. Businesses shut down, families were torn apart.

Anya told them of non-humans who had been pressed into service by the Royals, those with unique abilities being used as tools or weapons. Ron wondered aloud at how the Royals were able to exert such control over these individuals, and LeiRain thought of her conversation with Riv. If the Royals were using Pearl to force Eaton's compliance, perhaps they were using this tactic to force their will on other blends as well.

'The water elves—' LeiRain's voice caught and she had to stop to clear her throat. 'They think that the Royals have one of their own, that they are using her to control someone.'

As heads turned toward her, LeiRain drew strength from the understanding she saw in Silver's eyes. His magic brushed against hers, reassuringly.

'There was a blend,' LeiRain went on, 'a son of tempest, named Eaton. He was the one who aided the Royals in destroying our ship,' she explained to everyone. 'The elves believe that the Royals have taken his mate. Eaton would never help them unless he feared for her life. The elves' – she drew in a deep breath – 'they want us to get her back. Without her, they won't be able to control Eaton. He will be free and the waters will be safer for everyone.'

No one said anything. LeiRain twisted her fingers together.

She could hear the ocean hissing behind her as the tide slowly came in.

'The elves saved many lives today.' Rain's voice was pleading as she looked at Dearvian. 'They saved your ship.' He stared back at her, his brow furrowed. 'You would have nothing to piece back together if it weren't for them. And your crew—'

'Demi,' Ron interrupted her, 'I don't think any of us feel it is an unreasonable request. It's just that, well, we came prepared for a reconnaissance mission. In the last five minutes, it's turned into a rescue mission. There's a big difference.'

'I would have it be a rescue mission, anyway,' Anya chimed in.

'The thing you want from the other side of the island,' Silver raised an eyebrow. 'It's a person.'

'A friend.' Anya let out a long breath. 'Some of the people here were forced to leave family members behind when they fled the Royal side of the island. My friend, Muckjaw – he wanted to free them, to bring them all here.'

'And yet we are now to rescue him,' Silver replied, the crease in his brow signaling his worry.

'Just coming to this island,' Anya answered, 'turned this into a rescue mission for you.' Her voice rose as she continued. 'The only reason there are so many people here is because they can't leave. There are no vessels docked in our harbor because they have all been torn to pieces by the Royals. And now that you've brought a ship here, or what's left of one, there is no way that you can leave without taking some of these people with you.' LeiRain heard the confused grunts of men waking up as Anya's words grew louder. 'Besides the fact that many of them don't want to be here and wish desperately to return to their homes, this place cannot continue to support this many residents.' She threw her arms wide in a frustrated attempt to gesture at the island. 'They are *expecting* you to rescue them.'

'They thought we were coming for the refugees?' Dearvian asked. His eyes were wide as he took this in. He ran a hand over his face, looking overwhelmed as he rubbed the stubble on his chin.

Anya nodded. 'There is not a single ship that comes or goes from the whole of this island that doesn't fly the Royal flag. They wouldn't have been half as effective if it weren't for that son of tempest they have. If we liberate his mate, perhaps we also liberate ourselves from the Royal fleet that keeps us all island-bound.'

'Why do they not take this side of the island as well?' Silver asked. 'How is it that you've protected yourselves from them for so long?'

'As I said before, we put up wards. To be precise, Muckjaw put up wards. Most of his people have the gift of healing, but he has the gift of protection, of warding.'

LeiRain thought of the last time she'd entered a warded city. Was time passing differently here like it did in Corallis?

'What exactly do these wards do?' Ron asked, as if he were thinking the same thing as LeiRain.

'They keep people out, that's it.' LeiRain felt her shoulders relax in relief. 'Well, they usually keep people out. Your presence here is a pretty significant indication that the wards have begun to fade.' Anya sighed before continuing. 'And the fact that Muckjaw hasn't been able to renew the wards is a pretty significant sign that he is fading, too.'

53

'It looks awfully narrow,' Ron said as the four of them peered into a dark hole in the ground.

The turned earth reminded LeiRain of the little holes she'd seen crabs dig into the sand, the ones that filled with water every time a wave crashed ashore. She'd always enjoyed watching salt water bubbles rise up along the beach as the ocean retreated and the sand absorbed the moisture. Now the thought made her palms sweat. They were a few miles inland and there was no chance of the ocean washing over these tunnels, but LeiRain couldn't stop imagining them flooding. She would be fine, but her friends – she shuddered.

'There will be places where it's necessary to –' Anya eyed Ron's broad shoulders, 'squeeze through,' she finished. 'But I do not believe you will get stuck, if that's what you're worried about.' She shook her head dismissively. 'Many saurian are much thicker than you,' she concluded.

'Maybe,' Ron grumbled, 'but they've got the ability to dig themselves out if they get stuck.'

Silver lifted a thoughtful eyebrow. 'The saurians might be able to dig their way out,' he replied, 'but we are not without advantages.' With a wave of his hand, Silver made another, smaller hole in the dirt near the tunnel, demonstrating his power.

The gesture failed to comfort Ron. 'What are you doing, Forest God?' The dwarve asked, alarmed. His face reddened as he gestured toward the disturbed soil. 'You start moving soil around here and you have no idea how it will impact the integrity of the tunnels!'

Silver filled the hole back in with a flick of his wrist. His face remained blank, but there was something about the stiffness of his features that made LeiRain think he was trying not to roll his eyes.

'I don't understand,' LeiRain said, 'what is the difference between this and the tunnels we walked through in the mountain?'

R on let out a humorless laugh in response. 'Dwarves didn't just *dig* those tunnels out of the mountain. They were chiseled, carefully and over many years. We reinforced them with scaffolding and magic. And what isn't reinforced is carved out of stone, not *dirt*.' He gestured toward the dark soil with an open hand. 'Underground tunnels are much less predictable. The saurians made these by wriggling through the ground, not through careful craftsmanship.' He shook his head.

'Ron,' LeiRain began, but paused when the dwarve looked up to meet her eyes. She saw resignation on his face.

'Agh, it's fine, Demi,' he said. He tugged on his beard and cleared his throat. 'It's too slow and risky to go by foot above ground, and impossible to go by sea seeing as we have no vessel.' Ron shrugged, 'I guess if it caves in on us, we'll spare everyone the trouble of a burial.' He winked at her, one corner of his mouth lifting as he did so.

LeiRain smiled and let out a strained laugh. She was trying to think of a reply, another joke to ease her own nerves about traveling this underground route, but was distracted by the sound of scraping footfalls. She looked over her shoulder and saw a saurian, one of the lizard-like creatures that LeiRain had first seen at The Speared Sheel, approaching. The saurian shuffled toward the group, most of its body covered with a tattered robe, and stopped in front of Anya. He held out a clawed and scaly fist. Anya stretched out her own hand and, as she did so, the fist opened and dropped two small vials into her palm.

'Thank you,' she said, dipping her head respectfully. The figure nodded, then turned and walked away, its thick tail dragging through the dirt as it went.

'We'll likely need these,' Anya said as she inspected the vials she now held. LeiRain's brow furrowed as she tried to determine what made these so valuable. Noting her confusion, Anya went on. 'They're healing tinctures. Muckjaw's affinity is for ward-casting, which won't do him much good if he's injured. And if he is in the hands of the Royals, it's more likely than not that he is.'

Muckjaw's wards were the only thing protecting Beachspire from the Royals and they were failing fast. Anya took a cloth out of her satchel and carefully wrapped the vials before placing them in her bag. Silver and Ron were both rifling through their own supplies, double and triple checking the contents of their bags before they set out. LeiRain took a few steadying breaths and gently patted her sword for reassurance.

'Alright then,' Anya said, 'shall we?'

Sitting on the ground and sliding, feet-first, Anya dropped out of view. Silver followed behind her and LeiRain went next. The opening was at the base of a small hill and the first several feet were almost entirely vertical. LeiRain felt her stomach lift and flutter as she dropped and her body shuddered as the shield on her back skimmed the walls. Falling into darkness was disorienting but the sensation didn't last long and she managed to land on her feet, bending her knees as the soft earth absorbed the shock.

The air inside the tunnel was cool and moist and scented with the decay of plants. Ahead of LeiRain, the tunnel stretched much wider than the opening through which she'd just dropped, though it was still narrower than the mountain caves they had traveled before. The inside of the mountain had smelled like damp stone. This tunnel smelled like organic decay. In the mountain, there had been occasional whiffs of fresh air carried through the cave by trickling mountain springs. Here, the air was still with no hint of a breeze. LeiRain swallowed, trying to ignore how stifling it felt. As soon as she had her bearings, she searched the space for Silver and found him watching her with one corner of his mouth slightly upturned.

Hearing a rustle above, LeiRain darted to the side just as Ron tumbled through the mouth of the tunnel. Heavy clumps of dirt fell as his thick frame forced its way through the entrance. The dwarve landed heavily on his bottom, grunting as he made impact. He scurried to his feet, dusting off his backside. Ron's eyes scanned their surroundings and the creases on his forehead softened slightly as he took in the width of the tunnel before them.

LeiRain was watching Ron's face when a dim, blue glow began to emanate from the tunnel walls. She turned back to

Silver and saw the shining slate of his irises winking in the glow of the fae light. With a few quick steps in his direction, LeiRain was able to brush her hand lightly against his. Silver's head tilted to the side and his magic grazed hers in response. Silver studied her in the dim light, and her knees trembled under his gaze. His eyes narrowed in satisfaction as her heart sped up.

'Right,' Ron said, drawing LeiRain's attention away from the fae. 'Let's get this over with then, shall we?'

LeiRain looked down the length of the tunnel ahead of her. The fae light improved visibility, but it seemed as if the tunnel swallowed much of the glow. She pushed away her desire and focused on what lay ahead. Every dangerous situation she'd found herself in before had been by chance or accident. This – this was on purpose and there were others relying on her. Not just her friends, but the entire population of Beachspire. She couldn't afford to freeze this time. Nervous energy hummed through her body and LeiRain wished that they could move time forward. She wished that she could be in Royal territory now, facing her demons. But miles of dark tunnel stretched ahead of them. Anya and Silver had already started walking so LeiRain took a deep breath and fell into step behind them.

The saurian-made tunnels were surprisingly wide at times. The reclusive creatures, native only to this island, burrowed into the ground when they slept or when heavy storms passed over. Their tunnels ran beneath the entire island and before the Royals had taken over nearly half of the land, the saurians had done an excellent job of avoiding the other inhabitants. It was only with forced proximity, Anya explained, that the saurians began to associate with the residents of Beachspire. It had been the saurians' idea to use the tunnels to infiltrate Royal territory.

'Have you, um, *used* these tunnels before?' Ron asked as the group made their way through the earthen passage.

'No,' Anya replied, simply.

'So we just follow you, trusting that you'll be able to navigate us through these tunnels?' Ron asked as he squinted into the hazy blue fae light. It had taken only a few minutes of walking for them to come upon a series of branch-offs in the tunnel system.

LeiRain watched Anya inspect each opening, each available route.

'It's this way,' she said. 'This is the way he went. I just ... *feel him*.' LeiRain and Silver exchanged a knowing glance, and both sent a gentle pulse of magic down that invisible cord that connected them. The link Anya had with Muckjaw sounded very similar to what she had with Silver. *Magicae Canentis.* Whatever connection Anya and Muckjaw had, it wasn't romantic the way theirs was, but it was clear that magic sang between the two of them.

LeiRain kept quiet as they moved, holding her breath at times to hide her discomfort. She found it a bit unnerving to be squeezing through passages made of damp soil. Sometimes, small crumbles of dirt would fall in a shower from overhead and LeiRain would wonder how far she was from the surface. The fae light was a comfort, but the occasional narrowness of the passages bothered her more than the darkness. LeiRain spent most of the day staring at Silver's back, while Anya's soft footfalls moved quickly at the head of their column. The soil absorbed their voices whenever they tried to speak to one another so they interacted little and LeiRain spent the first few hours lost in her imagination. She tried to picture what they would find in the Royal compound and how she would feel when she saw the Royals. Would they find a prototype of the weapon the Royals were rumored to be building? What would it look like? The anticipation of what lay before them was almost unbearable.

They stopped to rest for the night when they reached another large opening at the intersection of three tunnels. As tired as she was, LeiRain wished they could press on. It was difficult to imagine sleeping here, beneath the earth. And even more difficult for LeiRain to imagine sleeping when the next day would bring them into danger. Despite these restless feelings, it was good to get off her feet.

Anya paced back and forth around two of the tunnel branches, pausing with her eyes closed in front of each one. 'Here,' she said, finally. 'It feels strongest here.' She gestured to the tunnel on the right.

They had been traversing the tunnels for close to twelve hours. Twelve monotonous hours. No conversation. Just the soft thunk of feet, the steady huff of Ron's breath behind her, and the occasional glug of water as one or another of them drank from a flask. Though the tunnels were cool, the lack of moving air and dampness of the soil made it humid and LeiRain's skin felt sticky; she longed to feel a breeze on her face.

'It will likely be a few more hours traveling underground from here,' Anya told them, 'at least, if the tunnel conditions are similar. We should rest now, though. We need to arrive fresh and strong.'

None of them disagreed. Even if nerves made LeiRain want to press on, she knew they all needed the rest. She settled back against the cool wall of the chamber. Rogue strands of hair had curled and sprung free of her braids and were clinging to her forehead and neck. She dreamt of fresh air and the night sky, but reminded herself that the journey through the mountain had been much longer and she had endured. Of course, that journey had been toward safety, whereas this one moved her toward danger. LeiRain brushed the thought away, refusing to be overcome by fear.

They all began pulling food from small satchels. Their stores on *The Mad Return* had been lost when the ship was attacked, but the residents of Beachspire had provided them with sustenance. It was more dried meat, dried fruit and nuts, but a different variety than they had on The Continent. The fruits were unique to the Arborris Enclave and, instead of dried venison or goat, they had strips of dried fish. The new flavors were welcome, especially after weeks of mushy stew and hard tack. The fish was a bit chewy but LeiRain enjoyed the saltiness and the fruit was far sweeter than any she'd eaten before. *Except longing fruit*, she thought. Despite the humidity, LeiRain inched toward Silver while she ate her dinner. He sat on the dirt, stretching his neck and shoulders as he chewed. LeiRain and Ron had been able to walk upright for most of the day, but Silver and Anya were tall enough that the tunnel had often forced them to bend in unnatural ways. LeiRain could have eaten her entire stash of food then and there, but knew that she needed to save some. She'd want breakfast tomorrow and then they would have the journey back. *Assuming we survive*. The thought had popped into LeiRain's head without her permission and she pushed it away, drawing closer to Silver instead. He spread his cloak out on the soil and the two of them laid on it.

'Only the dead are meant to sleep underground,' Ron grumbled as he drew his own cloak tightly around him. He didn't lay flat but propped himself up against the wall with his legs out in front of him, as if he didn't really plan to fall asleep. Anya, who was laying on the ground not far from Ron, snorted at his remark, before rolling over to face the opposite wall. Despite his protestations, and his reluctance to sleep in the tunnels, it wasn't long before Ron's snores filled the space.

LeiRain and Silver didn't speak, at least not with words, but magic rippled between them as they lay next to each other. Despite the looming challenges ahead of them, LeiRain eventually fell asleep with her arm pressed against Silver's and one foot draped over his ankle.

After several hours, she woke to Silver shifting beside her. He sat up and stretched his neck again, and his back this time as well. When he saw that LeiRain was awake, he offered her his waterskin. Ron rolled on his back, snorting himself awake. He sat up from where he'd slid down the wall and onto his side, rubbing his eyes. The dwarve looked between her and Silver. The fae was rifling through his satchel for breakfast but Ron caught LeiRain's eye and smiled at her with a nod of approval.

54

T he group paused and stared ahead at where the tunnel narrowed and began a steep, upward climb. Anya stood with her arms crossed over her chest, mouth pinched. She hadn't eaten much breakfast at all, despite her earlier insistence that they all be fresh and rested. LeiRain had watched the blend choke down a few mouthfuls of nuts and chug some water. LeiRain could relate. Breakfast sat heavily in her stomach as well. The few hours that they had walked this morning had been in total silence. There was a tension in the air, a coiled energy that was ready to spring. When Silver extinguished the fae light, they could clearly see a thread of bright yellow making its way down to them. Unless they turned back, there was nowhere to go but up.

Anya cast a nervous glance over her shoulder. Her eyes met LeiRain's and for the first time, LeiRain could clearly read fear in them. Taking a deep breath, LeiRain lifted her chin toward the blend in acknowledgment of the danger they were about to face. She felt a wave of affection for Anya, and admiration for her bravery and hoped Anya could read these feelings on her face as they stared at each other. A few more seconds passed before Anya blinked and her eyes hardened, the fear in them giving way to cold determination. She turned around to face the opening again, tiny strips of light glinting off polished horns as she stepped forward. With a series of quick movements, the blend disappeared as she scrambled up the tunnel opening.

There was a long pause. Silver, LeiRain, and Ron all held their breath and LeiRain's stomach twisted with anxiety. The silence stretched, tension growing with every second that passed as they waited to hear that Anya had made it and that it was clear. There was no way of knowing where this tunnel exit was located in relation to the various structures on the Royal compound. For all they knew, they were crawling out into the middle of the Royal barracks. LeiRain jumped as Anya's whisper carried through the tunnel.

'It's safe to follow.'

LeiRain sighed in relief and Ron's shoulders dropped some of their tension. Silver was already moving to follow Anya out. LeiRain felt a pulse of his magic and knew that he was urging her to take her turn. She stepped forward and began to crawl upward. The tunnel was so narrow and steep at the top that she was forced to pull herself through on hands and knees, sword and shield both dragging across the tunnel's edges. She dug her hands into the dirt to maintain her purchase, all of her muscles shaking with the effort. She squinted as loose soil crumbled and fell around her. LeiRain felt clumsy, clawing her way up, after Silver and Anya had exited so gracefully.

She shimmied up the last few feet of tunnel, sucking in a deep breath as the cool night air hit her face. Resting on her haunches near the hole, she took a few seconds to catch her breath before whispering down to Ron. As he began to climb up, LeiRain took in her surroundings. The daylight she had expected to greet her was absent and in its place she found thin strips of pale moonlight cutting through dark clouds. Despite the light of the moon, this open space felt darker to LeiRain than the fae-light-illuminated underground they'd been traversing. As her eyes adjusted, she saw that Anya was crouched near the opposite side of the tunnel opening, her arms spread wide as she held back a thick bramble that would otherwise cover the exit. There were a few scratches on her face where she'd pulled herself through the brush on her way out.

LeiRain's eyes wandered as she listened to Ron's quiet grunts coming from below. She could make out evenly spaced buildings of similar size, although large portions of the landscape were lost to night and shadow. They had broken free of the ground in the thickly wooded area that surrounded the periphery of the Royal complex. The row of small wooden buildings she saw sat between the group and the rest of the Royal facilities. Behind her, Ron let out a guttural sigh as he pulled himself clear. She heard his deep inhale and knew he was appreciating the fresh air. Silver was beside her, making his own survey of the area. He raised a hand toward the brush that Anya had been pressing back with her body. The branches pulled away from her and Anya relaxed her arms. LeiRain could clearly see the blend's features as she scanned the area. Her face was pinched with tension, her eyes narrowed. What might the two of them be able to see that was invisible to her and Ron? Even as they crouched behind the cover of brush, the sky lightened. Shadows were shrinking as the moon disappeared and orange sunlight began to glow from the other side of the Royal complex. Dawn had arrived. They needed to move.

Anya hissed to get their attention and gestured to one of the buildings off to the right. She thought that Muckjaw was there. So, so close. Anya led them as they crept from the heavy brush. Silver moved easily, keeping low to the ground. LeiRain stayed close behind, moving with slightly less ease but with the advantage of being shorter. She didn't turn to look behind her but she could feel Ron following. LeiRain's arm brushed Silver's as they pressed their backs against the nearest building. Ron nudged her foot with his and he gave LeiRain an encouraging wink when she looked back at him. Men could be heard in the distance, but no voices came from nearby. Anya peered around the corner of the building to ensure they were clear to move. When she moved, the rest of them followed, darting between the structures. They moved as quickly and quietly as they could, racing against the rising sun and the growing buzz of activity on the Royal compound.

'He's here,' Anya whispered as they slid along the back of another building. 'I can feel him. We have to get inside.'

There was no entrance from the back so they slunk around to the side. All they found there was cool, smooth brick.

'We can't break through this without drawing attention,' Anya whispered. 'Even if there aren't Royals waiting inside for us, someone will come running. We'll have to go through the front.'

They crept around the side of the building, crouching low. LeiRain's thighs burned as she inched along with her knees bent. Anya moved ahead of the rest and peered around the front corner. She turned back and waved the rest of them on. LeiRain gritted her teeth, grateful for the strength she'd gained from all those hours of sword drills.

They moved as a group toward a set of double doors, huddling close to each other at the front of the building. Anya reached for the door handle and tugged. The door didn't budge other than a slight rattle. LeiRain watched the blend's mouth turn down as she studied the lock, her own hands sweating and heart beating fast. Her eyes looked between the door handle, and the open space between their group and the other buildings. LeiRain could have sworn that the voices of men were growing louder. They were so exposed here, pressed against the front of this building. She shook her head at Silver, eyes wide, to signal her anxiety. The warm glow of morning sun was growing brighter. He drew his eyes from her to Anya and nodded his head in the same direction. *Look*, he seemed to say. LeiRain obeyed. Anya was eye level with the lock, long, thin pieces of metal in each hand. LeiRain could hear the it creak and whine as Anya shifted the tools around. *Click.*

With a satisfied smile, Anya pulled her hands away from the door and slid the tools into her tunic. She gripped the iron handle and tugged. The door creaked slightly but it opened. They all froze. LeiRain worked to slow her breathing. She felt each rise and fall of her chest as they waited. Several seconds passed. There was no response. Anya began to pull the door open a bit further. The morning sun cut a thick line through the dark interior of the building. It seemed unlikely that there would be Royals waiting inside in the pitch black.

Anya opened the door by only a few feet and slid inside as did Silver. LeiRain swallowed her fear and followed. Ron had to open the door a bit wider to slip through the crack. Despite his bulk, he moved gracefully and light on his feet as he came through. LeiRain tried to see into the dark space as the strip of light expanded with the opening door. They were standing on a paved ramp looking down into a cellar. Most of the space was underground, so it was much larger than it appeared from outside.

There was a dampness to the room, different from that of the tunnel in that it smelled not only of earth but of something rotten. Like spoiled meat. The humidity in this space made her skin feel sticky. LeiRain could sense the water in the air; it felt *wrong*.

She searched for Silver who had come in just ahead of her and found his lean form in the near-dark. He'd moved deep into the space as soon as he entered. Anya remained by the door as everyone passed. After Ron came through, she stepped around him and closed it, shutting out the morning sun. LeiRain heard her turn the lock. She wanted to ask Silver to illuminate their surroundings, but they needed to take the measure of this place first. His herb garden scent was a sharp contrast with the sour air of the cellar. She found her way toward him as her eyes were again forced to adjust to low light. As she blinked, LeiRain saw that there was a bit of light – a single torch burning in a bracket near the bottom of the entrance ramp.

They were standing on a stone-paved floor. The walls beneath the ground were constructed of neatly laid bricks. The space was maybe a hundred feet long and sixty feet wide and mostly empty except for the far third of it where she could see a stack of wooden crates on one side. Opposite the crates, she saw what looked like a discarded bathing tub and four livestock pens, two of which contained hunched figures.

They stepped carefully, quietly, as they investigated. LeiRain cringed as she thought of possible explanations for the awful rotten meat smell. Was there livestock here that had been neglected? This was no place to keep animals. There was no place for their waste, no fresh air. Even worse, the pens were terribly small. LeiRain recognized them from her days in Harbor Village. Their small size was meant to protect the animals, to prevent them from harming themselves should they become distressed during a sea journey. They were not meant for keeping animals long-term.

Anya continued pushing forward. Her feet slapped against the hard floor as she took a few running steps toward the cages. LeiRain cringed at the loudness of her footfalls. When she reached the cages, Anya fell to her knees in front of them, wrapping her hands around the bars. LeiRain could just make out a crumpled figure shifting from inside.

'What have they done to you, my friend?'

A wet rasping noise came from the figure. It took a few seconds for LeiRain to realize that it was a laugh.

'What have they not done to me,' came the reply. A clawed, reptilian hand reached through the bars and wrapped its fingers around Anya's.

'I'm so sorry I did not come sooner.'

LeiRain's heart broke at the pain in Anya's voice. She knew that pain, could empathize with Anya's feelings of guilt. LeiRain wanted to move closer, to see the saurian who'd risked his life to save others from the Royals. But this moment between Anya and Muckjaw felt intimate so she watched from where she stood.

Anya's face was mostly in shadow, but LeiRain could still see the anguish there and hear it in her voice. Ron, having no reservations about breaking into this private moment, moved past Anya. He stood before the double doors and drew his ax. Silver moved away from LeiRain's side to further inspect the room. With a hand on the pommel of her sword, LeiRain moved closer to Anya, too. Though it was difficult to tell in the dim light, the saurian's scales appeared gray rather than the bright green and yellow she had seen on his kin. His eyes were dull and covered in a milky haze, and she wondered if that was normal; the other saurians had all hidden their faces within the hoods of their cloaks. Muckjaw stood, leaning against the bars of his cage for support. His features were too different from her own for LeiRain to decipher the emotion on his face, but his hazy eyes looked weary.

'These friends have fared far worse than I have, I'm afraid. Once I was placed here, I tried to ward all of us. But it's become – *difficult*. And they were not in good condition when I arrived.'

LeiRain's eyes flitted to the small figure that remained crumpled on the floor in the pen next to Muckjaw's. Large dark eyes stared vacantly into the dark room. The figure's face was thin, and sunken. Her hair, which had probably once been a shining gold, was straw-like, dull and matted. LeiRain choked back a sob when she realized that what she had at first taken to be the loose fabric of a cloak was actually the shredded remains of a broken wing, hanging limply from the pixie's back. Her other wing was severed entirely and laid on the floor at the female's feet, a jagged piece of bone sticking out from her back where it had been torn away.

'I thought there would be more,' Muckjaw whispered. Anya patted his hand.

'How do we get them out?' LeiRain asked as she stepped forward and tugged on the heavy lock that held the door to the pixie's cage closed. But before anyone could answer this question, Silver spoke.

'We can't take them back the way we came.'

He was looking down at the dingy bathtub that sat against the wall. LeiRain followed his gaze and started when she realized that the washtub was not empty. Slowly, afraid of what she would see, LeiRain came to stand by his side. Her throat squeezed tight as she tried not to be sick. A thin, pale blue figure was curled on its side in the tub. There was webbing between her clawed fingers and toes. Dark blue gills flared along her neck. A few feet of murky gray water was not enough for the elf within to remain entirely submerged. Part of her hip and upper arm were exposed to the air. The exposed flesh was nearly white, the skin flaking. The Royals hadn't needed a cage to hold her; water elves couldn't survive long out of water.

'Pearl?' LeiRain asked, her voice barely a whisper. The sickly elf gave a stiff, barely noticeable, nod. She looked nothing like the beauty LeiRain remembered from her time in Corallis.

Silver was right; they could not go back the way they had come, not with Pearl in this fragile state. Not with the sickly Muckjaw and broken-winged pixie.

LeiRain was pondering their options when she began to smell smoke. Her head snapped around, searching for the source. She scanned the cellar but saw no sign of fire. Then, Anya shifted slightly from where she stood in front of Muckjaw's cage, and LeiRain knew where the smell came from. The blend's long-fingered hand was wrapped around the lock, the metal turning a bright orange and then blue before it began to melt. A sulfuric scent filled the air as the remnants of the lock dripped from Anya's hand and formed a silver-gray puddle on the floor.

Muckjaw pulled open the door to his prison and shuffled out. His gait looked stiff, although LeiRain was not sure if this was simply a result of abuse or if it was natural for the saurian. His tail dragged behind him, limply.

Anya moved to the next cage, the one that held the pixie, grabbing hold of and melting the lock just as she had done on Muckjaw's prison. But when the lock had pooled on the floor, the pixie remained where she was, staring blankly ahead. Even when Anya pushed the door open, the female did not respond. LeiRain looked back and forth between the pixie and the water elf, trying to decide who was in worse shape. Pearl would probably recover if they could just get her back to the ocean. But the pixie – she would never fly again.

LeiRain turned toward the pens, to see if she could offer Anya some help. Before she could take a step, cold, wet fingers clutched at her pant leg. Pearl slid her hand back into the water as soon as LeiRain looked down. *Don't leave me,* the elf mouthed. LeiRain knelt and put her hand in the filthy water, wrapping her fingers around Pearl's. Silver knelt beside her, but LeiRain was the only one who could command the water and Pearl knew it. LeiRain looked back to the pixie as she squeezed the elf's hand.

'What is your name?' Anya asked, softly.

The pixie's eyes flitted briefly to Anya's face and then back toward the nothingness she had been staring at before.

'Take my hand,' Anya said, stepping into the pen.

The pixie did not move, did not even look at her rescuer this time. Anya gripped the girl's upper arm, careful of her damaged wings. Slowly, she pulled the girl from the floor. Now that she was standing, the pixie's feet shuffled along obediently, but there was no other indication that she knew or cared what was happening.

LeiRain, Anya and Silver all exchanged looks while Ron stared ahead at the door.

'What do we do?' Anya asked, looking toward the murky tub. 'We can't … I won't leave her.'

'No, that's not an option,' Silver replied.

LeiRain looked down at Pearl and offered a reassuring smile before prying her fingers out of the elf's grasp. She stood, pulling the shield from her back and gripping the handle.

'We are close to water. I can feel it.'

'How long can she last once we take her out of that tub?' Anya asked, sounding skeptical.

LeiRain let out a long, slow breath, before speaking. 'If I don't have to concentrate on anything else, I think I can get her to the shoreline. But she won't survive long entirely out of the water.'

'How?' Anya asked.

One corner of Silver's mouth turned up in a half smile and he nodded at her. He understood what she intended to do but Anya had not yet seen LeiRain demonstrate her power. Just as LeiRain was opening her mouth to explain, the thin sliver of light cut through the middle of the room and widened, spreading across the cellar as one side of the double doors swung open. It happened so quickly that there was no way to prepare for it, no time to hide. Only Ron had his weapon drawn. Anya frozen while Silver and LeiRain did their best to fade into the shadows.

55

G et back,' Ron growled under his breath as he adjusted the grip on his ax. A figure entered – a man, judging by the broad-shouldered silhouette. LeiRain waited, shield held out in front of her, and hand gripping the pommel of her sword. She itched to draw her blade. Her heart pounded and her limbs tensed in all the right places, readying for action. She expected him to draw a sword or shout for help. The figure did neither of those things. Instead, he stumbled toward the nearest wall and placed his hand on it as he walked further into the cellar. The door swung shut behind him and they were once again left in almost total darkness.

He can't see us, she realized. His eyes hadn't adjusted to the dark yet and he was completely blind. Her own dark vision had been disrupted by the splotch of bright light streaming in through the cracked door, but they were readjusting quickly, her dark vision not entirely ruined. As she watched the figure, LeiRain found something familiar in his features.

The man seemed to sense something was wrong, to realize that there was a presence with him in the cellar even if he could not yet discern their shapes. He opened his eyes wide, trying to force his vision to improve. He looked like a man who might be handsome if he weren't so gaunt, so tired. LeiRain studied him, trying to discern why he felt familiar...

'Bren?' LeiRain gasped.

The man froze and turned his head toward where she stood, still obscured by darkness.

Voice shaking, he called into the dark. 'Who's there?'

Once she heard his voice, there was no doubt in her mind that it was him. Her friend, her former lover. The ambitious young man who was going to marry the merchant's daughter and settle down. The man who'd stood by as her mother's throat was slit and their home burned. LeiRain felt a jolt of pain in her chest as she remembered. For a brief moment, anger flared in her. Then, she recalled the fear in Bren's eyes when he'd seen her in the woods and the look of horror on his face when Ethan slit Alarra's throat. She remembered the many years they'd spent together as friends, and the way they had both giggled during their first kiss. Bren wouldn't hurt her and he wouldn't turn them in. At least, she didn't think he would. And maybe, just maybe, he could help.

'It's me,' she said, her voice cracking slightly. LeiRain took a step toward him. 'It's Rain.'

She felt tension emanating from where her friends stood quietly in the shadows. Ron let out a small growl, and the air shifted as the dwarve moved to stand near to her. He, too, remembered Alarra's death. He, too, recognized Bren.

'No, Rain, no!' Bren's sobbed, his face crumpling. 'They found you. I'm so sorry, Rain.' He shook his head, 'I'm so—'

'No, Bren, listen—'

He took a few steps toward her, hands held out. He stopped just shy of touching her. 'I can try to get you out, Rain. I can get you to the water, I think, without being seen. They'll kill me for it, but I'm dead anyway. Let me help you.'

'Bren—'

'How did they get you?' He went on without stopping to listen to her. 'When?'

'Bren, shut up and listen!' LeiRain clapped a hand over her mouth, shocked at how loudly she'd spoken.

Bren's eyes widened and he looked warily over his shoulder at the partially open door. But when he turned back to her, she saw a bit of sparkle in his eyes that hadn't been there before.

'Rain,' he whispered. 'I can't tell you how much I've missed you telling me to shut up.' He moved closer and looked intently at her face. His eyes seemed to have finally adjusted to the lack of light. LeiRain was able to get a better look at Bren as well, and she was disturbed by the ashen pallor of his skin and the thinness of his frame. He opened his arms as if he intended to hug her. LeiRain heard Ron grind his teeth.

'Bren, stop.' She held a hand out in front of her. LeiRain had been relieved that it was him and not another Royal, but she hadn't yet forgiven him for doing nothing as her mother lay dying.

Bren obeyed, coming to a halt a foot in front of her. He didn't embrace her, but ignoring her upraised hand, he rested his palms on her shoulders before sliding his grip down to her upper arms. His fingers tightened, squeezing her biceps as if to make sure she was real. Even in the darkness, she could see the circles under his eyes, the way his cheeks caved in. How had he ended up here? What had he endured?

LeiRain threw her arms around him. They wrapped easily around his malnourished frame, and his own arms felt thin and bony when he hugged her back. They held each other for several seconds, not as lovers, but as old friends who had found each other again. No, she hadn't forgiven him but she could appreciate his loneliness and fear. LeiRain pulled back, taking one of his hands and patting his fingers before she stepped away.

'How did you end up here, Bren? How did you end up there – *that day* – working for the Royals?'

'They commandeered the ship,' he said, his eyes losing focus, as he looked back through time. 'They killed the captain – they refused to believe he was human. They said he must have been a shifter offspring, but in all the years I sailed under him' – he shook his head – 'he was human and it didn't matter. He wasn't a Royal and it was just an excuse to take another ship. I kept my ears covered, like always, so they didn't know. What else could I do? They killed all the crew who weren't human and they killed anyone who didn't want to stay on and work for the Royals.'

LeiRain noticed the strip of fabric tied around his upper arm. Even in this lighting, she was certain of its color: Royal blue.

'How have you hidden it for so long?' LeiRain asked.

'It's been hard,' he replied. 'I keep to myself as much as I can. Some of them are starting to suspect though. I come here, sometimes, to check on the ... the people they keep. I bring them extra food and water when I can. I think some of the men may have noticed.'

'He's telling the truth,' Muckjaw croaked from where he stood beside Anya. LeiRain hadn't doubted Bren, but she was grateful that Muckjaw had spoken up on his behalf. Ron let out a sigh and she knew that the saurian's statement had put him somewhat more at ease with Bren's presence.

'And there was a fire one night,' Bren continued. 'Everyone got up in a hurry to help put it out. My ears weren't covered as well as they usually are. I realized it part way through fighting the fire, and I pulled my hat down to better cover them. I had hoped that no one noticed, with the confusion of the fire and everything.' Bren wrapped his arms around his midsection, holding himself. 'But the next day, one of the men said he thought I was part elf, that he had seen my ears in the chaos. He laughed about it, joking that I hid it well. I tried to laugh it off too, but I don't think he was joking. He knows. He's just waiting for the right opportunity to use it against me.'

LeiRain looked back at her friends for the first time since the reunion had begun. Despite Muckjaw's reassurance, Ron stood ready to pounce on her ex-lover at the first sign of trouble. Anya was studying Bren, but also casting concerned glances at Muckjaw who stood unsteadily beside her. There was no sign of jealousy or unease in Silver's eyes, just a steadiness in his gaze that told her he trusted LeiRain to make the right choice.

'Bren,' she said, turning back to him. 'Can you help us get out of here?'

He looked over the entire group, seeming to notice their number for the first time. 'It will be difficult with so many of you,' he said, biting his lower lip. 'But I don't think it's impossible. How did you even get in here?' His forehead creased. 'The Royals are all over the place.'

'There are tunnels – underground tunnels – but with their injuries,' LeiRain gestured to Muckjaw and the still silent pixie, 'we can't take them. They won't make it. 'And the elf,' LeiRain nodded toward Pearl, 'won't survive more than a few minutes out of the water.'

'It will take more than a few minutes to get her to the water from here if we're going to remain unseen,' Bren replied.

'How long?' LeiRain let her magic probe the murky bathtub water.

'Maybe ten, fifteen minutes,' he said.

'I can handle that,' LeiRain said.

He raised an eyebrow.

'Oh, right,' she said, noting his confusion. Bren had not seen her since the day before her majority when she had disappeared to Corallis. He had no idea what she could do. 'Just trust me,' she said. 'There isn't time to explain it all.'

'Alright,' he tilted his head to the side. 'If you say so.' There was a hint of a smile on his face.

'Do you know the layout of the settlement well?' Silver asked, stepping forward to stand beside LeiRain.

'Yes,' Bren answered confidently.

He looked back and forth between LeiRain and the fae as Silver's shoulder brushed against her. Realization dawned on Bren's face as he took in the body language between them. LeiRain held her breath, afraid of how Bren might respond. To her surprise and relief, he met her eyes and smiled broadly.

Looking back at Silver he said, 'Let me show you.' Bren knelt down, placing one knee on the dirt floor. He traced a finger through the earth, drawing a rectangle. LeiRain bent forward, straining to see what he was doing as Silver produced a warm ball of fae light and brought it to hover over their heads. 'This is the structure we are in now,' Bren said, looking up. The others circled around and watched him as he continued tracing lines in the dirt, drawing a map of the Royal compound.

Fear and excitement coursed through LeiRain and it took everything she had to maintain her focus on the bubble of water surrounding the elf in Silver's arms. She walked behind Silver with a hand clutching his tunic and her eyes staring at the center of his back – she needed absolute focus to keep the water elf entirely engulfed as they moved and couldn't afford to worry about their surroundings. In her sickly state, Pearl could likely tolerate even less time out of the water than a healthy water elf might. LeiRain had tried to pull moisture from the air to form a clean pocket of water for the elf, but there hadn't been enough to adequately cover her so there'd been no choice but to use cloudy tub water in which Pearl had been submerged. The sediment in the water made it more difficult for LeiRain to control, but she was managing to keep her hold on it.

Behind her, Anya walked with the saurian, Muckjaw, leaning into her shoulder. LeiRain was vaguely aware of his shuffling feet and scraping sound of his tail dragging through the brush. Ron brought up the rear with the nearly catatonic pixie slung over his shoulder. The pixie had let out a small whimper when the dwarve had thrown her over his shoulder, but seemed otherwise indifferent to her rescue. Bren walked in the lead, several paces ahead of them all, stepping around corners, pausing when the way was not yet clear and signaling when it was safe to continue.

Bren had drawn out a detailed map of the Royal compound. There were four other storage cellars like the one in which they had found the Muckjaw, the pixie, and Pearl. He confirmed that all of the others held only goods, no prisoners. Royal management's most pressing concern during the day was preventing their own employees and followers from stealing or slacking off their duties. There was little concern about the residents on the other side and no thought given to what risks they might pose. Many of the men in the Royal compound were crew from ships that had been forced into Royal service, and they were not enthusiastic about their new employer. To prevent unrest, the Royal leadership tried to keep most of them busy throughout the day with labor and at night, the men not on watch were given a generous allotment of alcohol from the Royal distillery.

The lax security allowed the group to move easily behind the cover of buildings and foliage. They made their way through the camp with relative ease, but the cover thinned as they got closer to the shoreline. Gaining access to the pier presented a significant challenge, but they would need to disable the Royal ships if the Beachspire residents were to have any chance of escaping the island. The pier was bustling with workers, sailors coming and going from the ships, and crates being loaded and unloaded. There were no walls to hide behind, but Bren managed to get them near enough to hide the group behind a large stack of barrels that had been left on the pier near the shoreline. LeiRain could hear the lap of water against ships' hulls, but they were still too far away to get Pearl into the water without being seen.

They stayed hidden behind the barrels with Muckjaw, Ron and the pixie while Bren and Anya left them to make their way to the other side of the Royal property and create a distraction. They had debated their plans for several minutes before finally deciding on a course of action. Muckjaw and the pixie would have to return to Beachspire by boat. There was no way they could drag the despondent pixie through miles of underground tunnel and going above ground would be too dangerous. And as long as the Royals had all of the ships, the residents on the other side of the Arborris Enclave were still trapped. It would only be a matter of time before the Royals gained access to them or the Beachspire resources ran dry. They would steal a small ship to send back the wounded, and destroy as much of the Royal fleet as possible while they had the opportunity. It was the only way the Beachspire refugees had a chance at survival, at escape.

LeiRain brushed away the beads of sweat that were forming on her brow, leaving a damp spot on her sleeve. She just had to hold the pool of water around Pearl for a few more minutes, until Anya and Bren drew the men away. She tightened her grip on her shield, drawing its magic to hold on to her connection to the water.

The sudden boom of a man's voice behind her made LeiRain jump.

'Hey! What—'

Ron's ax swung and the man's words were cut off by the severing of his head from his body. LeiRain felt her connection with the water falter and she fought to hold on to it. The Royal's now limp form remained upright for a few seconds, teetering just like LeiRain's grip on her magic. Then, the body fell, thudding loudly on the wooden planks. Dirty water splashed around Silver's feet as LeiRain's hold on it slipped entirely. Wide-eyed and panting, she looked at the gasping water elf in Silver's arms and the dampness on his tunic and pants. LeiRain grasped for her magic but it pulled away from the desperation and panic in her mind.

Silver could read it all on her face. With a knowing look, he lifted the water elf slightly and tossed her high into the air. Pearl's pale form sailed over the edge of the pier and into the water, hitting the surface with a loud splash.

56

S omeone shouted from the pier. 'What was that?'
They'd heard the splash. Ron adjusted the grip on his ax. LeiRain's hand went to the pommel of her sword, preparing for what was to come. Just then, a loud *boom* reverberated through the wooden dock.

'The distillery!' one of the men cried. Footsteps thudded on the wooden planks as men ran from their ships and toward the explosion that Anya had created. Sailors and dockhands ran past LeiRain, Silver and Ron where they crouched behind the barrels. The loud splash was forgotten as the men raced toward a coil of black smoke rising from the treetops. The distraction was a success.

Most of the men were fleeing the dock, but one curious sailor seemed determined to investigate the splash. LeiRain watched as the young man ran to the side of the pier. Bubbles still rushed to the surface where Pearl had been plunged into the water and the sailor's eyes narrowed as he looked at the disturbance. He unsheathed his sword, even as men rushed past him, heading to the fire. LeiRain's breaths came fast as she watched. Just one more step to his right and the sailor would have a clear view of their hiding place. She looked over her shoulder to see that Silver and Ron were focused on the treeline where men were disappearing on their way to the distillery. She had to do something about the sailor before he had a chance to raise the alarm.

LeiRain reached over and gave Silver's forearm a light squeeze to get his attention. Their eyes met and power thrummed between the two of them.

'Have my back,' she whispered and launched herself over the barrels and onto the pier.

LeiRain landed on the wooden planks with a light thunk and the sailor's head immediately swiveled to look at her. There was a brief few seconds of stillness between them and then the man lunged. The suddenness and recklessness of the sailor's attack surprised LeiRain. She stumbled back, nearly losing her footing. When they had sparred, Ron was deliberate in his attacks, precise. The sailor was frightening in his unpredictability. She shuffled back as he swung at her, his blade narrowly missing her shoulder. But as she dodged, all of LeiRain's training seemed to kick in. She widened stance and raised her shield as she placed herself between the sailor and dry land. LeiRain moved lightly over the planks, her weight on the balls of her feet. She was careful to keep her weight centered and her feet carefully placed, remembering all of the times that Ron had knocked her off balance. The sailor glanced between her and the shoreline and, realizing he was being trapped on the pier, lunged again. This time, LeiRain noted the way he pulled back his arm and she saw the strike coming. She swatted his sword away with her own. He stumbled, exposing his ribs to her, but she saw the opening too late. The sailor regained his balance and swung at her head.

She ducked, just missing the sharp edge of his weapon as it hummed through the air above her. The man's movements were sloppy and disorganized, his footsteps uncareful, his swings wild. The sailor staggered, his weight thrown off as his swing missed its target. Still in a crouch from dodging the blow, LeiRain swiped at his legs with the broad side of her sword. She and Ron had always been careful to use the flat of their blades in practice, and she'd done this without thinking – but the sailor went down nevertheless. His sword clanked against the pier as he fell onto his back. LeiRain took a few shuffling steps toward where he lay and kicked the hand that held his sword. The sailor gave a cry of pain as the sword slid a few feet down the pier, spinning as it went.

Weaponless and desperate, the man scrambled to his feet. Not wanting to mortally wound him, LeiRain was at a loss for what to do next. Taking advantage of her confusion, the sailor grabbed at her wrist and twisted, causing her to drop her own weapon. He reached into his boot and withdrew a knife as he yanked on LeiRain's wrist to pull her closer. Something clicked into place at that moment, one of her earliest lessons coming back to her. *Don't fight force against force,* Ron had said. *Use an attacker's momentum against them.* So, instead of resisting the tug on her arm, LeiRain moved with it. The sailor pulled her forward and she used his own strength against him as she swung her shield into his face. The sailor's fingers released their grip and he crumpled onto the pier before falling off the edge and into the water. LeiRain staggered forward, barely catching herself before she could fall in behind him.

Bubbles rose from the water where the sailor had fallen. The blow must have knocked him unconscious. The Royals might have gladly killed her, but LeiRain couldn't bring herself to let the man drown. She called to the water and drew his limp body to the surface. A halo of red formed around his head as his wound bled into the waves. She lifted her chin as she urged the water to carry him away. The man bobbed on the surface, borne by an unnatural current, until he was at least a quarter of a mile away from the pier. LeiRain directed the water to nudge him to shore and his body came to rest in damp sand. Even if he woke soon, and she doubted he would, the sailor wouldn't be able to climb the steep embankment until the tide came in to aid him.

LeiRain picked up her sword and, panting, stared in disbelief at her reflection on the blade's surface. She felt a surge of pride; she'd been in a real fight and she hadn't frozen. Her hands shook with the adrenaline that coursed through her veins and she might have stood there for hours, lost in the excitement of her triumph if she hadn't felt the pull of Silver's magic. It was a gentle tug, an inquiry. *Are you alright?* She sent a pulse of her own in response, more forcefully than she'd intended. *YES.* Sheathing her sword, LeiRain ducked back behind the barrels. Silver still scoured the treeline, but he cast a smile over his shoulder as she knelt beside him. Ron placed a hand on her arm and smiled brightly.

'Well done, Demi,' he whispered.

'I thought maybe you'd come to help me,' she replied, still breathing hard. Things had nearly gone very wrong.

Silver kept his eyes on the treeline as he spoke. 'We didn't think you needed it,' he said.

'You used your training in the chaos of a fight,' Ron added. 'That's as good as it gets, Rain.'

She smiled back at him, her cheeks burning.

'Bren and Anya are here,' Silver said in an urgent whisper, interrupting LeiRain's thoughts.

They all shifted to make room for the two just as Bren slid behind the barrels, panting. They'd chosen the distillery as their target for two reasons: it was very flammable and it was on the opposite side of the compound as the piers.

LeiRain looked over Bren's shoulder questioningly when Anya did not immediately appear beside him.

'Anya's already on the dock,' he said, in answer to her confusion. 'She's probably ready for you.'

Clutching her shield, LeiRain tried to hold on to the energy the fight had given her. She scrambled over the barrels and searched the pier for Anya. Several large crates had been left discarded on the pier or part way up the ramps to the ships as men left in a hurry to respond to the fire. Anya waited for her at the far end of the pier. She was lying flat on the wooden planks, her arm stretched out to reach the hull of the ship closest to her. Her hand glowed red and then orange as she worked to burn a hole in the vessel's side, but with only her fingertips brushing against the boat, progress was slow.

LeiRain pumped her arms as she ran toward Anya, Bren's footsteps sounding loudly on the planks behind her. He ran past LeiRain to reach Anya first, kneeling to grasp her legs so that she could reach further without falling off the pier. The blend rolled onto her side, extending her arm as far as it would go, but still only her fingers grazed the hull. This had been Anya's idea and it was a good one – if they disabled all of the ships, the refugees in Beachspire might actually have a chance at making it off the island. The Mad Return, once it was put back together, might have a shot at making it back to the Continent. But they had to act fast – the fire would only provide distraction for so long.

57

LeiRain's heart pounded as she stood beside Bren and Anya, communing with the water. She felt the ocean answer to her, the water shifting and bending to her will. The ship shifted as well as the water pushed it closer to the pier. Anya rolled back onto her stomach, stretching both arms forward. She pressed her palms flat against the hull.

'Thanks,' she said breathlessly, keeping her eyes on her work. She was less winded than Bren, another example of how Bren was rather worse for wear after his time with the Royals. Anya's hands turned blue with heat and the wood beneath them began to glow brightly. The pitch that sealed the wood smelled unpleasant, the scent of hot tar filling the air as the hull began to smoke. Orange flames sparked and crackled around her fingertips. LeiRain drew in a deep breath, scenting something other than heated pitch. The air around them felt electric, humming with magic as LeiRain commanded the water and Anya set fire to the ship.

Anya kept her hands against the vessel, focused and unmoving, until there was a large, gaping hole in its side. LeiRain let the ship slide back and away from the pier, the lines holding it to the dock going taut once more. But instead of letting her magic go, she urged the water to flow into the ship's wounded side. She felt her shoulders sag slightly with the effort as she directed the water to disobey the laws of nature. LeiRain clung more tightly to her shield as she drew on its magic and the water obeyed her, running up the hull and into the hole. She urged the water on and it flowed into the wounded ship at a faster pace. Soon, the vessel flooded enough that it began to list heavily to starboard. LeiRain pulled back her magic and the ship continued to take on water without her help.

Sweat dripped from LeiRain's chin as the use of her magic ate away at her energy. But there was something revitalizing about using her powers in conjunction with Anya's. The use of her own magic depleted her, but the electric charge of Anya's magic seemed to recharge her a little. The hull of the second ship broke open and LeiRain called on the water to rush in just as before.

Anya and Bren continued moving down the pier as LeiRain came behind them to flood the ships. Their work was going faster than LeiRain's and it was only a matter of time before the sailors began to reappear so she decided to try something different, something more difficult. She split her attention between the ship before her and the one that Anya was working on. Water continued to flow into the marred ship in front of LeiRain but it slowed just a bit as her magic shoved the other vessel closer to Anya's hand. As soon as Anya withdrew from the vessel, LeiRain began to push water into it as well.

She kept pace with them this way, dividing the focus of her magic as they went. The strain was immense, but she held on to each thread of her magic, deliberately acting on every ship until it listed enough to flood on its own. She had never pushed herself this far, before, and if LeiRain hadn't been so focused, she might have laughed with pleasure at her success. By the time the sixth vessel had begun to take on water on its own, her clothes were soaked through with sweat and there was a throbbing pain behind her eyes. All of the large merchant vessels were now groaning with the press of water against their hulls and listing toward the pier. It wouldn't be long before their combined weight began to tear apart the pier itself.

Ron and Silver, seeing that the work of sabotage was complete, hurried their way down the pier with the pixie slung over Ron's shoulder and Muckjaw walking with Silver's aid. One ship remained tied to the pier, buoyant and unmarred by Anya's hand. It was a smaller, faster vessel meant only for passenger travel and it would provide a means of escape for the injured. LeiRain watched them make their way down the dock. With Silver's arm around the saurian's middle, the emaciated form beneath his weathered cloak became clearly visible. The pixie, still despondent, remained limply slung over Ron's shoulder. LeiRain took a moment to catch her breath as the escapees were loaded onto the ship. She took a long pull from her waterskin and turned her face into the ocean breeze, which sent chills over her body as it swept her damp skin. Ron and Silver returned to the pier after depositing Muckjaw and the pixie onboard, but Anya, who had followed them, stayed on the ship. She pulled in the mooring lines as Bren untied them from the dock. Someone had to steer the vessel back to Beachspire and Anya was the only one of them, aside from Bren, with experience crewing a vessel. They still needed Bren's help to complete their mission, making Anya the obvious choice.

Anya pulled the last mooring line aboard, coiling it around one of the bits as she called out. 'We're ready to get underway.'

With a deep inhale, LeiRain called on her magic once more to push the vessel off of the pier and move it quickly out of reach of any Royal weapons. It slid away easily, the water needing only the smallest bit of suggestion from her as the sails filled with wind and propelled the ship forward. Releasing her hold on the water, LeiRain bent over and rested her hands on her knees. There was still magic humming inside her but the pool of it grew smaller with each use. Thankfully, the rest of their plans did not depend on her wielding magic. When she righted herself, she noted the look of longing on Bren's face as he watched the ship pull away. He could have gone with them, he could be on his way to safety right now. But instead, Bren had chosen to stay and guide them through the compound. It was the most selfless thing she'd ever seen him do, and LeiRain felt the roots of forgiveness begin to take hold.

The planks beneath their feet shuddered and creaked as one of the ships began to tilt into the pier. Shouts from the not-too-distant woods could be heard as they all turned to run ashore. Fire was the most dangerous thing that could happen aboard a ship at sea, so the sailors would be well-trained in combating them. It might not be long before men began returning to the pier and they had to get into Mr. Odro's office and back out before everyone knew of the ruined ships. Once they all returned to their post and discovered the sabotaged ships, they would know that the distillery fire had been no accident and they would start hunting for the intruders.

LeiRain breathed a sigh of relief when their feet were once more on soft earth and not the collapsing boards of the pier. Bren ushered them all behind a storage shed where she, Ron and Silver ducked down to hide between the wall and the bushes until he signaled for them to move on to the next bit of cover. Bren had never been in the manor house so he would be of little help once they were inside, but thus far he had navigated them through more than half of the compound without being discovered. They moved on Bren's command and LeiRain found herself gazing at the manor as her back pressed up against the cool exterior of an ice shed.

The building was enormous, its walls of sand-colored brick appearing to reach toward the sky. It looked to be three or four stories tall – it was definitely the tallest building she'd ever seen – with countless windows, and nearly as many balconies. LeiRain began to feel disheartened about their task. How would they find what they were looking for with all of those rooms? Silver, sensing her unease, let his magic wash over her. *You're not alone*, it seemed to say. *We're in this together.* LeiRain's breathing slowed in response and she returned her attention to studying the manor. Light green curtains billowed with the ocean breeze, almost as if inviting the group to enter. Servants, well-dressed in pastel frocks, passed by windows on the first and third floor with great frequency.

'There,' Silver said, pointing to a third-floor window. 'See the bookshelves? That's either a study or a library. Either way, it's somewhere we might find important documents.'

'What exactly are you looking for?' Bren asked. They had not shared details with him about what they hoped to accomplish once inside the manor.

'Proof.'

'Of what?' Bren asked, one eyebrow raised.

'They have designs for new, deadly weaponry. I want to find their plans for it. And anything else that may prove they are planning to start a war and to pit race against race. Anything that will convince my people of the threat they pose,' the fae replied.

'I can testify to that last part,' Bren said. 'I've seen them frame others for their acts of violence. Mostly, they blame it on blends but I've seen them blame sole-bloods for their acts, too.' Silver gave him a grateful smile but shook his head.

'Thank you, but I can't trust that will be good enough for my people.'

'Then I guess we've got to figure out how to get inside,' Bren replied, resignation in his voice.

Carefully, they worked their way around the manor, remaining hidden while they noted where the activity was thickest. The back side of the building, the side that faced away from the ocean and looked out at the cellars and ware-houses, was absolutely teeming with servants. Loads of laundry were being hung to dry in the sun and LeiRain could smell the lye and rose oil of the sheets draped nearby. Hot buckets of dirty dish water were being carried out and discarded, sending up wafts of steam as water puddled on the ground. It would be impossible to enter here without being seen. But the front of the manor, with its breathtaking ocean views, was quiet.

'The servants probably went through these rooms early in the morning, before Mr. Odro and his guests were awake.' Bren rubbed at a knot in his neck as he spoke. 'I've never seen any servants in the windows of the ocean-facing rooms. I *think*,' Bren said, unsure, 'he has a wife, or a mistress. I've seen a woman with him at times, standing on one of these balconies.'

Silver narrowed his eyes at the building. 'I have not heard any rumors of a mistress.' His voice was tinged with curiosity. 'And unless his circumstances have changed very recently, the younger Mr. Odro does not have a wife.' His lips pressed together tightly, telegraphing his unease.

'Let's be mindful of her possible presence, anyway,' Ron said, and Silver nodded in agreement.

The exterior of the building was lined with thick rose

bushes that were heavily dotted with yellow and white blooms. There was no way that these flowers were native to the Arborris Enclave, and LeiRain was certain they had been chosen to adorn the building as a mark of Odro's wealth. She normally enjoyed fresh flowers, but now the scent of them seemed sickly sweet.

They slid along the wall behind the bushes in a single file. Silver's fingers twitched slightly at the plants and their branches pulled away, leaving space for them to inch by without being snagged by the jagged thorns. They moved carefully, backs pressed against the brick, until they came to an open bay window where there was no sign of guards or servants. It seemed that Odro and his men were so certain in their control over the island that they didn't even bother to provide security on the ground floor of the manor. Silver entered first, stepping through silently. His figure seemed to melt into the pale green curtains that hung on either side of the window.

LeiRain went next and was followed by Ron who pressed up beside her where she hid behind the curtains. When she looked over her shoulder, LeiRain was surprised to see Bren coming through as well. They had planned to meet him back at the cellar where he'd found them ~ it was simpler this way and safer for all of them. Bren was not stealthy and even now he rustled the rose bushes as he moved. LeiRain gave him a confused look and whispered over Ron's head, '*What are you doing*?'

'I just—' He looked at her with pleading eyes as he whispered a little too loudly. 'I don't want to be alone out there again.'

Ron spun around and clamped his hand over Bren's mouth, eyes blazing with fury. When he moved his hand, he brought a single finger up to his own lips in a violent *shushing* motion. Bren was invaluable to safe navigation of the compound, but he moved clumsily and carried no weapons. In the manor he would be a liability, but they could not argue about it now. Somewhere inside, a floorboard creaked. Every second they stood here, every word they whispered to each other, brought the risk of discovery.

The four of them crept along, Ron making Bren walk a few paces ahead of him in an effort to better manage the risk. Somewhere ahead of them, they heard the shuffle of feet. The group crowded into the shadows beneath a nearby stairwell as the footfalls grew closer. LeiRain's heart pounded so furiously in her chest that she worried they could hear it. She held her breath, afraid even that would give them away. But the footsteps approached, and a woman in a light coral dress passed by without noticing them. She carried a silver tray and was dressed just like the servants they'd seen in the back of the house. At least it wasn't a guard.

When the servant disappeared around the corner, there was a collective sigh of relief from all of them except for Silver. His eyes narrowed as he peered down the hall in the direction the girl had gone and he shook his head, pursing his lips. *Something is off about this*, his eyes seemed to say.

She saw a similar look on Ron's face, his eyes dark with wariness and concentration. Bren looked no more unsettled than he had when they entered, oblivious to the fact that this had all been a bit too easy. LeiRain's stomach turned with unease as they crept down the hall to a set of ornate stairs. Silver, who was leading the way, hesitated. With his back pressed to the wall, his eyes ran over their surroundings, looking up and down and along the stairs. There was no one in the hallway, but the staircase felt too open, too visible. His throat bobbed as he swallowed and he gestured for them to move on. They stepped from the shadows and crossed the hall to stand on the steps. They moved quickly and quietly up the stairs, which were covered in lush red carpet. The banister shined with fresh polish and LeiRain let her eyes wander over the woodwork, studying the delicately carved flowers that adorned the mahogany. The carpet was so plush that LeiRain could feel the fibers of it shift and crunch beneath her feet. The richness of the manor belied the danger of what lived within.

They crept away from the stairs once they reached the third floor, Silver scanning the hallway as the rest of them pressed against the wall behind him. They moved forward only on the fae's command, sliding from one shadow to another. Every door they passed was open, but the first two rooms were empty bedrooms, stripped of linen and unlikely to hold any secrets. The third door led them to the library they had seen from outside. One at a time, they stepped inside and slid into the dark corners of the room. LeiRain looked around as she pressed her back against a set of shelves. Books and boxes of loose paper lined the room from floor to ceiling and LeiRain felt her stomach knot up as she realized how long it would take them to sort through all of this. She turned and looked at the shelf against which her back had been pressed and pulled a box of documents from it. As the others spread out through the room, LeiRain knelt on the floor and began to comb through the papers. Her hands shook as she pulled each one from the box and held it up to the light. It was not easy to focus on what she was reading when her mind was preoccupied with the threat of discovery but she did her best, sometimes reading a page more than once before she could discard it as irrelevant to their search.

LeiRain looked up frequently, eyeing the door and checking in on her friends' progress. The room consisted of three walls filled with books and documents, and a fourth that was floor to ceiling windows. Silver was nearby, combing through the same wall of shelves that LeiRain was working on. It was the longest wall and the shelves were densely packed. Ron and Bren had each taken one of the other two walls. Bren was kneeling on the floor, flipping through loose documents while Ron ran a finger slowly along the spine of each book shelved before him. The only illumination in the room was the sunlight streaming through the windows and LeiRain watched a few dust particles float through the golden rays before returning her focus to the task at hand.

She looked through the titles on the next shelf as Silver pulled several boxes of scrolls and documents from higher up. He set the boxes gently on the carpeted floor and then began to methodically examine the contents of each one. Carefully, he unrolled a scroll, scanned it briefly, then rolled it back up and returned it to the box. He paused occasionally, tilting his head to the side as he listened to something that only he could hear. Each time he did this, LeiRain felt her heart skip a beat, but he always went back to his work without a word to the others so whatever he heard wasn't, at present, worth mentioning.

LeiRain unshelved another box that turned out to be more financial ledgers and expense reports; nothing useful. She ran her fingers over the books that lined the next shelf, in between boxes, noting a familiar title, *Before the War*. This book was in much better condition than her copy had been – there was no water damage to the pages, no crinkling of the spine. Until this moment, LeiRain hadn't realized how much she missed her books and she had to resist the urge to slip it inside her tunic. Next to *Before the War* was an even newer-looking volume, *Why the War of Sorrows Wasn't Enough*. She pulled it down and flipped through the pages. LeiRain wasn't sure what she'd expected to find, but the book was full of hateful Royal rhetoric. She replaced it on the shelf, disappointed, and let out a slow breath, trying not to think of what would happen to them if they were discovered.

Beside her, Silver's face was unreadable but LeiRain noted that he'd tucked a scroll into his tunic. Had he found plans for the weapon? Silver reshelved a set of documents and she watched, hopefully, to see if he would signal their departure. But whatever the significance of the scroll he held onto, it wasn't enough to satisfy him. Silver pulled down another box.

LeiRain glanced at the other side of the room as she replaced the box she'd just examined. Ron seemed to sense her eyes on him and lifted his head to meet her gaze. He raised an inquisitive eyebrow before his eyes darted to the door. Her palms became slick with sweat as she watched him, thinking that he had seen someone pass by. But seconds later, he met her eyes again and offered a reassuring wink. LeiRain tried to wink back at him as she wiped her sweaty hands down the sides of her legs, but he had already returned his attention to the stack of papers he was holding.

As she withdrew another pile of documents, LeiRain checked in on Bren. He was slightly less organized in his approach and a series of open boxes sat before him on the carpet. He sifted through the parchment so quickly that it sometimes made a crinkling noise. LeiRain held back her warning for fear that her words would be even louder than the raucous he was already making. She could feel her pulse leaping in her throat as she looked down at the papers in her grip.

Time seemed to stand still as they sifted through each box and tome in the generously stocked library. Once they had combed through every shelf, Silver motioned for them to move toward the far side of the library. There, half hidden behind the thick folds of the window dressing, was another door. It stood slightly ajar and LeiRain peeked around Silver to see the study that lay beyond. Silver stood at the threshold of the other room, eyes unfocused as he tapped into his other senses. LeiRain's hands shook as the group waited for him to determine whether or not it was safe to enter. He tilted his head to one side, listening intently, then eased the door further open.

Bren sighed loudly behind her and she cast a scathing glance over her shoulder at him. He held up his palms in apology. She saw what had made Bren sigh: this room would be much more difficult to search. Gone were the neat rows of books and tidily stored scrolls. A large desk sat in the center of the room, covered in unevenly stacked paper, crumpled scrolls and an overturned inkwell. The wooden surface of the desk was barely visible beneath the chaos of everyday business dealings. And there were still more messy piles of paperwork, set on a small table near the door. A tea tray rested precariously on top of this pile of documents.

LeiRain felt exhaustion pressing down on her even as she looked at the room. She'd pushed her magical abilities nearly to their limit when she'd helped sabotage the ships and now her mind felt foggier with each minute that passed. The shield on her back felt heavier than she remembered, and it was a strain to keep her shoulders up under its weight. A bit of Silver's magic coursed through her then, like fingers running up her spine. LeiRain turned and smiled at him, her magic too tattered right now to send any coursing back to him in response. He gave her an understanding nod.

She and Silver approached the desk and Ron and Bren set to work on the tea table. There had to be something here that would point to the destructiveness of the Royal Merchant Marine Company, even if the sheer volume of loose papers felt overwhelming. Hopeful at first, LeiRain rallied her resources to focus on the work at hand, but despair began to set in as she searched through the mess of documents. With each irrelevant page she examined, it became less and less likely that they would find anything of significance. When she looked up at the others, none of them seemed to have made much progress either. She tried not to notice the discouraged slump to Ron's shoulders or the tired frown on Bren's face. LeiRain picked up another document and was skimming through information about sailors' rations when Silver sent a jolt of magic to attract her attention. He motioned for her to come closer and held out the document that he'd found. Her hands trembled as she read over the pages.

It was a contract for the sale of land and, at first, LeiRain could see nothing untoward within its pages. Then, Silver pointed his finger at a paragraph near the bottom of the second page.

'*It is imperative that the Royal Merchant Marine Company acquire this particularly valuable piece of land and the resources within it. It is currently occupied by a small dwarve clan who, despite their dwindling population and inability to fully appreciate the worth of the property, refuse to sell. This land must be acquired and the current residents expelled regardless of any potential resistance, by the second month of the new year.*'

Worse still, it seemed that the Royals had already constructed a plausible explanation for the sudden disappearance of an entire dwarve clan, one that would implicate other non-humans:

'*There are a number of reasons why this clan might come to no longer occupy said territory, including rivalries with a neighboring clan with whom hostilities have previously occurred, and a neighboring settlement of forest elves with whom the clan occasionally competes for resources.*'

'Let's check the desk drawers and then go,' she whispered.

'This,' she pointed at the scroll, 'is at least something.' She swallowed, then added, 'We've been here too long.'

Door hinges creaked loudly before Silver could reply. LeiRain jumped at the sudden noise and, assuming it was Bren, turned to scold him. She gasped and grabbed at Silver's sleeve – Bren was nowhere near the door, which now stood wide open, a dark silhouette standing in the entrance.

58

A middle-aged man in a smart black suit stepped into the room. He was almost handsome but the grayish pallor of his skin and the dullness of his eyes seemed to steal away his beauty. His irises were an other-worldly matte black and LeiRain felt as though he was staring through her.

With a forced brightness in his voice, the man spoke. 'I heard that you have an interest in my business,' he directed at Silver.

Ron sunk into a defensive stance, one hand resting on the handle of his ax as the man walked stiffly past him. Bren looked like a cornered animal, his eyes wide and limbs shaking. The man brushed past Silver, whose body tensed in response, and came around the desk. LeiRain saw a flash of slate fire in her lover's eyes as they followed the man's movements. He stopped behind his desk and placed his hands on the back of the chair.

Ron took a few steps forward and pulled the ax from his belt. LeiRain reached for her own weapon but Silver held up a hand.

'Wait,' Silver said, his voice steady. The dwarve stilled but kept his ax readied. LeiRain left her hand resting on the pommel of her sword. 'Let's not shed blood if it isn't necessary.' Ron's throat bobbed as he swallowed, narrowing his eyes at the stranger, but he took a step back.

'Please,' the man said, gesturing to the two chairs that sat opposite him on the other side of the desk. 'Have a seat. I'm afraid that I don't have enough chairs for everyone but I can ring the help and have more brought up. Maybe some fresh tea as well?' The man's smile made LeiRain's skin prickle. 'You all look as if you're in need of refreshment.'

'That won't be necessary,' Silver replied.

LeiRain saw Ron's fingers twitch on the handle of his ax.

'Very well,' the stranger replied. 'Suit yourselves.'

Ron seemed to relax slightly at this. The last thing they needed was for more people to become aware of their presence here.

The man – Mr. Odro, LeiRain presumed – made a show of pulling out his own chair, the legs whispering as they slid against the carpet. LeiRain and Silver had been on opposite ends of the desk and in the process of coming around to look in the drawers. Mr. Odro had now placed himself between them and LeiRain stepped back, warily. He looked back and forth between LeiRain and Silver, gesturing toward the other chairs.

'You've come into my home without invitation and now you're refusing my hospitality? At the very least, have a seat.'

LeiRain and Silver exchanged a glance, fingers of magic reaching between them though it was a strain for LeiRain to call on hers. Odro twitched in his chair and eyed them suspiciously as if he could feel their power at work. The two of them moved to sit opposite the man and, though this situation wasn't much better, LeiRain felt a wash of relief at no longer having the stranger standing between them.

They both sat. LeiRain felt Ron shift to stand behind her, placing himself between her and whatever might come through the door. Bren followed suit, moving to stand behind Silver, though likely more for his own sense of safety than anything else.

Odro set his hands on the desk, interlacing his long, thin fingers. 'Well, you've likely guessed, but I'm Ulrek Odro. Who are you and to what do I owe the pleasure of this clandestine visit?'

Several seconds passed by without a response. LeiRain felt the heat of Ron's body nearby and could hear the steady huff of his breath. She wanted to reach out to Silver with her magic, but the pool of it inside her was refilling so slowly that she dared not draw more.

'I was wondering,' Silver said, breaking the silence, 'why have you forced the indigenous population of this island to cower in fear on a small strip of land?'

'I have done no such thing,' Mr. Odro scoffed. 'I have been a resident of this island for years and when my father passed on – *gods rest his soul* –' he said, with an exaggerated frown, 'and left the business to me, I simply transformed this way station of sorts into a headquarters. I generously offered employment to the locals, but they all seemed to take great offense to our presence here.' He raised his eyebrows and shook his head. 'I can only assume that it is their intolerance for humankind that has driven them to isolate themselves on the other side of the island.'

'There are humans among them,' LeiRain replied. Silver's voice had been even and calm but hers was cold and cutting. She made no effort to hide her disdain.

'Why some humans would choose to dwell with – with those not of their own race is beyond me,' he replied. 'But it is a choice that they have made for themselves.' He lifted his chin indignantly, looking down his long nose at her.

'I have some other concerns about your business practices,' Silver went on. LeiRain felt his magic pulsing outward, searching for something of the earth. Despite his mask of serenity, Silver knew they were not safe here and he was preparing himself for battle. But what good was earth magic here, LeiRain wondered, on the third floor of a brick building?

'Oh,' Mr. Odro said, condescension evident in his voice. 'Do tell. I am quite eager to discuss my business practices with an individual who is currently trespassing on my property. And thieving, too, I believe.' Mr. Odro's gaze ran briefly over Silver's tunic where he had tucked away one of the found documents. He flashed a chilling smile as he reached into his desk.

'I apologize for the intrusion,' Silver said, leaning forward to stand. 'Perhaps it is time we made our exit. We can arrange another time to call on you and discuss my concerns.'

'No,' Mr. Odro commanded. Then, in a more polite tone, 'Please, continue. No time like the present, fae.'

LeiRain felt the blood drain from her face and her throat grow tight. Odro knew what Silver was. Odro had been the one to send those Royal henchmen after him, equipped with the ash of foxglove. LeiRain pressed her weight into the balls of her feet and prepared to stand. Heart hammering, her fingers dug into the arms of her chair as she waited to follow Silver's lead.

'This,' Odro looked up and winked at LeiRain, catching her off guard, 'you'll want to see.' His focus darted back and forth between Silver and the object he had withdrawn from the desk. An unfriendly slash of a smile stretched across his face. 'It's quite an interesting new invention.'

LeiRain watched his hands. He held an object of metal with a wooden handle, carefully carved to match his grip. Odro grasped the object and rested one of his fingers over a small metal loop, inside of which LeiRain could see a tiny lever. Rather than forming the shape of a blade, the metal of this object was formed into a tube, which Odro now pointed at Silver's chest. The object was less than a half-foot in length and LeiRain could not see how it might pose a threat, especially from a distance of several feet.

'Very resilient creatures, the verdaant,' Odro continued. 'After you dispatched with my men, I knew that it was only a matter of time before you showed up here.' He shrugged. 'Thankfully, I'm already prepared.'

It was then that LeiRain realized what Odro held – she opened her mouth to warn Silver, to tell him that this was it, *this* was the weapon they'd been looking for. Silver was watching the man, his eyebrows knit together as realization dawned on his face. He moved so quickly that the chair beneath him fell back on the floor. Standing, he grabbed LeiRain's hand and, fear flashing in his eyes, pulled her to her feet as well. She'd never seen the fae display such blatant emotion on his face before and it made her insides turn to ice. LeiRain looked back at Odro in time to see his finger close around the tiny trigger.

Silver's glowing blue shield slammed into place just as an ear splitting *bang* sounded in the room. Just as quickly as his shield appeared, it flickered out of existence. LeiRain's hands flew up to cover her pointed ears. Time had not sped back up yet and she watched smoke curl in the air, coils rising lazily from the object in Odro's hand. Silver crumpled to the floor on her left. At the same time, she noticed movement to her right and she became vaguely aware of Ron's raised weapon. *Bang.* The weapon went off again. The arc of Ron's ax fell short of its mark, leaving a slash in the desktop before the dwarve stumbled backward.

Time returned to its normal speed as LeiRain dropped to the floor beside Silver. She screamed his name, her ears buzzing so loudly from the noise of the weapon that her voice was barely audible even in her own head. Blue blood gushed from a hole in the fae's chest and she pressed her shaking hands to the wound. The blood was coming fast, pouring out between her fingers and running down the side of Silver's tunic. Her head throbbed, and her ears were still ringing as her entire world shrank to the size of Silver's chest wound. All LeiRain could see was blue as blood coated her hands and ran in rivulets down Silver's neck before spilling onto the floor. She leaned into him, pressing her body weight into her hands as she tried to staunch the bleeding. Any minute now, the wound would mend itself. He was fae, afterall. But the blood continued to flow.

'Silver. Silver. Silver...' She called his name over and over, her own voice more audible now but still sounding far away. His fae blood should have been repairing him, but instead it ran hot and thick over her hands and soaked into the carpet. LeiRain felt it pulse against her palms with every beat of Silver's heart. And she knew. She knew that he couldn't heal himself. Whatever Odro had used to penetrate Silver's body, it had been laced with ash of foxglove. That's why it had broken so easily through his shield and why the bleeding would not stop.

Ron's roar sounded somewhere nearby and Odro answered with dark laughter. On the other side of Silver, there was a blur of movement that might have been Bren. But none of it mattered to LeiRain; Silver was all that existed for her at this moment. She thought of his words the other night. *We'll have time to enjoy each other later.* Would they?

Blood spread over the floor, pooling on the carpet and soaking into the knees of her pants. Still, LeiRain kept her hands pressed against Silver's chest, willing him to survive. She didn't dare look at his face, too afraid of what she might see. She could feel the warmth leaving his body with each weakening heartbeat and still the blood flowed. He'd lost so much of it now, she wasn't sure how he was still bleeding. Every drop that ran over her hands was more precious than the last. LeiRain watched blood stream down Silver's paling neck in thick, blue lines and wished she could capture it, put it back inside of him. And then she remembered how she had been able to pull water from his lungs to save him from drowning. LeiRain recalled how she'd sensed the water in his body, how she had known what belonged there and what belonged to the sea. If she could draw water out of his body, could she not hold it in?

The weight of LeiRain's shield pressed against her back. Usually, she would grip it tightly to draw from its power, but this would have to be good enough because she didn't dare take her hands off of the wound. Staring at her blue-stained fingers, LeiRain reached out to the water. The tether to her magic felt feeble, like an overexerted muscle, but she pushed through the discomfort. Her mind brushed up against the pooling blood, and she sensed the moisture rattling in Silver's lungs. It was different than before. Warmer, denser than the salt water she'd pulled out of him. His heartbeat was only a subtle thrum now, but LeiRain could feel the lifeforce still flowing in his veins. Her magic threatened to pull away but she opened her whole heart to it this time, not just her mind. *Please*, she thought. *Please do this for me. For him.*

The bleeding began to slow.

At first, LeiRain feared it was because Silver had already bled out. But then his chest strained against her hands as he gasped. The water within him was bending to her will, offering itself to her cause. She forced herself to look at Silver's face. His skin was pale, lips nearly white, and his eyes were closed, eyelids fluttering slightly as he tried to open them. Silver wasn't safe yet, but the bleeding had at least stopped. LeiRain's fingers tightened around the fae's blood-soaked tunic and tears ran down her face as her body shook with emotion. She strained not to let her feelings of relief distract her, afraid that the magic might lose its hold.

When she was certain that the bleeding wouldn't resume, LeiRain stole a glance at Ron. He was kneeling in the corner of the room, having fallen back against a set of shelves. Blood seeped from his left thigh and he pressed a thick-fingered hand to the wound as he tried to stand up.

'Rain.' Her snapped back around to look at Silver. He blinked as his eyes focused on her face. Bren called out beside her and there was another blur of motion nearby but LeiRain ignored it, instead leaning in closer to better hear her lover's voice. He said something else, but it was too soft for her thrumming ears to hear. She watched Silver's color-drained lips when he spoke again. His message was clear: 'Run.'

Crack.

LeiRain sucked in a breath as pain shot through her back and then down her arms and legs like lightning. Even her teeth hurt as the shield shuddered against her. She turned and stood on shaky legs, tugging the guige over her head and letting the shield drop to the floor. Deafened once more by the weapon, LeiRain couldn't hear her own anguished cry, even as it vibrated in her chest.

In front of her, the shield lay with its handle against the bloody carpet. At this angle, the opal should have reflected back the light streaming through the window. Instead, its remains coated the shield in a shimmering blue dust and jagged pieces of blue green were scattered over the floor. The magic that had felt so solid and tangible only moments before slipped away. LeiRain looked back at Silver and saw a fresh bubble of blood rise from the hole in his chest. Her heart sank.

Hands fisted at her sides, LeiRain turned to Odro. Her fury was so complete that it felt as if a fire burned in her chest. The man stared at her, his smile still in place. Bren was at her side, tugging on her sleeve and nearby, Ron's leg collapsed under him as he tried and failed to right himself. LeiRain felt the impact of the dwarve's body vibrate through the floor. Odro held the weapon in front of him, pointed at LeiRain. Bren continued tugging on her arm but she resisted him. The man in front of her had taken everything from LeiRain. Her mother. Her home. And now, her lover. She was going to tear Odro apart with her bare hands. She took a step toward him not caring that he adjusted the barrel of the weapon to point at her chest. LeiRain struck out at him with a clawed hand—

Crack.

The weapon fired once more. At the same instant, Bren's grip on her arm tightened and he shoved her away. The blast rattled LeiRain's teeth and her head felt like it might explode with the force. She would join Silver, helpless and bleeding on the floor. She hit the carpet, but nothing pierced her body as she fell and when LeiRain ran her hands over herself, she found no wound. Bren stood over her, swaying. He clutched his stomach with one hand and clung to Odro's desk with the other. His dingy white shirt turned a deep red and the hand at his stomach was slick with blood. He had thrown her out of the way and taken the blast instead.

Bren dropped to one knee, letting his head rest next to the hand that remained clinging to the desk. LeiRain sat up, head spinning with the movement, and placed a hand on his arm.

She looked at him, eyes wide in disbelief. Bren could have fled with Anya and the others, but he'd stayed to help them and now he was paying the ultimate price. His eyes shifted to meet hers.

'Bren,' she felt his name in her chest as she said it. A name she'd called out so many times. A name she'd said in jest. A name she'd groaned in pleasure. A name she'd spoken with bitterness. Now, it was laced with desperation. 'Bren,' she whispered. 'What did you do?' He watched her lips as she spoke and LeiRain slid a hand up to his face, cupping his cheek. Her thumb left a streak of blue blood along his jawline.

'What I should have done a long time ago,' he said. Her hearing was beginning to return but his words still sounded muffled, distant. LeiRain watched his mouth move to be sure she understood him. 'I stopped being a coward.'

She choked on a sob. A loud grunt drew her attention to Ron who was once again kneeling on the floor. He leaned into his ax, panting, but at least blood no longer flowed from the wound in his leg. She refocused on Bren who was not so well-off. LeiRain reached for her magic, pleaded with it to save him as it had saved Silver. There was sorrow in the water's reply. *Too late. Not enough.* He was too fragile, too human for her to save.

Bren's blood began to pool on the floor, his red mixing with Silver's blue. 'You're not a coward,' she said, as she continued to stroke his cheek.

'Not anymore,' he replied, the corners of his mouth tilting up as he tried to smile at her. Bren took his hand away from the desk and used it to pull the stocking cap off of his head. One of his ears stuck out between dirty strands of blonde hair. His head slipped off the desk and he fell onto his elbows. Bren's ears were the only vestige of his elf heritage and he'd spent his whole life, at least his life since meeting LeiRain, hiding them. He possessed no magic. No heightened senses. No advanced healing. His mostly human body would not survive this.

'Don't let them take anything else from you, Rain.' Bren winced as he dropped from his elbows onto his side. He curled his arms around his middle and lay panting. His body convulsed with a frantic final breath and then he fell still.

Bren sacrificed himself for her. Just as her mother had done. LeiRain wouldn't let their sacrifices be in vain. She looked around the room and found Silver still breathing, though just barely, his eyes once again closed. His wound leaked but more slowly than before. She reached out with her magic, lamenting the absence of her shield as she struggled to sense what was happening inside of him. As best as she could tell, even with her lost concentration and the absence of the opal, the water magic had continued to keep him alive.

But she could not count on this to last forever, not when he was so close to dying. They had to get out of here and fast. Ron had finally made his way to standing, though he leaned heavily on his uninjured leg. His eyes were focused on where Odro stood behind the desk, his ax held out in front of him defensively and his jaw set.

LeiRain pulled herself to her feet, using the desk to haul herself up. When she came back into view, she saw that Odro had the weapon pointed at Ron. The man quickly swiveled around to point it once again at LeiRain. Seeing this, Ron dared to take a few steps closer. The movement drew Odro's attention and he swung to point the deadly thing at the dwarve again.

Odro was beginning to look tired and he seemed to be unsure where to focus his attention now that Ron was back on his feet. Sweat ran down the man's neck and dampened the collar of his pristine white shirt. He was panting for breath.

LeiRain could see his eyes widening with panic but couldn't understand why he was suddenly in such poor condition. None of them had come close enough to land a blow and the weapon he held didn't seem like it would take much of an effort to wield. As she examined him, the edges of his body began to blur. LeiRain blinked and shook her head in an effort to clear her vision, but she wasn't seeing things – Odro's figure began to glow.

Light pulsed from Odro's body sending waves of heat through the room. His silhouette flickered and the flashing of light grew faster. Then just as suddenly as it had started, the pulsing stopped and a flash of bright orange filled the room. Odro was no longer blurred – his body looked solid though somewhat shriveled and his face had gone entirely white. He still held the weapon but it dangled limply from his fingers as both arms hung at his sides. The weapon fell from his hand and hit the carpet with a soft *thunk* at the same time his well-dressed frame slumped back into his chair. Standing in the space that Odro had occupied seconds before was a tall, lean woman with ash gray skin, a sneer on her lips and death in her violet eyes.

59

'W ho are you?' LeiRain willed her voice to steadiness as she spoke. The woman looked her up and down and LeiRain took the opportunity to study her as well. Coal black hair hung to the woman's slender waist and framed either side of her heart-shaped face. Her features were beautiful but sharp and her thin red lips were so dark in color that they bordered on purple. When LeiRain looked into the woman's eyes, she saw orange and blue fire flickering in her pupils.

'I am a forgotten cousin of your dying friend,' she said in a cool voice. A lock of hair slid in front of her shoulder as the woman tilted her head toward Silver.

'You're fae?' LeiRain tried to puzzle out this woman before her. Bren was gone. Silver lay dying. Ron was alive but injured, and Odro was subdued. Where had this woman come from and why would she have anything to do with Odro, a man whose disdain for anyone non-human was readily apparent? LeiRain was desperate to look at Ron, to see how he fared and how he was reacting to this woman, but something told her that looking away was dangerous. She kept her eyes on the gray specter before her. LeiRain searched for something in the woman that reminded her of verdaant or tempest, something that would clearly mark her as fae. The only thing she could find was the fire burning in the woman's eyes. It matched the glint she'd seen in Silver's when he was angry, and the storm in her father's.

The woman's burning eyes narrowed. 'I am a blaze,' she said. 'A *god*. You may call me Aed.' She lifted her chin arrogantly.

Ron growled from behind her and LeiRain felt him shift forward, closing the distance between them. Good. That meant he was staying on his feet, he could walk.

'You are no god,' LeiRain replied. 'I've never heard of your kind before, but I can see how it would be easy to think so highly of yourself when you prey on the weak.' LeiRain cast her eyes toward Odro whose breaths had become shallow as he leaned back in the chair, his eyes closed. The man's skin looked like it was too tight for his body and his lips pulled back from his teeth in a grimace.

Aed leaned forward and placed her hand on top of the desk. She flattened her palm against a stack of papers. The pile quickly began to smoke and, within seconds, her hand had turned them to ash. The remnants of the paper had only just settled when the sepia wood around her fingers began to glow orange. Flame erupted from the desk and LeiRain flinched as searing heat rolled over her.

'All other beings are weak when you're a god,' Aed said, stepping back from the desk. LeiRain shook her head in confusion.

'Why are you doing this?' she asked. 'Are you helping the Royals? I –' she threw her arms wide, gesturing to her fallen friends and the gasping Odro, 'I don't understand.'

'She has been using them.' Ron said, his voice gravelly.

A cruel smile spread across Aed's face. 'The dwarve is correct,' she said.

'But why?' LeiRain felt her brows knit together. 'What use could the Royals possibly be to a fae?' Aed's smile fell when LeiRain once again referred to her as fae.

Ron swore as another flash of heat hit them both, this time coming from behind her. She turned to look and saw that, where there had once been a doorway, there was now a wall of flames licking the ceiling. The study window, three floors from the ground, was now the only exit. Could any of them survive a jump from this height? No sooner had she asked herself this than bright orange flames broke out along the windowsill as well, completely sealing them in. The fae's laughter was soft and disconcertingly sweet and LeiRain was surprised that she could hear it over the thrumming in her ears. She coughed as she wiped at her watering eyes. Thick smoke began to roll over the ceiling. The heat was becoming unbearable and LeiRain felt her chest tighten as she tried to breathe but got only mouthfuls of smoke. Head spinning and mind reeling, she clutched ineffectually at her throat.

Smoke poured into the corners of the room and began to fill up the spaces in between. Even as a white-gray haze surrounded the fae, LeiRain kept her eyes on Aed, watching the woman delight in their suffering. LeiRain jumped as she felt something close around her ankle and was relieved to look down and see that it was Silver's hand. He was still prone and very pale, but LeiRain thought she saw some color beginning to return to his lips. Something stirred in her chest as their eyes met through the thickening haze. There was absolute tenderness in his gaze. LeiRain strained to send a wave of magic toward Silver and winced as it met with emptiness – the foxglove ash had stolen their *magicae canantis*. LeiRain swallowed, her dry throat painful, and rubbed her burning eyes.

'*Why*?' She coughed, looking at Aed.

'I don't know what has befallen you before today, little demi-god, but your path now seems an impediment to my own.' The woman took a step closer to LeiRain, displacing clouds of smoke. She ran a hand through her hair, long gray fingernails poking out from between the strands. 'My sisters and I want to be restored to our rightful place and nothing will stop us. We *will* be recognized and respected as gods once more.'

'I've never even heard of you until today,' LeiRain choked out. She struggled to keep her eyes open and her head spun as the air around her thinned.

'Exactly my point,' the woman replied.

The smoke in front of Aed dissipated enough for LeiRain to see her clearly, to look her in the eyes.

'We were forgotten, written out of books,' Aed's voice darkened. 'When other beings began to learn the secrets of fire, we were no longer revered or respected. Our brethren remained in a place of honor – *none can hope to tame the earth or the waters*, men said. Even as their place in the order of things was preserved, the verdaant and tempest made no effort to ensure that we, *the blaze*, were remembered. They did not care when the society we had built crumbled. My sisters and I are all that remain of it and we remain only because we've adapted.'

LeiRain wanted to argue with Aed, to explain that the verdaant and the tempest were far from the thoughts of men, that they had retreated into obscurity, but she felt as if her skin were melting from the bone. The air was growing thin as the fire blazed around them and LeiRain fell to her knees, gasping. Ron was coughing loudly somewhere behind her, but she could no longer see him through the thick smoke. This was the magic that had burned the elder Odro in his sleep, the source of the fire that had touched only him and left everything around the man untouched. The elder Odro had just been another obstacle for the blaze to remove.

Aed continued to speak and LeiRain fought to maintain consciousness. 'We feed the fears of men such as Ulrick. We provide kindling for the fire of hate that already burns within them. His father was too level-headed and too weak of body to be of any use to us, but Ulrick's youth and ambition were enough. His insecurities practically drew him to me.' Aed's voice was sharp and clear, unaffected by the smokey room. 'All I did was nurture the fear that lived in his heart, cultivated it, until it eventually grew on its own. It blossomed into hate, which burns just as fiercely as any fire.' LeiRain stared at the blaze's slippered feet as she rested her cheek on the carpet. 'My sisters are doing the same on The Continent and soon enough, that hate will turn to conflict. Enough conflict eventually leads to war and where there is war, there is fire. We will rebuild the blaze civilization and we *will* reign again.'

LeiRain strained to think clearly, even as the world blurred. Silver's hand had grown loose on her ankle and somewhere in the smoke-filled room, Ron's coughing had halted as he succumbed to the smoke. *Think, LeiRain. Think.* This could not be the end, not when so many lives depended on her. She lifted her head, peeling her cheek away from the carpet, which had grown sticky with drying blood.

Her shoulder brushed up against Bren's body and she shuddered. His skin was cool and waxy. His stocking cap still lay in the palm of his hand, his fingers no longer able to grip it. She took the hat and held it against her cheek, letting it soak up the tears that now streamed down her face. Her lungs felt as if they had caught fire; breathing was misery. LeiRain closed her eyes against the pain, pressing her face into the fabric that had for so long hidden Bren's true identity from the world. As the rough cloth of the cap scratched her skin, his last words came back to her.

Don't let them take anything else from you, Rain.

'I won't,' she promised him.

Tired and desperate, LeiRain reached for the water. Not just with her mind, but with her entire being. She reached for her magic with her whole heart open to it, just as she had when she'd brought Silver back from the brink of death, demanding nothing, but pleading with the element instead. She let the magic see all of her, know all of her, and decide her worthiness.

The water didn't just rise to her touch. It *rushed toward it*. LeiRain could feel the bits of water in the air throughout the room. The spilled blood on the floor, the tiny particles of water that she and Ron and even Silver continued to exhale. There was water in Bren's lifeless body, and she drew from that as well. Carefully, she called to it, pulling just a little from each source so as not to take too much from any one of them. Gently, she drew it in, twisting the particles of it together as one might braid a rope. The water seemed to know her desires, to hum with her will.

LeiRain managed to draw herself up, clinging to the desk for support. She only had to think about the fires and the water began to douse them. White smoke rolled off the desk and from the windowsill as flames sputtered out. The smoke drifted, revealing Aed's face. Her eyes were wide and bright with fury, her forehead wrinkled in disbelief. She thrust her hands out before her, trying to produce more flames, but the water now surrounded Aed, a thin film of liquid that moved with her. Her hands turned orange and then blue with heat, but only steam rose up from them as her fire fizzled out.

'What are you doing?' Aed cried, swatting at the water that floated around her.

LeiRain smiled and tilted her chin up as she'd seen the blaze do before. 'I am the daughter of Alarra, bender of steel and weaver of enchantments. I am a daughter of tempest.' LeiRain took in a gasping breath, coughed, and stepped closer to Aed.

'Stop it, you little *bitch*!' The fae's expression was frantic now. Aed's fingers curled into talons. She bared her teeth at LeiRain. 'I'll *kill* you.'

LeiRain drew her shoulders back as she pulled moisture from the steam and fed it into the thickening wall of water that surrounded Aed. The woman could not move without coming into contact with moisture and LeiRain smiled when the damp sizzled at the blaze's touch.

'I am LeiRain of Harbor Village.' Her voice was husky with smoke inhalation. 'And I will not let you take anything else from me.'

Aed let out a howl and lunged for LeiRain, whose body was shaking with the effort of holding on to her magic. LeiRain tried to side step and nearly fell as Aed's clawed hands grabbed for her throat. And then Ron was beside her, roaring as he swung his ax. His blade, the one her mother had mended with skill and enchantments, caught the light of the dying fire as it made a wide arc through the air. LeiRain followed its path and, as it drew near the fae, she made the water ripple and part so that the weapon passed through without resistance. Aed's eyes went wide as Ron's ax sliced. At first, nothing happened and LeiRain thought that he had missed. Then azure blood bubbled from the fae's throat. Steam rolled off of it as it dripped onto the desk and then the floor. Aed's body wobbled where she stood before her head fell forward, splashing through the wall of water, a curtain of black hair streaming behind as it hit the floor.

LeiRain cringed at the wet thunk, and again when the headless body toppled backwards a few seconds later. Something very warm and wet seeped into her shoes. More blood. But this time it was the blood of an enemy, and not that of another friend.

A wave of exhaustion swept over LeiRain and the wall of water that she'd been holding in place around Aed splashed onto the floor. Her mind reached out, weakly, toward Silver and was relieved to find the water still holding her will, not letting him bleed out. His magic remained absent, though, and without the *magicae canentis*, her mind felt empty.

Sbe wobbled and her vision narrowed. Ron was in front of her now, his hand on her arm, holding her up. She could hear his voice and knew that he was speaking to her, but there was a whooshing sound in her ears that made it impossible to understand him. LeiRain exhaled a shaky breath just as everything turned black.

'Rain, come on! Wake up!' The distant voice sounded familiar.

LeiRain felt herself being jostled. Felt her head sway back and forth against the surface beneath her. Her chest burned with each breath and her body felt hollow.

'Rain!' The voice sounded closer now.

LeiRain opened her eyes. The air was still hazy, but much of the smoke had cleared. Ron knelt over her, a hand on both of her shoulders. His brow was furrowed, his face so red with exhaustion that it was almost the same color as the dark scar that marked his cheek. He withdrew his hands when he saw her eyes open and as he leaned back, LeiRain felt a cool breeze come in from the open window behind him.

'You've got to get up, Rain. We need to leave. *Now*.'

'Silver?' Her voice came out as a croak.

'Still alive, but just barely.' His eyes were bloodshot. 'You have to get up!'

LeiRain's head rolled to the side and she found herself looking right at Bren. He lay on the floor, crumpled against the desk. His clothing was soaked through with blood, both his own and Silver's.

'Rain, you *have* to get up. I don't want to leave Silver, but if you make me choose, I'm leaving him here to carry you.'

This broke through the fuzziness of LeiRain's thoughts. She sat up, pausing briefly to let a wave of dizziness pass. She looked at Silver as Ron helped her to her feet. He still was so pale, the color she'd seen coming back to his lips had disappeared. Ron took one of the expensive-looking window drapes and tore it into wide strips, then wrapped them tightly around Silver's body, covering the wound on his chest. The strips quickly became spotted with blue blood, but the bleeding had slowed so the spot did not keep expanding. Ron had tied a strip around his own leg where he had been shot through with the Royal weapon.

'We can't leave him,' LeiRain said, gesturing toward Bren. She was exhausted, scared. She wanted to get out of there as soon as possible, to get Silver to the saurians who could care for his injury. But it felt wrong to leave Bren's body among their enemies. His enemies in the end, too. Ron looked down at Bren before his eyes flicked to Silver.

'He's gone, Rain. And we have to get out of here.'

She shook her head, tears springing to her eyes. 'I won't leave him.' Before Ron could say anything else, LeiRain bent down and grabbed Bren's arm, trying to pull him over her shoulders. The body barely moved, and she nearly fell over with another wave of dizziness.

'Fine,' Ron growled in frustration beside her, 'move, I've got him.'

Ron picked Bren up and threw him over his left shoulder. LeiRain watched him kneel on his injured leg and prepared to throw Silver over his right.

'No, wait!' LeiRain exclaimed, waving her hands frantically as she looked at Silver's broken body. He was so weak and fragile now, she worried that he couldn't withstand such rough handling. 'You can't carry him like that with his wound.'

Ron shook his head: 'Rain, it's the best I can do if you want me to take them both.'

She looked at Silver, watching the disturbingly slow rise and fall of his chest. He'd slipped into unconsciousness again and his eyes were closed. LeiRain drew in a deep breath and let it out slowly. She felt as though she might collapse but she willed herself to remain standing.

I am the daughter of Alarra, bender of steel and weaver of enchantments. I am a daughter of tempest. I will not let them take anything else from me.

LeiRain drew in the water that had held the blaze at bay. She drew it into a pool beneath her lover, her *friend*. And slowly, knees wobbling with the effort, LeiRain lifted the water up so that Silver floated in a small pool, several inches off the ground.

Her hands were fisted at her sides as she turned to nod at Ron. He nodded back and, though his eyes crinkled with worry, the dwarve led them from the room with Bren over his left shoulder and his ax gripped in his right hand. LeiRain followed him, Silver's unconscious body floating between them.

They left the mansion with substantially less stealth than they had entered, focusing instead on speed. They moved as quickly as LeiRain could manage while maintaining a hold on her magic, darting from one building to the next. LeiRain made no complaints as rose thorns slashed the skin on her hands and face and snagged her clothes. She thought only of Silver and how he had brushed the thorns aside for them on their way in. The building, which had looked so beautiful when she'd first seen it, now looked hideous. LeiRain was glad to move far away from its tan brick walls.

Shouts could be heard as they moved. The distillery fire must have been under control now because they could hear men returning to the docks in a rush and only a thin stream of smoke broke through the treetops. Curses came from the waterfront as sailors found their ships sinking, hulls torn open and lower decks flooded. LeiRain would be surprised if there was anything left of the pier beyond a few floating planks.

She breathed a ragged sigh of relief when they made it around the back of the row of storage cellars. Ron shoved his way through the brush that hid Muckjaw's tunnel. He held back the thorny branches for LeiRain so that she could pass through first, her magic still holding Silver's body aloft. She stumbled and slid down the decline into the tunnel, more focused on keeping the fae's body steady than on her own steps. Without Silver's fae light, the tunnel was black except for the light that crept through the opening. She moved into the dark, calling up to Ron when they were free of the entrance. The dwarve dropped through the hole behind her, showing no hesitation this time. He landed on his feet with a loud thunk and a cloud of dust.

EPILOGUE

LeiRain took a sip of her coffee, closing her eyes as she savored its bitter warmth. Her throat still felt raw from the confrontation with Aed, and the heat of the drink was surprisingly soothing. She was deeply touched that Anya had broken into her coffee stores just for her. Silver was remarkably well after being so near to death, but the saurians insisted that he continue to rest. Ironically, the heavy bleeding that had almost been the death of him had also flushed most of the foxglove from his system, making it possible for the saurians to aid his healing.

Muckjaw gave her a solemn nod as he passed by. Color had returned to his scales and there was a bright shine to his eyes. It had only been a few days, but he'd insisted on repairing the wards around this side of the island even before he was healed. The residents of Beachspire seemed relieved to have their wards back in place.

Others had not fared so well. The day that they had set Bren's funeral pyre ablaze, the pixie had tried to throw herself on it. Islanders had taken turns checking in on her since then but they still did not know her name or how she'd come to be in the possession of the Royals. She refused to speak and spent most of her days staring off at nothing. She had at least begun to drink in small amounts and had taken food a few times, so maybe there was hope.

Anya seemed doubtful. 'Some people can't move through the past,' she said. 'They stay in the pain and make a home there. I hope she moves through,' she concluded, eyes softening.

The more time LeiRain spent with the blend, the more LeiRain appreciated Anya's wisdom and resilience. She hadn't been able to bring herself to talk about the blaze with Anya just yet. About how similar Anya's powers were to the fae's. Maybe it was just a coincidence, but LeiRain thought it unlikely given the rareness of such magic.

LeiRain emptied her mug and left it on the bar before exiting The Speared Sheel. The saurians had taken to shooing her away from Silver, insisting on his rest, but she had a great deal to discuss with him and no desire to be apart. The documents he'd uncovered had all been ruined, soaked in his blood. Ron had taken the weapon, but it had been damaged by the fire, all of its wooden pieces burned away.

LeiRain was relieved to find Silver alone in the tent when she returned. He gave her a half smile and started to sit up, but before he could get far, LeiRain nudged him over on the cot and slid under the covers beside him. Curling on her side, she draped one leg over his and wrapped her hands around his bicep. She longed to lay her head on his chest and listen to his strong heartbeat, but his wound was still tender. She contented herself with nuzzling into his neck.

'You didn't bring any coffee for me?' Silver asked. Of course he could smell the pungent stuff on her breath.

'Sorry,' she said, giving his arm a light squeeze. 'The saurians don't think it's a good idea.'

'Neither do I,' Silver quipped. 'That stuff is awful, especially without milk.' Livestock were scarce in Beachspire.

'I thought you liked it,' LeiRain laughed.

'I think I like the *idea* of coffee,' Silver said, thoughtfully. 'It *smells* as though it should taste good, and I love the extra bit of energy, but overall I think it's quite disgusting.' She laughed.

'More for me, then,' LeiRain whispered into his neck. He placed a hand on top of hers where she held his arm. Gooseflesh covered her body as Silver sent a wave of his magic washing over her. LeiRain returned the gesture, appreciating their connection all the more for having lost it while foxglove coursed through his veins.

The Royals were still a threat, not only to Beachspire but to the entire Continent. They had seen the evil behind the Royals and only LeiRain and her friends knew how truly dire the situation was. She – they – would stand up for those who could not stand up for themselves. They would come to the aid of those who thought that they were alone in their suffering, the outcasts who scraped by with no rights or protections under the King's rule. They would stop this war before it started. There was no other choice.

But not today, not now. Today, for this moment, LeiRain allowed herself to relish the joy of lives saved and love found.

THE END

ACKNOWLEDGMENTS

This book is literally a childhood dream come true and the first person I have to thank for that dream is Carol Kemna. She brought the Young Authors program to our school district. Ms. Creason (as she was known at the time) was fiercely supportive of my creativity. Carol left this earth in November 2020, the same month I finished my first draft of Water's Calling. This book was possible because of her and I hope that Carol's family and friends find comfort in knowing that her legacy lives on through the students she influenced. Thank you, Carol, for everything.

Thank you to Joe and Jesse, and all of the other members of the Sigurd's Foley campaign for inspiring LeiRain's story. Thank you to my sister, Kelcey, and my friends Pete and Tara for subjecting yourselves to a very rough initial draft. Your time, feedback and encouragement are so very appreciated. April and Tim, thank you for always supporting the weird and creative things I pursue, and for including us in many of your own weird pursuits. Thank you, April, for letting me steal much of your D&D character's persona. Grace! Nobody else in my circle of friends and family has read as many genuinely crappy drafts as you and yet not once did your belief in me waiver.

Thank you for all of your feedback, encouragement and your priceless friendship. Thank you, Renee, for never doubting that I could do what I set out to do and for always sending me love when I need it. Thank you to everyone at

White Dragon Martial Arts for your patience and enthusiasm. I stepped into the world of kung fu because I wanted to be able to write more realistic combat scenes, but you created an environment that made me fall in love with the art. I promise to always make my fight scenes as realistic as I can, to pivot on the ball of my foot, and to continue working on my balance (shake-shake-shake bash).

I owe a debt of gratitude to my editing team, Lore, Megan and Emma. Water's Calling would never have lived up to my vision without your expert guidance. More than that, your encouragement and genuine love of my story and its characters kept me going when I might have otherwise been overcome by discouragement. I'm a better writer because of you. Thank you. Thank you to the members of the SmashBear author chat, especially Sam and John, for making me feel like all of my struggles were normal and surmountable.

Mom and Dad, thanks for just generally telling me I was capable of stuff. It took me a long time to believe it, but it matters. You matter. I love you.

Tibby - You were cuddled into a tiny little knot against my hip for nearly every minute I spent writing the first draft of this book. Every time I sit down to write, I feel your absence.

And finally, thank you to my husband, Justin. Ours is not a perfect romance, but it is one built on friendship, humor and solid teamwork. This book would not exist without you. My life as it is now would not exist without you. I love you. I'm so glad we're on this adventure together.

Thank you for supporting SmashBear Publishing and our authors.

For more information about our authors, upcoming releases and what we publish, you can check out our website

www.smashbearpublishing.com

Or find us on:

Welcome to Tír na nÓg

We've been expecting you

Relive your childhood

Explore the forest

Finding your soulmate should be easy

Until you have to pick between two

Printed in Great Britain
by Amazon